THE

VIPs

MAR 2012 CH

Also by Scott Poulson-Bryant

What's Your Hi-Fi Q?: From Prince to Puff Daddy, 30 Years of
    Black Music Trivia
Hung: A Meditation on the Measure of Black Men in America

THE

VIPs

SCOTT POULSON-BRYANT

Broadway Books

New York

Copyright © 2011 by Scott Poulson-Bryant

Published in the United States by Broadway Books,
an imprint of the Crown Publishing Group,
a division of Random House, Inc., New York.
www.crownpublishing.com

BROADWAY BOOKS and the Broadway Books colophon are trademarks of Random House, Inc.

Library of Congress Cataloging-in-Publication Data
Poulson-Bryant, Scott.
   The VIPs : a novel / by Scott Poulson-Bryant.
      p.   cm.
   1. Rap musicians—Fiction. 2. African American men—
Fiction. 3. Birthfathers—Identification—Fiction. 4. Fathers
and sons—Fiction. I. Title. II. Title: VIPs.
   PS3616.O8573V5 2011
   813'.6—dc22

                        2010037518

ISBN 978-0-7679-2974-5
eISBN 978-0-7679-3224-0

Printed in the United States of America

Book design: Donna Sinisgalli
Cover design: Chris Sergio
Cover composite: © Getty Images/© Media Bakery

10 9 8 7 6 5 4 3 2 1

First Edition

I finished this book about a group of dear friends during my second chance in the city of Providence, so I think it would be, well, *providential* to dedicate it to a few dear people I met there who taught me some new things about friendship:

Hudson
Ivan
Jimmy
Max
Michael
Molly
Reade
Stefan

"Love takes off masks that we fear we cannot live without and know we cannot live within."

—James Baldwin, *The Fire Next Time*

"One shot to your heart without breaking your skin
No one has the power to hurt you like your friends."

—India.Arie, "Get It Together"

Acknowledgments

I'd like to thank a few people for helping to bring *The VIPs* to life:

First, my profs, friends (and students) at Brown University who understood my ridiculous circumstances and gave me space to see to all the busy-ness, especially: Andy, for the music; Frat, for the laughs; Sean, for the writing; and Annie, for summer '09. Tanya McKinnon for being the greatest, most patient agent on the planet. I want to thank Janet Hill for seeing the potential in *The VIPs,* and Christian Nwachukwu Jr. for his patience. A big (Brown) hug to Annie Chagnot, editor extraordinaire, who helped me see the real story inside the wall of words and thoughts that originally made up this book, and helped to chisel it into the lean, clean thing that I hope it is now. I owe major thanks to the Bryant family for their unwavering support and love during the crazy period of the last few years. I should thank all the peeps who stopped by my blog, Scott Topics™, and asked about the progress of *The VIPs*; knowing you guys were thinking of the book helped me to get it done. And for providing a bookish '80s teenager with lots of page-turning fun (and the idea to get this project going), I should give a shout-out to Jackie Collins, Judith Krantz, Harold Robbins, and Shirley Conran, whose famous quote from *Lace*—"Which one of you bitches is my mother?"—inspired *The VIPs*.

THE

VIPs

1

Barry Chambers sat in the backseat of the sleek Mercedes Maybach, sipping a Scotch on the rocks and watching through the dark-tinted windows as Manhattan rolled majestically by. This was Barry's second favorite view of the city, comfortably ensconced in the car's fine leather seat, a driver behind the wheel taking him wherever he needed to be. Second only to the view he got from his thirty-fifth-floor office. Both views, each of them a privileged perch of high living, made him feel like a king. And when you're the CEO of one of the biggest companies in New York, when you're doing one of the biggest mergers New York media has ever seen, when you're about to close on the duplex penthouse of your dreams in a beautiful Central Park West building, you *should* feel like a king. Or so Barry told himself. But, never afraid of a good cliché, he'd also started to tell himself that success was nothing if you had no one to share it with. So, in Barry's mind, all he needed was a queen by his side to make the pretty picture of his royal life complete.

There were just *so* many potential queens to choose from.

There was Erica Davies, the hot attorney at Conran, Collins & Krantz with the Tina Turner legs, in the D.C. office who came to (and *in*, Barry liked to remember) his bed every time she visited Manhattan for meetings. Then there was Amy Vincent, the TV soap star with the cocoa skin and emerald eyes that he'd met at a barbecue in the Hamptons two weeks ago. And who could forget Cheyenne Montgomery with her heart-shaped face and long curly hair and an ass that could stop traffic on the West Side Highway?

So many women, so little time.

And time was what it was all about. At thirty-nine years old, Barry was about three one-night stands and thirty orgasms away from the big 4-0, and the playboy ways that had lubricated his twenties and thirties were going to dry up and make him look a little *desperate* in his forties. At least that was what Heather Lindsey told him, just after his alarm went off that morning but *before* her words mutated into pleasured moans while she was straddling him and gyrating her tight hips. Then she came, hard, fast, and loud like always, shook her blond hair out of her pretty face, and pecked him on his cheek. Barry watched her taut legs as she scurried into the bathroom, mumbling something about her Town Car arriving any minute.

But Barry would never be desperate, he told himself. He'd just learned early that it was far easier for him to give a woman an orgasm than it was to give her his heart. Part of him wanted to say that to Heather as she waited for the hot water to steam up the bathroom. Instead he just said, "Don't rush. You can ride in with me."

She stuck her face around the door jamb. "Now, how would that look?" she purred, playing up her Southern accent. "Us strolling in together after a night of fucking? You want everyone talking about us?"

Barry just lay there in bed, listening to Heather sing her way through her shower, and let her words play in his brain. *Desperate*. Barry Chambers? *Desperate?* Nah, never that. But he had to admit to himself that he did feel as if some chapter in his life was ending. He wasn't sure if that meant that something new was starting, but he did feel some sort of end was near.

Maybe it was because of that phone call. Why in the hell had TNT called him? Considering the one and only time they'd ever been in each other's presence was a complete social and professional disaster, Barry couldn't believe his ears when his assistant Marcie buzzed him and told him the rapper was holding on line one. He'd picked up the phone and the first thing he said was, "Why the hell are you calling me? You finally see that deodorant deal was wack? You realized you need me anyway?"

There was a long silence before TNT's booming "Fuck you" filled the void between them. Then he laughed. "You still stuck on that shit? I told you the rules just like I told the rest of them. Whichever one of y'all beat me one-on-one was the one I'd give my business to. You lost, man. And I can't help it if your old ass sprained your ankle in the process. Get over it."

"Then why are you calling?"

"You need to come to a meeting."

"What kind of meeting?"

"A private one," said TNT. "As in 'don't tell nobody you coming.'"

"I'm a busy man," Barry said.

"No kidding," TNT said, then cracked up laughing again. "Look. Just be there. I'll e-mail the address to your secretary."

And now Barry sat in the Maybach, sipping his scotch and still wondering why he'd been summoned to the Hotel Gansevoort to meet with some silly-ass rapper. Considering how massive TNT's fortune had grown since that terrible day three years ago at the Chelsea Piers basketball courts, it was still a sore spot for Barry that his aging knees and lackluster hoops ability prevented him from bringing TNT's talent into the company's fold. A rapper with a fashion company, a record label, video-game production—when did the powers-that-be decide that thugs selling the worst images of black men to white kids were supposed to be the multimedia moguls? Barry just shook his head and sipped some more Scotch. Maybe TNT had changed his mind. *Maybe he'd changed his mind about working with us. Maybe the silly-ass rapper wasn't as silly as I originally thought.*

The chauffeur pulled the Mercedes over to the curb near the hotel and the pretty boy valet with the asymmetrical haircut came over to open the door. Barry gulped down the last of the Scotch and grabbed his briefcase. This was going to be interesting.

2

The last time Leo Bradford had been at the Hotel Gansevoort, two years before, he'd snuck into Manhattan for a short meeting with his agent and lawyer to work out a deal for the movie version of his second novel.

And he felt himself pulled into a movie of his own.

There, right across the luxurious expanse of the Gansevoort's sexy roof deck, sitting on a bench, sipping a vodka rocks, was his ex. Greg Finch, all 6'7" of him, stretched out like he was the king on a throne and all other guests were his minions.

And, as Leo expected, he wasn't alone. A muscular guy in baggy Diesel jeans was sitting a few inches away from him, not too close, but Leo could tell that they were together. That was Greg's style. Any guy he was dating couldn't be seen too close to him in public. Paranoid basketball star Gregory Finch, always scared that the paparazzi were after him, lying in wait to catch him doing something he shouldn't be doing.

Like being in love with a guy.

A ringing phone pulled Leo out of his memory. It was TNT calling again.

"Yo, man, you coming, right?"

"I said I'd be there. I'm downstairs. I'll be up in a minute."

TNT said "Cool" and clicked off.

Leo swigged back the last of his ginger ale and threw his cell phone into his bag, checking to make sure he'd remembered to bring his digital recorder for the interview with TNT. He had no clue what TNT wanted to tell him, but he figured it must be some kind of exclusive. Leo had been one of the first journalists to interview TNT when his debut album dropped four years ago and he'd run into him at a couple of parties and functions since then. Every time they saw each other, TNT made a point of telling Leo how much he liked the article Leo had written about him, how Leo had "gotten" him better than any other journalist he'd talked to. Leo always thanked him and moved on, never overly interested in getting too close to the celebrities he interviewed (well, except for Greg, but that's a whole other story). So it surprised him when TNT called him on his cell phone and invited him to the Hotel Gansevoort for a meeting. "And don't tell anyone you're coming," he'd added.

Leo hoped that TNT really *did* have some kind of exclusive announcement. As crazy as the magazine business was getting these days, they needed something to spruce up sales in the coming months. An exclusive from TNT could go a long way toward satisfying both the readers and the ad sales team. And that would be a good thing.

3

"All work and no play is going to make Joey a very dull boy."

Joey Ramirez stood up from the bed and looked down into Melanie's green eyes as he yanked up the zipper on his jeans. "You tellin' me that was dull?" He sat down again and reached around in the dark for his sneakers.

"*That* wasn't dull," Melanie said, stretching her slender arms out in a dramatic postcoital yawn. "But if you don't slow down . . ."

"I told you when you called me that I had a meeting at four," Joey said. "Sometimes a quick fuck is the best I can do."

Melanie sat up and pulled the sweaty sheets close to her. "You're never gonna settle down, are you?"

"Too much to do." He turned to face her. "Yo, what does TNT stand for? You know, the rapper TNT. What do his initials stand for?"

"That Nigga Troy," Melanie giggled. "Why you ask that?"

"No reason."

"Is that who you're meeting with?"

"Why you all up in my business?"

"'Cause you were just all up in mine."

"Funny," Joey mumbled, without smiling. He stood up and went over to the dressing table. He flicked a switch on the dresser and twenty bright bulbs lit up around the mirror. He shook his head. *Strippers*, he thought. *Wannabe movie stars.* He looked at himself in the mirror and ran his fingers through his wavy hair.

Melanie said, "Don't you even wanna take a shower?"

He could still smell her sex on him, but he didn't want to waste any more time in her apartment than he had to. "I'll take one at home."

"What's wrong? My place not good enough for you?"

No, he thought, *it's not*. He said, "Melanie, I wouldn't be here fucking you if I thought that." He turned back to her. "Would I?"

"I don't know what you think, Joey."

"And that's just the way I like it," he said and went to the bed to kiss her goodbye. "You need anything?"

Joey watched her eyes look up at the ceiling, like she was thinking hard. She ran her fingers through her dyed red hair and tilted her head to one side like a coy child. "I could use some new Manolos," she said.

Joey reached into his pocket and pulled out a wad of bills. He tossed three hundreds on the sheets. "Be good," he said, and turned to go.

"Call me," Melanie said.

"If you don't call me first," he said.

Outside, he jumped into his Land Rover and pulled out into the traffic on Seventh Avenue. Luckily his apartment was only ten blocks away. He'd have just enough time to get a shower, change his shirt, and meet TNT at the Gansevoort.

Please God, he thought, *please let this TNT thing work out*. Then he mentally slapped himself across the face. Who the hell was he turning into whining like that? "I'm Joey Ram," he said aloud. He looked into the rearview mirror and said it again, louder this time. "I'm Joey Ram."

And I still need a savior, he thought. What had being "Joey Ram" done for him except make him tons of money, make him a fashion star (whom *Page Six* called the "Latino Calvin Klein"), give him power and sex and access?

It had bored him, that's what.

What had Jacob told him when they met about the online arm of the company in Miami? "Women in Iowa want to look as chic as women in South Beach, Joey, and they spend almost as much money as the lips-on-sticks who walk around this silly Florida town every day." It had inspired him to build a new bridge line, another JoeyRam brand that would cater to young women who couldn't afford his couture and top-of-the-line sportswear.

But creatively he needed a new outlet.

So he'd started a men's line. No one was doing anything new these days with jeans and pullovers. He could put the JoeyRam stamp on those basic pieces and make a new fortune. But he needed a new star, someone young and raw to introduce the new line to the world, someone who could rock the JoeyRam name the way Marky Mark rocked Calvin all those years ago.

He was watching BET one night when it hit him: TNT. The sexiest rapper on the scene. Hip, young, funny, and smart, his music crossed over to white kids in the burbs and foreign kids overseas. Everyone thought he was best thing since Adam fucked Eve. And about to launch a movie career, from the gossip Joey had heard. He was perfect.

And the hardest fucking guy on the planet to get a meeting with.

Until today.

Joey pulled up to his building, jumped out, and tossed the keys to the burly doorman standing out front. "Hold it for me, Manny," he said. "I'll be back down in twenty minutes."

"Anything for you, Mr. Ramirez."

Can you make TNT my new star? Joey thought. *I'd suck your dick if you do that!*

Joey kicked off his sneakers and took his shirt off in the private elevator up to the penthouse and by the time he was in his loft, he was yanking down his jeans. His assistant Gertie, a petite Colombian woman in stern schoolmarm glasses, was sitting on the couch in the living room. "You're late," she said. "Your meeting's at four."

"I know. Did TNT call?"

"Yes, he did," she said. "He said, 'Don't be late.'"

"You didn't tell anyone about this meeting, did you?"

Gertie shook her head. "Didn't even put it in your day planner."

When he was all showered and dressed, he rushed back into the living room. Gertie handed him his BlackBerry and a brand-new brightly colored JoeyRam prospectus. She straightened his collar and wiped a speck of dried shaving cream from his cheek.

"Where would I be without you, Gertie?" he said to her in Spanish.

"Just where you are," she said with a smile. "Just where you are."

As nervous as he felt, he had to smile. "Can you believe he called *me* for a confidential meeting?" Joey said. "That's a good sign, right?"

Gertie nodded. "Think positive," she said in Spanish. "You'll be fine. Everything will work out fine."

Joey hoped so.

4

"You're thirty-nine years old," Duke Maynard's mother said. "You need some kids."

"How many grandkids do you need, Ma? Marie got two, Mike has one."

"Goes to show how much you know," his mother said. "There's no such thing as too many grandchildren."

"I'm not married."

"You *were*."

"I don't wanna talk about that, Ma."

He pulled over past the line of taxis idling outside Manhattan's bustling Penn Station and leaned over to kiss his mother goodbye. But she wasn't done.

"I mean, I'm getting old, Duke. By the time *you* give me some grandbabies I'm gonna be damn near on my death bed."

"We can only hope," said Duke, with a sly smile.

"You are so fresh," his mother said, reaching over and running her hand through his chestnut brown curls. "You need a tan. You're looking very pale." She opened her door and stepped out of his Mercedes. "Thanks for lunch, baby."

"I'm sorry I can't drive you home. I got this big meeting."

She waved off his words. "I know you have things to do, baby. Just call me before you get on that plane tomorrow." She closed the door and headed toward the escalators.

Duke watched until he couldn't see her descending head anymore, then pulled out into the Eighth Avenue traffic.

He'd love to be a father. But how could he do that? He wasn't interested in having a babymama and the attendant drama that went along with that. He wanted a settled situation, a new career, a new wife, a house, a family. He'd had the career, speeding across the gridiron, one of the fastest white guys the NFL had ever seen, according to anyone you asked. But now he was an *ex*–football player. He'd had the wife. But now he was an *ex*-husband, not that his marriage lasted that long. He'd had the house but now that belonged to the ex-wife down in Silver Spring, Maryland. So, he'd told himself, if he was going to have the family, he'd first have to find a new situation to erase the memories of the old one.

But, as usual, work was his real focus.

So it was a big surprise when he got a call from TNT. "Wanna have a meeting," the rapper had said to him. "We need to talk over some things."

He'd met TNT a couple of times before, once at a party in

L.A. right before he retired from football, and once at the ESPY awards the year before that, when TNT's debut album first came out. He seemed like a nice enough kid, a little thuggish perhaps, but weren't all the under-twenty-fives that way these days? Just like all the rookies he'd played with over the last few years—talking loud, strutting around, wanting everything before they deserved it. Whatever. He knew how to handle a kid like TNT. Why *not* take a meeting? At least he liked the kid's albums. If nothing else he could get his autograph for Marie's kids. They all loved rap music the same way he had when he was a kid.

Duke tossed his keys to the skinny valet outside the Hotel Gansevoort and stepped inside. He was a little early so he took a seat on one of the couches in the sunken waiting area and checked the messages on his cell phone. It had been a while since he'd been in the Hotel Gansevoort. It brought back memories of his old NFL life. It made him think of flying into Atlanta to play the Falcons and checking into the Four Seasons in Buckhead because his contract allowed him to stay in five-star facilities even if the team was staying somewhere else. His contract. To think that once his entire life was dictated by "the contract": what he could do and couldn't do, how he couldn't water-ski or deep-sea dive, how he had to be at camp on this day, at this time, ready to do what the coach and staff and captain said to do. It was a regimented life that, for all its limitations and standards, he loved nonetheless. Right up to the call he got just before camp two seasons ago.

"They're cutting you," his agent Morton had said. "They're going younger, rebuilding. They'll still pay you out in full. But you're out."

"Any offers around the league?" Duke asked, knowing the answer would be no. He was old. His numbers had slipped the last four seasons. Everyone was "rebuilding," no one wanted a thirty-six-year-old receiver who didn't receive as much as he used to.

"Duke?"

A familiar voice yanked him out of his thoughts. He looked up at the guy standing over him, dressed in black jeans and a black suede jacket with a brown leather bag thrown over his shoulder.

"Leo?"

"I thought that was you sitting there, man."

Duke stood up and the two men hugged tightly. Then Duke put his big hands on Leo's suede-clad shoulders and pushed him back to get a better look at him. "I think about you every time I come to the city. You still in Paris?"

"Yes," Leo said. "And you could call sometime. I'm sure you can afford a long-distance call, man." They both laughed. "You staying here at the hotel?"

"Uh, no," Duke said, "I have a meeting."

"Me too," said Leo. "Guess the Gansevoort's the place to be."

He and Duke sat down.

"How long you in Manhattan for?"

"Coupla days," said Duke. "Saw my mom, doing this meeting, going back to D.C. tomorrow night."

"Then we gotta have dinner," said Leo.

"I'd love to."

Leo looked closely at his old friend. "You looked sorta deep in thought for a second," he said. "What's on *your* mind these days?

"My future," Duke said, laughing.

"You too, huh?"

"Guess it's that time of life, right?"

"That, 'I'm-about-to-be-forty-in-a-coupla-years-will-somebody-please-tell-me-what's-next' time of life?"

"Exactly, bro," Duke laughed. "Yeah, let's get a meal and you tell me your story and I'll tell you mine."

Leo looked at his watch. "I gotta get to this meeting," he said, standing up. "How's six tonight?"

Duke nodded and followed Leo to the elevator. Inside, Leo pressed the button for the penthouse. Duke said, "You going to the penthouse?"

Leo said, "*You* going to the penthouse?"

"You going to see TNT?"

"Are you?"

Duke nodded. "This is weird, man."

"I got a call from him last week saying to meet him here today at four. Told me not to say anything to anybody. Don't tell me you got the same message?"

Duke nodded again. The elevator doors opened onto the penthouse and Duke and Leo stepped into the huge loft-like space. Incense burned somewhere in the room and instrumental jazz pulsated from speakers hidden in the shiny crevices of the lush suite.

A voice said, "That you, TNT?"

"Nah, it's not TNT," said Leo. "Is that—?"

Barry Chambers came around the corner and stopped in his tracks. "Leo? Duke?"

Leo froze. He wasn't expecting this. "Barry? What the hell are you doing here?"

Duke said, "Nobody told me this was some kind of reunion."

Barry laughed. "I was told to be here at four for a meeting."

Leo and Duke looked at each other then stepped down the three short steps into the suite.

"No one was here when I got here, so I made a drink," said Barry. "You guys want something?" He waved his hand toward the fully stocked bar.

Duke went right to it. He poured himself a straight Scotch and turned back to Leo and Barry. "Leo?"

Leo said, "Any beer?"

"In the fridge," Barry said.

"Just like *you* to case the joint," said Duke.

"Nice to see *you* again too, man," Barry said.

"Yeah," Duke said. "Whatever." He grabbed a Heineken from the refrigerator and handed it to Leo. Duke took a seat on a soft couch near the bar. "You set this up, Barry? This some kind of joke?"

"Believe me, Duke. If I'd set it up, I wouldn't have invited you."

Tension seeped around the lush suite like the central air had been poisoned with it. Before anyone could say anything else, the elevator doors opened, defusing some of the charged energy. Leo and Barry turned to see someone step into the suite. Expecting to see TNT, Leo stood up. When he saw who it was, he almost dropped his beer.

Duke said, "Joey?"

Joey said, "What the fuck?" He stepped into the suite as the elevator doors closed behind him.

Barry went right to Joey and grabbed him into a bear hug, nearly lifting Joey's thin frame off the ground.

"What the fuck?" Joey said again. "What are you guys doing here?"

"That seems to be the question," said Duke, standing up from the couch and coming over to Joey. "Joey Ram!" He and Joey embraced.

"You living in Manhattan now?" Joey asked Duke.

"D.C."

Leo said, softly, "Hey, Joey."

Joey winked at Leo and smiled. "Leo the Lion. My man."

There was an awkward pause as they stepped closer to hug each other. Then Joey followed Duke to the bar and poured himself a glass of red wine.

They all took seats on the soft sofas, staring at each other, their eyes taking in the present while their minds grew full of past memories rife with both pain and joy. It was as if there was so much to say that no one knew where to start.

"Damn," Joey said. "We haven't all been in the same room together since Leo found out—"

The sound of the elevator bell stopped him. They all turned to face the opening elevator doors, to see TNT strut into the suite.

He wore a Dwyane Wade basketball jersey, his muscular shoulders and arms glistening like they'd been plied with baby oil, and a pair of baggy Sean John jeans over dark brown Timberland boots. His neat goatee and dark eyebrows gave his light cinnamon brown face a menacing look, though his high cheekbones hinted at a prettiness at war with the menace. His head was shaved bald. He took a few steps into the suite, looked at the four men sitting there, then went over to the bar. He took a Heineken from the refrigerator, yanked the cap off, then tossed the bottle opener on the bar. He went back to the top step near the elevator, hovering there over the four men like some sort of carved statue dipped in bronze. He let his hazel eyes wander over the four of them: Leo in his artsy, uniform-like, all-black apparel; Barry in his slick custom-made suit and elegant Gucci loafers; Joey with his tailored JoeRam shirt open at the collar, the expensive True Religion jeans and Versace slip-ons; Duke in his simple Levi's and cotton oxford. TNT looked them over, taking his time before finishing the entire bottle of beer in three long gulps.

And when he spoke, basically a stranger addressing a room full of lifelong friends, his voice as rough and rhythmic as it was on his records, he asked, calmly, softly, but with an edge: "So, which one of you bastards is my father?"

1

"Happy Birthday, Leo!"

"Thank you," he said, eying the chocolate cake like it was three courses of a meal and not just three layers of dessert.

"I thought this was a welcome home party," his cousin Carla said. She looked at the others seated around the huge oak table. "I thought we were celebrating Leo coming home from Switzerland?"

"That too," said Lillian Bradford, Leo's mother. "But we don't really want to talk about that right now, do we?"

"But I thought—"

"Never mind, Carla," said Lillian, never one to discuss potentially unpleasant things when a celebration could easily take its place. "Can you pass me that knife, please?"

Leo watched Carla pass the knife to his mother. It was clear to him that Carla, who wasn't really his cousin but the daughter of his mother's dead best friend from college, didn't know how his mother could be when she didn't want to discuss something. In Leo's mind, though, this was very much a multipurpose party. He was not only celebrating his controversial release from that stuffy private school in Switzerland, where he was the only black boy and only one of five Americans. Nor was he just celebrating the fact that he was turning sixteen. He was celebrating the fact that he was about to spend the entire summer in Sag Harbor, far away from the city, far away from his battling parents. That had been the one thing he hadn't missed while he was studying in Switzerland: his parents' constant fighting. Ever since his father had decided to close down the CoCo Cosmetics production plant in Detroit and move the family to New York, things hadn't been the same. There was more money, which meant more furs and jewelry for his mother and bigger cars and fancier trips. But the move meant only one thing for his father: more access to his mistress. And for some reason, the furs and jewels and cars didn't seem to distract his mother from his father's mistress like they used to. Which meant many loud arguments when they thought Leo was in bed or out of earshot in some other part of their huge Central Park West apartment.

"Make a wish, dear," his mother said.

She didn't have to remind him. Leo had been wishing since he sat down at the table and tucked a napkin under his double chin, ready to dig into his favorite steak dinner. He'd wished for a summer full of three-quarters sunny days and one-quarter rainy days. He'd wished for Carla and her boring aunt to go back to the city as soon as they could. He'd wished for as few visiting relatives as possible so he could have as much chocolate cake as he wanted all to himself.

And he'd wished that this was the summer that he'd lose his virginity. He had come close in Switzerland. But, as his grandmother used to say, close only mattered in horseshoes.

He blew out the candles and leaned to one side so his mother could slice into the heaping cake. She passed him the first slice and he dug right in.

"This is nice," she said. "But only one piece for you, Leo."

"But, Ma—"

"One piece, I said. If you're going to be out here the whole summer, you should get some exercise and eat right. You don't want to be a butterball for the rest of your life, do you?"

———

Barry Chambers piled the rakes and hoes into the back of his father's old pickup truck. Then he snuck another glance across the pristine green-ness of the Bradford estate's plush lawn and stared into the large bay window of the house, where the girl of his dreams was sitting at the big oak dining table with some fat kid and two other rich-looking ladies. She looked just like the girl in the CoCo Cosmetics ad he saw in *Ebony* magazine. As his father started the ignition he pulled his eyes away from the bay window and jumped into the passenger's seat.

"Who was that tall girl?" he said to his father. "High cheek-bones, hazel eyes?"

"That's a cousin, in from the city. Why you wanna know?"

Barry shrugged and looked out the window as his father pulled out of the Bradfords' driveway onto Ninevah Lane. "Was her name Carla?"

"I think Mrs. Bradford did call her Carla. But like I said, why you wanna know?"

"Just asking." He couldn't help smiling. He shot his father a sly grin. "You know who she is, right?"

"I don't give a shit who she is. And don't be tryin' to mess around with that girl, you hear me?" Earl Chambers pulled a New-port cigarette from behind his ear and stuck it in his mouth. "I brought you on this shift so you could start makin' some money, not go chasin' tail."

Chasin' tail. *Who in the world,* Barry thought, not for the first time, *decided that I had to be saddled with* this *man as my father?* "Ain't chasin' tail. I just asked a question."

"And I gave you the answer." He lit the cigarette and blew a plume of smoke out the window. "Besides, there's enough fast-ass girls around here for you to climb up on without messin' with my clients' relatives."

"We going straight home?" Barry asked, changing the subject.

"I'ma drop you off, then I gotta run over by Walter's."

Of course, Barry thought. *Gotta have a drink or six before the night's over.* "I think Ma's cooking something good for dinner tonight."

"If you don't eat it all up I'm sure there'll be some left by the time I get there."

Barry sat back against the worn leather seat and cursed himself again for his own stupidity. He had planned to spend the summer in Vermont at the mock trial camp he'd heard about from his debate coach. He'd thought it was a free trip, open to all smart high school kids. But two days before the deadline to apply he found out that the program cost three hundred dollars. And when he'd brought the subject up at dinner that night, his father had turned him down flat.

"I'ma waste three hunnerd bucks for you to sit around with some white kids and pretend like you in a courtroom?" Earl had laughed and taken a sip from the can of Pabst resting next to his plate of fried chicken and collard greens. "Fuck that."

Barry's mother Hattie had tried to help him out. "It's for school, Earl," she said, her eyes downcast as she fiddled with the frayed edge of the old tablecloth. "This'll help him get into a good college."

"Which I also ain't payin' for," Earl said. Then he burped. "Y'all act like I'm made of money."

"We *act* like you could spend it on something other than beer and trips to Atlantic City," Hattie said quietly.

Barry froze, surprised by the anger and venom in his mother's voice. He could feel his chest constrict with fear as he waited for his father's response, which, if it was like all the others, would be a sharp smack across his mother's mouth. But Earl merely took the last few sips of his beer, picked up his keys, and walked out of the kitchen. After the door closed, Barry could see his mother's chest deflate with a long exhaling sigh.

Now, riding in the pickup, Barry tried to resign himself to the fact that he'd again be spending a long boring summer around the house, mowing other people's lawns and cleaning other people's pools. He thought again about the tall, slim girl with the long cocoa brown legs who'd passed him while he was digging weeds out of the Bradfords' front garden. Carla. Well, if he wasn't going to be in Vermont preparing to be a good lawyer, he could at least spend some time preparing to be a good lover.

Forget what his father said. Carla was going to be his.

Duke Maynard flipped through the records in the plastic milk crate. He pulled out a couple of albums by the Jacksons and Prince's first album.

He looked up at his friend Henry. "Where's Shalamar's first album? And the Dazz Band?"

"Check the orange crate," said Henry, flipping through an *X-Men* comic book. "You better not scratch up my records either."

"You know I'm a pro." Duke found the Shalamar album in the orange crate and stacked it with the others on the coffee table. He found the 12-inch singles he wanted, as well: D Train, the Commodores, and Stevie Wonder's "Do I Do." "You still don't have any Grandmaster Flash?"

"You know I ain't into that rap shit, man."

"Not even Run–D.M.C.?"

Duke had discovered Run–D.M.C. at his cousin's house in Queens a few weeks before and now it was all he liked to listen to. Something about the guys rapping over that scratched-up beat got him really excited. And he'd discovered other artists, too, whose tales of inner-city strife resonated with him. Even if he was a white teenager out in the far eastern reaches of Long Island, he still understood hard times. He sighed. "I can't deejay a party without a *few* rap records, Henry."

"Then I guess you better go buy you some records instead of borrowing mine all the time, right?"

Henry did have a point. And if Duke had had the money that's exactly what he would do. Take the train into the city and buy up all the hits he could find. At least then he could do some parties bigger than the little birthday jam here or after-school set there. Which would mean a little more money coming in. But he didn't really have time because of football. Now that he was first string, he had to concentrate. That's what Coach had said. He didn't want any of his first-stringers having any other hobbies. No girls, no parties, no nothing. It was football all the time, and if it wasn't practice it was watching film of the competition. If Coach got any inkling he was thinking about doing anything other than football, that would be his ass, most definitely.

"You coming to the party?" he asked Henry.

"Nope." Henry turned a page in his comic book. "Them bourgie niggas don't want nothing to do with me."

Duke looked up from the crate. That N-word always bothered him. "Henry, why you gotta use that word?"

Henry smiled. "You run the football like a nigga, you deejay like a nigga. You poor like a nigga. You more a nigga than them bourgie folk you be spinnin' records for. Sometimes I forget you's a white boy."

Duke sighed again. He'd been hearing that for a few years now, from the black guys he played football with and from the white kids at his school. Duke knew it was supposed to be a compliment, coming from most people, that he didn't seem like a white boy. But he didn't completely understand why. Sure, he thought some black dudes were cool. But he knew a bunch of them could be assholes, too, just like many of the white folks he encountered in his life. Especially the ones who accused him of trying to act black. Especially the ones who looked down on him and his mother because they didn't have money. Which confused Duke even more. He knew who he was, and he just thought he was being himself. Now that he actually had a black person in his family—his sister's boyfriend, his niece's father, was black—Duke found himself thinking about this stuff more and more lately.

"You should come and keep me company," he said to Henry.

Henry just shook his head. "Besides," he said. "I'm going to a comic convention out in Levittown early tomorrow morning."

"How you gonna meet any girls if you always in the house or at some comic convention?"

"I ain't worried about it, Duke. Besides, I ain't a football star like you. Ain't no girls interested in me." He pushed his glasses further up the bridge of his nose. "Not them bourgie ones who come out here for the summer, no way." He flipped open his comic book. "By the way, you need to stay away from them black girls, Duke. None of them gonna take a white boy that serious. Even if you do think you black."

"Henry, everything ain't about race—"

"See, now that's how I *know* you a white boy," Henry said with a sly laugh. "But you all right. I like you. I just don't want you gettin' your heart broke chasin' behind some sister who don't know that you all right."

Now this conversation was getting too confusing for Duke. He just shrugged and got up to go. "If you do decide to come to the jam don't worry about paying," he said. "I'll leave your name at the door. Okay?"

Henry just nodded and waved.

Outside, Duke got on his red Schwinn ten-speed and pedaled off. As he passed Walter's Bar and Grill, he saw Mr. Chambers's pickup parked out front. That was good, considering he had to stop by Barry's for some more records. It was always more fun at Barry's house when his father wasn't sitting around being mad at the world.

Mrs. Chambers was sweeping the front step when he turned into the little yard. She smiled at Duke and pointed around the house.

Barry was standing near the old garage out back, dusting dirt off his jeans as Duke wheeled his bike around the house. As he parked his bike, Duke could tell from the way Barry's lips were poked out that he wasn't in a good mood.

"I need your Run-D.M.C.," Duke said.

"How much you paying for it?"

"Paying? Man, you crazy. Since when I gotta pay to borrow records?"

"Since I'm moving outta here. Saving up."

"What'd your pops do now?"

Barry didn't say anything, just climbed the steps and went into the house. Duke followed him into his hot bedroom in the back of the house. A tiny fan managed to blow some of the stiff humid air around the little room. Barry flung himself across his bed, grabbed a football from the night table, and tossed it up into the air over him.

Duke sat in the desk chair and said, "You ain't moving no-where, man."

"Soon as I get the cash I'm outta here."

"To go where?"

Barry just shrugged. He sat up, tossed the football to Duke.

"Take the record, man. Not like I can play it anyway." He pointed to the shelves near the window that looked out onto the backyard.

The top shelf was empty. No turntable. No receiver. No speakers.

"What happened to your stereo?"

"What you think?"

"Your pops took it?"

Barry nodded. "Lost a bet to some kid at Walter's. My stereo was the prize. Said he was getting me another one but I ain't seen it yet."

Duke felt bad for Barry. There was always some drama at the Chambers's house, usually around money or Mr. Chambers's drinking. He could see why Barry would be planning some kind of escape, but at the same time, he wondered, Where could Barry go? Like Duke, he was only sixteen.

"You'll be in college soon enough," said Duke. "You suffered this long, you can wait another two years."

"Yeah," Barry said. "If I get a scholarship like you."

Duke flipped through the albums stacked against the far wall under the two pictures of Supreme Court Justice Thurgood Marshall that Barry had photocopied from a history book at the library. He found the Run-D.M.C. album and turned to Barry. "You coming to the party?"

"You know I'll be there." Barry stood up and looked at himself in the full-length mirror attached to the back of his bedroom door. He grabbed his crotch and shook his ass in a little grinding motion. "I'm getting me some pussy tonight."

"So what are you? You mixed?"

Joey stared at the skinny big-breasted girl in the tight pink tube top and thigh-hugging purple shorts. After five foster homes in four years he was used to this question, usually the first question he got from the new family he met when he arrived. The girl in the pink tube top rubbed at a scar on her knee and blew another bubble with the wad of Bubble Yum she chewed like a cow chewing cud.

"My mother's black and my father's Dominican," he said. He shifted the suitcase from one hand to the other. "What's your name?"

"Towanda," the girl said. "But they call me TeeTee."

"I'm Joey."

"I know who you are. Why you think I'm sitting here? I'm waiting on you."

Joey looked up at the harried-looking social worker in the wrinkled brown pantsuit who'd brought him here. She flipped quickly through a date book, then stole a glance at her watch. She said to TeeTee, "Is your mother here?"

"Like I said, I'm waiting. My mother be home in about an hour."

The social worker sighed loudly and looked at her watch again. "Okay, I guess it's all right. I'm really sorry," she said, not sounding very apologetic, "I have another placement. Will you tell your mother I'll be calling tomorrow to follow up?"

TeeTee just got up and went into the brownstone. Joey followed her inside, his eyes unable to avoid her seductively swaying hips. She certainly had a body on her. Joey didn't think he liked her personality too much, though. But she was going to be his foster sister for a while, at least until he did something wrong and got another placement, so he decided to make the best of it.

TeeTee pointed toward a slightly ajar door to the left of the living room. "You gonna be staying in there with Carlton." She flopped herself down on the couch. Joey watched her luscious body roll toward the cratered dent in the middle of the old couch. "What you lookin' at?" she said, though Joey could tell that she knew exactly what he was looking at. She pointed at the door again. "Go in there and get yourself settled."

Joey pushed the door open. It was a small, clean room, smelling of burned incense, with two twin beds, each pushed against the opposite wall. A bureau sat between the beds, with a mirror sitting atop it. Polaroids of various girls lined the edges of the mirror, stuck into the frame. At the end of the bed farthest from him sat a set of weights and barbells and a few pairs of sneakers. The wall on that side of the room was covered with posters: Jayne Kennedy in a tight one-piece swimsuit; a blown-up Diana Ross album cover; and an extra-large movie poster of Pam Grier as Foxy Brown. Joey opened his suitcase on the other bed and took out the plastic bag he'd been given for his toiletries. There was no space for his things on the bureau, covered as it was with Afro picks and cologne bottles and a huge boombox.

"You lookin' for something?"

Joey turned to see a short dark-brown guy with cornrows crisscrossing his bulbous head. He was short but he was big, his pecs popping forward and his stomach a flat board of muscles. He had a wet towel wrapped around his waist and was using another one to wipe beads of water from his shoulders and arms.

Joey said, "I'm guessing those weights are yours?"

"You guessed right, bro. You the foster kid?"

Joey nodded.

"How old are you?"

"Fifteen," said Joey. "I'll be sixteen in two months."

"You mixed?"

Before Joey could answer, the guy dropped the towel from around his waist and strode naked to the bureau. He took a pair of bikini briefs from the top drawer and stepped into them. Joey turned his eyes away.

"So where you from?"

Joey turned back to the guy, who was now sitting on his own bed. The bulge in his bikinis protruded out between his wide-spread legs.

"Born in Harlem," Joey said. He looked up at the posters. "I'm Joey, by the way."

"I'm Carlton." Carlton stood up and went to the edge of the bed and picked up two thirty-pound barbells. He lifted them over his head, then brought them down to his side. He did the same fluid motion ten times, his eyes closed, his sweat-glistened chest pumping up and down as he breathed in and out, before he spoke to Joey again. "These weights are mine. If you wanna use 'em, ask me first. You can put your shit in the bottom drawer and don't let me catch you going through my shit. You got that? Lessee, what else? Yeah, I don't get up early so if you get up, don't make no noise or I'ma be mad as hell. Sometimes I like to bring females back here and get my nut. If the door is closed, knock first and I'll let you know if it's cool to come in. If you wake up and you hear something sexy going on in my bed, just be quiet. I don't care if you get horny and jerk off, just be quiet while you doing it. Them's the rules. You got that?"

Joey nodded.

"You don't say a lot, do you?" Carlton said.

Past experience had taught Joey not to say too much when he was starting out at a new foster home, so he kept to himself until he felt comfortable enough to open up to the new "family" he'd been given. But that didn't happen too often. Usually by the time he felt comfortable enough to be himself, something had gone wrong and it was time to pack up and head to the next foster home.

"Well, I gotta get dressed for work," Carlton said.

"What kinda work do you do?"

"I drive."

"A truck?"

"Nah, man, I drive a limo," Carlton said. "And sometimes I do other kinds of driving. But that ain't none of your biz, is it?" He narrowed his eyes at Joey, then broke out into a loud laugh.

There were something sly and conspiratorial in his laughter and Joey could feel himself tense up at the sound of it. He turned to his suitcase and fingered a T-shirt packed on the top. He took a couple of deep breaths, and tried to shake off the weird feelings coursing though him. As he took shirts and shorts from the suitcase, he tried to calm down. He decided he was just being his usual suspicious self.

"You got something against limos?" Carlton said.

Joey said, "Excuse me?" He turned back to face Carlton.

"I like your quiet effect, Lil Joey," Carlton said. "Last kid we had here talked my damn ear off." He smiled and pulled a white T-shirt over his head.

"Oh yeah, one more thing," Carlton said as he stepped into a perfectly creased pair of black slacks. "Stay away from TeeTee. I know she's cute and all, but she's trouble. I can say that. She's my sister. And I know."

2

Carla burst into Leo's room. "Come on, you're taking me to a party."

Leo looked up from the tattered copy of *The Hobbit*. "We just had a party."

Carla lay down on the bed and entwined one long leg around the other like she was posing for a photo shoot. "You call *that* a party? You, me, your mother, and my evil aunt Beverly? Boring time, Leo. Nothing personal." She sat up and knocked the book from his hands. "I was on the beach this morning and I heard some girl named Renee was having a party tonight. Do you know her?"

Renee Cunningham, the oldest daughter of Reese and Tanya Cunningham, a short buxom girl with hair straight down her back. Actually he knew the Cunninghams from his building in Manhattan. They were the first black family to move in before the Bradfords. "If she's having a party," he said, "I wasn't invited." And he didn't like the sound of any party at Renee Cunningham's. Renee barely spoke to him in Manhattan and never spoke to him during the summer in Sag Harbor. She was a year older than Leo and she ran with all the good-looking kids. She called Leo "Fatty" once at a barbecue two summers before. Carla, with her long legs and the beautiful oval-shaped face that graced the publicity posters of his father's cosmetics company, would fit right in with the Renee Cunningham crowd. Actually, he was surprised that Carla didn't already know Renee, which he told her.

"Well, I don't really come to Sag, Leo, I *am* more of a Vineyard girl. And you've been away. She probably doesn't even know you're back from Switzerland now." She jumped up from the bed and twirled in front of the mirror hanging behind the closet door. "And spill it. What did you do to get sent back here anyway? What's the real juicy story?" She flopped back down on the bed and struck another pose.

Leo lay back against the pillows on his bed. How did you explain that you helped your friend Riyadh, the son of an Egyptian oil magnate, cheat on an exam? How did you explain that you did it because you had these terrifically confusing feelings about Riyadh, that you wanted to do whatever you could to make sure that he'd be back the next year so you'd have someone you could call a friend, someone who provided the only good times you had in Switzerland, sitting on the roof of the dorm, smoking cigs and playing Sugar Hill Gang cassettes on a tiny Swiss tape player? "It's a long story," he finally told her.

Not that Carla was all that interested. He could tell her mind was really on the night's plans. "Come on, Leo, I can't go to the party by myself. You have to take me. I'm gonna wear my new Jordache jeans."

Leo sighed. "Is the party at the Cunninghams' house?"

Carla nodded. "And one other thing, cousin. Who's the guy who was mowing the lawn today? So fine."

"Mr. Bradford? He's, like, forty years old. You into old guys these days?"

"Not *him*. A young guy, our age. Real cute. Tall, light eyes, high top fade."

Leo had no idea who she was talking about.

"You need to get out more, Leo," Carla said, still admiring herself in the mirror. "You need to meet people instead of reading books all the time." Suddenly, she turned back to him. "Leo? Are you a virgin?"

Leo could feel heat creep from his neck to his face. "What do you think?"

"I think if you take me to this party, you might meet a nice girl who'll help you out with that." Carla finally tired of looking at herself and opened the closet door. "I'll find you something nice to wear. By the time you get out of the shower I'll be dressed and ready to go."

As Duke was leaving the house he heard his mother shout, for the third time, "Don't be too late, Daniel. And no drugs! You hear me?" He grunted a yes and closed the door behind him. He sat on the step with his three crates of records and waited for Barry to pull up to the house. He breathed deeply. Every time he left his house, whether going to school in the morning or practice at night, he felt like he was escaping the womb. It hadn't been hard to figure out that he was only paying the price for the wild teenage years of his older brother and sister, but that didn't stop his mother's over-protective nature from getting to him. He silently cursed his father, as he tended to do in suffocating moments like this. He knew it was horrible to think it, but he did: If his father hadn't died seven years ago, things might not be the way they were. His brother Michael might not have gotten into cocaine and his sister Marie might not have gotten pregnant at sixteen. But his father did die. And now his mother was this sad, depressed person whom he barely recognized as his mother, depending on him like he was the parent and she the child. She didn't even use the nickname she'd given him as a boy. She called him Daniel the day his father died and she called him Daniel to this day.

And as much as Duke was enjoying his summer, he couldn't wait for fall. School would start, which meant football would start, which meant the college scouts would soon be out in full force, hovering around to see if the fastest white boy any one had seen was seriously Big Ten material. Because as hard as it was and as time-consuming as it began to be, football was his ticket out. And he couldn't wait to punch that ticket.

Rich girls.

That's what Barry was thinking about as he pulled his black mock-neck over his head and stared at himself in the mirror. Nothing like rich girls. Nothing like the smell of their expensive perfume when he was kissing them behind their ears. Nothing like the jangle of those heavy gold rich-girl bracelets when they're giving you a hand job in the backseat of Daddy's Mercedes or the feel of those pearl earrings in his fingers when they're going down on you behind the pool house at dusk. This summer that rich girl's name was going to be Carla.

Barry's thoughts were nowhere near the mock trial camp. All he could think about was making his entrance into Renee Cunningham's basement and knowing that all female eyes were going to be on him. Sure, he wasn't some private school Manhattan boy. He wasn't some scion of the uppity black middle class. He was a local, a townie. But he knew he was cuter than most of those soft rich boys who summered out here and acted like they were the best things the Good Lord had ever invented. He also knew that not many of them had his brains or his charm. So what if he'd spend the summer mowing their lawns and cleaning their pools? He'd learned two summers ago, the summer he was fourteen and his chest was starting to get some musculature and his braces came off, that the rich girls from Manhattan liked a local boy when it came to fooling around. And he was more than eager to play whatever role he needed to play.

Barry knew a lot less about the world than he thought he did, but there was one thing he'd managed to pick up, watching and observing the ways of rich folks: It was all about playing the right role. He knew he could do it. And he knew it would take him far.

He tiptoed to his parents' bedroom and peeked in. His father was fast asleep, one arm thrown across his mother's chest, his drunken snores threatening to rip the ceiling off the room. He reached his hand into the room, into the pocket of his father's dirty khakis, and slowly took the keys to the truck. Then he tiptoed to the front door and eased it closed behind him.

Carla, he thought as he started the truck, *get ready, baby, 'cause here I come.*

Joey sat on the couch between TeeTee and her mother Shirley, a big-boned, toffee-colored woman who thought *The Dukes of Hazzard* was the funniest thing in the world.

Joey had breathed a sigh of relief when his new foster mother came home, laden with grocery bags and department store carryalls. Carlton had gone to run an errand, which left Joey to spend much of the afternoon scooting away from TeeTee, who'd offered to rub his back before outright asking if she could give him a blow job.

"Don't eat me outta house and home and don't be askin' me for no money," was how Shirley had introduced herself to Joey. Then she went right to the kitchen and fried some chicken wings and mixed up a box of macaroni and cheese, singing along with a Millie Jackson tape in the boombox the whole time. "Soup's on," she'd yelled when everything was ready. Joey joined Shirley, TeeTee, and Carlton at the small kitchen table. He couldn't remember the last time he'd tasted such good fried chicken. It reminded him of his grandmother's cooking. Before she died and his life spun out of control. But he didn't want to think about any of that. So he pushed the thoughts away and concentrated on the chicken and the conversation around the table.

"Where you drivin' them rich folks tonight?" Shirley asked Carlton.

"Sag Harbor," he said.

TeeTee said, "Where's that?"

"Long Island," said Carlton. "Lotta black folks have vacation houses out there."

Shirley said, "These black folks you drivin'? Well, I'll be." She looked at Joey. "Take another wing if you want one, boy. I see you lickin' your fingers."

After Carlton left to pick up his driving partner, Joey joined

TeeTee and Shirley in the living room to watch TV. They were about to settle in for the second half of *The Dukes of Hazzard* when the front door flew open and Carlton ran into the apartment.

"Ma, you got Porgy's mother number? I waited half an hour. He ain't show up."

Shirley lifted herself from the couch and went into her bedroom. Joey sank deeper into the sagging couch, which caused TeeTee to slide closer to him, her arm landing on his thigh. She didn't move it. Shirley came back into the living room, shaking her head. "She say Porgy went down to Maryland to pick up his daughter. She say he called here and left a message."

Joey watched Shirley and Carlton both look at TeeTee. She shrugged. "Oh, yeah, he did call. I forgot to write it down."

"So what do you say to your brother?" said Shirley.

TeeTee shrugged again. "I forgot?" She tried to hold back a smile. "Just put the radio up loud if you think you gonna fall asleep. That's what everybody else do."

Carlton looked like he wanted to strangle TeeTee. He looked at Joey. "Come on, Lil Man. You coming with me. I know you don't say much but I need you to talk to me so I don't fall asleep on the road."

"Go 'head, Joey," Shirley said.

Twenty minutes later, Carlton had picked up two teenaged guys outside a brownstone in Brooklyn Heights. Soon they were speeding along the Long Island Expressway, heading for Sag Harbor.

As they passed through Suffolk County, Carlton turned down the music and said to Joey, "Can you drive?"

"Nope," said Joey. "Never really been anywhere long enough to learn."

"You wanna learn?"

"You can teach me?"

"We'll work something out. But you know you don't get nuttin' for free."

Who you telling? thought Joey. Being in the passenger seat as Carlton sped along the highway reminded Joey of the last time he saw his father, right after his grandmother passed away. Juan Ramirez liked to drive fast, too, with a can of Budweiser between his legs and loud salsa blaring from the tape deck, his long curly hair flying back in the breeze. They'd been speeding along that last night before they were stopped by a pair of cops who'd searched the car and found the stash of heroin that sent Juan Ramirez right to jail, for ten years. He died in a yard fight on New Year's Day of his second year inside.

"Y'all got any weed?"

Joey was pulled from his thoughts by the alcohol-laced breath of one of the kids from Brooklyn, sticking his head through the divider, looking from Carlton to Joey.

"I'm sure you can find some get-high where you going," said Carlton.

"What about you?" the guy said, peering close at Joey.

"He fifteen years old," said Carlton before Joey could answer. "Now sit back before I decapitate you with the window. Rich kids," he mumbled, shooting a look at Joey. "Nothin' but brats."

Joey laughed, as the guy sat back, his arrogant face blushing with a quick look of embarrassment. Joey couldn't remember a better first night at a foster home. TeeTee was a bit much, making eyes at him every chance she got, and Carlton's initial introduction with that sinister laughter still reverberated inside him, but Shirley had been fun, with her good cooking and loud laughter, and Carlton was acting like the big brother Joey had never had. Maybe this time would be different.

As they were getting off the exit for Sag Harbor about two

hours later and heading toward Main Street, the guy stuck his head through the divider again and said, "You do know where you're going, right?"

"Damn, Reggie, leave him alone already," the other guy shouted from the rear of the limo. "Just give him the directions Carla gave you."

"Carla didn't give me directions," Reggie said. "This is gonna be a surprise."

Joey moved himself closer to the passenger-side window, away from the violent fumes of Reggie's beer-laced breath. He tried to imagine what this Carla girl must be like if *this* drunk idiot was on his way to see her.

Leo was surprised that he knew as many people as he did at the party. He got hugs from Jill Robertson and Shelly Thomas, both of whom he'd gone to school with when he first moved to Manhattan. Todd Winston, whose father had gone to college with his father, seemed happy to see him and promised that they'd hang out over the summer since Todd was staying out in Sag for the entire season as well. While he was piling a small paper plate with chips and bean dip, he saw Robbie Mason, whom he knew through a cousin in the Detroit chapter of Jack and Jill.

The lights were low and the music was hot, but Leo still wasn't in the party mood. He would have been just as happy at home reading or watching videos. But reading and watching videos was never going to lead to what he wanted it to lead to: losing his virginity. He imagined himself the only virgin in the room. Everyone else seemed so in touch with their sexual energy, groping at each other on the dance floor, grinding against each other in the corners. What was wrong with him? *Other than being a big fat hog*, he thought, reaching for some more dip and chips.

He saw Carla, in her tight, hip-hugging Jordache jeans and black high heel shoes, slow dancing to a Prince song in the arms of the tall guy with the high-top fade. She looked positively orgasmic.

Then he heard a female voice say, "You see Carla Randall with that guy Barry? He mows our lawn. And I thought she was dating Reggie McFarland." He turned to see a short skinny girl with long curly hair talking to Renee Cunningham.

Renee said, "I've heard about her, Miss CoCo Cosmetics. She thinks she's the cat's meow because she's on all those posters. But what do you expect? She *usually* goes to the Vineyard."

"You know that guy Barry is supposedly hung like a horse."

"I've heard. I've also heard Carla's into big dicks—in both senses of the word."

"She's also my cousin," Leo said.

Renee looked at him like he was some creature the tide dragged in from the ocean that lapped at the beach right outside the house. "No, she isn't," Renee sneered. "I hear you just say that. And I thought you were in Europe or something."

"I'm back," he said. "And thanks so much for inviting me to your party."

"I didn't—"

"That's the point, Renee," said the other girl, making sexy eyes at Leo. "He's being sarcastic."

"Oh," said Renee. "Well, it certainly seems like that Swiss air did nothing for your weight, did it?"

The other girl stepped closer to Leo. "Hey, Leo, don't you recognize me?"

He looked closer. "Diane?"

"You got it. I look different, right?"

"What did you do?"

"Got my nose done. Grew my hair out. Boobs grew out."

Leo almost spit out his fruit punch.

"It's all right, Leo," she smiled. "I understand if you're a boob man." Then she looked at Renee and they both burst out laughing.

He grabbed a napkin and wiped the punch from the front of his shirt. Maybe it was time to move to the other side of the room. Or even go home.

As he watched Diane and Renee walk away he heard Diane say, "That white boy can really play some records."

"He can do more than that," Renee added, "You know *he's* been with Carla, too."

Leo looked over at the table where the DJ was spinning records. He didn't recognize him, but he figured that was because he really didn't know the Cunninghams to have too many white folks in their home. The DJ's eyes were right on Carla dancing with the guy in the middle of the dance floor. He looked pissed off. But his expression lightened up when Leo said, "Hey, you have any rap?"

The DJ held up a finger as he tried to catch the beat of a record playing on the left turntable to mix in a new record on the right. When he was done he leaned over the table toward Leo and smiled. "You like rap?"

Leo nodded. "You got any Spoonie Gee?"

"You like Spoonie Gee?"

"Not as much as I like Flash, but yeah."

The DJ held up his finger again and concentrated on the turntables. When he was done, he said, "You got any records?"

"Tons," said Leo. "My name's Leo."

"I'm Duke." He slapped five with Leo. "I'll talk to you later, okay?"

Leo nodded and let him get back to work. As usual, he felt much more comfortable talking to a guy. He didn't spit out his fruit punch once. And talking to Duke for those few seconds, he felt his heart speed up a few beats and heat rise from his neck to his face, which never happened when he talked to girls. Why was that? Leo swallowed hard and took a deep breath. Because he knew what it was about, it was the same way he'd felt talking to Riyadh. But knowing what it was didn't make it any easier to accept. It was still hard as hell to admit it to himself even though the idea of it had been ringing through his mind since before he left for Switzerland a year ago. Something about being at Renee's party, however, had shifted his feelings about the whole idea. He didn't know if it was Duke's open friendliness or Diane's abrupt flirting, or just the comfort of being back in Sag, the place he loved more than anywhere else in the world, but he decided to admit it to himself, to just say it.

"I like guys," he said. "I like *guys*." Then he exhaled. That wasn't so hard.

Duke leaned over the table. "What did you say, bro?" he shouted.

"Uh, ah, nothing, man. Just singing with the music."

Duke gave him another smile and a thumbs-up. Leo may have been ready to say it out loud to himself but he wasn't ready to tell anybody else.

"So," Barry whispered to Carla. "Why you ain't got a boyfriend?"

They were sitting on a soft felt-covered bench out on the veranda of the Cunningham house. The moon was high and bright in the summer sky and the sharp, salty smell of the ocean fell over them.

Carla ran her fingers along Barry's thigh. "Who said I didn't have a boyfriend?"

"You don't dance like you got one," said Barry. "I got radar for that kinda stuff."

"Imagine that," Carla said, with a wink. "Boyfriend Radar."

"You wanna go somewhere else?"

"Where else is there to go?"

Barry played with a charm on Carla's bracelet. "There's a whole beach out there."

"You feel like swimming?"

"I been swimming in your eyes all night. What's an ocean compared to that?"

"You are too smooth, Barry." Carla stood up. She leaned over the veranda railing. "I usually go up to the Vineyard. But I have a feeling I'm gonna spend a lot of time out here this summer."

"Good idea," said Barry. He stood up and stepped up right behind her, pushing his body against hers.

"You move fast, don't you?"

"I move at whatever speed you tell me to move."

Carla turned to face him, keeping her body close to his. She kissed him full on the mouth, her tongue reached for his. A soft moan escaped her lips. Barry took that as a sign and slid his hand up the back of her T-shirt.

"Maybe we *should* go somewhere else," Carla whispered in Barry's ear.

Carlton had barely parked near the curb when Reggie tumbled out of the limousine. Carlton jumped out and ran to the passenger side, propping him up against the long shiny car. Joey stood by in case Carlton needed help keeping Reggie standing.

"Hey!" Reggie yelled to two girls standing outside the Cunningham house. "Is Carla Randall in there?"

The girls just looked at each other and went inside.

Reggie turned to his friend Martin. "At least it sounds like some good music, right?" He stumbled forward, swayed a bit, but caught himself before Carlton and Martin had to catch him. He turned to Carlton and Joey. "Come on, guys. Have a drink. On me."

"No, thank you," said Carlton. "We'll wait out here for you."

Inside, Duke was on the mike, rousing the crowd. "To the beat, y'all, to the beat!" Reggie paused on the basement stairs, swaying there for a few seconds. He pointed at Duke and turned to Martin. "Oh, man. They got a white boy deejaying the set! Check it out!"

Reggie found the bar in no time, Martin quick on his heels, and poured two cups of punch. When Martin reached for one, Reggie yanked it back, spilling punch on his pink polo. "These are for me, man. Get your own." He swayed there to the beat of the music, taking long sips from the large plastic cup.

Renee Cunningham saw Reggie and Martin, and pushed her way through the crowded dance floor. "Reggie!" She grabbed him into a hug. "So nice of you to come."

"This punch is weak," he slurred. He looked over her head. "Where's Carla?"

"She's around here somewhere," said Renee, her eyes peeled for the first sight of Carla Randall. She knew her party was about to go from good to memorable. "I think I saw her out on the veranda a little while ago."

Across the room, Leo watched Renee talk to a ridiculously handsome light-brown-skinned guy with curly hair. He thought the guy seemed familiar. As he got closer, he realized it was Reggie McFarland, Carla's ex-boyfriend. Leo hadn't seen Reggie since a cotillion three years before. He thought of Reggie as The Phony. He didn't like him three years ago and he didn't think he'd like him now.

"Reggie?"

Reggie spun around to face Leo. He squinted his hazel eyes, then leaned closer. "Hey, Leo. Leo Leo Leo. My main man Leo." He grabbed Leo into a big beer-scented hug. Leo could feel punch spill from the plastic cups and moisten the back of his shirt. He pulled away from Reggie. "Can I buy you a drink, my Leo?"

"No," Leo said, rolling his eyes. "This isn't a *bar*. What are you doing here anyway?"

"I came to surprise my baby. Where is she? Where's my baby Carla?"

"I thought you two broke up?"

"What kinda question is that, my Leo Leo Leo?" Reggie turned to Martin, who was looking more and more embarrassed by Reggie's loud voice and wobbly posture. "You hear what he asked me? He asked me if me and my baby broke up."

"Carla and Leo came together," said Renee Cunningham.

"Then you *know* we're still together, my Leo."

"Did you check outside?" Renee said. "Maybe she's taking a walk on the beach."

"Actually," Leo said, "Carla already went back to my house. She was tired."

"From what?" said Renee. "She didn't look tired to me when I saw her earlier. She was the star of the dance floor."

"That's my baby," said Reggie. "The life of the party."

Out on the beach, Barry pulled Carla's T-shirt over her head and Carla reached for his belt, unfastening and yanking it through the loops in one expert move. They pulled hungrily at each other's zippers. Barry got out of his jeans first. It took a few minutes to get Carla's tight designer jeans past her hips. When he had them off, Barry reached down and rubbed between her legs. A hiccuppy giggle escaped Carla's lips and he knew he'd hit the spot. He moved his hands up to her breasts and played with her nipples, running them through his fingers, tightening, loosening, tickling. When Carla reached down to grab him, he swatted her hand away.

"Not yet," he moaned. "You first."

The quizzical look in her eye was exactly what he wanted. The

Jackpot Look, he called it. No girl ever hears a guy say those words, "You first." That's what he played to, and it worked every time. He grabbed both her hands and held them over her head with one of his, touching her lips with his own, brushing them with his tongue, licking her cheeks and earlobes and eyelids, as he reached down with his other hand, searching for that spot. Carla's hiccups had turned to soft moans, then louder ones, and Barry knew it was time to bring it all home. He bent her knees and pushed her legs back and began to lower himself to her.

"Carla!"

Barry looked up to see the moon-highlighted outline of some guy standing on the beach, shouting Carla's name at the top of his lungs.

Carla clamped her legs shut and sat forward. "Shit." She scrambled out from under Barry, grabbed her jeans and T-shirt, and skidded off down the beach.

"Carla!" the guy shouted. "It's me, baby. I know you're out here somewhere!"

Barry yanked his underwear and jeans up over his hard dick and stepped into his Pumas. After he pulled his mock-neck over his head, he could see a tall guy stumbling along the beach toward him. He stood there until the guy was close. Good-looking guy, Barry thought, in a light-skinned pretty boy type of way.

"Who are you?" said Barry.

"Reggie McFarland. And you?"

"Nobody, man."

Barry started back toward the Cunningham house.

The veranda was crowded with partiers, all of their eyes on him. In the middle of the crowd stood Renee Cunningham, looking quite amused. Barry climbed the stairs and pushed through the crowd. Inside he got a cup of punch and went over to the DJ table.

Duke said, "So you got what you came for?"

"I don't want to talk about it."

Duke just shrugged and went back to spinning records. Stevie Wonder's "Master Blaster" pounded from the speakers.

Suddenly there was a commotion out on the veranda. Barry put his drink on the DJ table and pushed through the crowded dance floor to see what was happening.

Carla was arguing on the bottom step with the pretty boy kid.

"What are you even doing here?" Carla screamed.

"I wanted to surprise you," said Reggie.

"You know I don't like surprises, Reggie. What, were you expecting to find me with another guy? Were you spying on me?"

Barry moved to the front of the veranda crowd. He stood next to a chubby kid with a stricken look on his face. "You're Carla's cousin, right?"

"Sort of," Leo said.

"Did you know she had a boyfriend?"

Leo just shrugged. "You fooled around with her?"

"A little," said Barry.

"That's him," said Renee, pointing at Barry. "The guy who mows the lawn."

All eyes looked to Barry. From the bottom step, Reggie and Carla looked up toward the veranda. Reggie waded through and squeezed himself between Leo and Barry.

"You messed with Carla?"

"You better take that up with her," Barry said. "If that's your girl."

"If?"

"You heard me, man."

Reggie turned to Carla. "Is this the dude you were with all night?"

"That's him," said Renee, getting even more excited. People would be talking about this party all summer. "This may pass for fun in Martha's Vineyard," she said to Carla, "but we don't conduct ourselves that way here."

"Shut the fuck up," said Leo. He noticed surprised eyes turning his way at the sound of his words. He was as surprised as anyone.

"Shut up," screamed Renee, "you tub of lard. Just because your cousin's a slut—"

Suddenly Reggie hauled off and swung at Barry. Barry ducked and landed a right in Reggie's stomach. Reggie stumbled back, already wobbly from too much drink, and fell right into Leo. Leo pushed him forward, right into Barry's left hook, which sent Reggie flying over the veranda railing right onto the soft sand in front of the house. A group of girls near the door screamed.

Someone said, "Move aside," and a stocky guy in a chauffeur suit pushed through the crowd and kneeled down over Reggie. A light brown Latin-looking guy in cut-off denim shorts and a tank top helped him get Reggie to his feet and everyone moved aside so the chauffeur could drag Reggie back around the house to the limo.

Carla gave Barry a long look, then followed the chauffeur to the car. Leo asked Barry if he was all right.

"I'm fine," Barry said.

Leo followed Carla to the front of the house. People were driving off, eager to get on the phone and spread the word about the first big party of the season.

Leo watched as the chauffeur and the other guy shoved Reggie into the back of the limousine and then stepped aside to let Martin climb in behind him. Looking at the Latin guy, Leo felt that familiar rush of heat as his heart beat a little faster. He'd seen some good-looking dudes at the party but this guy was absolutely beautiful, he thought. He moved closer to him. "What are you," Leo asked Joey. "The chauffeur's assistant?"

"Something like that," Joey said. "You live out here?"

The guy didn't seem to have any kind of accent. Maybe he wasn't Latin? "My parents have a house," said Leo.

"Oh," Joey said with a smile. "You one of the rich kids."

"My *parents* are rich," said Leo. "I'm not. I just have rich relations."

Joey laughed. "That's funny."

Carlton said, "Come on, Lil Man Joey. Time to break out."

"See ya," said Joey.

"See ya," said Leo.

Carla stepped up next to Leo. "You told him I'd gone back to your house?"

"Just trying to protect you."

"I'm seventeen, Leo, I don't need you to protect me."

"Sometimes, Carla, you really do," Leo said.

Duke came outside, still holding his mike, his DJ headphones resting around his neck. He went over to Barry. "Was it all worth it, man?"

Barry just smiled and put his arm around Duke's shoulder. "Come on, let's get your records so we can get outta here. I gotta get my dad's truck back."

Before Duke could follow him inside, he turned to Leo. "Hey, man," he said. "I still wanna get with you about those rap records."

Leo took a receipt from his pocket and wrote his phone number on the back of it. "Call me, bro. I'm around all summer."

"Be cool," Duke said, and headed inside. Barry turned back to Leo. "Hey, man, thanks for havin' my back out there."

Leo just nodded and watched the limousine as it pulled out of the Cunningham drive and drove away.

3

Late at night, in June of 1983, four teenaged guys had some private thoughts.

Leo Bradford fingered the buttons on the pajamas he wore only when there were female relatives visiting the house, and whispered the name in the dark, the name he'd been whispering the whole way home: "*Joey*." Then he caught himself. How did he know if this Joey dude even *liked* guys the same way he did? Maybe he was as straight as a guy could be. But then he decided he didn't care. He just wondered if there was any chance, any way, he'd ever see that kid Joey again.

Just before he fell asleep he realized there was.

Barry Chambers slipped his father's truck keys back into the dirty khakis on the chair and tiptoed into the kitchen to get some ice. His left hand hurt from slugging Reggie McFarland so he put the cold cubes in a dish towel and wrapped it around his hand. As he undressed for bed, he thought of his moments in the sand with Carla and his dick was hard again, pitching a tent in his boxer shorts. He stripped off the boxers and stood naked in front of the mirror. He thought about jerking off, then decided not to. Why waste a nut? He wanted to save it. And he knew exactly whom he'd be saving it for. Carla.

Duke Maynard checked in on his mother, then flopped himself onto his bed. He couldn't believe the way the night had transpired. He was on fire on the wheels of steel, doling out the funk like he never had before. He reached into his pocket and counted out the two hundred bucks that Renee Cunningham had pressed into his palm right before he and Barry drove off. Oh, man, Barry. Why didn't Barry tell him that the girl he was after was Carla Randall? He'd had a coupla nights of fun with Carla last summer. And another one, for old time's sake Carla had said, when she first got back. Carla was into playthings. He guessed it was now Barry's turn to be played with. He put Carla and Barry out of his mind. How 'bout that kid Leo? Name-dropping Spoonie Gee? It always surprised Duke that he didn't meet more black folks who were into rap the way he was. It was about time he met someone around the way who was also into the music. He put the receipt with Leo's number on his night table with the payment from the party. Maybe this was gonna be a good summer after all . . .

Joey Ramirez lay in bed, looking at the shadows on the ceiling above him. This was his usual process when getting to know a new home, lying still in bed on the first night, checking how the shadows moved from the streetlights, listening for the rhythms of the house, how the floorboards creaked or the heater switched on and off in the night. He told himself that he'd know if he felt safe or not, based on the sounds the house made when everyone was asleep. It was superstitious, he knew, but that didn't matter. He turned his thoughts to all the big beautiful houses he'd seen out on the east end of Long Island, and the salty spray of ocean air that hovered all around them, as he drifted off . . . and soon something felt really, really good, soft-and-wet good. So good, it felt like the entire lower half of his body was stiff with anticipation, ready to explode. Which it did, waking him with a start. He sat up. His stomach was damp, his underwear yanked down under his balls. He blinked, trying to adjust his eyes to the darkness. Then he felt the bed shake, and he saw TeeTee hovering over him, smiling down at him. She winked once, then climbed off of him. He looked over at Carlton's bed. The room was empty except for him and TeeTee, standing there pulling a tiny pair of panties up around her full hips, a big smile on her lips. Before he could say anything, the door swung open and Carlton was standing there, Shirley right behind him. Joey looked from Tee-Tee to Carlton to Shirley, then down at his almost naked body, his penis still rigidly erect.

Summertime, and the living was supposed to be easy.

1

"You're telling us," Joey said, looking around at the three men in the room he'd known since he was fifteen years old, "that one of us is your father?"

TNT nodded.

Barry said, "Are you fucking serious?"

TNT nodded again. "As serious as fucking cancer."

"That's impossible," said Barry. "Impossible."

"Why is it impossible?" TNT said. "I wouldn't have brought the four of you together if I wasn't sure it was one of you."

"So this isn't a business meeting," Duke said, standing up.

"Call it a 'personal' business meeting," said TNT. "As in my personal business. Sit down, Duke."

Barry went to the bar. The only sound in the suite was the clink of ice hitting his glass. "What makes you think it's one of us?" he said, his back to the rest of them.

"I have my sources."

"That's not good enough," said Barry. "You gotta come with something stronger than that, man."

"Or you do," said TNT.

Barry turned to face the room. "What does that mean?"

"I think it means," Leo said, "that unless we can *all* prove that *none* of us is his father, he probably has evidence that *one* of us definitely is."

"You and your fucking logic all the fucking time," Barry said to Leo.

Joey said, "Shut up, Barry."

"You shut up."

Duke cleared his throat. They all turned to face him. "I think that you don't have any proof. That's why you have all of us here. You need one of us to confess."

TNT stared hard at Duke, his eyes like sharp, angry rays. Then they softened and he sat down on the top step. "You might be right, Maynard. Score one for the jock."

Barry swigged back the last of his drink and slammed the glass on the bar. "I know I'm not your father." He picked up his briefcase and stepped around the couch where Joey and Duke sat. "And I have things to do and places to be—"

TNT said, "Sit down, Barry."

Barry ignored him and started past him up the steps.

"I said, sit down, Barry."

"Why? To play some game with you? Man, like I said, I got important shit to do."

TNT stood up, his foot knocking over the empty beer bottle. It rolled down three steps and smashed into pieces when it landed on the marble floor.

"Better get someone to clean that up," Barry said, pushing the elevator button.

Joey stood up. "Barry."

Duke said, "Let him go. I'm sure it's not the first time he's been accused of paternity."

The elevator doors opened. Barry stepped into the car, turned to face the room, and waved at them with a sarcastic grin as the doors closed. They all watched the numbers as the elevator descended.

"What's your mother's name?" Leo asked TNT.

"Where were you born?" asked Joey.

"*When* were you born?" asked Duke.

TNT held up his hands, a smile on his lips. "Too many questions. I brought *you* guys here to do the answering."

"Then maybe I should leave, too," said Joey. "I'm willing to hear you out, but I'm not into games."

"I was born in March 1984," said TNT. "So that means my mom got pregnant with me in the summer of 1983."

Joey and Duke and Leo looked at each other.

They remembered the summer of 1983. It was a wild summer full of good times and bad. But definitely the start of something important for all of them. They'd all become friends that summer. And here they were again, brought together years later.

I know who his father is, thought Leo.

He can't *be,* thought Duke.

I can't believe this is happening, thought Joey. *I should have left with Barry.*

2

Outside the Hotel Gansevoort, the guy in the red sweatshirt with the black baseball cap pulled down over his eyes watched the guy in the expensive suit climb into the Maybach.

Must be his lawyer, he thought. *He'll be thanking his lucky stars he got out of here, now won't he?*

After he watched the Mercedes drive away, he made his way to the reception desk, tucked back along the right wall. The blond girl standing there had blush high on her cheeks and a snippy look on her face.

"Can I help you?" she said, like she really didn't mean it.

But he didn't care if she meant it or not. "What room is TNT in?"

"Is Mr. TNT expecting you?"

Check her *out. Mr. TNT. Like he's some kind of VIP.* "Yeah, he's expecting me. I wouldn't be here if he wasn't, now would I?"

The blond girl looked through a folder on the counter in front of her. "I'm sorry, there are strict instructions from Mr. TNT. No visitors. And no interruptions."

"Check again," he said.

"I don't have to check again. Now, will you please step aside?"

He reached under the big red sweatshirt, letting his fingers tickle the heavy .45 stuck into his belt. *She wouldn't be acting so uppity if she knew what I had,* he thought.

"Sir? Would you please step aside?"

He stepped aside. Why waste what he had on her? She wasn't worth it.

This was all for TNT.

Mr. TNT.

He laughed. But then again maybe *Mr.* TNT *was* the best way to think of him.

Everyone should get a little respect on the day they were going to die, right?

1

"You knew I liked Carla," Duke said. "Why didn't you tell me it was her?"

Barry shrugged. "Figured it wouldn't make a difference. It's not like you all were in love or anything." He looked out the car window at two girls roller skating along Main Street. *It's not like she'd fall for you anyway*, he thought. *I love you, man, but Carla McFarland would never fall for a white dude. Anybody could see* that. *Anybody who was black anyway*. He just smiled and turned back to Duke. "Is this any way to greet your boy after I been away a whole month?"

"How was it anyway?"

"Great," said Barry, "just like I expected it would be."

They were in Duke's mother's station wagon, driving back to Sag Harbor from Islip airport, where Barry's flight from Boston had landed. As much as he'd enjoyed his three exciting weeks in Vermont at mock trial camp, Barry was very happy to be back home. If only to give his mother a huge kiss and hug.

The day after Renee Cunningham's party, he'd come home from work with his father, sweating and tired and dirty, to find his suitcase fully packed and sitting on a chair in the dining room. His mother was standing next to it, a huge smile on her face.

"Whose suitcase, Hattie?" his father had asked, heading toward the bathroom to wash up for dinner. "You goin' to see your mama in Norfolk?"

His mother just shook her head, her eyes meeting Barry's. "That's Barry's stuff."

"He ain't goin' nowhere," his father yelled from the bathroom. "We got houses lined up all summer."

"He can work with you when he gets back from mock trial camp."

"But—" Barry started.

His mother held up a hand. "Hush. I took care of it."

His father bounded out of the bathroom, throwing his wet towel on the floor. "You took care of it how? Didn't I tell you that boy wasn't—"

"Hush up, Earl. I got a bonus from some extra day work I did for Mrs. Carpenter up Dayton Street. I called Barry's debate coach and he said if we put him on a plane tonight he could be there for the second session and still get full credit. So I figured—"

In a flash, Earl was on top of her, slapping the palm of his hand against her face. Barry leaped on Earl's broad back, yanking him off of his mother and shoving him against the breakfront. Earl leaned there, the old china rattling behind him, spittle at the corners of his mouth, breathing heavily.

"Thank you, Ma. But I can't go."

"Yes, you can, Barry. You need to." She held one hand to her face where Earl's slap had landed. Barry picked up the wet towel and handed it to his mother. She pressed the coldness to her face.

"Not if he's acting like this, Ma. I can't leave you here."

"When'd you get so noble all of a sudden?" said Earl. "Spoiled brat."

"You're going," said his mother. She shot Earl a look that closed the conversation. "That's final. I can take care of myself."

"Any extra money comin' in *this* house goin' in my pocket," Earl bellowed as he headed into the bedroom. "Get my dinner on the table, I got places to go."

Hattie reached into her bra and pulled out a wad of cash. "This will take care of your personal stuff. Your flight is tonight at eight. Can you get a ride out to the airport?"

"Ma." Barry felt tears stinging his eyes.

His mother wiped away the lone tear to stain his cheek. "No, don't you do that, baby. You just go up there and show those people what you know. You let me deal with all this here, okay? Now go get ready, baby."

He just nodded and went into the bathroom. He cried through the whole shower and even found himself tearing up again at the airport.

Now, riding back to Sag Harbor with Duke, he said, "So, you seen Carla around?"

"You are ridiculous, man."

"I'm just being me," said Barry. "You wouldn't want it any other way."

Duke turned onto Barry's block. He could see Mr. Chambers's pickup parked out front. As they pulled in behind the pickup, Barry said, "So what up for tonight?"

"Goin' to chill with Leo," said Duke.

"Is Carla visitin' this weekend?"

"Carla's back with her boyfriend, Barry. If she ever *was* apart from him."

"He's a punk."

"Maybe," Duke said. "But he's Carla's punk."

"But Sunday's the Fourth of July. Of course she's coming out for that?"

Duke just shrugged. He wanted Barry to get out before Mr. Maynard came out of the house. "I gotta run, man. I'll call you later."

Joey watched Shirley count out the money, straightening out crumpled bills and piling the tens and twenties into separate stacks around the table. She took a drag off a Newport, put it in the ashtray, and blew a plume of gray smoke in Joey's direction. Then she laughed, one of her broad loud guffaws that showed every gold tooth in her mouth.

"Hand me them rubber bands over there, Joey, baby."

Joey got the box of rubber bands off the window sill and bristled at the sound of the nickname Shirley had been calling him for the last month.

It hadn't taken long for things to change in the Bogarde household.

That glorious dream of a first day, full of fried chicken and limo rides and *The Dukes of Hazzard*—unlike any first day he'd ever had at any of his numerous foster homes—had mutated into a nightmare. He shivered thinking about that first night, waking up, finding his hard penis exposed to the world, TeeTee standing victorious at the end of his bed, and Shirley and Carlton standing in the doorway, staring like two frozen sentinels. Joey had leaped up from the bed, blushing and scared.

"It was TeeTee," he'd yelled. "She did it to me in my sleep."

Shirley said, "Get outta here, Towanda," and came into the room. She sat at the end of Joey's bed and said, "You want me to believe that my daughter came in here in the middle of the night and pulled down your drawers to get at your little dick?"

Joey knew it sounded ridiculous and the sarcastic tone in Shirley's voice didn't make the situation any better, but it was the truth. "It's t-t-true," he'd managed to stutter.

Shirley looked back at Carlton, who just shrugged and took a

seat on his own bed. Shirley turned back to Joey. "What am I supposed to do? You here *one* day and you already all over my daughter? Don't you know she's only fourteen years old?"

"I didn't *do* anything," Joey mumbled. He felt sticky and cold.
He wanted to take a bath and change his underwear but he felt like
he couldn't move. "Really. I promise you. I was just sleeping. Even
Carlton said that I should watch out for—"

"I ain't say shit," Carlton said. He looked mean as hell, with his
arms crossed in front of his big pecs, his lips poking out. "I think we
got us a liar here, Mama."

"I can't go through this again," Shirley said, shaking her head.
"I guess I'ma have to call that social worker and tell her they sent
me a sex freak."

"NO!" Joey screamed. "I didn't do anything. Really."

Shirley just looked down at the drying wet spot on his stomach.

Joey had heard about what happens to foster kids who got
caught up in a scandalous situation with the foster family. He'd
heard of a guy in his last home who'd accidentally walked in on his
foster mother changing clothes after church and could never get
placed again. He spent the rest of his years before turning eighteen
in a succession of dirty group homes and detention centers. Joey
knew he couldn't bear that. The thought of it made him sick to his
stomach.

"I'm sorry," he begged. "It won't happen again. Please don't call
the social worker."

"Okay, fine. But you gonna help Shirley out and Shirley gonna
help Joey out."

Joey nodded. He liked the sound of that.

"If you help me out like I want I won't tell the social worker you
had sex with my daughter. You help Shirley out and everything'll
be fine."

And for a few days after that conversation, everything did seem fine. Shirley never brought up his sex with Tee Tee and for the most part, everything in the Bogarde household returned to normal. Tee-Tee acted as if she'd never slipped into his room that night. In fact, she was never really around, spending most of her time at the day camp or with a new boyfriend, a skinny, worn-out-looking guy named Romeo. Carlton went back to calling Joey Lil Man and even took him along on more limo assignments whenever Porgy had to take his son to a Mets game or stay at home with his pregnant wife.

Then one morning, Shirley trooped into the bedroom and said, "Joey, you speak Spanish, doncha?"

"A little."

"That's good enough. Get dressed. You coming to work with Shirley today."

An hour later he and Shirley got off the F train near the courthouse in downtown Brooklyn. This part of Brooklyn made Joey think of his father's court case and his grandmother's battle for custody of him and all those fights he'd had to live through when his mother was alive and his father was hooked on smack. The sun was shining and the sidewalks were crowded with shoppers and workers out on breaks.

Shirley had made him wear one of Carlton's old suits she'd dug out of the closet. Thick with the pungent stench of mothballs, it was a little big on Joey, so Shirley made him roll up the sleeves and cuffs. In that shining summer sun, Joey could feel sweat trickling down his back and his sides.

Shirley gave him very specific instructions. He was to go into the restaurant she pointed out and ask, in Spanish, if anyone could help him. When someone offered to help him, preferably someone Spanish, he was to bring the person out to the street and ask for directions to Washington Heights. Ideally he was to look for a person with some shopping bags, ideally a woman with shopping bags. Once Joey got the person outside, he was to take out a handwritten note and show it to the person, making sure that the person put down whatever shopping bags she was carrying. He was to engage the person in a conversation—"Act as dumb as you can," Shirley had told him. "People ain't scared of a dumb chile"—then walk away, as if the person had helped him as best as she could. Once he walked away, he was to wait for Shirley on the corner of Fulton and Flatbush.

It wasn't until the second try, talking to a large Dominican woman with three Modell's shopping bags and one stuffed Duane Reade bag, that Joey realized what was going on. While the woman leaned over Joey, trying to read the note he held in his sweaty hands, Shirley was replacing the woman's bags with her own, stuffed full of paper and old magazines and old clothes. Once Shirley got the bags, she headed in the other direction and met Joey at the agreed-upon location. Once it started to get dark and Shirley was sure she'd done enough business for the day, she and Joey headed back home, where Shirley laid out everything she'd gotten during the course of the day. Then she called up a guy named Melville, who came over, perused all the items, the clothes and electronics and personal goods, took what he could sell, and counted out money to Shirley.

When they had a good day, they had fried chicken. When the day hadn't gone so well, they ate grits and salmon croquettes or bacon and eggs for dinner.

"You," Shirley had told Joey after two weeks of solid work, "are a fuckin' gold mine. You gonna make Mama rich, Joey, baby. With those big brown eyes, can't nobody resist helping you out."

During one stretch of "good days" Joey found himself lying in bed at night, thinking about Sag Harbor. He'd never heard of the place before accompanying Carlton on the limo ride, but it had certainly made an impression. Even amidst all the drama of the drunk guy and his girlfriend, Joey was struck by how healthy and lively everyone seemed. Maybe it was their wealth? But there was a vibe out there, smooth and evened-out, problem-free, really, if getting drunk and fighting for your girl was the extent of the trouble you had when you spent time in Sag Harbor. He thought about that chubby kid who talked to him before they drove off. There was something about him that Joey liked, something in his smiling eyes that drew him in. Eventually, though, Joey started to force the thoughts of Sag Harbor out of his mind the moment one crept in. No use dreaming about Heaven when you were destined to spend your life in Hell.

2

Leo stepped on the scale. He stared at the bathroom wall, too scared to look down at the number. *I know Duke said I look thinner*, he thought. *My mother even said so. And my pants do feel a little baggier on me. But . . .* This was the first time Leo was weighing himself since he'd started his diet regimen. He told himself he'd wait a month, after switching to salads for lunch instead of cheeseburgers, and grilled salmon and snapper for dinner instead of the pork chops and pizza he loved so much. He ate breakfast every day, a bowl of granola and some yogurt, as Duke had told him he should. And he ran the complete length of the beach every day. But he hadn't wanted to weigh himself until he was sure he'd lost some weight.

He looked down at the number. And he almost fell off the scale. Fifteen pounds. He'd lost fifteen whole pounds in the month since Renee's party. *Hot damn.* He yanked at the elastic band around his boxer shorts and let it snap back against his belly. *My smaller belly*, he thought with a big smile. He couldn't wait to tell Duke. And his mother. But the congratulations of those two were nothing compared to the words of one person.

Joey.

He'd said the best thing in the world, the most wonderful words one human being had ever said to another human being, as far as Leo was concerned. Leo had walked out of the record store on St. Mark's Place in Manhattan and Joey had leaned out of the limo window and said, "Hey, man. Almost didn't recognize ya. You lost some weight?"

Leo had gotten the number of the limo company from Reggie by way of Carla.

"Why do you want that number?" Carla had asked, calling from a CoCo Cosmetics photo shoot in Cancún.

"I need a limo," Leo had said.

"I think you have some girl stashed away in Manhattan that you want to impress," she had said with a wicked laugh.

"Everything's not about sex, Carla."

"Yes it is," she'd said. "And don't forget I'll be there for the Fourth of July."

He called the limo company and told the dispatcher that he specifically wanted the drivers who'd taken the McFarland party to Sag Harbor earlier in June. Of course, Leo realized it was a long shot that Joey would show up, but there he was, grinning that fantastic grin, dimples indenting his cheeks, those dark eyebrows and that dark curly hair so much like they'd been in Leo's dreams.

The limo had picked him up at the record store and proceeded to take him all over Manhattan. He usually went into the stores and shops alone while Carlton and Joey waited outside in the limo. But when they went to his favorite comics store on Fourteenth Street, Joey went in with him.

"What's your favorite?" he asked Leo.

"*X-Men*," Leo said. "Sometimes I feel like I'm a mutant myself."

Joey laughed. "Me too, man. I know exactly what you mean."

After Leo bought the *Lord of the Rings* trilogy at the Doubleday Book Store on Sixth Avenue, he told the driver he was ready to head back to Long Island.

While they drove, Joey looked through the partition. "What records you buy?"

"Mainly some rap stuff."

Joey's eyes lit up. "Who you like, man?"

Leo moved up toward the partition and handed Joey the brown paper bag stuffed full of twelve-inch singles he intended to give to Duke. He watched Joey's eyes bulge at the site of the all the records. He let out an impressed "oh shit" when he saw the Fearless Four's "Rockin' It" 12-inch.

"I can b-boy," Joey said. "I used to go to parties uptown when I was living . . ." His voice trailed off.

"Living where?" Leo said, trying to find out as much as he could about this boy.

"Not important," Joey said, suddenly shy. He handed the records back through the partition. "You got some good taste, bro."

Leo said, "Where are your people from?"

"The Bronx," said Joey.

"I mean before that."

"You mean, am I mixed?" Joey said, laughing.

"I guess."

"My mom's black and my pop's Dominican."

"I figured you might be Spanish."

"You figured?" Joey laughed.

Leo blushed. *I said too much*, he thought. *As usual.* "No, I, uh, I just—"

"It's all good, bruh. You crossed my mind, too." Then, making sure Carlton's eyes were on the road and not him, he quickly winked at Leo then turned back to look out the passenger window.

Leo's heart raced. *Crossed his mind?* What had he meant by that?

And now, standing in the bathroom, fifteen pounds thinner, he needed to figure out a way to see Joey again.

Later, after dinner, as he was jogging on the beach with Duke, it dawned on him how he could do it.

Duke said, "I can pick Carla up from the train station if you want."

"She's taking a car from the airport," Leo said. "I ordered a limo for her."

"Oh yeah, I forgot," Duke laughed. "The princess."

"Something like that," Leo said.

They were chilling out on the Bradford deck facing the beach, a box of cassettes between them, a boombox sitting on one of the other chairs. The sun was setting over the ocean, the air fragrant with the smell of sizzling barbecue floating from the house next door. Leo sat back in his chair and had to smile at the thought of his quick new friendship with Duke. He couldn't remember the last time he'd made a new friend who liked so many of the same things he did. And since Duke and Barry were such good friends, Leo had begun to think of Barry as a new buddy as well.

Leo heard his mother talking to someone inside. He turned to see her ushering Barry out to the deck. Barry said, "Thanks, Mrs. Bradford," and plopped down in the one empty chair.

Duke said, "What you doin' here?"

"Looking for Carla, I'll bet," said Leo.

Barry grinned. "Just wanted to see what you fools were gettin' into."

"Just chillin'," Duke said. "Like I told you."

"Welcome back," Leo said. "You get into any fights up in Vermont?"

"Just one," said Barry. "The mock judge was a racist. Snobby kid from Scarsdale. Didn't think I made a good trial attorney. I had to bop him one, let him know how we do it down this way."

Leo said, "Aren't you supposed to be some kind of debate champion?"

"Yeah," said Barry. "And your point is?"

"You should be able to settle things with words, not fists."

"Tell me that when some guy is up in *your* face telling you *you* ain't good enough to do something."

"How do you know I haven't been in that situation?"

"'Cause you a rich Negro," said Barry. "You got everything in the world at your fingertips."

"That's not true."

"I ain't stressin' it, though," Barry said. "I'ma be a rich Negro too one day, and ain't nobody gonna be able to tell me shit."

"Money isn't everything," said Leo.

"It is if you ain't got none," Barry said. "Right, Duke?"

"I'm outta this conversation," Duke said. "My mother always told me you don't talk about money, politics, or religion." He tossed Leo a cassette. "Here, let's just play some music."

In Brooklyn, Joey was about to enter the kitchen when he heard Shirley mention his name. He held back and leaned his ear close to the door. Shirley said, "You can't take Joey on that Sag Harbor drop-off."

"Why not?" Carlton asked.

" 'Cause I'ma need him out here. Got a nice job planned out."

"You know I need him so I don't fall asleep. That's the only legal shit we got goin'. Mama, you better let him come with me." Carlton chewed on some pork chop. "Besides I got something in the works." He explained his plan to Shirley.

"Then, fine, take him. And don't get sly on me, boy. Everything you get you bringin' right back here for us to divvy up. You hear me?"

Joey stepped back from the kitchen door and tiptoed back to his room. He lay across the bed and looked out the window. Across Myrtle Avenue he saw a skinny girl in a tight skirt sipping from a 40-oz bottle of beer.

It was bad enough he was helping Shirley rip off innocent Spanish ladies on the streets of Brooklyn. Whatever Carlton was talking about doing in Sag Harbor, though, that was something else. That was getting arrested and spending the rest of his teens in a juvie hall if things didn't go right.

He needed to get out of there. Shirley claimed she'd be able to find him but the longer he'd been at the Bogarde household the more he realized that Shirley was mostly talk. She was a low-rent con woman, not some connected violent type.

Carlton pulled him out of his thoughts. "Sit up, Lil Man, we got some things to talk about."

Joey sat up and faced him.

"You gonna help me do a job," Carlton said. "You down for that, Lil Man?"

Joey nodded. He'd found that the less he spoke, the more they trusted him.

"Okay," said Carlton. "This is what we're gonna do."

3

Carla stood outside the American Airlines terminal at Kennedy Airport and watched the cute guy walk toward her. He had a large card with her name on it.

"Carla Randall?" he said.

"You're the limo driver?"

"Carlton's the driver, ma'am. He's pulling around now. I just wanted to make sure you were here."

"Please do not call me 'ma'am.' How old are you anyway?"

"I'll be sixteen next month," Joey said. He couldn't believe he was standing there talking to the chick from the CoCo Cosmetics ad. She was even more beautiful in person than she was in the billboard on Flatbush Avenue. "How old are you?"

"I'll be eighteen in two weeks," Carla said. "My luggage is over there." She pointed behind her.

As she got comfortable in the backseat of the car, Carla wondered why she hadn't heard from Reggie at all during her entire week in Cancún. The first thing she'd do when she got to the Bradfords' was call Reggie and make sure he wasn't planning any more summer surprises. She didn't need him showing up and cramping her style. Why didn't he just understand that eventually he was the one she was going to marry and be a good wife to? Why couldn't he comprehend that all the other boys were just practice?

"Why don't you have any money, Leo? Your father gives you a good allowance."

His mother stood over the buffet table, watching the caters prepare steaks and burgers and chicken legs for the barbecue.

"There's hardly anything to spend money on out here. Did you spend it all when you were in Manhattan?"

"Why does it matter where I spent it? I need some more."

"Go get it out of my wallet. I have too much to deal with right now." Before he could get inside, she said, "What time is your DJ friend going to be here?"

"Two."

"Please tell him we don't want any rap music, dear."

"Yeah, okay."

"And Leo?" She turned away from the table to face him. "I've been thinking about it and I was just wondering, aren't there any nice kids that you can hang out with while you're out here?"

"Nice kids?"

"You know what I mean—"

"You mean not locals? You mean not some white guy DJ and the son of the guy who cuts the lawn?"

"Leo—"

"What is it you always say to me, Mom? That you just want me to be—"

"Happy," she finished for him. She nodded. "You are happy, aren't you?"

"The happiest," he said. "And I'm only going to get happier."

"What does that mean?"

He thought of Joey, riding in the limo with Carla. He was counting down the hours. "Nothing, Mom. I just feel like it's gonna be a good day, that's all."

It was a rare time that Carla Randall paid any attention to the road signs when a limo was taking her where she needed to be. She was usually doing her nails or reading *Vogue* or giving Reggie a blow job. But this time, with no nail polish or magazines or boyfriend to occupy her, she was watching the green highway road signs flash by. So when the limo edged over to the right and smoothly took the exit to Sayville, she was surprised. She climbed forward to the partition and tapped on the window.

When it was all the way down, she said, "Uh, we're going to Sag, not Sayville."

"We're going where I take you," said the driver.

Carla looked at Joey. He wouldn't look back at her.

"Where are you going? I know you know the way to Sag."

"Just sit back and shut up," Carlton said, and he pressed the button to ease the partition window shut.

Carla had to yank her hands back. "Where the hell are you taking me?"

As he counted out a hundred dollars from his mother's purse, Leo watched her out on the patio. He had to admit that he was enjoying the summer, being here with just her. He thought he'd be sick of her by now. But she'd been cool, quiet, unobtrusive. She seemed happy, and that made him happy, even though he knew that all that happiness would probably change to something else with his father arriving for a full week.

After he got the money from his mother's purse, Leo went out on the deck. He saw Barry, doing a last minute paint job on the tool shed near the driveway. Why he was painting it was anybody's guess. Maybe Mr. Chambers told him to do it to give him something to do. From what Leo could tell, Barry didn't seem to enjoy his father too much. They never seemed to be fighting with each other but there was always a quiet edge to their interactions, as if they resented the fact that they shared the same language, let alone the same DNA.

Leo could see that dynamic between them so clearly because

he knew about distant fathers. Every time he saw Barry talk to his father in that sidewise way, Leo felt like he was looking in a mirror. They may have occupied different sides of the economic spectrum, but he and Barry had more in common that Barry would ever guess.

As if on cue, Leo heard his father say, "There's my boy." He turned to see him coming around the house with a small valise and garment bag.

"Hey, Dad," Leo said, climbing down the steps to give his father a hug. *Shit, I must have summoned him up*, he thought.

He wasn't surprised to find the smell of perfume on his father's collar. And it wasn't the breezy scent of Chloe that his mother wore.

Happy Fucking Fourth of July.

Joey looked around at the grubby shack where Carlton had dropped them off while he continued on to Sag Harbor, the pool house of a dilapidated structure that seemed to have once been an elegant old mansion. The house reminded Joey of the big house in that Civil War movie his grandmother used to watch all the time. He wondered if it had one of those great winding staircases inside like the one in that movie.

There had to be a way out of this. He tried to concentrate, which was hard since Carla would not be quiet.

"Tell me what this is all about," she said to Joey. "Where is he going? Why did he leave us here? Is this some kind of kidnapping?"

Kidnapping. That's exactly what this was. Carlton hadn't called it that when he was telling Joey what he'd planned to do, but that's what it was. It all seemed so slipshod and rushed. He didn't even tie the girl up. Joey could only imagine what Carlton had in mind. And if Carlton got caught, what would happen to him, out here in the middle of nowhere? *You have a brain, Joey. Think.*

There was something he could do, but he wasn't sure it would work.

"Are you listening to me?" Carla screamed. "I said, Why did he leave us here?"

"Please," Joey said. "Just shut up."

"I don't *want* to shut up. I'm supposed to be at a Fourth of July party in less than an hour and you and your driver guy have me in some deserted shack. Tell me what's going on. If it's money you want, I'll give you money."

Joey turned to face her. Exactly what he wanted to hear. But would it work?

"How much money?" he said.

Carla reached into her pocket and pulled out a wad of crumpled bills. "He took my bag," she said. "But I have about two hundred here."

"You think that will get us to Sag Harbor in a cab?"

"I don't fucking know," Carla shouted. "But I'm willing to try if you are."

Barry put the empty paint can in the back of his father's truck and went to the hose near the garage to wash his hands. He almost stuck the hose down his jeans to cool himself off. He'd heard Mrs. Bradford tell her husband that Carla was arriving any minute and he almost shot a load standing right there.

His father came up behind him. "Stop daydreaming and pass me that hose."

Barry turned and handed his father the hose, nozzle end first. Earl jumped back from the spout of running water. "Shit, nigga, watch out."

"Don't use that kinda language," Barry said. "The client won't like it." Then he walked away and climbed into the passenger seat to wait for his father to finish up.

He thought about what Duke had said as they drove back from the airport the other day. *Should* he have told Duke he was trying to get with Carla? He'd remembered that Duke had said something about kissing on some model-type rich girl. But it wasn't like he'd declared true love for her, had he? And Duke wasn't really into females like that. Not that he was gay or anything, he was just focused. Duke didn't let anything get in the way of what he needed to do, whether it was deejaying or football or taking care of his crazy mama. *I need to be more like that,* Barry thought. *About something other than pussy, at least.* He liked Duke. Hell, he probably loved him. Like a brother. But when it all came down to it, Duke was a white boy. And no matter how poor they may be, white boys do all right in the world because the world looks out for white boys. *There need to be more good things for me, too.*

Carlton pulled the limo into the driveway of 42 Ninevah Lane.

He went to the front door and rang the doorbell. The fat nerdy kid he drove around Manhattan came to the door, just as he'd hoped. He had this hopeful look in his eyes, looking past Carlton at the limo, like he was expecting Christmas, his birthday, and New Year's all in rolled into one. Carlton cleared his throat so he could use what Shirley liked to call his "Polite Nigga" voice.

"Hello," he said. "I'm sorry, but I thought I should come tell you this in person."

The fat kid said, "What's the problem?" His eyes were still on the limo, an expectant look on his face.

"I was dispatched to pick up a Carla Randall from JFK Airport this afternoon and transport her to, uh, 42 Ninevah Lane. This is that address, am I correct?"

The fat kid nodded, still looking over Carlton's shoulder.

"Well, I waited for a good while and Miss Randall never came out of the airport. I checked the arrivals and her flight did, in fact, arrive from Cancún, but she must not have been on the plane. Unless she took another car and arrived to her destination safely?"

"Uh, no, Carla's not here yet. I thought you were her car." He looked over Carlton's shoulder again. "Don't you usually have another guy driving with you?"

"Oh, yes, sir. That would be Joseph." *Why is he asking about Joey?* "He was ill today, couldn't make the trip."

"I'm sorry to hear that," said the fat kid. "Well, we haven't heard from Carla. So maybe she did decide to hang out in Cancún."

"Well, like I said, sir, I just wanted to make sure." And he turned to go.

"Wait a sec."

Carlton turned back to the door.

"You drove all the way out here from JFK just to tell me that you didn't pick up Carla? That doesn't sound right. Nice of you as it is."

"Oh, sir. I guess I forgot to mention. I did in fact pick up another fare coming in this direction. I guess there are lot of vacationers making their way to the Hamptons. Lucky me, right?"

"Yeah," Leo said. "Lucky you."

Carlton turned to go as the fat kid closed the door with a sad look on his face. He got into the limo and pulled out of the driveway. Now he had to find the spot for Phase 2.

He hoped Earl Chambers had given him good directions.

"You've got to be fucking kidding me," said Carla. She watched the trees along the highway zoom by as the cab made its way toward Sag Harbor.

"I am not kidding you," Joey said. "Now listen to me. When we get there are you going to give me the money?"

"So, in other words," Carla said. "You were supposed to hold me hostage till your friend got back. But now, since you're helping me go free, you want money?"

"I sold him out, you little princess. The least you can do is help *me* out."

He did have a point, Carla had to give him that. *What was a couple grand when his friend wanted to take the Bradfords for who knows how much? Besides, I can just call the cops when we get to Leo's house and this dumb little kidnapper will be taken care of.*

Then something dawned on her. This kid was fifteen years old. Fifteen-year-olds didn't kidnap people. "What are you going to do after I give you the money?" she asked.

"Let me worry about that."

"Are you sure you're fifteen?"

"Pretty sure," he said. "Why?"

"You seem older," she said. "You have a certain gravitas about you."

"Gravi-what?"

"Buy a dictionary with the money I give you and look it up."

As he and his father pulled into their driveway, Barry said, "Whose limo is that?"

"Don't worry about it," said Earl, silently cursing Carlton. Didn't he tell him to park in town and take a cab to his house? He pulled into the driveway and jumped down from the pickup. He waited for Barry to go inside before he went over to the limo, sitting there on their little street of drab houses like it was a rich kid mocking the less fortunate.

Carlton rolled down the window.

"What the fuck are you doing here, Carlton?"

"You said be here at two."

"I also said to take a cab." He looked up and down the block. "I don't need all this fuckin' attention."

"I didn't catch the cab part, Earl."

"Did you catch the other thing?"

"She's in the pool house at that house we used to clean in Sayville. Off Exit 30."

"You make the call yet?"

"Nope. Just got here."

Earl looked up at his house. The curtains in the front window ruffled. Hattie was in there minding his business as usual. "Gimme a sec and I'll be back out."

Inside, Earl found Hattie in the kitchen, pouring mix into a blender.

Hattie said, "I guess I'm not supposed to ask why there's a limo parked outside the house, right?"

"Right." He brushed past her and went into the bedroom. He quickly changed out of his work clothes and went to the bathroom to wash his face. He could hear Barry singing in the shower.

He went back through the kitchen and went outside. Carlton was leaning against the limo, whistling some tune. "Let's go," Earl said.

It was a habit he'd picked up in Switzerland. Any time he was sad or depressed or just plain pissed off by some slight from one of his haughty Eurotrash classmates, Leo would bum a cig from one of the cafeteria ladies and climb to the roof of his dorm to smoke. Now, not knowing whether to be pissed at Carla or disappointed in himself for thinking this plan to see Joey again would work, Leo got a Marlboro from one of the caterer waiters and searched his father's Saab for a match. As he was digging through the glove compartment, he looked up to see a cab pull up to the house. When Carla jumped out, he jumped out of the car. "I go through all the freakin' trouble of sending a limo for you and you turn up in a cab?" he shouted. But Leo stopped himself. He saw Joey near the cab's driver's side, counting out bills to pay the driver.

Carla said, "You will *so* not believe what happened, Leo—"

Leo said, "Is that Joey?" and Carla stopped talking. She watched Leo step closer to the cab. There was a strange look in Leo's eyes. And was he actually slimmer? Yes, he was staring at the Joey kid like he wanted to eat him up. Carla sighed. Leo was in love! Her not-so-fat-anymore little cousin was a fag! How fuckin' fabulous was that?! Too bad his first crush had to be a little criminal.

As Duke and Barry pulled up to the Bradfords' in Duke's mom's old station wagon, they saw two police cars parked out front. Leo was leaning against his father's Saab with Carla and some muscular little Spanish-looking kid.

Barry jumped out of the station wagon and went right over to Carla. "I'm glad you made it," he said.

"Almost didn't," she said. She pecked a kiss on Barry's cheek. "I'll explain later."

Duke said to Leo, "What's going on? You guys hired security or something?"

Leo shook his head. "Like Carla said, I'll explain later. You need to get set up. Head on back." As Duke started toward the deck, Leo added, "Oh, yeah, no rap."

As soon as the cab had pulled off, Carla dragged Leo inside to find his parents. Leo tried to listen to Carla's story but his mind was all over the place. He couldn't believe that the guy he'd been dreaming about for the last three weeks was standing in his house.

He'd only planned on catching a glimpse, maybe asking the chauffeur and his assistant if they wanted to stay for a hot dog or something.

Gary Bradford laughed, took a long sip of his Scotch, and said, "Kidnapped? But you're standing here in front of me. What kind of kidnappers are these?" He popped a cherry tomato into his mouth. He pointed at Joey. "Who's that?"

"He was helping the guy out at first," Carla said. "But he helped me get away."

"And he's standing here in my house?"

Leo said, "He's a friend of mine, Dad."

"So, a friend of *yours* helped to kidnap your cousin? I sent you to school in Switzerland to meet stupid people and say dumb things like that?"

Leo's mother said, "Gary."

"What? Don't 'Gary' me, Lillian. How *ridiculous* does that sound?"

Carla said, "In a way he was kidnapped, too, Uncle Gary."

"Now what are you talking about?"

Carla turned to Joey. "Tell him, Joey."

So Joey began his story, in halting, hesitant words. At first, he just told the Bradfords about Carlton's plan to extort money for Carla, about the house in Sayville where Carlton had left them to wait. He told them that he didn't know Carlton's accomplice in Sag Harbor; Carlton hadn't told him his name. But sitting there, looking into their faces, Joey felt something he hadn't ever really felt from strangers before. They really seemed interested in hearing his story. And before long, it all came rushing out of him. His mother's death, his father's arrest, his grandmother's death. His trip through Children's Services, his five foster homes in four years, and his eventual role as Shirley's con accomplice. As he told the story he realized that he sort of felt sorry for Carlton and TeeTee; how else could they turn out with a monster like Shirley Bogarde for a mother?

When he was done talking, Lillian Bradford went over to him and hugged him closely, a tear in her eye. She said, "You mean to say that man might be somewhere around town as we speak?" She looked at her husband. "Gary? That man needs to be arrested." She looked down at Joey. "Him and his mother."

Gary called the police and they were there within minutes. Joey described Carlton and the limo and an APB was put out immediately.

Two minutes later the telephone rang. Gary Bradford answered it.

"You want money for Carla?" He looked around the room. All eyes were on him. "Why would we give you money for Carla when she's standing right here in front of me? Describe what she's wearing, you say?" He looked at Carla. "My niece is wearing a denim skirt and a white halter top and a pair of brown espadrilles. How's that? I hope you're still somewhere in Sag Harbor and you'd better hope the cops find you before I do because I won't be responsible for—Hello?" He put the receiver down and popped another cherry tomato into his mouth. "Imagine that. The fuckin' idiot hung up."

The Bradford barbecue was in full swing when a young policeman came around to the beach side of the house and asked for Gary. Leo joined his father as he talked to the policeman near the tool shed. He told him that they'd arrested a Carlton Bogarde and wanted Leo to come down to the precinct to identify him. They all agreed that the next day would be fine.

Gary turned to Leo, his eyes glassy and celebratory with the sheen of Scotch. "How did that kid Joey become a 'friend' of yours?"

Leo told him how the limo service had been used to chauffeur Carla's boyfriend to Sag Harbor.

"He's a brave kid," said Gary. "Your mother and I would like to help him out somehow. Sometimes you have to help those less fortunate than you, son. Remember that." He hugged Leo.

This time, the only perfume Leo smelled on his father was Chloe.

Leo watched his father walk away, toward the frolicking guests on the beach. He went back to his father's Saab to find the matches he'd been looking for when all the drama started. He sat in the driver's seat, lit the cigarette he hadn't gotten to smoke earlier, and pondered what exactly he would say to Joey, now that he had him, so unexpectedly, in his presence. When he finished the smoke he slammed the car door shut and headed back to the barbecue. Duke was on the turntables, mixing Chaka Khan's "Papillon" into Boz Scaggs's "Lowdown." He saw Barry dancing with Carla. He saw Renee Cunningham standing next to her pouty-mouthed mother, also watching Barry dance with Carla. He saw Diane with her big breasts trying to talk to Duke as he mixed records. He saw his parents standing at the edge of the water, holding hands. He knew this happy period wouldn't last but he also knew that the one thing he and his mother had in common was enjoying when his father behaved like a good man for a change.

And he saw Joey, standing near one of the big pit grills, a plate in his hand, an open hot dog bun waiting to be filled. In that moment, Joey turned and saw Leo standing there. He smiled. And winked.

4

In Brooklyn, Shirley Bogarde sat on the steps of her brownstone, watching the hamburgers sizzle on the little grill she'd hustled away from some Chinese woman out in the Flatlands a couple of weeks ago.

Shirley looked at her watch. Carlton should have been home by now. She wanted Joey to get a good night's sleep. She had big plans for him tomorrow. Day after the Fourth? Everybody and they mama was gonna be on Fulton Street spending money like it was going out of style. Thank God Children's Services saw fit to bestow Joey upon her. He was the perfect age and he had the perfect temperament. Not like that stupid child they sent her last time or the uncontrollable one with the one short leg they sent her before that. As far as she was concerned, neither one of those foster kids was worth the cum TeeTee had fucked outta Joey to get him into the game.

When the first police cruiser pulled up in front of Shirley's brownstone on Myrtle Avenue, she figured somebody on the block must have got to fighting. Niggas don't know how to chill out on a holiday, always starting some trouble. When the second cruiser pulled up, right in front of her building, Shirley felt her heart beat a little faster.

She thought about all that silver jewelry she had stashed in the closet.

She thought about all that flatware under the bed.

She thought of those four ColecoVision video games stacked up in the shower.

Carlton and TeeTee, let alone Joey, never even crossed her mind.

1

"I never really knew my real mother," said TNT. "I only met her once. A friend of the family looked out for me. Then I was in the system."

Leo and Duke both looked at Joey.

Joey said, quietly, "I know what that's like."

"Then you know," said TNT, "that looking for my father is only part of it. When you spend most of your childhood in the system, you spend a lot of time looking for yourself first."

"You got that right," said Joey.

Duke said, "How'd you figure it was one of us?"

"I found out I had a living aunt. When she died, I went through all her shit and I found a picture—"

Joey interrupted him. "Why don't you just tell us what your mother's name was?"

TNT went over to the bar. He reached down into the fridge and dug out another beer. "Any of you want anything?"

Duke said, "I'll take a beer."

"You?" Leo said with a smile. "Drinking a beer?"

"Since I ain't playing ball no more, what's the point in being a saint?"

TNT tossed Duke a Heineken and came back over to the three of them. "I don't want to tell you my mother's name," he said to Joey. "Not yet, at least."

"Then I don't see how any of this is worth our time," said Joey.

"Joey's right, man," said Duke.

TNT yanked the cap off his beer with a bottle opener, then tossed it to Duke. "Yeah, he might be right. But maybe I want to hear more about all y'all before I tell you everything I know."

Duke said, impatiently, "What's the deal with this picture you found?"

TNT got up and went over to a duffel bag sitting on a settee near the balcony windows. He pulled something from it and came back over to the others. He held up a worn photograph. "This is it."

He handed it to Leo. Leo stared at it for a few seconds, nodded, then handed it to Duke. Duke looked at it, smiled, and handed it to Joey. Joey glanced at it. "Wow."

The photo showed the four of them, Leo, Duke, Joey, and Barry, on the beach, the ocean behind them, their teenaged faces full of hope and summertime fun. Barry had turned away just as the shutter clicked and he was caught looking at the bikini-bottomed strut of a girl strolling by them on the beach.

"This was taken at the Labor Day barbecue," said Leo. "1983."

"I almost missed it 'cause my coach wanted me to meet Jim Brown," said Duke.

"I'd forgotten that," Joey said. "That's right." He looked up at TNT. "Now will you tell us who your mother is?"

"I'd like to. But, yo, I really think Barry should be here to hear the whole story, don't you?"

2

The Mercedes Maybach sat outside the Imperial Theater, four blocks from the Hotel Gansevoort. Barry had called in to the office and told his second assistant Lisa that he wouldn't be back for the rest of the day. Then he had the driver take him to Serendipity, a posh eatery on the East Side, where he sent the driver in to get a frozen hot chocolate.

Then he called Melody Monique and left a message for her on her voice mail. "I'll be outside the theater after the matinee. Come give me some head."

And now there she was, tall leggy Melody Monique, air-kissing the other *Hairspray* chorus girls as they all flew off in different directions to take breaks before the evening show. She climbed into the Maybach and offered her cheek to Barry, careful not to smudge her stage makeup.

"Sorry, big guy," she whispered. "No blow jobs today."

"But I so need one," Barry whined. "Pretty please?"

"I have another performance tonight," she said. "And I don't like to perform on a full stomach. But you sounded so down on my voice mail. I checked it right after I came offstage. What's wrong?"

"Nothing," said Barry, frowning. "Everything." He stared out the window. "You ever feel like your past can slap you right in the face?"

"I don't spend much time thinking about it one way or the other."

"Good for you," said Barry.

"So?"

Barry watched a group of tourists flock past the theater and another group crowd into an upscale pizza restaurant for a preshow meal. "So, if there's no blow job being offered, I'm gonna have to say farewell, dear Melody."

"Some other time?"

"Yeah. Some other time."

He watched Melody's tight little showgirl rump as she climbed out, watching her as she knew everyone else was watching her step out of the expensive car. She gave him a five-fingered wave and sashayed off down the block.

The driver dragged his own eyes away from Melody's legs and said, "Where to now, Mr. Chambers?"

Barry took one last sip of his frozen hot chocolate.

"Take me back to the hotel."

3

"Uh, excuse me. Sir?"

The guy in the red sweatshirt and the black baseball cap looked up from the magazine to find a balding guy with tiny owlish glasses staring down at him. He was wearing a black sports jacket and his name tag said "Warren."

"What you want, Warren?"

"I want to know if you're waiting to meet someone in the hotel."

"How you know I ain't a *guest* in your fuckin' hotel?"

Warren looked over his shoulder at the blond woman from the front desk. She nodded and stepped back behind the desk. "I know because you talked to Gail a little while ago and she said you were asking about someone who might be staying here."

"If you know alla that already—"

"Please leave, sir. Please excuse yourself from the premises."

"Says who?" He again fingered the loaded gun he had hidden in his belt. He so wanted to yank it out and blast this bald-headed fuck to the moon. "You know what? Don't worry 'bout it. I'll get out."

"Fine."

"But I'm coming back soon as I find out what room he's in."

"Well you won't be finding out from anyone here."

The guy in the black baseball cap stood up. Now he was looking down at Warren. "Don't be so sure about that."

1

Lillian Bradford cried the day she and Gary drove Leo to Yale. She started tearing up as soon as the Saab pulled out of their parking garage on Central Park West and was still at it by the time they were on the Henry Hudson Parkway. There were no tears from Leo. He couldn't wait to get out of New York City and he gave a mental middle finger to the building and the doorman standing under the purple awning outside it as they pulled out of the garage. The only thing he'd miss in NYC, the only thing he felt like he was leaving behind, was Joey. But he wouldn't be missing him for long. Joey was due to drive to New Haven in October so they could all go see Duke play football in Syracuse.

After his parents drove off, Leo unpacked his suitcases and waited for his roommate to arrive. He tacked his Talking Heads poster to his closet door and taped a huge *Purple Rain* poster over his bed. He was organizing his underwear and socks in the top drawer of his bureau when a voice behind him said, "How's that for luck?"

He turned around to see a thin, scruffy white guy standing in the doorway, an ancient-looking Army-issue duffel bag slung over his shoulder. He had long, messy hair and his jeans looked filthy, like he'd just trudged through the Amazon trying to find his way to Yale. He flung himself onto the bare mattress, landing with his long legs splayed and a mischievous smile on his face. "Lucky me," he said. "Another black dude."

"Another one?" Leo said.

He sat up. "Must be something in me, but check this out. My roommate at Groton? Black dude, from Louisiana. My roommate at my post-grad year in London? Black dude, from Pennsylvania. My roommate at the Peace Corps? Black dude, from Chicago. And now, you. Another black dude. I must be some lucky sonofabitch, huh?"

"I think you're thinking of black cats," Leo said. "Not black guys. And black cats are supposedly *un*lucky."

The guy on the bed barked out a loud laugh. "Good one." Then he held out a grimy-looking hand. "I'm Peter Anthony Reynolds. Call me Pete. You must be Leo?"

Two hours later, they were huddled in a back booth at The Cherry Picker, a dark, little ale-soaked bar on York Street. By the time the waitress brought the third round of beers, Leo felt like he'd gotten Pete's entire life history. Born and raised in Arkansas, though he'd lived all over the globe because his father built hospitals in impoverished countries. Parents divorced when he was seven. Older sister was in rehab in Minnesota. And his girlfriend Hilary was a sophomore at Brown, so if Leo needed the room to himself on the weekends, that was cool, because Pete intended to be on the first train to Providence every Friday morning.

"So, Leo, you got a girl?" He took a sip of his beer. "A guy?"

Leo swallowed a gulp of beer and looked away. "What makes you ask that?"

Peter shrugged. "Why the fuck not? I fucked a dude for most of senior year." Then he shrugged again and downed a long gulp of beer. "But I'm not really sure I took to it, so here I am, Hetero-city. Not that I'm all that into labels, ya know?"

That made Leo think of Joey. And the first time they'd had sex.

It had been much easier than Leo expected to keep Joey in his life. Thanks, surprisingly, to his father's rare moment of generosity.

Gary Bradford put a lawyer on Joey's case, which resulted in Gary's assistant Edna becoming Joey's legal guardian. Joey spent summers with the Bradfords in Sag Harbor, and lived with Edna in Spanish Harlem during the school year. Leo and Joey had spent the rest of that first summer together, swimming, reading comics, playing rap records, and, whenever they were lucky enough to get some time alone in the house, kissing and jerking off.

But the first time? It was the last Friday in July. They'd come in from the beach, soaked and sandy, and raced each other to the shower. Joey got there first, stripped out of his trunks and stood there, holding his hand under the spray, waiting for the pounding water to heat up. Just before he stepped into the shower, he realized that Leo was still standing there, completely nude, watching him. Joey knew what he was thinking. He'd thought the same thing. So he stepped into the shower and he left the curtain open. Leo stepped in behind him and they enjoyed the longest hottest shower either of them had ever taken. They didn't talk about it afterward. They'd merely gotten into their pajama shorts, popped some Jiffy Pop on the stove, and settled down in the den to watch *Diff'rent Strokes* and *The Facts of Life*.

There was an unspoken agreement never to tell anyone about their times together; their clandestine sex was just between them. Though it became clear to both of them that Carla had figured it out when she came to visit during Labor Day. She kept making eyes at them and giggling. Once, she asked Leo if he'd ever read a book called *Giovanni's Room*. When he asked her what it was about she just giggled and didn't respond. Leo found the book in a store in Sag Harbor and he read passages to Joey late at night on the beach by flashlight.

"But those guys are gay," Joey had said, looking out at the ocean.

"And what are we?"

"I'm not into labels." He tossed a stone into the water. "I just like what we do. We don't have to call it anything." He wouldn't even say bisexual, which Leo thought might have made sense since Joey liked girls, too.

But that's where they left it for two years. During the summers, they hung out with Duke and Barry out in Sag; the rest of the year, they were inseparable in Manhattan, going to ball games and rap shows, discovering each other and the newness of their feelings. They just didn't need labels. They had, as far as Leo was concerned, each other, and that was more than enough. Now Leo was up in New Haven while Joey was down in Manhattan, studying accounting at City College.

Peter signaled the waitress for another round of beers.

"S'okay if you don't want to tell me," he said. "Not really my business anyway."

Leo felt a sudden rush of emotion. He hadn't expected this openness from Peter, and it excited him to think that he'd be able to speak openly about Joey if Peter knew his story. So he smiled and said, "Sure, I've been with a guy before."

"There ya go, dude," said Peter, high-fiving Leo over the table. "As long I don't wake up one night and find you groping my package." He winked and took a sip of beer.

"Can we keep it between us, though?" Leo asked.

"Who am I gonna tell? It's not like I know loads of people here yet. Do you?"

It wasn't loads of people Leo was worried about. "A friend of mine is a sophomore," he said.

"And you don't want him to know?"

Leo shook his head.

"Well, then. I'll be sure never to mention your sexual proclivities if he ever calls or drops by. What's this dude's name anyway?"

"Barry," Leo said. "Barry Chambers."

2

"Oh, Barry," moaned the girl on the bed. "Don't stop."

Bang. BangBangBang.

"*Please*. Don't stop, Barry."

BangBang. "Please DO stop, Barry. I can't hear myself think in here!"

Jealous, Barry thought as he quickened his stroke. How was he supposed to get his nut if that idiot next door kept banging on the wall? Fucking dorm rooms. He couldn't wait till next year, when he'd be in an upperclassmen's college. He opened his eyes and looked down at the girl beneath him, her own eyes shut tight, her fists pounding against his back in rhythm with his strokes. *What was her name again?* He was almost there, close to the very edge, and he couldn't remember the chick's name to save his life.

"I'm coming," she moaned. "Oh, Barry, fuck me. Harder. I'm coming!"

Of course you are, he thought. *Wouldn't have it any other way.*

Afterward he lay on the single bed, wishing the girl would hurry up in the bathroom. He had to meet Leo for dinner and he didn't want to be late.

It still amazed Barry that he and Leo had ended up at the same college. As ambitious as he was, Barry had always assumed, considering how hard-nosed his father was about money, that he'd end up at a state school on a scholarship. But the best thing to come out of his father's Fourth of July disappearing act was that Barry really was poor now, which meant he was even more qualified to get into an Ivy League school looking for a fatherless black kid with good grades and a jones for the good life. Barry knew that Leo was destined for an Ivy League education, so he barged himself even further into Leo and Duke's friendship, enamoring himself to Leo's father, who himself had once been a poor, fatherless black boy with Ivy League dreams.

Not that Barry was using Leo to stay connected to Gary Bradford. He genuinely grew to like Leo, funny, smart Leo, who cracked them up with his imitation of snooty Renee Cunningham and the way he made up names for all the girls parading their lithe bodies across the beach all summer and the corny summertime lotharios that followed them around. He began to spend as much time with Leo as he did with Duke, particularly as Leo got slimmer and slimmer and became quite the chick magnet for all those rich honeys looking for a handsome husband. The weird thing was that the slimmer and more attractive he got and the more all those honeys started to hover around him, he seemed to grow less and less interested in trying to pin one of them down for himself. Maybe the coolest thing about Leo turned out to be the way he'd managed to chill Duke out. Barry liked the change in Duke, who'd mellowed out a bit, cracking jokes and seeming so much more relaxed about so many things.

The one thing Barry never completely understood, however, was Leo's relationship with that kid Joey. Sure it was cool that the Bradfords looked out for him after all that drama with his foster family. And Joey was a cool guy, if a little too quiet at times for Barry's taste. But there seemed to be some other connection between him and Leo that Barry couldn't quite put his finger on.

Whatever it was between them, Barry liked the fact that he was a Yale upperclassman to Leo's new status as freshman. Maybe now that he had Leo all to himself in New Haven he'd be able to teach him a thing or two about life. After all, hadn't Mr. Bradford told him to look out for Leo? To make sure he met some cool girls, to help him come out of his shell? Anything Gary Bradford wanted from Barry, Gary Bradford would get. Because Bradford's letter to the board of directors of CoCo Cosmetics had gotten him a scholarship to college. His well-timed phone-call recommendation as a Yale alumnus had certainly helped Barry get a spot in the class of 1987. Barry would need one more thing from him: A letter to the Yale law school four years from now would be money in the fucking bank.

Barry said, "What's with all the white kids?"

Leo looked around. "What are you talking about?"

They were sitting in the Foyer, a snack bar on campus, a month after classes had started, and Barry was curious. He figured that he hadn't ever seen Leo's potential Oreo side in Sag Harbor because there were so many black folks around, but that didn't stop him from wondering, Why *did* Leo spend so much time with white kids? He had to do something about that.

"If you wanna pledge a frat, you better pull that shit together, man."

"I don't think I'm pledging, Barry. Not interested."

Barry sipped his coffee. "But your father—"

"Is Super Kappa, I know," Leo said. "And like I said, I'm not real interested. As for all the white kids, as you put it, I hang out with cool people, I don't care about race."

"I bet you they do."

"Meaning?"

"Meaning I bet they all think of you as their 'black' friend. And you walking around acting like race isn't important."

Leo laughed. "Okay. You find me some cool black folks to run with and I'll run with 'em. Till then I'll just do what I do."

Barry tore off a piece of bagel. "You fuckin' white girls, too?"

Leo laughed again. "I ain't fuckin' nobody. Haven't really been thinking about it either. Look, man," he said. "I'm sure my father asked you to keep an eye out for me, but I promise you, I'm doing okay. Just trying to get my bearings with classes and all, but I'm fine. Okay?"

Barry sighed. This looking-out-for-Leo thing was going to be harder than he thought. "Whatever you say, man."

For all his concern, what Barry couldn't see was that Leo *was* fine. Yale was everything he'd expected it to be, and more. He felt comfortable among the "best and the brightest," particularly since no one at Yale felt the compulsion to strut his or her stuff around so that everyone knew it. It was so different than the wealthy, jaded, snootier-than-thou atmosphere of his exclusive lycée in Switzerland. He'd gotten one of the freshman slots at the radio station, hosting a show that mixed his beloved rap records with imported alternative rock tracks that he loved as much as rap. He liked the people in his dorm more than he expected to, staying up late discussing politics and books and movies. He even enjoyed running into Barry around campus. He and Joey spoke on the phone every other day and as time went on, he felt less and less compelled to jump on a train and go down to Manhattan to see him.

But then something happened.

3

About a week after his dinner with Barry, on his way to his Religious Philosophy seminar, Leo ran into Barry outside the Student

Union. Barry was talking to a short pecan-brown girl in a pink beret and pea coat. Barry's face lit up like a light as Leo approached.

"This is the brother I was telling you about," Barry said to the girl. "Leo Bradford. Leo, this is Lynn Davis."

Leo smiled and shook Lynn's hand. She was a softly pretty girl with a bright, toothy smile. Leo had seen her around campus.

Lynn tilted her head to the side. "You're Gary Bradford's son, right? I saw that article about your father in *Ebony*. CoCo makes the best cosmetics for sisters."

Barry said, "That's him all right."

Leo looked at Barry. *What the hell is he doing?*

"I was telling Lynn," Barry continued, "how much you love that shitty British music like Depeche Mode. Lynn loves that stuff."

"I've lived in London for the past six years," Lynn said with a smirk. "What's your excuse, Leo?"

Barry said, "You two should get a meal and compare autographs or something."

"Or something," Lynn said, laughing.

"Yeah," Leo said. "Sure. Anytime." He turned to Barry. "Joey's driving up early Saturday morning so we can get a good start to Syracuse. You still going, right?"

"Hell, yeah," said Barry. Then he turned to Lynn. "You like football? We're taking a road trip to see our buddy play. You should come with us, Lynn."

"I love football," she said. She tore a piece of paper from a notebook and wrote down her name and number. She handed it to Leo. "Call me," she said. "See ya, guys."

Barry watched her stroll away. "She wants you bad, Leo."

"She's not my type."

"What is your type?"

"Just be up and ready to go Saturday," Leo said, and he started off toward class, laughing at Barry's attempt to play matchmaker. He couldn't wait to tell Joey.

But he didn't get the response he expected when he called Joey that night. "You there?" he asked into the silence.

Joey said, "I'm still here."

"It's funny, right?"

"Maybe you should check her out, man."

"Why?" Leo said. "I ain't into her. I'm not into any girls."

"I'm just sayin', man . . ."

"Just saying what? Yo, what's up with you? You jealous? You know I ain't trying to get with anybody else."

"I know." Then he was silent again. Leo could hear the TV somewhere behind Joey, blasting out the theme song from *Magnum, P.I.*

"Well," Leo said. "Don't seem like you got much to say. See you Saturday?"

Joey said, "I'll be there." Then he hung up.

Leo hovered over the silent phone, willing it to ring again, ignoring the weird looks he was getting from Pete. But Joey never called back.

4

The first time Joey saw her, the second day of classes at City College, she was sitting two rows ahead of him in his Econ 1 class. The first thing he'd noticed was her ear, small and brown and pierced with one simple pearl. Nothing wild like the contraptions most of the girls were wearing—long, dangly accessories that made noise and just looked sloppy. A pearl. But it wasn't just the pearl. It was that the rest of her was so different as well. Joey had never seen a girl with pearl earrings also wear motorcycle boots and tight black Levi's. The mix of the rough and the gentle intrigued him.

The second time he saw her he was standing outside of the Arts building, and there she was, striding across the campus, a textbook in the crook of one arm, a heavy-looking shoulder bag swinging from the other.

He had to meet her.

But he didn't try to meet her, partly because he truly didn't know how to approach a strange girl and start a conversation. But it was mainly because of Leo. He loved Leo. He loved how Leo talked and what he talked about. He loved how compassionate the dude was, how he'd invited him into his house and family, even if it did start off because he was horny as hell and thought Joey was the cutest thing in the world. That was cool, Joey had thought he was pretty cute, too. He had fun with Leo. As different as their backgrounds were, as different as their upbringings had been, they shared many of the same ideas about the world, they had the same tastes in music and movies and silly TV shows. And Leo was by far the best kisser he'd ever met. Not that either of them had had all that much experience before they reached for each other in the shower that night.

But he had told Leo that he liked girls, too. He liked their softness. He liked the way girls thought differently than guys. He'd only been with two girls before his dreamtime experience with TeeTee at Shirley Bogarde's house, but he remembered how strong he felt with them, the way they'd held on to him when they kissed, the way they expected him to be firm and a little distant.

Things had been good with Leo. Even with him going away to Yale, Joey felt like what they had was real and strong and deep, that nothing could come between them.

But then he saw the girl with the pearl earring.

And then Gary Bradford took him and Edna out to dinner.

Sitting there in Spencer's Steak House, they'd mostly discussed CoCo Cosmetics stuff that Joey didn't understand. Mr. Bradford asked him a few questions about school, which Joey answered politely. But during coffee and dessert, Mr. Bradford asked Edna about a guy named Tom who worked on her staff at CoCo. Why had he quit so suddenly?

"His boyfriend got a job in L.A. and Tom wanted to relocate with him," said Edna, sipping her tea. "They'd been having problems. A new start will be good for them."

Mr. Bradford laughed and said, "Good for them? They're homosexuals, Edna, you expect them to ride off into the sunset and have a nice happy life?"

"They're nice guys, Gary."

"I just don't get the gay thing." Then he turned to Joey. "I was scared that Leo was gonna turn out gay the way he spent so much time in his mother's skirts. I'm glad you came along, Joey. You've helped me make a man out of him."

Joey smiled and drank down the last of his soda. He didn't know what else to do.

"I just don't see how they can be happy. And now this AIDS thing is happening?"

Edna said, "It's not just gay men getting sick, Gary . . ."

But by then, Joey had tuned them out. He went to the men's room and ran the cold water and tossed some onto his face. He had no idea that Mr. Bradford felt the way that he did. Did Leo have any idea? Would he still pursue the life he seemed to be pursuing if he knew his father felt the way he did? Gary Bradford's words played in his mind as he stared into the mirror. But when he thought about it, Joey wasn't completely surprised by Gary Bradford's words, and he cursed himself for not expecting it. He always credited himself with being a good judge of character, that he had to be a good judge after spending so much of his entire life witnessing quick changes and abrupt shifts, the biggest shifts often made by the people with the most power over him, like his father and Shirley Bogarde and Carlton. Why should anything be different now? Just because Gary Bradford had a lot of money and the connections to make Joey's life a little better? As he wiped his face off with a paper towel, Joey also wondered about something else. Was he imagining things or was there something more familiar than usual between Mr. Bradford and Edna? He pushed the thought away as quickly as it had come, deciding then and there not to get involved.

He went to school the next day and the first thing he did was talk to the girl with the pearl earring. Her name was Beth. They had lunch. They talked about how hard Econ 1 was. They went to a movie that night. And they had sex the night after that.

They were lying in bed after Joey finished his phone conversation with Leo about Barry introducing him to some girl named Lynn. There was so much Joey wanted to say to Leo, but he couldn't find the words. He had, however, made a decision. What he couldn't say to Leo he'd show him. It was, really, the only way.

He turned toward Beth and looked into her brown eyes and ran his fingers through her mass of long braids. "What are you doing this weekend?" he asked her. "You wanna go to a football game?"

5

Syracuse beat Rutgers, helped along by three touchdowns by star wide receiver Duke Maynard. But it didn't seem as if anyone else was in a celebratory mood when Duke caught up with his friends at the Root Beer Inn after the game. "I know it wasn't the Yale-Harvard game y'all always talking about," he said as he got to the table and saw the dour looks on most of their faces, "but come on, guys, gimme a little bit of dap."

"Good game," Barry said, hugging Duke when he came over to the table.

"Yeah, bro," said Joey. "Good game." He took his arm from around the funky-looking girl seated next to him and stood to grab Duke into a hug. "This is Bethany," he said, turning to the girl, who smiled and offered Duke her hand.

Duke shook it, then turned to Leo, seated next to a cute, shy-looking girl in a beret. Neither of them seemed too happy. Leo introduced her as Lynn, then said, louder than he needed to, "Now, can we order some food already?"

The small talk around the table stayed pretty small while they waited for their food to come. Duke talked mostly to Barry, since Joey seemed to be completely wrapped up in Bethany and Leo seemed not interested in anything.

Finally, Duke said, "This is the first time I've seen any of you since Labor Day and this is the welcome I get?"

"Considering we almost died driving up here," said Leo, "I guess we're all just trying to catch our breaths again."

"Almost died?"

"Joey was more into teasing Beth than keeping his eye on the road," said Leo.

Barry said, "Can we talk about something else? We made it here, didn't we?"

"I just wish people would be honest already," said Lynn.

Everyone looked at her. "Honest about what?" Duke asked.

She cleared her throat. "I don't really know any of you all that well, but it does seem to me that there's something else going on here, something that's not being said."

"Like what?" Barry said.

"Maybe I shouldn't say anything," she said, and sat back. "Like I said, I don't know any of you all that well."

"No," Leo snapped. "You don't." He took a sip of water. "Then again, I don't think I know some people as well as I thought I did either."

Joey said, "You talking about me?"

"If the shoe fits," said Leo. Then he stood up and walked toward the bathrooms in the rear of the restaurant.

Duke said, "What the hell is going on?"

"I'll be right back," said Joey. He followed Leo's path to the bathrooms. When he got back there, he found Leo leaning against a brown wall smudged with ink from years of collegiate graffiti. "You're not handling this well at all, man."

"That why you wanted me to date Lynn? 'Cause you're with this Bethany chick?"

"Leo, you know how I am. You've known all along."

"And you couldn't give me some kind of warning? I was just supposed to get in the car with you and your—what is she, your girlfriend?—and understand everything? How fucking disrespectful is that, Joey? Huh?"

"Lower your voice, Leo. I'm standing right here."

Leo pushed past him. "You're not anywhere, Joey."

Joey grabbed Leo's shirt and pulled. "At least act like a fucking man, Leo."

That stopped Leo faster than Joey's yank on his shirt. "*I* need to act like a man? Me? Joey, a *man* doesn't spring a new lover on his current one and expect the one he's with to sit back and be cool about it."

"You and me were not lovers," Joey said, looking away.

Leo looked closely at Joey, at his beautiful brown eyes, at the long lashes that he'd kissed on so many occasions. "Then what were we? What are we?"

Joey hesitated. "Boys," he said. "You're my boy. You know that. You knew I liked girls, Leo. You knew it. I never lied about that." He looked at the table over Leo's shoulder. "Let's talk about this later." Joey went back over to the table.

As Leo joined them, the waitress was serving their food. They all ate in silence for a few minutes. Then Duke said, "I'm so glad to see y'all. I miss you guys."

Barry said, "I miss you, too, bro. But I don't see how you have much time to be missing anybody with all these honeys around here."

"Only one honey for me," said Duke. "She should be joining us soon."

Barry said, "You got a woman?"

Duke smiled and nodded. "Of course I do. What, you think I turned gay when I got to Syracuse? From what I hear, that only happens to you Yalies." He playfully poked Leo in the arm.

"Certainly does," said Leo.

All eyes turned to Leo.

"What does that mean?" said Duke.

"And some of us already knew we were gay when we got there."

"Now," said Lynn. "That's what I meant by being honest."

Barry said, "You telling us you're a fag?" His fork clattered on his plate.

"Well, that explains that," said Bethany.

Leo said, "Excuse me?" His eyes were on Joey as he spoke. "Explains what?"

Bethany smiled and fingered the pearl earring in her left earlobe. "Seems pretty clear to me that you sorta have a crush on Joey." She giggled and looped her fingers around Joey's hand. "I think it's really cute."

Barry said, "Where the hell do you get that from?"

"Seems pretty clear to me, too," said Lynn. She turned to Leo. "So are you, as they say, 'coming out of the closet'?"

"What the hell is going on here?" Barry said. He pushed his steak away from him. "Please tell me you are not a faggot, Leo. What would your father say?"

"He'd hate it," Joey said, his eyes right on Leo. "He'd hate it. He'd stop paying for Yale. He'd disown you. He'd leave you bleeding in the street if he saw you laying there begging for help."

Leo said, "How can you talk shit about my father? After everything he did for you?" He regretted the words the moment they came out of his mouth.

"So you're saying I was just something your father bought for you to play with?"

"You got as much out of my father's generosity as I did, Joey." He pointed at Bethany. "But apparently not enough, right?"

"I never promised you anything," Joey said. "But if you don't believe me about your precious fucking father, get on the train when you get back to New Haven, go to his fancy fucking office on Forty-eighth Street, and tell him that you like boys. See how he responds."

And suddenly, sitting there looking at Joey sitting next to Bethany, Leo knew that Joey's words were for real. He did have to admit that much to himself: he knew his father well enough to know that his being gay wouldn't exactly be embraced with open, welcome arms. But something else became clear to Leo. Hearing Joey's words about his father in such clear tones, and seeing the exhausted and, Leo thought, sad look on Joey's face, Leo realized the harsh truth of everything else. It explained everything.

"He said something to you," Leo said. "My father said something to you and that's why you're with her."

"Joey's with me because he wants to be with me," Bethany said, her lips pouting with fury. "How dare you accuse him of being like you?"

"I don't think he's accusing him of anything," said Lynn. "Sounds like it's already been done. Weren't you listening?"

Duke sat back in his seat, then suddenly jumped up from his chair, a big forced smile on his face. "Everybody? I want you to meet Amanda."

They all turned to see a pretty cheerleader standing at the table. "Duke," she said with a tight grin. "You didn't tell me your friends from home were so, uh, friendly."

6

For all their melodrama—*Leo and Joey? Having sex?* It was going to take Duke a few days to get his head around that—Duke was sad to see his friends drive away from Syracuse. But as he waved to the retreating car, his other hand tightly gripped by Amanda, Duke felt even sadder that he now had to go back with Amanda to her dorm, where her parents and brother waited to say goodbye. It had been two years since he and Amanda had started their friendship, two years since the third day of freshman year when they'd stayed up all night after a Getting to Know Your Dormmates party and debated the political genius of Grandmaster Flash versus the b-boy lyrical skills of LL Cool J. Even though he found her more and more attractive as freshman year sped by, Duke constantly reminded himself that Amanda was just a buddy, someone to temporarily replace Leo in his life as a devoted rap fan. And he kept telling himself that after he and Amanda met for lunch in the student union one day and suffered through a series of long, mean stares from three white members of the Syracuse basketball team. Then, late second semester, one of Amanda's friends asked her, as Duke sat on her dorm room floor sorting through a box of rap cassettes, if Amanda's father knew she was spending so much time with a white boy.

"A *fine* white boy," Lisa said, shooting a look at Duke as she moved to the door to go. "But still a white boy."

Duke asked Amanda, "Would your father have a problem with us being pals?"

At first, she didn't speak, as she kneeled down to the floor and helped him organize the cassettes, her head hovering close to his. Finally she said, "My father is what you might call a Race Man." She fingered the edge of a Kurtis Blow tape. "He thinks—"

Duke smiled and scooched closer to her. "He thinks white people are devils."

Amanda laughed. "He just doesn't trust white people."

"If I was a black man from the South," Duke said, "I probably wouldn't trust too many white folks either." He looked at Amanda. "But some of us ain't so bad."

"I know that," Amanda said. "And I think he knows that, but you know, I've been through this with him before. I dated a white guy in high school. He didn't take it well."

"So then he wouldn't like it if I did this," Duke whispered, and he tilted her head back and kissed her gently. Amanda didn't resist. She leaned into his lips and soon they were lying flat on the floor,

Amanda on top of Duke, grinding and kissing as Roxanne Shanté rapped in the background.

On his way back to his dorm across campus that night, Duke realized he really liked this girl, this smart, funny, cynical, beautiful rap-loving Georgia girl. Even as they became comfortable with each other, however, he hadn't told the guys from home about her, mainly because now that her family had relocated to Manhattan, they were a part of New York's upper class black society and there was every chance that her parents would know Leo's parents. They still hung out on campus, but they didn't tell anyone at Syracuse about the next step their relationship had taken. During the summer after freshman year, while he deejayed all over Sag Harbor, resisting Amanda's pleas to visit his hometown, he snuck into Manhattan every chance he could to chill with Amanda in the East Village apartment she was sharing with her cousin while they interned at the *Village Voice*. They went to outdoor concerts in Brooklyn and street fairs in Queens, figuring they could blend into the metropolitan cityscape of New York City, where no one seemed to look twice at the big white jock and the beautiful young black girl on his arm. For all their clandestine attempts at keeping things secret, the Holland family eventually found out about their relationship thanks to a slip of the tongue by Amanda's cousin. Duke suffered through a stilted dinner with the family, answering a fusillade of questions from Thomas Holland about his upbringing and parents and grades and future plans.

Now here they were standing outside Miller Hall, Duke feeling awkward by the hostile glances Amanda's father wasn't shy about tossing his way, yet feeling embraced by the looks of embarrassment her mother cast all over the place. He watched Amanda and her family as they hugged and kissed and said their goodbyes.

"What about Thanksgiving?" Mr. Holland said before getting

into the car, a smudged rental that, from the smirk on his face, he obviously considered beneath him. "When should we be expecting you?"

"It's still a little early for that," Amanda said, shooting a quick glance at Duke, "isn't it, Dad?"

Mr. Holland said, "Never too early to make holiday plans."

"Isn't Syracuse playing Northwestern that weekend?" piped in Sean, Amanda's fifteen-year-old brother, his eyes stuck to a portable video game. "You guys kicked their asses last season."

"Who cares?" Mr. Holland said. "What's a football game have to do—"

"Tommy," said Mrs. Holland.

Mr. Holland looked from his wife to his daughter. "Don't tell me you were planning on going to that game, were you, Amanda?"

Amanda looked at Duke again. He shrugged and raised his eyebrows. She turned back to her father. "I was thinking about it, but maybe—"

"Sweet," yelled Sean. "Can I come, too?"

"Get in the car, Sean," said Mr. Holland. "Whatever, Amanda. It's fine with me."

Amanda smiled. She took Duke's hand in hers. Duke could feel all eyes go to their entwined hands. He held Amanda's tighter.

Amanda screamed. "Really, Dad? Mom?"

"Whatever your father says, Mandy." Her mother kissed her on the cheek, then went back to the car. "So long, Daniel," she said to Duke. "Come on, Sean."

When they were all in the car, Mr. Holland backed out of the space. Before turning out, he stopped the car and rolled down the window. "Amanda? I meant to tell you. That internship with *New York* magazine that I told you about? I spoke to Bill Young and he said there weren't any more spots left." He rolled up the window before Amanda could say anything and pulled off, out of the visitors' parking lot.

"That's my father's version of tit for tat," said Amanda.

Duke could see the tears forming in Amanda's eyes. The resolute tone of her voice told him she'd experienced this before. "You don't think . . . He wouldn't—"

"I know my father, Duke." The tears came harder now. "It's either you or him."

Duke pulled her into a tight hug and they stood there in the parking lot, her head on his shoulder, as a flurry of snowflakes suddenly dropped out of the sky.

1

Duke sat on the edge of the tub. The room service buffet of sushi and salad and steak sandwiches that TNT ordered had just arrived and he could hear the rest of them out in the suite, talking food choices and carbohydrates. Duke had excused himself to wash his hands, but as he sat there watching the water splash from the ornate faucet into the elegant basin, he was thinking about sex. As in the sex he had in 1983, the summer he met Leo and Joey, the summer before he started Syracuse, the summer TNT was conceived. He listed in his mind all the girls he'd slept with that summer.

There was Teresa Hughes, the sexy girl voted Most Likely to Get Divorced Twice, who had slept with virtually every boy in the senior class of Sag Harbor High.

There was Stephanie Tyson, a plain Jane–type black girl who was not plain at all when they got busy in her parents' basement after she finished tutoring Duke in trig.

There was Carla, whom he eventually did fuck, even though he never told Barry. He'd given her a ride from Leo's house to the railroad station and they ended up doing the deed in the backseat of Duke's mother's station wagon.

Three girls that spring and summer. Teresa hadn't had any kids, if he could remember correctly. She went to Vanderbilt that fall and eventually became a doctor. Last he'd heard she was living in Los Angeles doing plastic surgery.

He knew Carla didn't have a kid. He didn't see much of her after he left for Syracuse, but he did see her in magazines and on billboards, and she certainly didn't look pregnant. Besides, if Carla had gotten pregnant by him, Duke was sure he'd have heard about it from somebody in the Bradford family.

He took out his phone and dialed his mother. She answered on the second ring.

"Ma—"

"Duke? I just walked in! How'd your meeting go?"

"You remember Stephanie Tyson?"

His mother laughed. He could hear her breathing hard as she took off her shoes or something. "I haven't thought about her in years. Why?"

"Do you know if she has any kids?"

"Duke, I don't—"

"Actually, do you know if she got pregnant right out of high school?" He looked at himself in the mirror over the sink. He could only imagine what his mother was thinking from all these questions.

"Duke, what are you asking me—"

"I know it sounds strange, but, I—I just need to know if she . . ."

His mother asked quietly. "You think it was yours?"

Duke breathed deeply. "So she did get pregnant?"

"Last I can recall, she did have a baby, but . . ."

"But what, Ma?"

"Her baby died as an infant."

There was a long silence between them. Duke knew his mother;

he knew she was considering the possibilities. Finally he said, "Ma? I have to go. Sorry I bothered you."

"How did your meeting go?"

Duke sighed. The words echoed in his head: *Which one of you bastards is my father?* "It's still going. I'll call you later, okay?"

2

TNT watched Duke come out of the bathroom, slipping his cell phone into his pocket. Either the dude is a real clean freak and washed his hands five times or he was on the phone with someone. TNT wondered who he'd called. He watched Duke go over to the buffet setup and pile salad greens onto a china plate. Then he looked from Duke to Joey to Leo, and for a moment he wondered if his gambit would pay off. Would they stick around long enough to figure this all out? Considering how fast Barry had jetted out of the suite, TNT was surprised none of the others had done the same. But then, still watching the three of them huddle together across the room, TNT realized that they were probably enjoying this trek down memory lane as much as he was enjoying it. Sure, there was a lot he knew about all of them, but there were details he still needed filled in. Details about them as a group, but also details about the one who'd fathered him, the teenager who was now a man. A man he needed to have a relationship with now.

But he wasn't ready to bare his soul to any of them yet. They still needed to know who was in charge of this meeting.

He walked to the middle of the suite and popped open another beer. "Hey, Leo," he asked. "Exactly how long were you and that basketball player together?"

Leo laughed. How much did this kid know about them? "Let me ask you a question," Leo said. "It's obvious you know that I'm gay. So why keep *me* here?"

"Just 'cause you suck dick," TNT said, "don't mean you ain't had some pussy in your life." He turned to the couch behind him. "Right, Joey Ram?"

Duke said, "Listen, man, torture might work in some places but we respected you enough to show up here and we've sat through your accusations. Will you just get to the point you want to make?"

TNT walked over to the huge wall of windows, looking out at the rococo highlights of the Manhattan skyline. He stood there for a few minutes, then turned back to the three of them. "You know what I find interesting?"

"What's that?" Duke said.

"All of you, all four of you, have achieved so much, and none of you have any kids. Why is that?"

"None that we know of," Joey said. "If this meeting is any indication."

"Exactly," TNT said, a sarcastic smile creasing his lips. "Were you all too busy making your careers happen? Do you all have, how do they say it on TV, like, intimacy issues? You don't stay with a partner long enough to make a real family? Huh? What is it? All y'all about to be forty and none of you got a family."

"Life got in the way."

They all turned toward the elevator. Barry stood there, his briefcase in one hand, a bottle of Scotch in his other hand. "I had to get some liquor," he said. "They didn't have my brand here."

TNT laughed. "Barry. So fuckin' slick we didn't even hear the elevator open."

"That's me," Barry said. He stepped farther into the penthouse, taking tentative steps. "I've never been as fast as Duke or as smart as

Leo." A hint of slurring dented his words. "Or as sexy as Joey." He winked at Joey. "But I've always been slick."

Leo said, "How much of that Scotch have you had?"

"Enough to come back here and face our young accuser." He sat down on the couch next to Duke. "You mind if I sit here, Duke, my brother?" Duke stood up and walked over to a chair on the other side of the room. "So, back to the game y'all were playing. Someone gonna deal me in?"

1986–1987

1

"Thank you for seeing me on such short notice, Mr. Bradford."

"No problem, Duke," said Gary. "I told you anytime you needed anything to call me right up."

Duke tried to sit tall in the slick leather chair across the huge oak desk of Gary Bradford, who was sitting back in his throne-like chair, his fingers steepled in front of him as if he were considering some major decision. It was the first time in his life Duke had encountered the man outside of Sag Harbor. Out there, in shorts and sandals, grilling at the barbecue or reading on the deck, Mr. Bradford was friendly but distant. In his Armani suit and silver watch, sitting behind the mammoth desk, he was like some terrifying statue. Duke got the distinct impression that Bradford liked it more this way.

"Well," Duke began. "I've made a decision about going pro—"

"Look, Duke, I have to say something, before we go further."

Duke nodded.

"I am a major advocate of education. Especially for young men from backgrounds like yours. Sure, I know the Horatio Alger stories about poor boys working hard, conquering obstacles, but at the end of the day, anyone of any kind of stature will look at you as someone below their level and class if you don't have an education, if you don't have that sheepskin hanging somewhere in the world that says a university saw fit to award you a degree. You understand what I'm saying, Duke?"

Duke nodded again. His eyes instinctively went over Bradford's head to the two degrees on the wall behind him. Yale College. Harvard School of Business.

"Now, Duke. I understand that you are a talented young man. I know all about the things you accomplished on the football field for Syracuse. But notice. I said 'for Syracuse,' not 'at Syracuse.' Do you know why I made that distinction, Duke?"

"I think so, Mr. Bradford."

"Because at the end of the day, what you did—the numbers you put up, the footballs you caught, the yards you ran—you did that for the men who own and run Syracuse. *For* them, Duke. You got nothing from them except accolades and awards and wins instead of losses. Now that you've made the decision that you've made, where are those men to help you really make sure the decision is the right one? And if it is the right one, where are they to make sure that you get the best possible representation that a young man can get at such an important juncture in his life? They're not here, and that's why you came to me, requesting that I help you. Which I'm glad to do. No problem at all. You're going pro. Wonderful. But I have to ask you once more, Duke: Are you sure you don't want to finish your Syracuse career instead of leaving now for the NFL?"

"With all due respect, Mr. Bradford, you just told me that everything I accomplish at Syracuse is *for* Syracuse rather than *at* Syracuse." Duke sat straighter in the chair and cleared his throat. He continued, "If I stay to get the degree you deem so important I will keep doing just that. Things for Syracuse. If I leave now and sign with the Redskins, I'll be able to write my own ticket. I can always finish my education."

Gary Bradford steepled his fingers again. He looked at Duke, hard and for a few long seconds. Then he smiled. "It's a quandary, isn't it, Duke?"

"Not really," said Duke. "I've made my decision."

"Well then, good for you," said Bradford. He pressed another button on the panel. "Hannah? Please get numbers for Hank Millerman, Kevin Ford, and Frank Gilstrap for me. Quickly." He took a cigarette from the tray sitting on the right corner of his desk and lit it. "Can I ask you another question, Duke?"

Duke nodded. "Sure, Mr. Bradford."

"Do you plan on marrying Amanda Holland?"

Duke swallowed. He wanted to ask Bradford how he knew about Amanda. But instead he said, "I'm not sure yet. I do love her, but we haven't talked about marriage. We're both still young."

"But you've dated since your freshman year, Duke. It must be pretty serious."

"It is serious, sir."

Bradford said, "She's a beautiful girl."

"Yes, she is," said Duke. "Thank you."

Bradford took a drag off the cigarette, blew out a plume of gray smoke that hovered between them before disappearing into the air. "Does her father know about the abortion she had?"

"Excuse me?"

"The abortion. Does Tom Holland know you knocked up his daughter?"

"How did you know about that?"

At that moment a short pretty woman in a long black skirt and white blouse came into the office and placed a folder on the desk. She smiled at Duke, then crept back out of the office. Bradford opened the folder and took the lone sheet of paper from it. He pushed it across the desk at Duke. "Those are the numbers," he said. "Hank Millerman is the best sports lawyer in the business. Kevin Ford and Frank Gilstrap have the best sports marketing agency in the game. They're doing something no one else in the game is doing. They're thinking of athletes as stars beyond the field. They'll make you a lot of money if your agent allows them to. I went to business school with both of them. They'll be expecting your call." He took another drag from the cigarette, then tamped it out in the shining silver ashtray next to the phone. "Glad you came to see me, Duke. I appreciate the friendship you've given Leo and as I said, if there's anything I can ever do . . ."

Duke got the impression then that the meeting was done. He stood to go. He waited for Bradford to stand. He didn't. He just reached out his hand to shake with Duke.

"Please give my regards to Amanda," he said.

"I will," said Duke.

"So does he?"

"Does who what, sir?"

"Does Holland know about the abortion?"

Duke shook his head.

Bradford smiled again. "Good," he said. "Make sure it stays that way. You won't be able to play football for anyone with both of your legs broken in three or four places."

Outside on Forty-eighth Street, Duke watched the midtown pedestrian traffic hustle along in a blur of a movement. *Does Holland know about the abortion?* He could feel his heart knocking against his chest with a fierceness he'd never experienced. How could Bradford have known about that? He'd only told Leo and Barry about it. Leo because he was the most logical person he knew, and Barry because he needed the five hundred dollars that Barry owed him to take care of the situation. He could feel his fingers trembling, and the trembles creeping up his arms. That had been the hardest week of his life, that week in the summer of 1984—terrifying, confusing, and painful but ultimately clarifying his love for Amanda and her love for him. It had been her decision and he vowed to stand by her, whichever way she wanted. She made her choice and they made a pact to deal with it and move on as best they could with their lives. Every so often, the details of that week played through Duke's mind: the tears and embraces, the all-night conversations that led to more heartbreaking tears, the trip to the doctor, the hard seat in the waiting room, the sullen look of blankness on Amanda's face when she came out afterward. It had been hard, but they'd gotten through it, quietly, privately, just as they'd wanted it. *But how does Mr. Bradford know about the abortion?* Maybe they hadn't been so private, after all.

After a few more minutes, Duke got up and took his place in the bustling Manhattan foot traffic along Sixth Avenue. He looked down at the paper, with the names Bradford had given him. He now knew something his mother had told him since he was a kid. Advice is never free.

2

"Leo? Leo Bradford?"

Leo put down the bag of carrots and turned toward the familiar voice, one he hadn't heard in a long while. He took in the sight of the tall, gangly white guy, hair to his shoulders, stud earring in each ear, unkempt goatee masking his thin lips.

"Pete?"

"Yeah, man. How you doing?" Pete grabbed Leo into a big hug, then stood back to take a look at him. "You lost weight, man!"

Leo smiled. "What are you doing here? Shouldn't you be up at Yale?"

"Shouldn't you?" Pete grinned. "I never saw you around, then

I heard you weren't there anymore. You never struck me as the dropout type, bro."

Pete was the first Yalie Leo had run into since leaving school months ago, and it felt good to see his old roommate, someone from those happy New Haven days. "What are you doing here?" Leo repeated.

"My band got a gig at Brownies, man. Our first real New York City date. Can you believe it? Shit goes well, maybe I'll be a dropout like you, bro." Pete's infectious smile and eager energy hadn't diminished at all from that first day of freshman year. "You should come to the show. It's tomorrow night. We blew off classes all week to come down here and get ready. It's damn near finals anyway. Anything I don't know now I'm not gonna know in two weeks, ya know?"

Pete's words struck Leo with the memory of how much he'd loved his classes, loved studying, especially during finals, haunting the libraries and discovering the words he'd always dreamed of discovering. But he forced the thoughts of Yale out of his mind. It had taken long enough to get himself past the painful part, the decision he'd made, the mourning of the loss of the thing he worked so hard to get and dreamed so long to have. Nope, he wouldn't let any of that past stuff invade his brain. He decided to let this accidental meeting with Pete mean good things for the future.

"Can I bring someone with me?" Leo said.

"Bring everybody you fuckin' know, bro. The more heads we get in there drinking beer, the better chance we get another gig." Pete looked over Leo's shoulder at the carrots. "You cooking for yourself these days?"

"Who else is gonna do it?"

"I would think you'd be at your folks place. Don't they still live in Manhattan?"

Leo nodded. "Just trying to be independent, ya know?"

"Gotcha," Pete said, hugging Leo again. "I gotta run. See you tomorrow night, bro. Don't forget, okay?" He dashed out of the store.

"I won't," Leo said to Pete's retreating back.

"He didn't even mention Leo," Duke said to Amanda. "Sitting there talking about how important education is, finishing school and all that. Seemed a little hypocritical to me."

Amanda stirred the pot of broth on the stove. "Pass me those onions," she said.

Duke said, "Did you hear me?" He pushed the onions across the counter.

"I heard you," she said. "But did you really expect him to bring up Leo after everything that's happened?"

"Who didn't bring up Leo?"

Amanda and Duke turned to see Leo coming into the kitchen. He plopped the bag of carrots in a bowl in the sink and turned on the faucet to clean them. He looked from Amanda to Duke. "So who'd you run into? Somebody from Sag?"

"Nobody," Duke said. "So what else is gonna be in this stew anyway?"

Leo said, "Don't change the subject."

"Duke had a meeting with your father," Amanda said quietly.

Leo continued washing the carrots for a few seconds. Then he turned off the spigot and put the bowl close to Amanda's elbow. "You saw my father? Why?"

"I had to get some info," Duke said. "I'm sorry, bro. I just figured that if I—"

"If you what? If you snuck into town and had a secret meeting with my father I'd never find out? And you stay at my apartment while you're sneaking around?"

"First of all," Amanda said, putting down the big wooden spoon. "This isn't *your* apartment, Leo. My cousin's letting you sublet it."

"As long as *I'm* paying the rent on it, it's mine," Leo said. "Just be glad I'm not asking you to pay me to stay here."

"We'll go to a hotel if you really feel that way," Amanda said.

"Yeah," Leo said, "It's not like you can stay at *your* father's house, right?"

Duke saw the heat rise in Amanda's face. "Come on, man, that's not necessary."

"But it's necessary for you to go to my father for help after the way he's treated me? At least you got a fucking college to go back to, Duke. You too, Amanda. Your pops may not like you being with Duke but he didn't take Syracuse away from you, did he?"

Duke jumped down from the counter stool and went over to Leo. "Listen, man—"

Leo shrugged away from him. He turned and went into his bedroom.

As he lay on the bed in the tiny bedroom he stared up at the framed Public Theater poster on the wall and listened to Amanda and Duke try to talk in hushed tones. He tried to tune them out, not easy to do in that tiny apartment, the only place he could afford if he was going to stay in Manhattan and live on his own without help from his parents. Which, he had to admit, is what made him so pissed about Duke going to see his father. Or any of his friends doing it, for that matter. In trouble? Need some help? Go to Leo's dad, he's a Fixer, he'll help you out. It didn't always bother Leo so much, the rescue missions his powerful father always seemed to accomplish for his friends; of his whole crew, he was the only one with a real father figure in his life. It wasn't like Gary Bradford was such a prize that Leo couldn't bear to share him if he had to. But how did that father figure behave when the truth became known about Leo? How did the powerful Fixer fix things when he found out his only son was gay?

Leo could still remember the tense meeting months ago in the den of the Bradford apartment on Central Park West one week before classes started at Yale for his junior year. He could still picture the three of them—his father, his mother, and himself—spread around the huge Laura Ashley–decorated room, like players in some stiff, badly directed drawing room play, his father chain-smoking Camels, his mother crying softly, one hand in her lap, the other one grasping at the string of pearls around her elegant neck.

His father had asked, "So is this true, what I hear?"

"I guess not," Leo had said. "Not if you can't say it, Dad."

"I've—We've, done so much for you. And this is what happens? Who did it?"

"Did what?" Leo asked him.

"Who introduced you to this shit? Who gave you the idea that you were . . ."

"Gay?"

"Where did it come from?"

"Is that important, Dad? Can't it just be?"

"I refuse to believe that it just happens like that."

His mother said, "It isn't like he's been bringing girls home all these years, Gary."

He swung around to face his wife. "Are you saying you've been, what . . . preparing yourself for this moment? Because there were no girlfriends?"

"I'm saying you need to calm down and just deal with this."

"I will not." He just stood there, not saying anything, just sipping from his Scotch and staring at Leo.

The silence irked Leo, but the stares bothered him more, like he was some exhibit in a museum or an animal in a zoo.

"I know a shrink," Gary said finally.

"I don't need to see a doctor," Leo said. "I'm not sick."

Gary snorted sarcastically, and sat down on one of the couches.

Leo felt his mother's eyes on his profile. He didn't want to look at her. He felt like he'd burst into tears if he saw even the slightest sense in her face of how much she loved him. And he refused to show his father any vulnerability.

Gary took a sip of his Scotch and lit another cigarette, and at that moment, as he blew out a plume of smoke, Leo knew exactly how his father had found out about him.

"Barry told you, didn't he?"

Gary didn't respond at first. "Does it matter how I found out?"

Leo shrugged. "Not really," he lied, feeling his insides coil up, a sharp and fast anger beginning to boil in his brain. He stood up.

Gary said, "Where are you going?"

Leo went over to the bar. He poured a glass of water and stood there with his back to his parents. "I gotta pack for school."

"You're not going back to school," Gary said.

"What are you talking about?" Leo said. "Classes start in a week."

"You'll see this shrink—"

Lillian said, "Or what?"

"I'm not paying for him to be up at Yale running around wasting my money."

"What does his sexuality have to do with Yale, Gary?"

"Lillian, you don't understand. This happened up there. Somebody up there got to him and put this gay crap in his brain. You think I'm gonna continue to subsidize that?"

Lillian sighed. "Go finish packing, Leo."

"Are you going to the doctor?" Gary demanded.

"No," Leo said. "I'm not."

"Then you're not going back to Yale. It's that simple. It's your choice." Gary and Leo locked eyes, daring the other to back down, to relent to his strength. In that moment, in the heat of this battle with his father, Leo felt more like a man than he ever had in his life. He knew somehow that when he walked out of the den, giving up Yale and his friends and studies and freedom, what he would gain in self-sufficiency would take him far. He knew it in his gut.

"No," he said again. "I'm not going to any doctor."

"Then that's that," Gary said, his lips a thin line. "He made his choice, Lillian."

My choice, Leo thought now lying on the bed, smelling the heady blend of onions and carrots and beef broth floating in from the kitchen with Duke and Amanda's chatter. His choice: a tiny dusty sublet in the East Village, a shitty job at a radio station retrieving tapes for an arrogant DJ. He breathed out a long sigh. *This is my life,* he thought. *And I chose it.* Just like Duke had chosen his life, walking away from college for an indefinite future in football. Leo could only imagine what it must have been like for Duke to be sitting there in that hostile office of Gary's, probably in front of that huge desk with its telephone panel of demands being made while you tried to have a conversation. Leo almost laughed. He hoped Duke got what he needed out of the meeting because Gary Bradford would never let him forget that he'd helped him in some way.

In the kitchen Leo found Duke and Amanda leaning against the sink, their words melting into soft kisses, which they quickly stopped when they heard Leo return.

"I'm sorry about what I said," Leo said.

"Forget it," Duke said. "I wanted to tell you—"

"But I jumped the gun," Amanda said.

"Don't worry about it," Leo said. He picked up the wooden spoon and listlessly stirred the pot of stew. "So, we gonna eat this or we gonna go out and get Indian food?"

Sitting in Delhi Eats on St. Mark's Place, they had chicken tikka, basmati rice, and good conversation. Then Duke said, "He asked me about what happened last October."

"He asked you about it?" Amanda asked, a piece of naan bread hovering near her mouth. She put her fork down. "How did he know?" She pushed her plate aside like it was a memory of that awful week. "And why did it have to come up in a conversation about you finding an agent?"

Duke shrugged his shoulders. He reached over and massaged Amanda's neck. "I wasn't going to say anything, but it's been going through my mind all day."

Leo said, "How else does my father find out anything about us? How do you think he found out I was gay?"

Duke sighed. "I didn't want to think it."

"Barry," said Amanda. She turned to Duke. "You told Barry about it?"

Duke didn't say anything. "I had to. He—"

Amanda put up her hand to stop him. "He was the only one *not* in a bad mood the day I met you all for the first time," she said. "And I didn't like him then."

"Barry has issues," Duke said. "His family situation—"

"We all have family shit," Amanda said. "That's no excuse to betray people."

Leo raised his glass of wine. "Well, all I can say is 'Welcome.'"

Duke and Amanda exchanged a look. "To?"

"The Betrayed by Barry Club. You're now officially members."

They clinked glasses, but there was no joy in it. Duke said, "I've known Barry longer than any of you. I joined that club a long time ago. What'd you used to say about him? 'Be-Wary-of-Barry.'"

They all laughed and Leo felt good again. For a little while at least. Maybe it was hearing Amanda and Duke lovingly, automatically, finish each other's sentences, maybe it was his earlier thoughts about his father's role as Fixer to his friends, maybe it was being reminded of Barry's nickname by Duke, but for some reason one person kept popping into his brain, the person who'd hurt him worse than anyone in the world ever had, in that bathroom in Syracuse, the person he hadn't spoken to since that day in the restaurant. For some reason he could only think of Joey.

3

"The stitching's for shit and that color you chose is absolutely disgusting. Other than that, it looks okay."

Joey put down the blouse he was sewing and tried his hardest to stare daggers into the back of the bitchy teaching assistant, who was now standing at the next work station, berating another student. When the daggers didn't work, Joey just wished he wasn't there at this tacky-ass night class where he didn't feel like he was learning anything anyway, except how to take bitchy criticism from nasty queens who'd never gotten too far in their own fashion careers. So he packed up his self-respect, his sketch book, and the absolutely disgusting pieces of fabric he'd been using to sew the blouse, and left the classroom, not looking back to see if Evil Queen Teaching Assistant was watching, but secretly hoping that he was.

Out on Twenty-sixth Street, Joey realized that for once in a long while, he didn't have anywhere to be. The store where he worked was closed for remodeling for three days. He didn't have to run any errands for Edna. And he wouldn't be seeing Greta, the girl he'd been dating for the last few months, since her prep school friend's band was playing a gig downtown this week and she was spending time with him. So he just decided to walk.

And as he walked, Joey had to ask himself a question. What was it about him that always got him into these relationships with slumming rich kids? From Leo to Bethany (which had lasted another whole year after the debacle at Syracuse that fall; she'd actually been turned on by the fact that some guy wanted her man as badly as she did), to Yanique, the stunning model he'd dated next, who'd turned out to be the daughter of Nigerian royalty, escaping her parents' strict rules and jetting around New York like some lost African Audrey Hepburn princess on her own little *Roman Holiday*. And now Greta, half Greek and half Haitian, prep school princess, Barnard dropout, growing her dreadlocks and writing music reviews for the *Village Voice*, who spoke fluent Spanish because her parents kept a home in Costa Rica throughout her youth, who demanded that she and Joey speak only Spanish to each other whenever they were alone. She was crazy as hell. Everything she did, from her painting, to their frequent fights, to her mere way with words, was completely, flamboyantly dramatic, but she was also incredibly smart, extremely creative, with a good artistic eye, and she knew how to have fun.

If only he could corral his own creative impulses. After suffering through boring classes at City College, thanks to the flowing generosity of Gary Bradford, Joey realized that fashion was what he loved more than anything. He got his best grades in the architecture and design classes he took at CCNY, but he realized that if he was going to get a real design education, he'd have to go to a real design school. So he told Edna that he was going to transfer to the Fashion Institute of Technology, down in Chelsea. When Edna told Gary, while he lounged on the couch after one of his and Edna's rendezvous that they didn't bother to keep secret from him anymore, Gary laughed and said he wasn't going to pay for Joey to leave City College, where he could get a solid, well-rounded liberal arts education. Joey was disappointed but he was at least relieved to hear that his reason wasn't because of all the fags in the fashion biz. So, Joey took on another job and enrolled himself in a night class at Fashion Studies, a bootleg fashion academy that had planted itself in upper Chelsea so it could inhale some of the flavor of FIT's rarefied air and breathe it back onto the poor or unconnected students who couldn't afford to get the real thing. Joey figured he would do FS for a year, then apply for a scholarship to FIT and see what happened.

"The stitching's for shit." What did that idiot know about stitching? Nothing that he could teach Joey, who'd learned how to sew at his grandmother's knee before she'd died and the city system swallowed him into its belly. He'd forgotten all about sewing until one day that first summer in Sag Harbor when Carla was whining about a skirt that she didn't think was short enough. While Carla was back in the city overnight for a model go-see, Joey found the skirt and re-hemmed it, stitching together a cute little halter to go with it, from a pattern he found in the local fabric store on Main Street. Carla screamed with surprise and delight when she returned, even calling up a friend in Manhattan to rave about the halter and "the sturdy stitching" in particular. Carla wore the halter more than she wore any other piece that summer, and Barry and Duke teased him about his sewing ability—until they needed some fly clothes to meet girls the next summer and didn't have the money to buy them. Joey smiled at the memory.

As he strolled down Sixth Avenue, still remembering those summers in Sag Harbor, the beginning of what he always thought of as his new life, he wondered if perhaps those memories were returning for a reason. Or two. First, he wondered if perhaps he was supposed to do what he'd done then: go to a fabric store, get some material, and sew some pieces. He wouldn't use a Butterick pattern, but one of his own, based on one of the many sketches he had in his notepad or waiting to be emptied from his brain. He could show his pieces to some stores or designers, and perhaps get an internship or get some store to carry his stuff. It was a pipe dream, he knew, but it excited him, the thought of making a living from something he'd created in his mind, from his own imagination. Which led him to the other thing.

Leo.

Whenever he felt creative, he thought of Leo. Leo, who always encouraged him to pursue whatever he felt passionate about. He could always turn to Leo when he felt slow or meaningless or empty. He could always look to Leo to fill him up with something graceful or special or even say something sarcastic, to prick the bubble Joey could often create around himself, to step inside it and urge him to do something good.

But what was the point of thinking about Leo? He'd broken the kid's heart, and cruelly, right in front of his boys, neither of whom Joey saw or spoke to or heard from anymore. Did he even deserve to be thinking of Leo in any supportive capacity? Or was that his selfishness leading him there, that bubble he could create, to invite Leo's good blessings in while still leaving Leo himself outside?

Whatever. He'd leave the Leo bit alone. But he'd definitely buy the fabric and start sketching and stitching. Maybe he'd make something for Edna. Or maybe for Greta. Would she appreciate that? Her boyfriend handing her a box with clothing inside and saying, "I made this for you?" No, he'd hold back on sewing something for Greta. No need to rock the boat this soon into the relationship. The sex was still too good.

4

Driving back to the university in the cherry-red Maxima he'd been loaned for the season by a car-dealer alumnus in Syracuse, Duke noticed that the economics text stayed unopened on Amanda's lap as she constantly changed radio stations, yanking their ears from honky-tonk country tunes to easy-listening ballads that almost put Duke to sleep. Duke hummed along with the songs when he could, mainly because he didn't know how to address Amanda's silence and obviously nervous demeanor, and he needed to hear *one* of their voices or he'd go crazy. He mentally chastised himself for telling her that Gary Bradford had brought up the abortion at their meeting, but it was important, he thought, that she knew that someone outside of their close circle knew. It was a decision they'd promised never to discuss again, and he'd broken it. Now there was another major decision to be made and Duke really wasn't sure if that was weighing on Amanda's mind as much as the abortion.

He was definitely going to skip his senior year and go pro. His mother had told him to do what he thought was best. His brother Mike seemed giddy with anticipation, already dropping hints that he'd want to be on the Duke Maynard payroll. His sister Marie cried and hugged him, suddenly detailing just how much work needed to be done on the little house she and Starkeisha and her new little three-year-old son rented in the middle of a crack-infested Queens neighborhood. He had his family taken care of. Now he just needed to find out what Amanda wanted to do.

Duke watched Amanda stare out the car window, rubbing her fingers as she always did when she was nervous about something. "What's the deal?" he asked her, reaching out to stop her fiddling hands.

"Thinking about finals," she said.

"Your very last finals if you come with me," he said. She smiled weakly and continued to stare out the window. "You know you don't have to come, Mandy," he said softly. "You can stay here, finish school, then join me in D.C. next year."

She nodded. "I know that, but I want to be with you."

"Listen, let's just concentrate on Pick an Agent Day, okay?"

Amanda nodded. They drove on. Duke knew there was something else; Amanda had never in the three years he'd known her ever worried about an exam. But he didn't push her on it. She'd open up when it was time.

The knock at his apartment door two days later surprised Duke. Everyone he hung out with, including Amanda, who said she wanted to give him room to think about things before the big Pick an Agent Day, was carpooling it down to Connecticut for the big basketball game against UConn. He was even more surprised to see his coach standing there in the doorway, his usual look of disapproval etched even deeper across his face. He barged right in and said, "You signed with an agent in New York, didn't you?" He went right to the refrigerator in the tiny kitchen and took a beer from the six-pack on the top shelf. He popped the top and dropped himself onto to the old couch in the living room.

"Not yet," Duke said. "I told you I was investigating. I have until next week."

"We need you," Coach Callahan said. "You know that."

"And I need to move on," Duke said, sitting in the leather chair across from the couch. He stared up at the map of the United States that his roommate Clarence had taped to the wall. He let his eyes travel from Syracuse to New York City to Washington, D.C.

Coach sighed. "Washington's gonna take you, ya know."

"They need me," Duke said, smiling. "They should take me."

Neither of the men spoke for a few seconds. Duke listened to the hum of the dishwasher in the kitchen. Coach sat forward and put the beer bottle on the coffee table.

Coach raised his eyebrows and sat back. "I wanted to talk about Amanda."

Duke sat up. "What about her? She hasn't made any decision yet."

"What did she tell you?"

"She's torn," said Duke. "Either she'll come with me and we'll get married or she'll stay here, get her degree, then come down. Either way we're getting married." He smiled at the words that had come out of his mouth. He hadn't yet articulated them to anyone except Amanda. Saying them out loud, he felt like a man.

Coach said, "I think you better come with me."

Amanda's room was empty, cleared out of everything but the bed that came with the place and the steel clothes rack her brother Sean had brought up from New York. Her posters were gone, as well as the huge postcard collage she'd made of her friends' dispatches from around the world. The only thing of interest was the envelope on the bare mattress, addressed to him in Amanda's squiggly handwriting: "Duke."

Duke looked over at Coach, who just shrugged and went back into the living room, where his daughter Pammie, Amanda's roommate for two years, lay wrapped up in a comforter, a bowl of chicken soup on the coffee table in front of her.

"She begged me not to say anything," Pammie had said when Duke and Coach came into the apartment. "I'm sorry, Duke."

Duke read the letter:

Dear Duke

I love you. Please know that this is not about how much I do
now, and always will, love you. But I can't marry you. I can't move to
Maryland with you, now or after I finish school. I had a choice to make.
And I think you know what that choice was. I can't see living my life
without having you in it. And I can't see myself living a life without my
family in it. But I have to choose one. And I choose my family. Please
forgive me. Please don't hate me. Please understand. Do not try to contact
me. I will get in touch with you when it's best for us to talk. I love you.

Mandy

Duke felt his body collapse into a hard chair next to Pammie's
couch. "I have to find her. She must have gone back to New York,
right?" He looked at Pammie. "Right?" He could hear panic in his
voice; he could feel his heart pumping wildly, like it was threatening to break and explode inside him. Tears erupted from his eyes.
"Huh? Where else could she have gone?" It was like something in
his muscles and bones was resisting his mind's desire to move. He
hated the feeling of tears on his cheeks, embarrassed to be so na-
kedly emotional in front of Coach and his daughter. But his body
wouldn't move, only the tears would. He felt like the severe pounding of his heart controlled the increasing volume of the tears.

5

A few days after Duke and Amanda had returned to Syracuse,
Leo met up with Carla at the Dojo Restaurant on St. Mark's Place.
She strolled into the collegiate vegetarian hang-out wearing heels,
hip-hugging tight blue jeans, and an expensive-looking scoop-

necked peasant blouse that showed everything she wanted the world to know about cleavage.

Noticing Leo's surprised look, she said, "Didn't you say it was a concert?"

"At an East Village dive," Leo said, laughing. "You look like we're going to see Luther Vandross at the Garden."

"Well," she said, sitting down and picking up a menu, "You never know who's gonna be there." She looked over the menu. "I don't eat bean sprouts."

"You'll find something."

"So where's Duke? You know I used to mess around with him, right?"

"Duke is back at Syracuse," he said. "Left a coupla days ago."

"Oh." She looked disappointed for about twenty seconds. Then she brightened up. "Well, did I tell you your boy Barry called me?"

"Like I'd care."

"He said that he still thinks about me."

"When he's not thinking about himself, I guess."

"It's gonna be weird with him working at CoCo next year."

Leo dropped his menu. "What did you say?"

"He's going to postpone law school for a year and work for the company."

"I'm not hungry anymore," he said. "Let's just go."

Brownies was packed. Leo held tight to Carla's hand and forced his way through the crowd of sweaty, black-clad downtowners. Through the huge halo of cigarette smoke that hovered over the crowd like a rain cloud on the verge of letting loose a storm, Leo could see Pete and his bandmates tuning up their instruments on the tiny stage.

"That's Pete," he told Carla, pointing toward the stage. "My old roommate."

"He's cute," she yelled. "For a skinny white boy."

To Leo, cute didn't really do Pete justice anymore. He'd grown into his gangliness and there was something about him now that Leo couldn't put his finger on.

At the bar, Leo asked the mohawked, serene-looking barmaid for a Corona and a glass of white wine for Carla, who was twisting her head back and forth, taking in the scruffy East Village vibe that was worlds removed (though only sixty blocks away) from her Upper East Side roots.

"I love your hair," she screamed at the barmaid. "Very punk rock."

The barmaid smirked, gave Leo his change, and moved on to the next patron.

"I love the attitude down here," Carla said. "It's so . . . so . . ."

"I know," Leo said with a smirk. "Punk rock."

"I was gonna say skanky."

The squawk and rumble of a bass guitar signaled the start of the show and most of the heads in the tight room turned to watch the band rev up into a fast, ragged cover of the Beatles' "Mother Nature's Son." Leo bobbed his head to the beat, his eyes on Pete, surprised by his old roommate's vivid stage presence. Pete hopped around the stage, mike stand in hand, like a sexy but slightly damaged windup toy. He looked good.

Carla said, "Was he that sexy when you were sharing a dorm room with him?"

As he turned to respond into Carla's ear, he caught a face out of the corner of his eye, a face he didn't expect to see in Brownies watching a rock show.

It was Joey.

————

Greta yelled into Joey's ear, "Who the fuck are you looking at?"

He didn't answer her, just smiled and planted a kiss on her cheek. He pulled her around so that she was in front of him and he wrapped his arms around her waist. She grabbed his beer and took a sip, her dyed-green dreadlocks hitting him in the mouth as she threw her head back to sip.

With Greta in front of him, Joey knew she couldn't see him looking to his left, watching Leo and Carla at the bar, drinking and yelling to hear each other's words. Carla was still beautiful in that sly, pampered way of hers. And Leo. He'd lost more weight. And he'd been working out, it seemed, his shoulders broad and round in the tight black T-shirt he sported. Had he conjured Leo up, thinking about him after class earlier in the week? Joey wanted to go over and say hello, but then reconsidered. Leo wouldn't want to see him. It had been too long at this point. What would they say to each other? And just then, two minutes into the first song, his eyes still on Leo, Joey saw him turn to his right and look right at him. First, he turned back toward the stage. Then he turned back, watching Leo continue to watch him. He nodded a hello, and smiled, and waited. Eventually, Leo did the same.

After the show, Joey waited in the back of the club while Greta ran up front to talk to the band. He watched Leo and Carla hang out near the bar, knowing that Carla's pokes into Leo's shoulders were urges to get Leo to talk to him. Part of him wanted Leo to maintain his resistance; another part of him wanted Leo to break down and come over. Sipping down the last of his beer, Joey decided to make the choice for everyone. He grabbed his beer, stepped over a passed-out guy in heavy eyeliner, and went over to Leo and Carla.

"Hey, man," he said. "Hey, Carla."

Carla threw her arms around his neck and screamed. "Joey!"

She stepped back and looked at him. "I really shouldn't even be talking to you after the way you treated my cousin. But fuck it, you are so talented! Are you still sewing?"

"How are you's" turned into "Where have you been's" and eventually the three of them were having a stiffly casual, getting-updated conversation. Carla did most of the talking, relaying responses to each of them as if she were translating their words from one language to another one that they both understood but refused to share. The tension was broken only when Greta found them, dragging Pete and another ruggedly pretty guy with her. She introduced the other guy as Wayne ("Whose dick I used to suck behind the gym at Choate many years ago!") and wondered aloud how Pete and Leo managed to get along in the same dorm room.

"We sucked each *other* off," Pete said with a wink. "That's how."

Leo noticed the stricken look on Joey's face as everyone else laughed.

Greta announced that the evening was just starting, that they were all heading over to the Cat Club to see another band. Carla begged off, saying she had another party to go to. She gave Joey another tight hug and whispered into Leo's ear: "*She's* not fierce, and *he's* ripe for the picking. I'm sure you can steal him away from her if you try hard enough, baby."

At the Cat Club, they crowded into a tight VIP booth, designated as such because Greta's father was the vice president of A&R at Columbia Records, and Greta had told the door guy that he'd be joining them that night. Leo sat squeezed between Peter and Wayne, sipping a vodka tonic and watching Greta grind herself into Joey while she perched on his lap. Pete pulled a thick joint out of his pocket and lit it up, passing it to Leo and kissing him on the cheek at the same time. Leo took a hit of the joint and passed it to Wayne. He couldn't help but notice that Joey's eyes were right on him.

"You look good," Pete told Leo. "I missed you, man."

"I missed you, too," Leo said. Up close, he felt even more the energy Pete had spread around Brownies, a rock-star rhythm that emanated from him like a seductive scent. He'd always thought Pete was a handsome guy, but there was something different now, an edge, some kind of sexy vibe brought on by maturity. Or was it just confidence? Whatever it was, Leo liked it.

"You're different," he said to Pete.

"You are too," said Pete. He leaned closer. "Remember that first day of school when I told you that I fucked around with a coupla guys but I figured it wasn't for me? Well, I've decided it is for me."

Leo said, "Uh, okay."

"And I wanna fuck around with you." He planted another kiss on Leo's cheek.

"I gotta piss," Leo said, and squeezed his way past Wayne and out of the booth.

In the bathroom, he stood at a urinal relieving himself, wondering where Pete's sudden come-on had come from. The door swung open and Joey came in. He stood near the sink, waiting for the guy pissing next to Leo to wash his hands and leave.

"You were fucking him at Yale?"

Leo blinked a couple of times and zipped up his jeans. "Are you serious? *You* were with some girl, Joey. You cannot be serious."

"Just tell me, Leo." He was serious. So serious, Leo could only burst out laughing. Joey jealous of some dude, all this time later? After all that had happened?

"You notice," Leo said, "that we always have these conversations in bathrooms?"

As he reached for a clean dry paper towel, Joey rushed toward him, wrapped his arms around him, and kissed him, hard, on the lips, pushing Leo back toward the urinals.

Leo pushed back, still kissing him, until they were smack against the graffiti-marked, sticker-covered door. As they kissed, they could hear pounding on the door. Leo pulled away from Joey, which allowed the guy outside to shove his way inside. He gave them both a long look, then went to the urinal.

Leo said, "I can't do this."

"Why not?" Joey asked. "It doesn't have to mean anything."

"See," Leo said. "That's exactly why." He slammed the door and headed back to the booth. He saw Pete on the dance floor, his hands in the back pockets of his tight jeans, watching the all-girl band onstage tear through some funky, bass-heavy jam. As he went up to Pete, he felt a hand on his arm. He turned to see Joey standing there.

"What is there for us to talk about, Joey?"

His brown eyes bore into Leo's. "Everything."

Leo dug into his pocket and took out one of the cards he'd had made with his name and number. He handed it to Joey. Then he turned, took out another one, and handed it to Pete. "I'm outta here, guys. Have a great night."

1

"You're full of shit," Barry said. "I think this is a hustle and you want something." He thought for a second. "Something other than knowing who your father is."

TNT just looked at him. Then he said, "The VIPs."

"What?" Barry said.

Joey said, "Huh?"

Leo and Duke exchanged glances.

"Damn," said Joey. "I haven't thought about that name in years."

"Neither have I," said Duke.

"How do you know about that?" Leo said.

"I have my ways," said TNT. "Like I said—"

Barry didn't let him finish. "Who put you up to this?"

TNT didn't say anything.

"So someone did put you up to doing this," Barry said.

"I didn't say that."

"You didn't have to," Barry said. "It's all over your face."

"You don't know me well enough to—"

"I'll tell you what I do know," Barry said. "I know a bullshitter." He sat down. "Why don't you just tell us what you want?"

"I told you already what I want," TNT said. "I wanna know which one of you is my father. And what if someone did clue me in? What if somebody did put me up to this? You think I wouldn't do my own research? You think I'd take four very busy dudes away from their lives to tease them?"

"Feels like a tease," Joey said. "To be honest."

"I don't care how it feels," TNT said. "I just wanna know what I wanna know."

"I want to know who put you up to this," Barry said. "Tit for tat."

Leo said, "Did you show that picture of us to anyone?"

"Of course he did," Barry said. "And I'd bet you money that that's the person who's behind all this shit."

"Well," TNT said. "You might be right about that."

2

The guy in the red sweatshirt and the black baseball cap stood outside the Twenty-fourth Street offices of Revenge Records and waited. According to what he'd learned, she'd be out any minute.

But he could wait.

If she was due out three hours from now, he could wait.

The name of the record company made him laugh. Was that what that lady next door to his grandmother used to call poetic justice? Or was that irony? One or the other, or maybe a little of both. He didn't want to think too hard about it. It hurt his head when he thought too long or too hard about something that didn't really mean a whole helluva lot in the long run. Hell, it hurt his head to think about *anything* too long or too hard. He knew that about himself. And that was why he was going to win this war. Because he knew himself. He knew what he could do. He knew what he could accomplish once he set his mind to it. And most of all, he knew when you had to teach someone a lesson, when you had to let someone know that they couldn't get away with things just because they thought they were someone special.

Like TNT.

That Nigga Troy.

Yeah, right. Not even his name is for real. He even stole that.

More like That Liar Troy.

Yeah, that's what he intended to call him when the time came, when the clock struck and it was time to do the deed.

A woman came out of the building. Short, cute, close-cropped hair, brown skin, Coach bag, maroon suede jacket. Just who he was waiting for.

He jumped down from the mailbox he'd been sitting on and hopped into step with her. "Hey, shortie," he said, trying to make his voice as flirty as possible.

She didn't even look at him.

"Yo, shortie," he said. "I'm talking to you."

She sped up her stride.

"I'm talking to you," he said. When she still didn't say anything, didn't even acknowledge his presence, he reached into his pocket, pulled out the gun, pressed it close to her side, and said, "If you scream I'll kill you."

"My wallet's in my bag," she said.

"Oh, so you do have a voice?" He shoved her to keep her walking, glad that most of the people on the street were white people shopping for flowers who paid little or no attention to a couple of black faces passing by. "It's about Troy."

He pushed her toward a car he had parked at the end of the block. He unlocked the door and helped her in. He went around the car and got in on the driver's side.

When he closed the door, she asked, "What do you want?"

"You're gonna help me get in to see him," he said.

1

Barry sat at his desk in the inner row of cubicles and wished, not for the first time that year and not for the last, that he had been given a window seat. Which meant an office, like a real person making real decisions, not some low-level gofer. When he had accepted the job from Gary Bradford, postponing law school for a year, and then two, Barry had assumed that Gary wanted him as some sort of Gen X go-to guy, a sharp mind to provide feedback about the young consumers whom CoCo desperately needed if they wanted to stay competitive in the modern cosmetics game.

I went to Yale, Barry thought, again. But it didn't seem to make a difference to the ridiculous old-school soldiers in the Gary Bradford army, not one of them under thirty-eight, and all of them, in Barry's eyes, remnants of some past time when black folks were still "Colored," trying to play catch-up with what the white folks were doing. Damn near every product on the CoCo Cosmetics menu of offerings seemed to be some blacked-up version of a mainstream white product, with nothing hip and happening that the new generation of black and brown women would find exciting and cool.

Barry watched Gail Oliver strut by, probably on her way to another marketing staff meeting with Gary and Vernon Franklin, the supposed "head" of marketing who was still stuck in the seventies as far as product marketing went. Tall and light brown with slanted eyes and a perpetually down-turned mouth, Gail was rumored to be the person Gary turned to for anything that he thought of as "young and hip." Barry remembered her from Sag Harbor, jogging around the pier with her husband Anthony, both of them holding their heads up and backs straight, their arms pumping with the knowledge that they were the next power couple to lead black folks into the future. When Barry told her that he'd seen her in Sag, she asked where his family's house was located. When he told her he was a local guy, not a summer guy, she promptly put her nose back in the air and said, "Ah," suddenly remembering that she had a meeting to attend.

Whatever. He went to Yale. *And I'll be in Yale Law School in a matter of months,* Barry thought. *And I can fuck you like your silly dentist husband never could.*

But he had just three more months left of his CoCo Cosmetics hell. Then, finally, off to law school, the holy grail of his higher education ambitions, the days he'd looked forward to since he was sleeping on that hand-me-down twin bed in that hot back bedroom of their tiny house on Reservoir Lane. Which reminded him that he had to call his mother back.

The first thing she said was, "How is Duke doing?"

"Uh, he's good, Ma. You saw the touchdown he made in the Super Bowl, right?"

"Chile, I was too happy," she said. "I only watch the Redskins 'cause they have a black quarterback. But I must say, it was nice seeing Duke out there doing his thing. Brought back so many memories of you all throwing that filthy ball all over the yard."

"Yeah," Barry said. "Listen, I'm calling 'cause I don't know if I'm gonna get out there before I leave for L.A."

"Why not?"

"Work, Ma. You know how it is." His message buzzer rang. "Hold on, Ma." It was Gail Oliver on the line, requesting that Barry be in her office in five minutes. "Gotta go, Ma. Call you later this week, okay?"

After he sat down in the hard chair opposite Gail in her sparsely decorated office, Barry observed her as she finished a call. He noticed the small diamond in her ear. He noticed the maroon polish on her nails as she played with the diamond in her ear. He noticed her ear. He had an erection.

"Barry? Are you listening to me?"

"Uh, yeah," he said, shifting in his seat. "Something about *The Cosby Show*?"

"We're doing a product placement there," she said.

"CoCo Cosmetics? Product placement?"

Gail nodded. "I know," she said, a coy smile on her lips. "Not like us, right?"

"Seems a little modern for CoCo," he said.

"I agree. Hopefully not too modern."

"No such thing," Barry said. "Not these days."

"Maybe," said Gail. "But listen, we want you to take the product over to the set in Queens. I can't go. And Vernon hates Bill Cosby, so it's gotta be you."

Barry beamed. "Just say when."

2

An hour later, Barry had crossed the Fifty-ninth Street bridge in a CoCo Town Car and was standing in Queens at the Silvercup Studios. As he waited for the producer who was supposed to take him to Set Number Four, a cute, heavy-set black woman with her head in a paisley print turban rushed up.

"I'm Liza. Are you Barry?"

As Barry nodded, she grabbed his elbow and pulled him behind her onto Set Number Four. "Sorry to rush you," she said. "But Mr. Cosby just called another rehearsal, so we have just enough to time to get this stuff to set design before they start blocking." She looked back at Barry. "You ever been on a TV set before?"

Barry shook his head.

"Just follow me, okay?" She sped up to a trot.

By the time they got to the set design room, Liza was out of breath. She put her hands on her hips and craned her neck to find someone in the mess of plywood and tools and sawdust. "Manny? You back there?"

A guy with a Nike headband popped his head up from behind a steel workstation. "I'm right here." He saw Barry standing behind Liza. "That the guy with the cosmetics stuff for detail? Give it to George. He's over in costume with KiKi."

They rushed out of there. Barry had to smile. He'd only been there for a few minutes but he already liked it. This was his speed: fast, energetic, and loud, not like staid CoCo Cosmetics. He followed Liza down the hall into another room, where the walls were covered floor to ceiling with bolts of fabrics and garments. Two model dummies stood to the side, straight pins sticking out of their torsos. The petite tan woman pinning a African print dress to one of the model dummies nodded at Liza and Barry.

She called to the back of the big space. "Joey! Can you come up here?"

Barry and Liza waited for a few seconds before a handsome, young guy came rushing up from the back, a stack of jeans in his hands. He said, "Barry Chambers?"

"Joey? You work here?" Barry tried to hug his old friend, who still held the jeans in his arms. Liza grabbed the jeans so the old friends could embrace.

They sat on a low concrete border in the parking lot near Set Number Four, sipping coffees. "My eighth cup of the day," Joey said. "They keep a dude running around here."

Barry said, "Wish I could say the same."

"It's a cool place," said Joey. "And I get to use some of my designs on the show."

"You design clothes?"

Joey laughed. "You forgot about The VIPs?"

Barry almost spit out his coffee, laughing. "Oh yeah. Those clothes you made for me and Duke for that party! Those shirts were dope."

They watched some girls walk by, sipping on their coffee, then Joey said, "You see Duke on the Super Bowl? He wrecked it, huh?"

"Hell, yeah. You see Leo at all?"

Joey shook his head. "Ran into him and Carla about a year ago. We don't really stay in touch. You?"

"Not really."

Barry remembered that day in Syracuse and wondered if Joey was gay or straight. Then he wondered why it even crossed his mind. Joey was Joey. He was cool. Barry remembered the quiet way he'd insinuated himself into Sag Harbor life (considering the awkward way he'd been introduced to it) and how easily he became a part of all of their lives. Considering he wasn't speaking to Duke or Leo—or, at least, since neither of them seemed to be speaking to him—Barry was happy to see Joey.

He said, "Yo, you wanna get dinner one night?"

"Sure, man. You can meet my girl. Just give me a good heads-up. Like I said, they keep me real busy out here."

———————

As he watched Barry head off the lot toward the waiting Town Car, Joey had to smile. Barry Chambers. After all this time.

Life was strange indeed, he thought as he made his way back to the costume room. Here he was, twenty-three years old, working and living in Queens, his life pretty much wrapped up in going to work, sketching designs at night, and watching Greta build her massive art installations, and nothing was what he'd expected it to be.

As he sorted through the new arrival of multicolored sweaters that had to be distributed around to the cast dressing rooms, he recalled the last time he and Leo had hung out, a week after that drunken, club-hopping night. What had Leo told him when he showed up at his tiny apartment the night after that kiss in the Cat Club bathroom?

"We shouldn't be doing this." They'd been lying in bed, in Leo's East Village sublet, the threadbare sheet on top of them fluttering in the breeze from the open window. "You're in love with Greta," Leo said.

"And I guess you'll end up with that guy Pete," said Joey. He ran his hand softly across Leo's chest.

"What makes you say that?"

"I know you, Leo. Why wouldn't you want to? He's smart, creative. And most important, he likes the hell outta you." They listened to the whine of a cat somewhere out in the courtyard where crackheads slept during the night. "And I never said I was in love with Greta."

"Just like you never said you were in love with me."

"I didn't have to," said Joey. "You already knew I was."

Leo got up from the bed and went over to the bureau near the window. He took a cigarette from a soft pack that was slightly crushed from being in his pocket, and lit it.

Joey said, "You look really good." He patted the bed. "Come back over here."

"We shouldn't be doing this, man."

Joey said, "Just tell me what you want, Leo." He sat up.

"I want you to leave. I want you to get dressed and get out of here," Leo said. "The only way I'm going to completely get over you is for you to leave right now, Joey. Leave right now and don't come back until you can tell me what *you* want. You know what I want and what I need. You asking me that hurts as much as that day in Syracuse."

Joey hesitated, then got up from the bed. He took the cigarette from Leo's fingers, took a drag on it, then handed it back. As he was looking around for his boxers, the doorbell rang. He watched Leo go into the living room. He didn't have anything to say.

He heard Leo say, "What are you doing here?"

In the living room, he found Leo hugging Duke, leading him over to the couch.

"They made her choose," Duke was saying. He was close to tears. "She had to fucking choose, man."

Those words reverberated around Joey's mind now, as he continued separating sweaters for each of the cast members. There was always a "they," and it felt like "they" did always want you to "choose." That's what you never got taught about life, he thought. No one teaches you that the things you want oftentimes are not the things that "they" want you to have. *I'm a coward*, he thought, just as he'd thought it in Leo's apartment, watching Leo attend to Duke. *I was a coward and I'm still a coward.*

He remembered getting dressed, saying hello to Duke, then leaving silently, not even saying goodbye to Leo.

"You have anything you can whip up for Clair for three weeks from now?"

He looked up to see KiKi rolling the dummy model toward the full-length mirror.

"She and Cliff are going to a formal ball and Phylicia wants something couture but not cliché. Can you come up with anything like that?"

Joey smiled. "I think I can." He might have been a coward about loving another man, but he wasn't a coward about designing.

3

"Can't we go someplace else, Barry?" Carla said. "You know how hard it is to eat barbecue when you're wearing a white Mizrahi tank dress?"

Barry craned his neck to get a look at the door of the restaurant. "Wear a bib."

"But it's Mizrahi."

"I'm sure he won't mind."

Carla said, "Who are you looking for? I thought you said Joey and his girl were gonna be late. Chill out, Barry."

At that moment, Barry saw exactly who he was really waiting for, as Gail Oliver stepped into Houston's with her husband, Anthony, close behind her. Since the day he took the CoCo products to Queens, he'd been spending a lot more time with Gail, sitting across from her in her office, his dick hard, his hands sweaty, picking her brain about the marketing end of the business, eavesdropping on her phone calls, trying to remember any important names or dates she might say or jot down. Part of him felt like a weasel for exploiting this new access, only because when he allowed himself to think about it, he wasn't sure if he was staying in her mix because he wanted to fuck her or because he wanted her job. Eventually, in Barry's mind, it wasn't getting into Gail's panties versus setting himself up to usurp her duties in the marketing department. Because Barry had decided that he wanted both.

"Oh, look," Carla said. "There's Gail and Anthony." She waved as the maitre d' showed them to their booth across the restaurant. "I'm sure you know, Gail, right?" Then she smiled. "Of course you do. That's who you were looking for, isn't it? That's why you asked me to dinner tonight?"

Barry wasn't surprised Carla had keyed into his motivations. Sex never seemed too far off her radar. But he stayed cool. "We've worked on some projects together," he said, standing as Gail got closer to the table, relieved that he hadn't gotten an erection watching the smooth twist of her hips. "Hey, Gail," he said. "Imagine seeing you here!"

Gail introduced Barry to Anthony and both of them leaned in to kiss Carla hello.

"You two dating?" Anthony asked.

"We're just friends," said Barry with a wink

"Watch out for this one," Gail said to Carla. "He's a slick one."

"We go way back," Carla said with a sly look at Barry. Under the table, she reached over and grabbed his thigh. "I can handle Barry."

As Gail and Anthony went over to their booth, Joey and Greta were being escorted to the table. Barry almost fell off his chair. Why hadn't Joey told him he was dating some poor struggling art student? The light brown girl with the multicolored dreadlocks was pretty enough but she looked like an East Village refugee. She had on a sleeveless old-fashioned knee-length dress that openly displayed the ragged tattoos that decorated her skinny upper arms. Carla jumped up and gave Joey a big hug, lamenting how long it had been since she'd seen him, and launching right into the kidnapping tale that had brought Joey into her life.

"He never told me that story," Greta said, reaching over to run her hands through Joey's wavy hair. *"Tu es ella savior?"* she said to Joey. *"Bueno hombre."*

"What did she say?" Carla said. "I get back from Mexico and forget all my Spanish."

"I think she's trying to say how nice of me to be your savior," Joey said. "Now can we order some food before I get completely embarrassed?"

After the waiter took their orders, Barry excused himself. "Men's room," he smiled, and headed across the restaurant, making sure to pass Gail and Anthony's table as he made his way to the rear.

Carla said to Greta, "I love that dress. What thrift shops do you go to?"

"This?" Greta looked down at her dress. "Believe it or not, Joey made it for me."

Carla laughed. "Actually, I believe it." She told Greta the story of her hemmed skirt in Sag Harbor and the halter Joey made to go with it. She leaned across the table and ran her fingers over the dress's fabric, looking closely at the stitching and detail along the bias. "This is fabulous. It looks like the real thing, but it's also so modern and funky," she said. "Can you make me a few?"

Joey shrugged.

"I'm serious," Carla said.

"Serious?" Barry said, returning to the table. "You're never serious about anything."

"I am about fashion," said Carla.

"Except fashion," he said.

Carla said, "What were you doing at Gail's table?"

"Work stuff."

"I bet."

"I'm serious."

"About what? *You're* never serious about anything," Carla said.

"*You* know that's not true," Barry said coyly.

Carla let out a squeal and slapped Barry's arm. "Just watch out with Gail," she said. "Homegirl's a shark."

And all she needs is a fin to prove Carla right, Barry thought a week later, stepping exhaustedly into his boxers as he watched Gail re-apply her makeup in the mirror over the bureau in Barry's bedroom.

"What a nice lunch," said Gail, turning back to Barry. "I think we'll need to schedule another one for next week, what do you think?" She added, "Carla won't mind."

"I told you we're not together."

"Okay, Barry," she said. "Whatever."

"Listen," Barry said. "Can we keep this quiet? I mean, between Gary and—"

She ignored his words. "You want to walk back together?"

"I'm gonna make a stop," he said. "I'll see you back at the office."

"I have a three o'clock with Gary. You should be there."

"About *Cosby*?"

"The show's in a week. There's a company event to watch it together."

After she left, Barry tied his tie and sat on the bed. A CoCo Cosmetics group event? This he'd have to see to believe. He checked himself in the mirror, admiring his ability to accomplish the goals he set for himself. All he'd had to do was invite her to lunch. And she knew exactly what he'd wanted. Instead of the hotel room Barry suggested, she said she'd rather go to his place. So they ended up there in his little fourth-floor walkup around the corner from CoCo that Gary Bradford had loaned him for the summer. He finished the wine left in the glass on his bureau and left the apartment. To think all he'd done was ask her to lunch.

Would life always be this easy?

4

A week after dinner with Barry and Carla, Joey came home from work to find a huge gift-wrapped box on the dining room table. It looked oddly glossy and chic sitting on the worn oak carpenter's table which was surrounded by assorted mismatched chairs they'd bought at a Salvation Army in Forest Hills right before they'd moved into the place. Greta was nowhere to be found. There was no card attached to the gift, so he didn't know who it was for or who it was from. Greta's father had a tendency to send them things like coffeemakers and toasters, which Greta would promptly re-wrap and send right back to him. Was this something waiting prettily just to be returned?

It was a sewing machine. A Singer. Brand new. Ultra-deluxe. Now this couldn't have come from Greta's father; he didn't even know Joey sewed. Then he saw the card, taped to the flat pane of the bobbin deck.

"Joey, Greta told me about the machine you've been using. If I'm going to be your patron, you will HAVE to work on the most modern instrument your artful hands can access. Consider it a gift. AND GET ME THOSE DRESSES ASAP!!!! Love, Carla."

Joey dropped into the nearest dining room chair, his eyes stuck on the machine. This thing was faster, sleeker, much more sophisticated than anything he'd ever used. He got right to work. He found the original sketch of the dress Greta wore to dinner. It would have to be altered for Carla's tall, voluptuous frame yet still retain the pseudo-Victorian elegance that caught the eye of every fashion-savvy person who commented on the dress whenever Greta wore it.

Four days later, he had two dresses almost done, one in maroon with eggshell piping, the other a deep brocade print with crimson inlay.

Greta said, "You know you should be doing this for a living, right?" She rinsed the remaining paint smears from her hands and ripped a length of paper towel from the rack. "Carla will love those."

And she did. Screaming at the top of her lungs and dancing around his tiny living room the next day, Carla told Joey, "I'll need five more. I want two for my friend Jillian's wedding and the other three for a friend coming in from Europe in two weeks. Can you do that? In two weeks?"

"I should pay you back for the sewing machine," he said.

"It was a gift, Joseph. Now all you have to do is gift the world with your designs."

Joey asked her, "You really like my stuff that much?"

"Like it? Joey, baby, that's my point. Now that I'm stuck here in Queens till my driver comes back, sit with me"—she plopped herself on the couch and patted the cushion next to her—"and bring those sketchbooks. I want to see *everything* you have."

Six hours later, after Carla had gone, Joey and Greta lay in bed. Wrapped in the sweaty sheets, Joey said, "I can't do this for a living if I'm going to *Cosby* every day."

"We'll figure something out," Greta said.

But they didn't have to. The next day, Joey showed up at work to find KiKi furiously shoving sweaters into a series of shipping cartons. When he asked her what was going on, she glared at him. "What does it look like? I'm sending these sweaters back."

Joey noticed they were the same sweaters he'd divided up before he took a week off to finish the dresses for Carla. "I just separated all those for the cast members," he said. "Why are they going back?"

KiKi tossed one to him. He caught it with one hand and looked at it. It seemed fine until he looked at the label on the inside of the crew neck. The size was odd; no one in the cast wore that size. And it was crew neck. There'd been a direct order to have only V-neck sweaters to better show off the collars of the shirts underneath.

"I'm sorry, KiKi. I didn't even notice."

"Obviously not, Joey. I think you're too busy dreaming up designs for your own line," she sneered. "Like *that's* ever going to happen."

"Excuse me?"

"You heard me. I give you the simplest tasks and you fuck it up because you're too busy doodling ideas for dresses in that damn sketchpad like you think you're Oscar de la Fucking Renta."

"I don't have to take this," Joey said. He threw the sweater back onto the pile near KiKi's elbow. "You can't talk to me like that."

"Fuck you. Do you know what it was like sitting in that damn office listening to them berate me because of a simple job I passed on to my so-called assistant?"

"Is there someone I need to talk to?" Joey asked. "We can fix this, KiKi."

"Talk to Human Resources," she said curtly. "You're fired. Get out of my sight."

"It was an accident," he pleaded. He thought of his conversation with Greta just that morning, as they tried to come up with a plan for Joey to use her work space late at night, so he could create dresses after he got home from work. He felt all of his dreams disappearing, getting socked away into a box like those sweaters KiKi was slamming around angrily. "KiKi," he said. "I need this job. You know I've been good for you—"

"Just go, Joey." She wouldn't even look at him.

"Please, KiKi," he begged.

Joey knew KiKi had real bitch potential. He'd seen how she treated some of her co-workers. And everyone on the set who'd greeted him when he first started working for her ten months before had given him a sad, rueful look when he told them which department he worked in. Now he knew why. He just never thought she'd turn her venom in his direction. But KiKi only knew Nice Joey, Joey Who Needed a Job, Joey Who Obeyed Her Wishes. She didn't know the Joey who'd lived with four different foster families by the time he was fifteen years old, the Joey who watched his father overdose and his grandmother waste away from cancer because her Medicaid didn't cover the best possible treatments she could get. KiKi had never met the Joey who could be as manipulative and mean as the best of them when it came to protecting himself against nasty foster mothers and careless social workers, the Joey who heard the pleading tone in his voice and said, "Then I guess I'll have to take my sketchbook with me to Human Resources and show them all the dresses I designed for the show that have your fucking name on them."

That got KiKi to look at him.

"You wouldn't," she said, dropping the sweater. "You wouldn't dare do that."

"See if I won't."

"You'd be ruined in the fashion industry before you even got started," she said, her hands on her lips, her eyes wide. "I know people, Joey. I could ruin you."

"You do costuming for a TV sitcom on its last legs," said Joey. "If you really knew anybody, you wouldn't be here in Queens packing sweaters into FedEx boxes." He turned to go.

"Joey," she said quietly. "Wait."

He turned back to face her. "What am I waiting for?"

"We can work something out," she said. "Stay. I'll talk to Human Resources."

Joey looked at her, hearing her sudden attempt at diplomacy, watching her trembling hands, the obvious desperation pouring off her like flop sweat, and he knew he'd hit a nerve. He didn't feel particularly good about insulting her, but he felt something like power coursing through his veins. "Don't talk to anybody for my benefit," he said. "I wouldn't work for you again if Diana Ross was hired to play Rudy Huxtable's fairy godmother and begged me to knock off a Bob Mackie original for her death scene. Fuck you, KiKi. You just did me a favor."

With that he turned and walked out of the room, thinking, *At least I hope you did.*

5

Leo sat in the window seat of the Barney Greengrass on Amsterdam Avenue and waited for his mother to arrive from her hairdresser. He needed this time with her. Not just because he hadn't seen her in months, but because he needed a few hours away from Pete. If anyone had told Leo that dating a rock star would be as exhausting as it was, he would never have signed up for the job. In two years, Crazy Pete and the Wild Men had gone from a group of Yale kids playing a couple of nights at Brownies to opening for

Guns N' Roses to headlining their own European tour. Thanks to Greta's father, the band's own gift for self-promotion, and Pete's unerring ability to craft massively melodic anthems that grabbed the attention of MTV executives and the kids who kept the channel in business, the Wild Men were one of the biggest bands in the world. And Leo, who went from "best friend of the lead singer" to "biographer" to "co-lyricist" in those two years, enjoyed every minute of the ride.

Except, that is, for when he didn't.

He loved the travel, something he and Pete had in common dating back to Yale, and he loved the random, decadent gypsy-ness of their life, checking in and out of hotels, eating foreign foods, throwing away underwear and buying new shorts whenever they needed clean stuff to wear. But lately he'd begun to feel like an appendage on a hand that didn't really need him to make the fist it needed to be to pound its way to the top. Sure, he wrote words that Pete called poetry and sang like an angel. And he felt sure that Pete was completely into him, was in love with him even, in the way that Leo needed someone to be. But, really, what was he? He was never going to be, in the pages of *Rolling Stone* or *Spin* or the *Village Voice*, the lover of one of the world's biggest up-and-coming rock stars: He and Pete had mutually decided that it wasn't time for him to "come out." But two years in, Leo knew that there probably would never be a right time to proclaim their love in public, even if, as the band joked, they had one of the best "meet-cute" stories two people could have. The closet thing bugged Leo, but there was something else. In all the traveling and lyric-writing and party-going, he wasn't doing anything that said "Leo." Everything was about making sure the Wild Men were successful and taken care of. Leo had the urge to do something that was solely about his own creative impulses, something that was stamped with his own point of view, something that didn't require the vetting of agents and law-yers and managers and bandmates before it ever saw the light of day.

He'd been working on something, a journal of sorts, detailing his life up to that point, including his relationships and the strife with his father and his life on the road with the band. He didn't think it would ever see the light of day; there were too many people who'd hate to see their exploits in print, who'd probably come after him with a chain saw if they did. What the journal did do was show him that he in fact could write, that he hadn't just been getting gassed by his high school teachers because he was the lone black boy in the class who was able to put a few words together when so asked. And since he hadn't had time to try any creative writing classes at Yale, crowded as his time was trying to fulfill the required courses to ensure graduation, he never had a chance to impress anyone in New Haven with his abilities.

"Such a waste of time," he said out loud, then took a sip of the delicious Colombian coffee the waitress put down in front of him.

"What's a waste?"

He looked up to see his mother taking a seat across from him, her hair in a striped purple and white scarf, protected from the drizzle that sprinkled the New York streets.

"Nothing," he said. "Talking to myself." He kissed Lillian, then sat back. "Why the big hairdo today? It's not Friday."

"CoCo Cosmetics event tonight," she said. "Your father's hav-ing a group of people over to watch *The Cosby Show*."

"I thought he hated Bill Cosby."

"He does, but the cosmetics are being featured on the episode tonight, so he's all excited." Lillian ordered a cappuccino from the hovering waitress. "You look good, baby. Still in love?"

Leo grinned, happy that he could be himself around his mother. He may have been banned from the Bradford household, but Lillian had put her foot down at never seeing her son again. "Pete says to tell you hello and that he's still waiting to do those tequila shots with you."

Lillian laughed. "Between you on the road all the time and Duke on the TV, I have to shake my head at the lives you boys are leading."

"You're surprised that we're college dropouts who didn't die the moment we left campus? Ma, you are so old school."

"So I am," she said. "I just worry."

"Well, don't worry about me. And Duke's doing more than fine. You see his commercial yet?"

"The one with the little girl?" She nodded. "It's so sweet. Your father cracked up for hours after he saw it during the Super Bowl."

Leo ignored her mention of Gary as the waitress returned with their drinks and a plate of biscotti. "I hear Barry's working at the company."

"He'll be there tonight."

"You never really liked him, did you?"

"I didn't like the way he was always creeping up behind Carla."

"Carla loved it."

"I have my issues with Carla," said Lillian. She shook her head. "That girl . . ."

"She's a modern woman, Ma."

"I guess." She sipped her own coffee. "You all are. Modern. Different than my generation anyway." She looked at Leo for a few seconds. "You know there was a time when a boy like you, who came from where you come from, would never have made the choices you made."

"The only choice I made, Ma, was the one my father gave me."

"True." She bit into a biscotti and delicately placed it back on the plate. "But you've survived, is what I'm saying. Flourished, even. There was a time when no one would have wanted anything to do with you. But you're doing fine."

"That's the Lillian influence," Leo said.

"You have some Gary in you, too," she said, laughing.

He couldn't resist asking: "What about me is like him?"

Lillian said, "How much time do you have?" She laughed. "You're both stubborn as hell. You didn't get that from me, I'm a softy, I'll relent in a minute to make peace. You're both—"

"Stop," Leo said. "I actually don't want to know."

"You're both handsome as hell," she said.

"Thank you, Ma."

"You look good." She ran her finger around the edge of her cup. "I'm sorry for calling you a butterball back then."

"No, you're not."

She laughed. "Just a little."

"I love you, Ma."

"I love you, too, Leo."

They sat there and looked at each other as if both were trying to recall good times, enjoying each other's company, not needing to make any more small talk, though they did ultimately, Lillian passing on all the gossip from the Sag Harbor–Martha's Vineyard–Silver Spring black society axis that had no room for Leo anymore, and Leo telling her all about the governor of Arkansas, who was planning a run for president, and who Pete was going to help stump for. When they got up to go, Lillian said, "Promise me you'll be happy, baby."

"I am happy," he said, and as he walked off toward the limo that waited for him at the corner of Amsterdam and Eighty-sixth Street, he thought to himself, *There are some things in my life that I'd change. But I am happy. How the heck did that happen?*

6

"Why do we have to go to this thing?" Greta asked, running a towel across her dreadlocks. "It's not like you work for CoCo."

"But I could," said Joey. "Carla wants to show off the dress. She wants me there."

"To show *you* off too." She tossed the towel on the bed. "Such a great patron."

Joey ignored the edge in Greta's voice and tried to ignore the wet towel on the floor. Ever since Carla's visit and his many meetings and phone calls with her since getting fired, Greta seemed to be getting less tolerant of her. And now that he was in the apartment twenty-four hours a day making dresses and spending much more time with Greta than he ever had before, he'd been getting much less tolerant of just how sloppy and immature she could be. It had been one thing to come home to a messy house and clean up behind her. The meniality of washing dishes and emptying garbage pails was somehow soothing when he needed to come down from the fast-paced TV high and prepare himself for some sketching or sewing. But it was a completely different situation to watch Greta all day as she left dirty dishes all over the place and treated the bathroom they shared like it was a public facility with a cleaning staff on call.

"You don't have to come," he said finally, heading into the bathroom to shave. "Stay here, get some work done."

"I think I will," she said.

Joey breathed a sigh of relief. At least then maybe he'd be able to enjoy himself as well as drum up business instead of standing in the corner with Greta, as she tried to prove her hipness and laugh away her class guilt with barbed insults about the black bourgeoisie.

———

"So what's the story?"

Barry looked at Gary Bradford over the rim of his glass and wondered what he was talking about.

"Why didn't you tell me the original idea to do product placement was yours?"

"I, uh—"

"I didn't hire you to be a schlep, Barry. I expected you to step up. Not settle for the windowless cubicle. We need to talk about your future," he said. "Find me later; there's someone I have to see."

Barry watched him grab Lillian by the elbow and maneuver her across the room toward an arriving couple. *His* idea? He'd mentioned a few things to Gail's assistant early on, but he'd never said anything to Gail. Had she told Gary that the idea was his? *Damn*, he thought. *Was my dick that good?* He saw Gail across the room near the fireplace, standing with Anthony and Vernon Franklin. She gave him a little wave. He nodded a hello, seeing that Anthony had turned to see who Gail had been greeting. He raised his glass in a toast. Barry nodded and returned the gesture.

This was going to be some night.

Pete said, "You're really not gonna make me watch *The Cosby Show*, are you?"

"I guess I still have a little bit of pride in the family business," said Leo. "It's not like anything else is going on tonight." He looked down at the newspaper in front of him. "For a change," he added.

Pete slid him a beer down the length of the counter in the kitchen of the loft space they rented while staying in Manhattan. "'For a change'? Do I detect a note of exhaustion in your voice?"

Leo said, "If the mic fits, sing into it."

"A night in the crib might not be too bad." He gulped down his beer. "Did you tell your mother what I said?"

"She said anytime you're ready she'll drink you under the table."

"You obviously didn't get your mother's genes."

"She told me I'm just like my father."

Pete laughed. "So if we have a gay kid you're gonna disown him?"

"You trying to get pregnant?" Leo said.

"Imagine that," Pete said. "Hey, we got any weed around here? If I'm gonna spend the night watching bad TV I gotta be at least a little bit high." Pete reached for the phone mounted on the wall near the refrigerator.

"Call Hank."

"I'm already ahead of you."

"**A**unt Lillian, you remember Joey, right?"

Lillian hugged Joey. "Of course I remember Joey, Carla. What kind of question is that?" She stepped back to look at him. "So handsome. All of you, really, you all grew up so well."

Joey blushed. "Thank you," he said.

"I had lunch with Leo today," Lillian said. "He's in town for a couple of weeks."

"Great," Joey said. "I'm gonna get a drink. You want anything?"

"I'm fine," said Lillian. When Joey was out of earshot, she looked at Carla. "Did I say something wrong?"

"No," Carla said. "I just don't think Joey and Leo are as tight as they used to be."

"Why not?"

"I don't really know. But enough about them." Carla did an

elegant twirl and struck a pose. "Joey made this frock I'm wearing tonight."

"It's beautiful."

"And you should get him to make you one."

"I couldn't pull off that look, Carla."

"You don't have to. Give it to someone. I'm trying to help Joey get a collection off the ground. We need all the investors we can find."

"*You're* going into business?" Lillian tried to stifle her laughter but failed, almost spilling her drink as she giggled.

"I'm not going to be the CoCo Cosmetics girl forever, Aunt Lillian."

"Don't get indignant."

"Then don't laugh at me," Carla said. "I have my Aunt Beverly for that."

Joey returned with a glass of champagne. "I saw Russell Simmons over there. Since when do the Bradfords socialize with the rap music set?"

Lillian said, "Who is Russell Simmons?"

Carla laughed. "The guy over there in the sneakers talking to Uncle Gary."

Joey said, "I didn't expect this kind of shindig."

"Carla was telling me you designed the dress she's wearing."

Joey nodded. "Carla's my biggest booster."

"I'll take three of them," said Lillian. "In various shades of blue."

"Carla told you to say that."

Lillian blushed, and looked at Carla. "I tried."

"Do you really like the dress, Mrs. Bradford?"

"I love it," she said. "It's a little young for me, but the design is fabulous."

"Then I'll make something more your style. Consider it a gift, after all you've already done for me."

"I insist on paying you for it, Joey."

Carla said, "Let her pay you, Joey. Didn't you know the Bradfords have a tree out in the garden that grows money?"

Across the room, Gary said, "It's just about that time, everyone."

And at that moment, the grandfather clock next to the Tiffany lamp struck eight.

At the first commercial break, Gary shushed the crowd to watch Duke's Coke ad, a remake of the famous Mean Joe Greene commercial with the little boy in the tunnel leading to the football field. Only in Duke's commercial, they'd cast an adorable little girl and added a little twist in which the little girl's mother already has a Duke Maynard towel for her daughter, only she doesn't explain that she got it on a date with the football star.

Everyone sitting around the screening room laughed.

"I knew Duke when he was just a kid deejaying parties out in Sag," Gary announced.

A few oohs and aahs rippled through the crowd.

"I knew Duke, too," Carla mumbled, and Barry pinched her shoulder.

"Yeah, you *knew* him all right," he whispered, just before the show came back on. He saw Joey over near the bar. He seemed to be in a tense conversation with an older gentleman in a porkpie hat. "Who is that Joey's talking to? I didn't think he'd know anyone here except us."

Carla shrugged. "I think that's his girlfriend's father. He's some music biz guy at Columbia Records. Shut up, the show's back on."

At the sight of the boxes of CoCo Cosmetics on Theo Huxtable's new girlfriend's bureau, a loud roar went up in the screening room. When she actually opened the box of face powder and held it right in front of the camera as she looked into the mirror, the roar grew even louder.

After the screening Barry could feel a real buzz in the room. It felt ripe with possibility and he felt like he might be standing in the future of CoCo Cosmetics rather than in the staid past that seemed to waft through the office like so much stale perfume. His eyes met Gary's, as he was standing in a circle with Gail and Vernon and an older man Barry didn't know.

Gary grabbed him around the shoulder as he stood there. "Tom Holland? This is Barry Chambers, one of the rising young minds at CoCo Cosmetics. It was actually his idea that we move into doing some product placements."

As he leaned in to shake hands with Tom Holland, Barry could feel Vernon Franklin's light brown eyes boring into him. But he tried to ignore that as he was trying to recall how he knew this Tom Holland person.

"This black man, Tom Holland, owns one of the biggest shipping companies in the country," Gary said. "We've been working together since he had one truck shipping out of Georgia and I had one factory up in Detroit."

"So this is Barry Chambers," Holland said. "If this young man's mind is as sharp as I hear, Gary, I might have to steal him away from you."

"I'll be starting Yale Law School in the fall," Barry said with a smile, "so I won't be available for a few years yet."

Gary put his arm around Barry's shoulder. "Barry graduated from the College two years ago," he said proudly.

"Must be the Gary Bradford influence," said Holland. "All you Yalies stick together. I'm a Harvard man myself." He looked around the room. "I should be getting out of here, we have another dinner to get to. Where is my daughter?"

"I'm right here, Dad."

Tom Holland said, "Barry, have you met my daughter Amanda? She's just graduated from Wharton Business School. Now that she's back in New York, maybe you can show her around."

Barry smiled at Amanda. Sure he remembered meeting her. "I'd love to," he said.

Like most things around the Wild Men, Leo and Pete's quiet TV night alone turned into a big loud party. Hank, the band's New York party connection, arrived halfway through *The Cosby Show* with three ounces of weed, three six packs of Corona, and three girls who, Leo thought, probably weren't old enough to order drinks in a public establishment. Fifteen minutes later Pete answered the door to find Curry, the band's bassist, stumbling in with a frail-looking girl in tight black leather pants and a dirty pink halter top. Ten minutes later the lead singer of a band called Crack Whore arrived with his entourage, a bunch of bong-headed collegiate types all dressed in cutoff denim shorts with their boxers exposed at the waist. They were like a traveling rock 'n' roll fraternity looking for their next kegger. And Hank was there to serve everyone anything they needed.

Leo found Pete lounging in the tub in the master bathroom, passing a joint back to the frail-looking girl in the dirty halter, which up close Leo could see was really not pink but actually stained with splotches of dried blood. She passed the joint to Leo, then pulled down her tight jeans to use the toilet.

"This is some place you guys got here," she said, the loud splash of her pee punctuating her words. "Curry's place is a dump compared to this."

"Thanks," Leo said, and passed the joint back to Pete, who, he could see, was trying hard not to laugh. "Maybe you and I can go house-hunting after the tour ends."

"That would be so hot," she said, her eyes drooping. "Freaking hot, man."

"I'll be out there," Leo told Pete. He went out on the terrace that overlooked SoHo from Houston Street and watched the buzz-seekers enjoy their Thursday night. He was there for ten minutes when a scream came from the living room. He bumped into Pete rushing from the bathroom. "What the fuck was that?"

In the living room, one of Hank's girls continued to scream, her hands clutching her face like she wanted to tear her skin off. Every-one was in a wide loose circle, surrounding one of Crack Whore's entourage, who was on his back on the floor, his body flopping and twisting like he was possessed.

"I think it's a seizure," someone said.

"Or a bad dose," someone else said. "Look at how red he is."

Leo pushed through the circle and knelt down over the boy. He felt his forehead. "He's burning up. Someone call 911." No one moved. "Call 911!" Leo shouted.

Still no one did anything. Leo jumped up and ran back to the bedroom to get the phone. Curry was right behind him.

"Leo, you can't call the cops. What if this guy's dosing? It'll be in all the papers."

"Then what are we gonna do?" Leo yelled. "If he is dosing, you want him dead here in me and Pete's apartment? It'll be in the papers anyway!"

Pete came into the room. "Hank knows what to do," he said. "He's gonna take the dude out of here."

Leo said, "Take him where?"

Pete shrugged. "I didn't fucking ask him, Leo."

Leo ran back into the living room. The kid had stopped his shaking.

One of the young girls said, "Is he dead?"

Leo grabbed his wrist to check for a pulse. "No." He leaned over to listen to the guy's chest. "He's still breathing." Leo slapped him a few times across the face. "Wake up, dude. Get up!" Someone tossed Leo a wet towel. Leo rolled it up and put it against the kid's face. Soon he started coughing, his body wracked with the effort. "Get me some water," Leo yelled. The guy stopped coughing. Leo looked into his eyes. "Can you hear me?" The guy nodded. "What's your name?"

"Jay," he said, his voice a croak. "My name is Jay."

Leo looked back at the Crack Whore singer, who nodded. Leo grabbed a cushion from the couch and put it under the guy's head. "You're gonna be all right," Leo said to him. "But you should go to an emergency room."

Pete said, "I'll take him."

"No," Leo said. "Not *you*."

"Just put him in a cab," said the Crack Whore singer. "I'll get him home."

"He needs to see a doctor," Leo said.

Leo saw that these people had no real concern for this kid. Now he just wanted them out of his home. "Party's over, people." He slammed the bedroom door behind him.

Soon, Pete came into the bedroom. Leo lay on his side, facing the window. He listened to Pete take off his jeans and toss them on the chair. He felt him get into the bed. Pete slipped close to him and put his arms around Leo's torso. Leo didn't say anything.

Pete said, "I know you're awake."

"I hope that kid is, too. Wherever he is."

"He'll be fine," Pete murmured against Leo's neck.

"I hope so, Pete."

7

HOW WILD ARE THEY??? screamed the headline of the *Post* the next morning.

Greta read the headline out loud again. "I have to call Pete."

"And say what?" Joey said. "'I read in the paper about the guy who almost overdosed in your apartment.' Then what?"

"Offer support," she said, scraping paint from her fingers and letting the chips fall on the table near her plate of grapefruit. "What's up your ass this morning?"

"You get any of that paint in that grapefruit," Joey said, ignoring her words, "and you'll be the one overdosing."

"Fuck you."

"Right back at you."

In the silence, Joey could hear the sneaker-on-concrete squeak of kids playing outside in the street. He sipped his coffee and read the newspaper article. Rock 'n' roll. Drugs. Underage girls. Police looking to talk to Pete Reynolds, lead singer of Crazy Pete and the Wild Men. *Who cares,* Joey thought, *when the woman you think you love's been lying to you for months?*

Suddenly Greta said, "So who was the top?"

"Excuse me?" Joey put down the paper.

Greta peeled another rind from the grapefruit. "You and Leo. Who was the top? And who got fucked?"

Joey just looked at her. "Who's getting fucked in this relationship?"

"I know who *used* to get fucked. But the one who *was* doing the fucking doesn't seem that interested in anything unless a sewing machine is involved."

Joey said, "Are you serious?"

"As cancer." With that, she got up and threw the grapefruit in the garbage can.

Joey watched her go. "Wow, I didn't think you knew where the trash can was."

He heard her slam the door of her studio. He thought about following her. He wanted to tell her that he'd run into her father at the Bradfords'. That, according to him, he'd been sending her money since the day they'd moved to Queens. That she hadn't actually sold a piece to a big collector in Amsterdam like she'd told Joey, but had been living off the good graces of her pops for the last seven months. Joey felt like he'd been living a lie with her all that time: all that show of sending back her parents' gifts and complaining about their bourgeois lifestyle, how much it conflicted with her desire to make art, to create a world where poor people wouldn't be exploited, and art, not commerce and politics, would be the center of community building. He considered confronting her, asking her for an explanation for her lies, but as pissed as he was, did he really care? Lying was what people did, wasn't it? What else was new? It came as naturally as breathing and kept them alive just as easily. He got up and went to the sewing machine. The only place he could find any truth.

"**W**hat did they do?" Pete said, throwing the newspaper across the room. The thin pages separated and floated all over the floor. "Huh?

What did they do? Call Crack Whore's publicist before going to the hospital?"

Sally Forsyth said, "That's what I would have done." She was the band's publicist. She'd been at the apartment for two hours now, her insistent doorbell ringing competing with the initial burst of phone calls that woke Pete and Leo up that morning. She had the phone in one hand and a bagel in the other. "Who was this kid?"

"Hanger-on," Pete said. "I didn't even meet him." He looked at Leo. "Did you?"

Leo shook his head. "Maybe I should have," he mumbled. "Since he and I have that in common."

Pete jumped up. "Will you stop saying that?" He lit the cigarette that had been hanging between his lips for the last ten minutes. "You are not a fucking 'hanger-on.' You were the one who kept things calm. To hell with what the *Post* has to say."

Leo could recite the paragraph by heart. "The lavish loft apartment, shared by lead singer Pete Reynolds and band hanger-on Leo Bradford, is known for playing host to debauched parties whenever the Wild Boys were in town. Reportedly Reynolds and Bradford, roommates at Yale in the '80s, were known for their wild partying there."

Sally Forsyth pulled her long, dark hair into a ponytail, then let it all drop against her back. She exhaled, blowing out her cheeks, then sat forward on the couch. "Who brought the drugs?"

"Hank McCoy," said Leo. "All we'd asked for was some weed."

"It was supposed to be a quiet night," said Pete.

"And to think it all started with watching *The Cosby Show*," said Leo. "How fucking ironic is that?"

"Well the police don't deal in ironies," Sally said. "And they'll be here any minute, so I need you two to pull it together and get

ready." She exhaled again. "I missed my fucking yoga appointment
for this shit."

The doorbell rang. "And there they are," she said.

8

Barry sat in the hard chair across from Gary. He didn't know
where to look, at Gary's angry face or the newspaper on his desk,
HOW WILD ARE THEY??? glaring from the front page. He didn't
know if this was why he'd been called down here, so he didn't say
anything, just waited for Gary to speak.

Finally, he said, "Are you in touch with Leo?"

Barry shook his head. "No, sir."

"Do you know anything about this guy he's supposedly living
with?"

"I met him once at Yale."

"Are they . . ."

"I don't think they're a, uh, couple, sir." Barry shifted in his seat.
What was Gary asking him now? "I believe they're just good friends.
I heard somewhere that Leo cowrote some of the songs on the
last CD the band recorded. Sold very well, actually, they're all over
MTV." He sat forward. "Which, speaking of MTV, is something I'd
like to run by you, sir—"

"Any money in that?"

"Sir?"

"Writing songs on a rock 'n' roll album."

Barry had to smile. "Actually, sir, yes, there is, if the record is a
big seller. Between publishing and radio plays and—"

Gary said, "What were you saying about MTV?"

"I think we might want to get some CoCo products into some videos. Word is that MTV might start cracking down on product placement in videos, but I think we can get in under the wire. They're playing a lot more black artists' videos now, and it would be good for us to start thinking young and hip that way."

Gary steepled his fingers and smiled. "Videos, huh? Speaking of videos, let me show you something, Barry." He got up. "Follow me over here."

They both took seats on the maroon leather couch on the other side of Gary's huge office. Gary pressed a button on the console next to the couch and a video screen rolled down from the ceiling, blocking the mirror that hung over the ornate fireplace.

Gary pushed another button and the lights dimmed. Suddenly the screen was filled with fuzzy videotape lead, which suddenly went blue, then popped into a shot of a bedroom. From a high corner angle, the room looked familiar to Barry, but he couldn't really tell where it was. Then he recognized the bureau at the top of the picture.

It was his bedroom. In the apartment Gary gave him to use for the summer.

"Mr. Bradford?"

"Just watch."

A full minute later, a door opened and Barry watched himself and Gail Oliver step into the room. In a flash, Gail was all over him, kissing his neck, running her hands over his back, pulling him out of the jacket and shirt he'd worn that day. She pushed him down onto the bed and climbed atop him.

Barry looked down.

"Watch, Barry."

By the time he could bring his eyes back to the screen, he and

Gail were already in the throes of sex, Barry pumping away, his ass the main focus of the shot, though he tried to look past it and focus on Gail's face, the orgasmic expression on it, which he could see over his big shoulder.

Gary pressed a button, and Barry's ass stopped in air, mid-stroke.

Gary turned to him. "Good work, young man."

Barry didn't say anything.

"Is that how you respond to a compliment? You say nothing?"

Barry said, "Why do you have this, Mr. Bradford?"

"Well," he said. "It started off as fun."

"It's fun to watch your employees have sex?"

"It's fun to watch me have sex."

"I don't understand."

"You think this apartment just sits empty when there's not some homeless CoCo employee who needs a place to stay?" Gary laughed. "This is my apartment, Barry."

"You and Mrs. Brad—"

Gary laughed, sarcasm coating the edges of his laughter. "Sure, me and Lillian scoot off to a love nest and make love all afternoon."

"I didn't mean—"

"You beat me to it, Barry."

"Excuse me?"

"Do you know how long I've been trying to fuck Gail Oliver?" Gary lit a cigarette. "I said last night that you were doing a good job here at CoCo and I meant that. I see now that you take it seriously."

Barry couldn't believe what he was hearing. Was he really being congratulated for sleeping with Gail Oliver? "I don't understand, sir."

"What I'm saying is this: How would you like to take on some more responsibility at the company?"

"What kind of responsibility?"

"More marketing," Gary said. "Working closer with me."

"I'm going to law school in the fall, Mr. Bradford."

"Yale Law School isn't going anywhere, Barry." He took a drag off his cigarette. "We need you here at CoCo Cosmetics."

Barry felt his heart beating in his chest. "I'll have to think about it, I guess."

Gary took a piece of paper out his pocket and handed it to Barry. "Think about this also while you're at it."

Barry opened the piece of paper. There was a number written on it with a dollar sign. It was a big number. Not quite as big as the number he expected to be offered three years from now when, he expected, every law firm in New York would come chasing after him. But pretty damn close.

"Call me within the hour," Gary said. "I'll be waiting."

9

Leo noticed, after the detectives left the apartment, that most of their questions had been directed at him. Sure, Pete was the rock star, and everyone knew rock stars indulged in drugs. But Leo, as he tried to explain later to Pete, was the black guy, and "black guy" trumped "rock star" whenever drugs were the topic of the conversation. So, of course, it had probably been Leo who'd brought the drugs to the apartment and gave them to the unwitting young white guy who almost overdosed.

Even Sally agreed with Leo. "Happens all the time. You should see how they treated another client of mine, a rapper. He'd been carjacked and all the cops wanted to do was search his car for drug paraphernalia when they arrived on the scene."

"I should write a song about that," Pete said, reaching for a bagel.

Leo said, "*You* should?"

Pete grinned. "We should."

Which gave Leo an idea. After Sally was gone and after Pete locked himself in the little studio they kept in the apartment to lay down some guitar parts, he sat himself at the computer and typed a sentence: "And to think, it started with a quiet night watching *The Cosby Show*." By nightfall, ignoring the ringing phone and only stopping once so he and Pete could order up some Thai food from the restaurant on the corner, he had written two thousand words of what he decided to call "The Hanger-On," an essay on what it felt like to be the no-name guy who hung out with a rock star. It left out more than he'd have wanted—no mention of their sex life—but it told an honest story of being "that guy," the guy people pushed aside to get an autograph or asked how to get a phone number for the star. "Somewhere between bodyguard and baby-sitter," he wrote, "to be a hanger-on is to be just visible enough to the world that you feel invisible to yourself."

"You really feel that way?" Pete asked him in bed that night. "I don't mean to make you feel that way."

"Maybe you should read it again," Leo said. "It's not how you make me feel."

Pete scanned the article. He dropped it between them and said, "Sometimes I wonder if we were fated to meet each other. You don't believe in fate, right?"

"I believe in connection," said Leo. "We had, we have, a good connection that we don't share with anyone else."

Pete said, "You think we'll be together forever?"

"Do you?"

"I want to be."

"Then maybe," Leo said, "we will."

Pete jumped up. "I have an idea," he said, grabbing Leo's printed pages and running over to the desk. He dialed a number on the fax machine and put the pages in the slot to be sent.

Leo said, "What are you doing?"

"Making you visible," he said, as the first page was sliding through the fax machine.

A month later, a warm, breezy May Saturday, Joey rang the bell at the Bradford apartment. Lillian's assistant Rachel led him to the den where Lillian sat on the couch, an elaborate tea set spread out before her, a hint of jasmine lingering in the air. Joey handed the garments to Rachel and took a seat. As Lillian tried on each dress, Joey sipped tea and jumped back and forth between the rooms, suggesting accessories, pinning alterations, congratulating Lillian on keeping her figure all these years.

He felt like a real designer.

As he gathered up the two dresses that needed altering, he watched Lillian gather up her jewelry, preparing things she'd be taking to Sag Harbor for the summer. She packed everything into a pile of sleek Chanel valises with locks at the end of each zipper.

"I miss Sag Harbor," he said to her, pulling his own garment bag shut.

Lillian said, "You are welcome anytime, Joey."

"Of course he is."

They both turned to see Gary standing in the doorway, a stout glass of Scotch in his hand. He came into the room, nodded hello to Joey, and kissed his wife on the cheek. He looked around. "So many dresses, so little time."

"There's enough time," Lillian said. "If I have to wear three a day, I'll fit them all in." She handed Rachel her bag. "Especially if they're designed by Joey. You should see his things, Gary."

"I'm sure they're spectacular," he said. He sat on the chair in front of Lillian's dressing table. "What's your plan, Joe?"

"My plan?"

"Yes," Gary said. He took a sip of his drink. "How do you plan to grow? You intend to do couture pieces for ladies who lunch like my wife? Or do you want to make dresses that the regular folks wear to family reunions and proms?"

"Both, I guess," Joey said, blushing. He truly hadn't thought about it much. He was enjoying himself enough and making a bit of money just making dresses to order for Carla and her rich friends. "Everyone wants to look nice, right?"

"Then you need to make a plan." Gary got up. "Come see me sometime. I'll help you in any way I can. Okay?"

Joey nodded. He and Lillian watched Gary leave the room.

As Joey picked up the garment bag to go, Lillian grabbed his wrist. She said, "Don't bother with him, Joey. Doing business with my husband is like doing a deal with the devil. And don't you ever tell him I told you that." She slipped a check into his hand and closed his fist around it. "Thank you, Joey. You'll be hearing from me. Carla and I have big plans for you."

"Another year off?"

Hattie Chambers placed the plate of food in front of Barry, then sat down across from him at the tiny table in her kitchen. "I'm so glad you came out here to eat, baby, but this is some news I ain't expect. You sure you wanna do that?"

Barry nodded, swallowing some macaroni and cheese. With all the money he was making now, he thought, he'd be renting a car and coming back out to Sag Harbor to eat all the time. "I couldn't resist it," he said. "Mr. Bradford offered me the moon."

"The moon is far away for a reason, boy. Ain't everybody supposed to go visit it."

"Meaning?"

"You know what I mean. I thought you wanted to go to law school."

"I do wanna go, Ma. But this offer . . . Law school will always be there."

"But I won't." She got up and took a pan of rolls from the oven. "I wanna see you graduate from law school. Soon."

"Oh," Barry laughed. "So this is about you?"

Hattie laughed and swatted him with the warm towel. "I just want you to be happy. Are you?"

"You know what happiness is, Ma? It's an office with a window. Happiness is a salary I'm getting now that I could probably only make with a law degree. Happiness is—" He wanted to say "fucking Gail Oliver all night when her husband is away at some wack dental conference," but he didn't. "Happiness is coming out here and eating up this potato salad and macaroni and fried chicken."

"If you say so, baby," she said.

"I don't think Pete will go for it," Leo said to the guy in the sunglasses sitting in front of him. He wished he could see the guy's eyes. It was hard to finally talk to someone in person when you still really couldn't *see* him or her; they might as well have been communicating on the telephone. "Really, Glen, I don't think Pete'll be into me writing about him. We're too close." Leo sat forward. "Is that a deal breaker? Does that mean you don't want me writing for you guys anymore?"

"Not at all," said Glen Yeager. "Ever since we published that

'Hanger-On' piece we knew we'd be in business with you for a long time." He smiled. But it didn't mean much to Leo if he couldn't see the dude's eyes. "So we'll just think of something else for you to do, okay?" He looked at his watch. "Excuse me for a sec?" He jumped up and ran from the little office.

Leo looked around at the walls, every inch of them covered with tour posters, promotional pics, magazine covers. Even the computer on the desk was covered, layered with rock band promo stickers. Leo almost couldn't believe he was sitting there in the offices of *Rolling Stone*. After doing the editing over the phone with Glen, Leo didn't expect him to call up and invite him into the office. He got nervous at first, wondering if perhaps he was supposed to bring Pete with him, that maybe the editors were only acting excited to work with him because he had Pete and the Wild Men to name-drop at meetings. But that wasn't the case, as Sally had to explain after she'd read the faxed pages and sent them right over to a friend at *Rolling Stone*, who called and said they wanted to run it in the next issue.

"They want you to do a few profiles," she'd said breathlessly. "They think you have a real voice and a great point of view."

"And a friendship with Pete Reynolds."

"Hush," said Sally. "Do you know how many starfuckers there are out there who think they can write?"

"From 'hanger-on' to 'starfucker,'" Leo said, "in the span of a minute."

"That's not what I meant and you know it."

"So?"

"So, have a good edit, do everything they say, and wait for your next assignment. Or better yet, come up with some ideas you can pitch them."

Now Glen returned to the office with a severe-looking young

woman dressed in black, her hair yanked back into a long ponytail. She introduced herself as Kimson and held out her hand to Leo. "You think you can interview Billy Joel? The writer I wanted broke his leg skiing with Don Henley, and we need the piece in ten days. You seem like you know your way around a sentence or two. And you seem to get how rock stars think. I'm trusting you because I liked your essay and Glen here says you're the man."

Leo nodded. "I am," he said. "I mean . . . Not I am the man, I mean I can—"

"Billy's out in the Hamptons. You gotta go out there and talk to him." She glanced at her watch and rushed out of the office. Over her shoulder she said, "Glen'll give you the details."

When Kimson was gone, Glen said, "Prove me right, bro."

"I will," said Leo. "I will."

By July, thanks to Carla, Joey had so many dress orders, including a first communion frock (as she put it) for Carla's goddaughter, that he put an ad in the *Village Voice*, looking for an ace seamstress who could match him stitch for stitch. By the middle of August, as he prepared for the trunk show Carla and Lillian were hosting for him in Sag Harbor, he and Greta were barely speaking to each other. Their sex life was nonexistent. She was sleeping in her studio room at night and making her art in there all day, only coming out to eat, and slamming things around when she found that Joey's busy schedule meant nothing had been cooked. Joey once almost suggested she go to her father's for dinner, but stopped himself. If she wasn't going to bring up her financial situation with her father, neither was he.

Besides, he had other things to concentrate on. Like hiring an accountant to start taking care of his burgeoning income. Looking for another seamstress to help with the growing load of dresses to get made and fitted. Deciding a theme for the fashion show. Finding models who'd be able to express what he wanted the clothes to say. Finding transportation to get everyone out to Long Island.

Finding models was the most fun.

On the third, and last, day of model interviews, Greta stormed out of the house, almost knocking down the first girl to show up. "I probably won't be back tonight," she shouted at him as she slammed the door.

Part of Joey hoped she'd stay away for longer than just one night, but he pushed Greta out of his mind and concentrated. He noticed that the fourth girl waiting had been to the house before, tagging along with one of the models who'd shown up on the first day. Not as tall as the others, with a great mess of curly brown hair shooting out in all directions, she was almost preternaturally beautiful, brown as maple syrup with piercing green eyes and cheekbones that looked like they could cut glass. Joey didn't remember her name, but he couldn't take his eyes off of her.

When her turn came, she stepped up to the dining room table, unwrapped the light sweater she'd tied around her shoulders, revealing a white halter top that covered perfectly shaped breasts, and said, "I thought I needed to make a second impression. First ones can often leave you mistaken." She held out her hand. "My name's Cheyenne."

Joey was already mentally designing a dress with her body in mind. If that wasn't love at first sight, Joey didn't know what was.

"Do you have a portfolio?" he said.

"No."

"Have you ever walked a runway?"

"I walk the streets of New York every day just like everyone else."

"That can mean something you may not want it to mean, Cheyenne."

"I'll let you take it the way you want to." She stared right at him, her eyes bulging with challenge. "So am I in or out?"

One of the models sitting on the couch exhaled a long exasperated sigh and got up and walked out.

"You're in," Joey said.

"Are you gay or straight?"

"Which do you need me to be?"

"Good in bed, whatever you are."

"Let's just do the show first," Joey said. "How 'bout that?"

"I'm down."

Over Cheyenne's shoulder, Joey could see the remaining model roll her eyes, quietly pick up her portfolio, and creep out of the apartment.

Joey said, "I think we're alone."

"So?"

There were no words. Joey stepped toward Cheyenne, pulled her close, and buried his face in her neck. She arched her back, pushing her body toward his, grinding herself against his growing hardness. Their kisses got rougher and longer as they stumbled toward the couch, falling to it as they wrestled each other out of their clothes. The world was silent around them; all Joey could hear was the beating of his heart as he fingered her breasts and felt her hand wrap around his dick.

He never saw Greta, peeking through the front window.

10

Duke watched the bikini-clad brunette pour suntan oil into her palm and spread it all along her brown arms and legs.

He turned to Rocky Tolbert, floating next to him on an in-flated blue pool raft, his arms behind his head, his eyes closed to the penetrating sun. "Will you look at that?"

"Huh?" Rocky lifted his head lazily, not so eager to move his sore arms since they'd started two-a-days at camp. "The one in the purple bikini? Hot."

"What you think she is?" Duke asked. "Puerto Rican?"

Rocky lifted his head again, squinted in the sun. He half-shrugged. "Brazilian, maybe? I don't know. Go ask her."

"Maybe I will."

Rocky said. "The rumor is you scared of girls, dude."

"The rumor?" Duke sat up on his own floating raft and let his legs hang over the sides. "Who started this rumor?"

Rocky half-shrugged again, as if to say, "Who knows?"

"Scared of girls," Duke muttered, his eyes still on the girl in the purple bikini. He hadn't seen her around the hotel since they'd checked in to start practice for the season, so he didn't expect her to be one of the notorious athletic supporters who hovered around waiting to catch the eye of a Redskin before the season kicked off. This one didn't even pay him and Rocky any attention and he knew their bodies were better than any other bodies she'd seen on a pair of guys in her life.

Scared of girls, indeed. Duke thought of a couple of things he could do with the one in the purple bikini that would prove to anybody anywhere that fear wasn't his problem. Duke's problem was simple: He knew what he liked and he wasn't finding it. Of course, he knew how to find sex when he wanted it; that was the easiest thing in the world, particularly when you're twenty-four years old, you play for the Washington Redskins, and you already have two Super Bowl rings. It was D.C., where women could be like cars or jewelry—you could have them whenever you wanted, but only if you were willing to throw around a lot of money. But that had never been Duke's thing. He craved stability, perhaps because of his own crazy family history, but also because it just seemed right. He liked smart women, independent women, not like the ones who cavorted around athletes, camouflaging their intelligence and stressing their physical attributes to hook a guy because they believed (rightly, it seemed to Duke) that that seemed to be what most men wanted. And so many of the women he encountered had that hungry look. Not like they needed a meal, but like they could devour him and keep on moving.

It also didn't help that, almost four years since it ended, he still missed Amanda.

Scared of girls? He'd been discreet, is all. There was Yvonne, the sister of one of his first-year teammates, a nice, churchgoing sister who bored him to tears. He'd dated Shelly Marcus, a Howard senior who talked only about herself, who was more concerned about pledging the next group of AKAs line than she was with sustaining any kind of real relationship. Sure, there'd been women, but none of them were Amanda Holland, smart, funny, passionate, hip-hop-loving Amanda Holland.

"You coming?"

Duke looked up. Purple Bikini was now lying, eyes closed, on a chaise longue. Rocky was swimming back to the pool steps. "Practice in half an hour, man," he said. "I'm heading in."

Duke slipped off his raft and swam in behind Rocky. Before he entered the hotel, he glanced back at the girl in the purple bikini. She was watching him, as well. He winked at her and ducked inside.

He decided to check his messages while Rocky was in the shower, singing something about "girl you know it's true . . . true . . . I love you . . ." Duke closed the bathroom door. He hated

Milli Vanilli on the radio and he hated them coming out of Rocky Tolbert's big mouth.

He had two messages. The first one was from a teammate who needed a ride to practice camp. The second one, from his agent, almost made him drop the phone. "Duke, this is Matt. Your sister called me to find you. Seems your mom's not doing well. She's in the hospital. Marie's trying to get out there now and she says she can't find your brother anywhere. Your mom's at Central Suffolk Hospital in Riverhead. I know you'll wanna get up there, so I already called the team. Amy here is making plane reservations for you. Call me when you get to Long Island."

Duke looked at the phone. He called info for the number of the hospital. The woman at the desk wouldn't tell him anything, would only confirm that a Eunice Maynard was in the cardiac care unit. She refused to put a doctor on the phone.

Who else could he call? Leo. He dialed Leo's number.

Pete answered the phone. "Hey, Duke. How's stuff in—"

"Is Leo there, Pete?"

"He's on assignment, man, talking to Billy Joel out in Long Island."

Duke couldn't believe his luck. "Can you get a message to him?"

"Should be able to. What's up, man?"

11

By the time Joey got to Sag Harbor, he didn't want anything to do with fashion or clothes or models. He wanted to strip off his jeans, run right past the Bradfords' house, jump right into the cool water of the bay, and swim off all the stress that lay before him.

First, Greta decided she wanted to go to Sag Harbor, that she needed to be there for his first real fashion show. Joey didn't understand. She had barely even spoken to him in close to two months and now she wanted to play the supportive girlfriend?

Then Luis called. He wasn't sure he'd able to get both vans in time for their agreed-upon departure time. Could Joey split the trip in two? Perhaps send the dresses first, then send the models later? After sitting on the phone for an hour looking for another van he told Luis that the one van would be fine. Luis responded by saying his wife had demanded she accompany him on the ride. Fine, Joey told him. Just be on time.

Then two models dropped out of the show. One of them didn't realize she wouldn't be getting her usual rate, which almost sent Joey over the edge. Her usual rate? According to her interview, she had only been in two other runway shows, and both of those had been in Schenectady. The other model couldn't find a sitter for her baby. Could she bring him along? No, Joey told her, she couldn't. She called Joey a fag and hung up.

Now here he was, standing on the pier out behind the Bradfords' house, exhaling deeply, staring out at the water when he felt a gentle tap on his back. He turned to find Carla there, a friendly smile on her lips. "You'll be fine, baby," she whispered and took him into her arms.

Joey felt like crying.

Barry parked his rented Jeep outside the diner on Main Street in Sag Harbor and ran inside. He didn't see Gail anywhere. He described her to the waitress.

"I know Miss Oliver," the teenager said. "She was here. Then her husband showed up and they left about fifteen minutes ago."

Barry drove slowly past Anthony Oliver's parents' summer house on Lincoln Street and, sure enough, he saw Anthony's Jaguar parked in the driveway behind Gail's pert little VW Rabbit. He idled there for a few seconds, staring at the gray clapboard house, trying to decide what to do. As horny as he was to be with Gail again, this wasn't even about sex. He actually wanted to talk real CoCo Cosmetics business with her. But it was becoming clearer that Anthony suspected something between them. Why else would he show up here so unexpectedly? Barry decided he could wait. He'd pull Gail aside before Joey's fashion show. He'd have to, or the whole thing would fall apart. No way was he going to embarrass himself in front of Gary Bradford.

Leo sat with Duke's sister Marie on a worn wooden bench in the visitors' lounge outside the cardiac unit at Central Suffolk Hospital. It was quiet at this early hour, except for the hushed squishy sound of the nurses' soft shoes as they passed by in the hall.

"Thank you so much for coming," Marie said. "Duke will appreciate this."

Leo couldn't believe how much older Marie looked. She was only four years older than he and Duke, but even with the chic clothes Duke had bought her and the long hair extensions that Leo was sure Duke also paid for, she still looked like an old woman. Her once-porcelain, cheerleader-happy skin now hung loose and dry-looking, her eyes drawn. He hugged her, running his hand down her arm, trying to comfort her. "He'll be here soon," he said. "Any update yet?"

Marie shrugged her thin shoulders in his arms. She spoke

against his chest. "I never understand doctors," she said. "But I think they said it's not so good. I'm praying for her, Leo."

He looked at his watch. He had told Pete that he'd meet Duke at the airport. It was time to head that way.

Outside in the parking lot, Leo remembered the only other time he'd been to this hospital. Carla had sprained her ankle playing tag with a bunch of the boys back when he was eleven. His father had rushed her to the emergency room and Leo had tagged along, thinking how strong and fast his dad had seemed, running to Carla's rescue like that, saving the day. He remembered his father stopped at the Baskin-Robbins on the way back to the house, and he and Carla both got pistachio cones with multicolored sprinkles.

As he pulled the car onto Route 4, he swerved to avoid hitting a car trying to merge right to his left. Leo shoved his fist on the horn. He blinked a few times and realized the guy pulling in front of him was giving him the finger and shouting some choice words from the comfort and protection of his big Jeep.

"Fuck you," he shouted to the guy, who had stopped the Jeep, and was now climbing down from it, storming over to Leo's Mustang. *Oh shit*, Leo thought, when he realized who it was.

"Barry," said Leo. "What are you doing out here?"

"Uh, I grew up out here?" Barry looked down into the Mustang. "You going to your mother's thing for Joey?"

Leo swallowed hard. Why did he have to run into Barry? Why did he have to bring up Joey? And what was his mother hosting for Joey in Sag Harbor?

Barry said, "Get out and give me some love, bro!"

"I don't give love to people who betray me," Leo said.

"Betray you? Me? How? When?"

"Don't start, Barry."

"That's why I ain't heard from you?" Barry leaned his hands on the door.

"Get off the car, Barry. I gotta get to the airport."

"Me too! Who are you picking up? Or are you leaving?"

"I'm getting Duke," said Leo. "His mom's in the hospital. Get off the car, Barry."

Barry leaned back dramatically, raising his hands in the air like someone had a gun on him. Leo sped off.

"How did I betray you?" Barry shouted to the car. "Tell me!"

"**A**re you nervous?"

Joey looked at Lillian Bradford's pleasant face and had to smile himself. "Nervous ain't the word."

"Don't be, dear. Everyone who's going to be here wants you to succeed. Show them some pretty dresses and you will." She squeezed his hand and headed over to her Saab. "Can I bring you back anything from downtown?"

"I'm fine," Joey told her. He turned his attention back to the crates of shoes and garment bags full of clothes. He directed Luis to take the top two bags to the last bedroom on the right. He carried the two crates himself and followed Luis into the house.

Through the huge bay window in the back of the living room, he could see the five models cavorting along the sand, laughing and giggling. They didn't seem nervous at all. Then again, he realized that their futures weren't dependent on this one night. He saw Cheyenne, her usually messy hair pulled back into a manageable ponytail, and felt something stirring in him again. He thanked God that he'd been able to talk Greta out of coming with him. He didn't need anything to distract him, not from the show and not from Cheyenne. All during the ride out, when he should have been thinking of accessories to use with the dresses, he was thinking about how he could get closer to her. He didn't even feel guilty. His relationship with Greta was basically over. He knew it. Greta knew it. But that didn't mean he was starting anything serious with Cheyenne beyond a few dirty screws against the wall. He'd had his last love affair. He was marrying himself to JoeyRam Fashions. They could fuck. They could see each other sometimes. But for Joey Ramirez, the relationship game was over.

Duke had only his carry-on bag, and he dropped it to the floor to give Leo a big hug when he saw him standing at the arrivals.

"Thank you," he mumbled. "How is she? Is Marie there? Did she find Mike?"

"I don't know yet," Leo said. "And no, Mike's still out there somewhere."

"I can't believe this is happening," said Duke. "I told her—"

"Duke!" It was Barry, crossing the parking lot. He seemed to be distracted, looking from side to side and over their heads. He stopped in front of them and tried to hug Duke hello.

Duke stepped back. "Leave me alone, Barry."

Barry looked from Leo to Duke. "What the fuck? You too?"

"Me too, what?" Duke asked.

"Leo claims I betrayed him," said Barry. "You taking his side?"

"I have my own side," Duke said. "And if I didn't have to be at the hospital to see my mother, I'd kick your ass right here for telling Mr. Bradford about the abortion."

Barry's eyes started to wander again, looking past them at the terminal. "I never said anything about the abortion to Gary."

Leo said, "You call my father Gary?"

"We work very closely," Barry said. "And he misses you, Leo. I can tell."

"So *that's* why I'm not allowed into my own family's house

anymore? Because he misses me so much? Come on, Duke, let's get to the hospital." They started off, then Leo turned back to Barry. "And Barry? Keep all of our names out of your mouth, okay? Part of me almost appreciates that you told my father I was gay, but at least you could have talked to me—"

"I didn't tell your father you were gay, Leo."

"Then how does he know? He said that I wasn't the only person he knew at Yale. Who else did he know there? You, Barry, that's who."

Barry looked like Leo had slapped him across the face. "I really didn't tell him that, Leo." He looked at Duke. "And I didn't tell him about the abortion. I thought you trusted me with that info, man."

Duke said, "Come on, Leo, man, we gotta go."

Barry sat on a bench outside the Islip Airport and waited. *My brain isn't big enough for all this*, he thought. Why would they think that he'd told their secrets to anyone? *There were a lot of things I'd do, hell, there are a lot of things I have done,* he thought. *But I'd never betray Duke or Leo.*

"Barry!"

He looked up. And as good as he thought he'd feel at this moment, staring at the approaching woman, the building block of a whole plan that had been in preparation for months, he had no idea what would happen now. He stared at Amanda and tried to gather his emotions.

"Hey, Amanda," he said, standing up, glad that Duke and Leo had already left the airport. "I'm glad you came. You're gonna love the fashion show. I'm sure Joey can't wait to meet you."

While Duke was in with his mother, Leo laid his head on the soft back of the couch.

It had to have been Barry.

Leo could still remember the beginning of the talk with his father:

"So are you a faggot?"

"Who told you that?" Leo had asked him. "Where did you hear that?"

"You think you're the only person I know at Yale?" Gary had said. "You *know* you're not the only person I know at Yale."

It had to have been Barry. Who else knew? Lynn had been sworn to secrecy—and, most important, she had whispered into Leo's ear on the ride back from Syracuse that she thought she might be a lesbian. Leo smiled at the memory of their secret hello-smiles on campus after that, like they shared a connection that no one could imagine. Leo sighed and slid down further on the hospital couch. If not Barry, then who?

Duke saw his mother try to smile when he came into her room in the cardiac ICU. He took her hand and felt tears come to his eyes. He blinked them back and sat on the stool next to her bed.

She moved her lips but Duke spoke first. "Don't, Mommy. Don't say anything, I'm here and I'm not going anywhere."

Later, as she drifted off to sleep, Duke went out into the visitors' area.

"You know what?" he said to Leo. "I think Barry was telling the truth."

Joey stood in the back of the living room, behind a paisley scrim Carla had hung across one side of the huge space to hide the models and create an impromptu changing area.

The first JoeyRam fashion show had begun. C+C Music Factory

played over the stereo, then segued into Color Me Badd's "I Wanna Sex You Up." Joey hoped the music wasn't too risqué as he tried to peek out at the proper-looking ladies there to see his line. But just as he did, a model yanked him back to fix the sash on her gown.

As Carla stood out front, a stack of index cards in her manicured hands, saying, "First, we have Cynthia in a fabulous JoeyRam minidress," Joey sent Cynthia down the makeshift runway in the middle of the Bradfords' huge living room. "Notice the fine tailoring and intricate webbing along the bias," Carla continued. "Joey says this dress was inspired by, guess who? Me!" Joey peeked out again from behind the scrim while Cynthia walked, amazed at the number of people grouped on both sides of the catwalk. On one side he saw a couple of editors from fashion magazines, whose faces he recognized from reading *Women's Wear Daily*. There were a couple of actresses, friends of Carla's, one a soap star, the other a Broadway diva. Interspersed among Mrs. Bradford's black society friends were some music biz people, and various employees of CoCo Cosmetics—thanks to Mr. Bradford—including Barry, who was sitting next to some beaming woman, who looked sort of familiar, applauding as the third girl came out. Cheyenne. Carla narrated the runway fashions, pointing out Cheyenne's "magnificently cut tank dress, perfect for holiday or evening. How many gowns can you say that about with any confidence this season? Or even last? Eat your heart out, Calvin."

The crowd laughed and applauded and Joey felt the pounding of his heart subside.

When Cheyenne came back to the dressing area, she said, "You rock, JoeyRam," and scurried off to put on her next ensemble.

By the end of the show, bathing in the applause as he himself walked down the runway, getting kisses and hugs from the five models, Joey felt like he was floating. This was what success felt like. This is what it felt like when people loved you and loved what you could do. This is what it felt like to be embraced. As he bowed, then turned to return behind the scrim, his mind was crowded with the faces of people to whom he'd always wanted to say "Fuck you." But there were also the faces of the good ones, the people to whom he wanted to say "Thank you" and "I love you" and—

Carla grabbed him from behind and yanked him into her arms. As he turned to face her, he saw a cloudy look cover Cheyenne's pretty face as she stepped into a pair of baggy beach shorts. He watched her cross her arms, turn abruptly, and go out the back door. She looked pissed.

"You're going to be a star, Joey," Carla gushed. "It went so well! What do you think?"

Joey started to tell her, but as he opened his mouth, he realized he could barely speak. He cleared his throat, opened his mouth to try again, but nothing would come out, except the tears that poured down his cheeks.

Neither of them wanted anything fancy for dinner, Leo having spent the better part of three days sailing and dining and chatting with the rock star and Duke not interested in dealing with the drama of any high-toned places, so they decided to get crabs at the Little Crab Hut near the pier, where they'd eaten so often as teenagers.

"I'm gonna have her moved," Duke said. "To a hospital in Manhattan."

"You think that's wise? In her state?"

Duke just shrugged.

They took their trays to one of the outdoor tables, and sat next to each other, facing the water, where the yachts of the East End wealthy, parked in their docks, seemed to stare back at them with haughty looks on their sterns.

Leo nibbled on a crab leg. "It's weird being back here, isn't it?"

Duke shrugged. "Probably more for you than for me. At least I can go to my house."

Duke went inside for more tartar sauce. Leo considered what Duke had said. Here he was, approximately two miles from the place he loved more than anything as a kid, and he was forbidden to be there. Or was he? What would his father do if he saw Leo on the property? Call the Straight Police to drag him away to some combination jail/rehab facility? He knew his mother would love to see him. Though he was curious: What exactly was she doing for Joey this weekend?

A couple of voices drew his attention. He looked to his left, and couldn't believe what he was seeing. Strolling up to the Little Crab Hut were four people (plus one he didn't recognize) who looked so completely odd together that Leo almost choked on his milk shake. Barry, Amanda, Carla, and Joey. And some sexy model-type chick whom Leo had never seen before.

Carla saw Leo first.

"Baby cousin!" she screamed, and ran over to Leo's table. "I have the greatest news about Joey! Come over here, Joey!"

Joey sat down and said, "Leo. Hey, man."

"Carla?" Duke said as he came out of the Hut. Then he saw who was standing next to Barry. *"Amanda?"*

She went up to Duke and kissed his cheek.

Barry said, "Surprise, everybody!" The sarcasm in his voice was thicker than the tartar sauce on the tables.

Amanda said, "So. How's your life?"

Duke didn't know how to answer that. *You mean since you*

walked out on me or since I started scoring touchdowns like they were going out of style? "I'm fine," he said. "And you? What are you doing here? With these guys?"

Amanda explained about meeting Joey at the Bradfords'. How she'd finished business school and was looking for investment possibilities. How Barry had suggested she meet some young designer on the way up who needed backing. "And I asked Barry to get me in touch with you. Never imagined I'd see you here."

"I haven't talked to Barry in a long time," Duke said.

"He said that," said Amanda. "But he said he'd try. He's a good friend, Duke." Amanda hesitated. "He didn't tell Gary Bradford about us. It's all he's been talking about since the fashion show ended, running into you and Leo at the airport." Amanda sat down on a stone bench near the ice cream parlor. She patted the bench next to her. "You told Mr. Bradford, Duke. He knew I was pregnant," she said. "What I never told you was that I told my mother when I found out. She told my father. He told Mr. Bradford about me being pregnant. I didn't even know they were friends, let alone that you had some connection to him."

"But he *asked* me if we told your father about the abortion."

"When I didn't have a baby, Duke, one would either surmise that I'd had an abortion or a miscarriage. He guessed abortion. You confirmed it."

Duke replayed the conversation in his mind; he remembered it like it had happened just the day before. Damn. He'd been played. Sitting there, hat in hand, asking for Bradford's help, he'd given away more info than he'd walked away with.

He said, "Why'd you leave?"

"I explained it in the note, didn't I?"

"The note? After all we had, a note was supposed to sum it all up for me?"

"That's not what I'm saying, Duke."

"Then what are you saying?"

"I'm saying I had to make a choice then. I can make my own choices now."

"Which means that I can make my own choices, too."

"Excuse me?"

"You left me so that your father would continue to pay for school," he said. "You left me because you and your family didn't believe in my future—"

Amanda put a finger to his face. "It wasn't that at all—"

Duke shrugged her off. "No? Then I guess it was my fault for being, what did your father call me? A piece of white trash, right? We were in love, Amanda."

"We were young," she said. "I was confused."

"I wasn't," he said. "I loved you. I was willing to risk so much to be with you."

Now Amanda stood up. "Yeah, you were risking so much, Duke. Don't give me that. You hadn't even told your family about me, Duke. Remember that? I couldn't even come out here to meet your mother. How do you think that made me feel?"

She took a business card from her back pocket and held it out to him. When he didn't take it, she slipped into the pocket of his jeans. "I'm leaving," she said. "If you want to contact me all my info's on that card. If not? I will say this. Thank you for loving me, Duke. And I apologize if you think I didn't love you enough. But that went both ways, whether you choose to remember it that way or not."

Barry watched Amanda walk away from Duke, down Main Street, and ran after her.

"Leave her alone," Leo said. "They'll figure it out."

Barry turned back to Leo. "So? That's it? You think I got home from Syracuse, ran to the phone, called Gary, and said, Guess what? Leo's gay. That's what you think? Well, I didn't. I'd never do that to you. To anyone I called a friend." He sat down. "Have you tried talking to your father?"

Leo shook his head. "He doesn't want to see me unless I agree to see a doctor."

"That was years ago, Leo, you think he still feels that way?" Barry took a sip of Leo's milk shake. "You should have seen him when you guys were in the paper about that overdose. He was asking how much money you made writing songs. He at least was concerned that you were eating and not in some gutter somewhere."

"Or he was just wondering if I'd inherited his ability to turn shit into something shiny and sellable."

Barry laughed. "Do you know how jealous I was of you when we first met? You had a successful father who cared about his family and handled his business. Do you know how much I would have loved to have that?"

"You only know one side of my father, Barry."

"I know enough to know that maybe it's fate that you're out here. Go see him."

Carla and Joey and Cheyenne came out of the Hut carrying trays. They squeezed around the table and dug into their food.

Leo stared at Cheyenne, watching her feed tiny shrimp into Joey's mouth. This was exactly the kind of woman he expected Joey to be with. Someone perfect-looking. He introduced himself and offered his hand to Cheyenne.

"I'm Cheyenne," she said. "I'm Joey's new muse."

Leo swallowed hard. So she wasn't just beautiful. She was dumb, too. "Is that right?" Leo asked, shooting a look at Joey. He looked embarrassed.

"I'm going to be a supermodel," Cheyenne said.

"Really?" Leo said. A thousand smart-ass lines came to his brain. He didn't know which one to use. "So," he said, "have you already filled out your application?"

"Oh shit," Cheyenne said, cole slaw dripping from the fork halfway to her mouth. "I didn't know I needed one." She looked at Carla. "Do you know how I can get one?"

Leo looked at Joey, simultaneously loving the embarrassed look on his face and hating himself for causing it. "How's Greta doing?" he asked.

"She's fine," Joey said. "As a matter of fact, you're reminding me of her right now." He sipped some soda. "How's Wild Man Pete? Saying no to the drugs, I hope."

Carla put down her fork. "Joey's show was fantastic, Leo."

"Glad to hear it," said Leo. He stood up. "I'm gonna get Duke and go. If any of you want to send his mom good wishes, she's at Central Suffolk Hospital."

Barry watched Leo head over to Duke, still sitting on the stone bench, his head in his hands, and felt the negative energy Leo had left in his wake after exchanging insults with Joey. There was something he could do about that.

Barry took a sip of his soda, sat up in his seat, and said, with a flourish, "Joey? How would you like to be the designer for the new CoCo Cosmetics fashion line?"

12

Joey lay in bed that night. It was strange to be sleeping at the Bradford house in the old twin bed he'd slept on back in those early

Sag Harbor days. Stranger still not to have Leo sleeping across the room, snoring.

But was anything stranger than Barry's offer? The CoCo Cosmetics fashion line? He wanted to jump up and call everyone, tell them the good news. But who could he call? Greta? She'd probably grunt a response and hang up in his face. Leo didn't seem all that interested. It was these times when he remembered how alone in the world he was, parentless, siblingless, just Joey, fending for himself out there.

He eventually fell asleep, feeling sorry for himself even as he still celebrated the day's achievement. Cheyenne's long legs were the last thing he remembered before he drifted off to dreamland.

Duke twisted and turned on the lumpy couch in the visitors' room at Central Suffolk, getting up every hour to look in on his mother, who didn't seem to be changing. His brain was full: When he wasn't praying for his mother's recovery he was thinking about Amanda. Had he been too hard on her? And she was right, wasn't she? He had never once introduced her to his family, all the while taking it personally that the Hollands weren't exactly treating him like the Prince Charming their daughter thought he was.

About three o'clock in the morning, he stretched his arms, got up, and went outside to get some air. He sat on the hard concrete steps in front of the hospital and clasped his hands in front of him. He needed to make a plan. If his mother recovered but needed care, what should he do? Move her down to Maryland or Virginia so she'd be comfortable? She'd already resisted his pressure to move her to a new place, even in Sag Harbor, insisting that she liked where she was. Marie couldn't care for her; she could barely care for herself and her own kids at this point. And Mike, cracked-out again after a long rehab stint Duke had paid for just after signing his deal with the Redskins, certainly couldn't help. He was nowhere to be found, lost to the world, out in the wind like a piece of garbage that missed the dump truck when the trash was being taken away.

He wished he'd rented a car. It was nice to see Leo at the airport, but it would be nice to just drive around, maybe ride out to Montauk, see the dunes, watch the sky change color as the waves splashed against the surf.

He got up to return to the visitors' couch. As he stood, he noticed a beat-up old Chevy parked in the first row of cars. The person behind the wheel was staring right at him. Duke had grown used to that, the stares of football fans and the curiosity of non-fans who knew his face from his commercials. He was just glad this person was parked in a car; he really was in no mood to be rushed for an autograph. He turned to go into the hospital. But something made him turn back to the car. He knew that face. It was different, but familiar still, like a caricature of a face he once knew. It was his brother.

He said, "Mike? That you, Mike?"

The car door opened and his older brother stepped out of the Chevy, but it wasn't really his brother, was it? This skinny, shrunken, ashen-faced guy with tears running down his face, his clothes like disheveled rags pieced into an outfit?

"It's me, Duke. It's me." When he smiled, tears still streaming down his face, Duke saw more empty spaces than teeth. "Is Mama here, Duke? She ain't dead, is she? Duke? Is Mama here?"

Duke hugged him, this thing that used to be his brother. The brother he used to toss a football with in the fall and play tag with in the spring, the brother he followed around like a worker ant until he left Sag Harbor for college. And Duke cried, for his brother, for his mother, for the hard decisions he knew he had to make.

———

Barry lay in the hotel bed, smelling the crisp freshness of the sheets, and like Duke, he was waiting. Sadly, he decided, in vain. He looked at the clock. It was past three. Gail wasn't going to show.

Fuck that. He got out of the bed, pulled a pair of jeans and T-shirt over his nakedness, and left the room. Downstairs, the lobby was empty except for a bellman who was sleeping on the guest couch near the front door. Barry went out on the veranda and found the teenaged front-desk clerk there, making out with a pimply girl in a polka-dot New Kids on the Block T-shirt. The clerk asked Barry if he needed directions somewhere.

"Nah," Barry told him. "I'm a native."

As he took a seat at the Olde Mill Inn on Route 4, Barry had to laugh at that. A native. Could he really call himself that now? He wasn't even staying at his mother's house while he was out there, choosing instead to crash at the chic New America Hotel on Main Street. He told himself he was staying there because it made meeting with Gail that much easier if one of them already had a room registered. But the truth was, he didn't want to be in that cramped house he grew up in. The first time he'd slept there since leaving, he'd woken up in the middle of the night, sweating and shaking, thinking he'd heard his father crashing into furniture, home from a bender, ready to take his frustrations out on either Barry's face or his mother's body. And staying there reminded Barry that he'd come from nothing. Which may have been a sign of pride for some people, but not him. There was no glory, for him, in being poor. There was no innate positive quality in being on the low end of things. That was a myth some old American made to encourage the nobodies to hope they'd be somebodies. Well, he thought, sipping the Scotch in front of him, he'd always been a somebody, even if his original visits to the Bradford home had been to mow their lawn and clip their hedges. He'd definitely always been a somebody; he'd just been dropped at the wrong address when he was born.

Leo put down the pen and threw himself on the bed. He looked up at the lattice-like detailing along the edge of the closet door. He'd always wondered what the rooms at the New America Hotel were like. He'd eaten there with his parents, many summers ago, but having a summer home less than a mile away there'd never been any reason to stay there. But as a kid, sitting in the diner across the street, he liked to watch who was checking in and checking out and make up stories about them and their lives after they left Sag Harbor. Now he was one of those people. What was his story?

Let's see:

Twenty-three-year-old college dropout. No, Ivy League college dropout; does that sound a little classier? But not just any dropout. This dropout is the son of, some say, one of the richest and most successful black businessmen in the world. He's also the son of one of the most beautiful black women to pass the so-called paper bag test, that's how beautiful she is. This son, this one-time rising star, loves men. Which is not good when you're the son of those kinds of people. You can't advance the black race when you're busy sucking dick or fucking a rock star up the ass, no matter how much you love him, no matter how good a citizen you are. You still run into family friends on the street in Sag Harbor, and when you lean down to tickle their new baby, they pull the stroller away, tight polite smiles on their faces the entire time, like you might pass on your awful ways. You then go back to your hotel room and try to write the best Billy Joel profile the music world has ever seen because, like you wrote in the article that made your name, you still feel pretty much invisible.

In love, lonely, and invisible.

What a way to describe yourself. "Hi, I'm Leo and I'm in love, but I'm also lonely and I feel invisible."

Except when I'm making catty comments to a model—who probably didn't even get the cattiness—because I think she's probably fucking the person I used to love.

Used to love. Yes. I just want Joey to be happy. I'm in love with Pete now. Skinny, fun, Wild Man Pete, who would do anything for me, would stitch the Bradford family back together with guitar strings if he could.

Which gave him an idea. Leo went back to the desk and picked up the pen. He turned to a clean page in the legal pad and wrote: "The love he had for his father was a long-distance affair, even when they slept three doors away from each other in a million-dollar summer home that sat on a Long Island bay." As he sat back, admiring the sentence, wondering what he could do with it, the phone rang.

"Yo, boy."

"Barry?"

"Meet me in the lobby."

Leo found Barry standing at the front desk, chatting with the gangly teenaged guy working there, a heady gleam in his eye that Leo recognized from many years ago.

"You're drunk," Leo said.

"Not yet," Barry said. "Sammy here is gonna get us some beers from the kitchen."

Sammy said, "I told you, sir, the kitchen has been closed for hours. It's locked."

Barry pulled three twenties out of his pocket and slapped them on the counter. "Looka there, I think I just found the key."

Sammy took the bills, his eyes shifting around the room as if he were searching for a superior who might leap out of the shadows and catch him being bribed.

"We'll be outside," Barry said, pulling Leo out to the veranda.

After they sat, Leo said, "What's up, Barry?"

"You were an asshole to Joey today."

Leo stood up. "I'm going back upstairs."

Barry yanked him back down to the soft couch. "I know you think I'm some kind of tattletale, but I'm not."

The attendant brought them each a beer. He sat them on the table in front of the couch and headed back inside. Barry popped his beer open and said, "You are so much like your father, man. An asshole."

"He's a bastard," Leo said.

"No, *I'm* a bastard. He's an asshole, like you."

"You're an asshole, too."

"No, I'm a bastard," Barry drawled.

"Fuck it, what's the difference?"

"The difference," Barry explained, "is that assholes like to hurt people to get the upper hand. Bastards are just looking out for themselves."

"Yet, somehow," Leo said, "you're the one my father cherishes. And I'm the one who hasn't been home in two years."

"So that's it, isn't it?"

"What?"

"You're as jealous of me now as I was of you back in the day."

Leo laughed. "I'm not jealous, Barry. Of anybody."

"If you say so."

Neither of them said anything for a while. Barry sipped from his beer and stared up at the stars. Finally, Leo stood up.

"I'm going back upstairs," he said. "See ya."

When he got to the door, Barry said, "It was Edna."

Leo stopped. "What about Edna?"

"I think she told your father about you."

"She couldn't have done that without telling him about Joey, too."

Barry shrugged. "Maybe she did. Listen, I already told you what your father is. He's an asshole. But here's what your father isn't, Leo: homophobic. How could he be? He's worked in the cosmetics business for years. He may be ignorant about shit, but do I think he *hates* gay people? Fuck, no. Here's what your father is, other than an asshole: he's a father. You think he gives a *fuck* who *Joey* screws? Hell, no. That has no bearing on who he is or what he's done in his life. But you? His son? Of course, he's going to make a big deal out of that."

Leo just stood there, one leg in the hotel, the other one still on the veranda. "You know what this means, right?"

"What?"

"He *wanted* me to think you told him," Leo said. "What does that tell you?"

Barry finished his beer. He put the empty bottle on the table in front of him and stood up. He stretched his arms out wide over his head, yawning loudly. "It tells me what I already knew, Leo. Your father's an asshole. And I mean that as lovingly as I can."

13

"The *entire* year?" Leo said.

Duke nodded as he put his bag in the backseat of Leo's rental car. "I have to," he said. "I can't have her in the care of Marie and Mike. And I don't trust some hired-hand nurse to take care of her the way I could."

"How will the team feel about that?"

Duke shrugged. "I don't really care." He looked at his watch.

"Let's go, man. I don't wanna miss this plane. The sooner I get there, the sooner I can be back here."

Mrs. Maynard had shown positive signs overnight. Her doctor told Duke that she'd survive the heart attack, that the damage to her heart had not been as extensive as they first thought. But she'd need some physical therapy and a complete change in her eating habits and general lifestyle. After letting Mike peek in on their mother, his ashy face marked where tears had tracked down his cheeks, Duke took him back to their mother's house and gave him something to eat. Sitting there at the small, rickety kitchen table, watching his brother wolf down eggs and grits and bacon like he hadn't had a solid meal in weeks, Duke decided to stay. He made a call to a realtor, inquiring about a larger house in the Sag Harbor area. He called his agent and told him the news.

"The *entire* year?" Matt Lipson had exploded over the phone.

"See what you can do," Duke said. "Meet me in Virginia. I'll be there by four this afternoon." And he hung up. He wondered if he was doing the right thing. Right or not, he just knew that he didn't really have a choice.

As they pulled into the airport lot half an hour later, Duke said, "You don't have to wait with me, I know you got work to do."

Leo nodded. "Call me when you know when you'll be back."

"I will." Duke opened the door. Then he looked back at Leo. "Thank you for everything, bro. Will you look in on her one more time before you head back to the city?"

"Of course I will, man."

"Looks like we'll be seeing more of each other," Duke said.

"What about you and Amanda?"

"One thing at a time," he said. He hugged Leo and got out of the car.

———

Barry watched Gail sit down next to Anthony and feed him bacon from her plate. He almost dropped his own plate of quiche and sausage.

"Stop that," Carla said, sitting next to him on the couch.

"What?"

"Staring at her." She took a bite of toast. "Move on, fuck someone your own age."

"I would but you keep rebuffing me."

Carla shrugged. "Been there, done that."

"And I hear Reggie's back in the picture."

"He's gonna propose this week," Carla said, beaming.

"And you know this how?"

"I found the ring."

Joey squeezed himself between the two of them. "What ring?" he asked.

"Carla's soon-to-be first ex-husband is about to propose."

Joey congratulated Carla, then looked around the room. "I don't recall brunches being this boring at the Bradfords when we were kids."

Barry looked around at the haughty expressions on some of the guests. There *was* something stiff about the room that did seem different than other occasions. Then it hit him. "These are all the ladies who weren't invited to the fashion show yesterday."

Joey said, "Why weren't they?"

"Second tier," Carla said. "But they've all heard about it, so they're pissed. They're all trying to figure out when and how they became second tier."

"Too complicated for my blood," Joey said. "I just wanna make clothes."

"Joey, you can let that shit go," Carla said. "Right now." She had her hand on her hip and a stern look on her face.

Joey said, "Let what go?"

"That whole *Stella Dallas* outsider-looking-in shtick."

"She's right," Barry said. "How do you think I've gotten as far as I have?"

"Kissing ass and fucking the right women," Joey said.

"Well, other than that," Barry said.

As Joey packed his cartons and garment bags into Luis's van to go back to the city, he thought about Carla's words. The Outsider-Looking-In? A shtick? Was that how he'd been presenting himself? Or was that just Carla's typically blunt way of saying he wasn't an outsider anymore? He had felt that way at times, even as he grew closer to Leo and the guys, and got comfortable as part of the "family" and enjoyed his time living with Edna. Now being back around them, he did still feel as if he was just visiting, hanging out with the cool kids until they realized he really wasn't part of the in-crowd. But was Carla right? Was to time to "let that go"?

As Luis made a U-turn to get onto the main road, he said, "What you thinking about, papa?"

"Nothing," Joey said. He was fingering the envelope Barry had slipped him before he left the Bradfords' home. He opened it to find a basic agreement outlining his responsibilities as the designer for CoCo Cosmetics Fashions. "Nothing," he said again.

"So you're gonna be a star?"

"Excuse me?"

"Come on, papa, I heard those models talking when I drove them back last night. All they were talking about was how you're about to be some big fashion star."

"Model talk," Joey said. He turned toward the window, so Luis couldn't see the big smile plastered on his face. "You know how women can be."

"Guess you'll be leaving the neighborhood now, *sí*?"

Joey didn't say anything. He just put his head back on the seat and forced himself to fall asleep. He needed to dream some more.

Three hours later, Luis was poking his shoulder. "Back in Queens," he said.

Joey jumped out of the van and went to unlock the apartment door while Luis opened the rear door of the van to start unloading the boxes. As he pushed the key into the lock he heard a scream.

From inside the apartment.

He shoved open the door and rushed in. Blood. There was blood on the floor near the dining room table. "Greta?" No response. He headed toward the back of the apartment, toward the bedroom and studio. He checked the bedroom first. It was empty. As he turned to go to the studio, he heard the scream again. It sounded like Greta.

He called her name again but the only response he got was a smash and a grunt, like someone had fallen to the floor. Blood covered the floor, leading from the bathroom to the studio. He slipped down in the puddle, covering his hands in it.

He pushed the studio door open and there was Greta, lying against the wall, holding her stomach. Standing over her was a medium-sized guy, his arm raised as if to hit her. Joey noticed that the back of the man's clothes was covered in blood and a short length of rope dangled from the wrist of his raised arm.

Joey said, "Greta?" As he crossed the room, the guy turned to look at him.

"Thank God," the guy said. "Help me, please."

"No!" Greta screamed. "He's gonna kill me, Joey. He's gonna kill me!"

A long look of confusion covered the guy's face and he yelled as Joey rushed him, shoving him against the wall, knocking over cans of paint and piles of plywood. The guy was strong. As Joey hit him across the face and chest, he pushed back on Joey, and they both fell to the floor. Joey managed to crawl over to Greta. But before he could reach her, the guy was up again, grabbing Joey, spinning him around to face him.

"Please," he said again. "Help me, please!"

Joey lost his balance, and almost slipped, but he didn't fall. He grabbed the lapels of the guy's blood-splattered jacket and swung him around, finally shoving him back. As the guy flew backward, his head hit the edge of Greta's file cabinet. Then he fell forward and there was more blood, spurting from the wound in his scalp where his head had collided with the cabinet's burnished metal. He lay there, his fingers spread, as if they were reaching for Joey's ankles.

"Yo!" Joey turned to see Luis standing in the doorway. "Papa? *Qué pasa?*"

Joey turned to Greta, still shuddering and huddled against the far wall. Joey went to her and kneeled down. "Who was this guy? Greta?"

Luis said, "He broke in?"

Before Joey could say anything, there was a commotion in the front room and suddenly Luis was shoved aside by three uniformed cops, pushing their way into the studio, all of them armed. "Put your hands up," one of them shouted at Joey.

"This is my house," Joey said. "He attacked my girl—"

Another cop boomed, "He said, put your hands where we can see them!"

Joey stood slowly, his arms raised, his eyes still on Greta.

The third cop was kneeling over the guy in the jacket, two fingers on his neck. "He's dead," he said. "Looks like the guy, too."

"He must have broken in," Joey started. "I just got back and I found him—"

"Be quiet," shouted one of the cops. To the other cop on the floor, he said, "You sure that's the guy?"

"Fits the descrip," he said, standing up.

The third cop, a tall burly guy, walked toward Joey, taking his cuffs from his belt. He grabbed Joey's arms and swung them down, slapping the cuffs on each wrist. "You're under arrest for kidnapping and murder."

Joey said, "What? Wait, I live here, who is this dude? I just walked in and—"

The sound of the steel cuffs encasing his wrists resounded in Joey's ears. And in the commotion of it all he thought he saw a hint of a smile on Greta's face.

14

"What else do you remember?"

The tiny room was still spinning. And it smelled of piss and stale coffee. Joey lifted his head from the table and tried to focus his eyes on the older guy sitting in front of him. His arm still hurt from the beating he took from the three cops; his eye was swollen where one of them had smacked him. He couldn't even remember the attorney's name, as full as his head was of so many things, including the up-close and coffee-breathed questioning he'd gotten from two detectives just an hour before. Fifteen hours ago he'd been eating brunch in Sag Harbor. Now here he was sitting in a holding pen with a lawyer, trying to explain that he had nothing to do with any kidnapping.

"It all happened so fast," Joey said. "Like I told you."

"You'd never seen this man before?"

"No," Joey moaned. In his own ears, his voice sounded like a whine. He didn't even feel like talking anymore. But he asked, "Where's Greta?"

"We'll talk about Greta in a sec, Joey. Please just think, was there anything else?"

Something had been ringing in Joey's mind since he'd been brought into the precinct. Something the guy had said when he first burst into the studio and saw Greta hunched against the wall. Hadn't he said, "Thank God"? Hadn't he said, "Help me, please"? Why had he said that? Help him? From what?

"You sure that was it? 'Help me'?"

"It was like he thought I'd broken into the apartment to rescue him or something." Joey sat forward in the chair. "Wait a second, you don't think Greta really kidnapped that dude, do you?"

The attorney didn't say anything, just scribbled some notes on the fresh yellow legal pad in front of him. "Then you fought," he said. "And you pushed him against the file cabinet."

Joey nodded again. "You'll be able to work all this out, right?"

Again, the attorney didn't respond, just wrote something down.

"Say something," Joey yelled at him.

Finally he put the pen down and looked at Joey. "Seems a guy went missing two days ago. He fit the exact description of the guy you fought in your apartment."

"And they think Greta and I abducted him? I was in Long Island the entire weekend. There were witnesses."

"I know." The attorney nodded. "Ms. Randall told me." He looked at Joey hard then, like he was demanding something he really didn't want to ask for. "But your girlfriend, Greta, she wasn't with you?"

Joey shook his head. "She had work to do on a new piece. She stayed in Queens."

"Did you talk to her while you were in Long Island?"

"No." He thought. "The guy had rope around his wrists," Joey said. "Maybe he escaped wherever he was and broke into the apartment." *But the door had been locked when I got there,* he thought.

The attorney started to gather his things. "I'll be in touch, Mr. Ramirez. Don't talk to anyone without me being here." He shook Joey's hand and left the room.

When the door closed behind him, Joey felt like the earth had stopped turning and thrown his body into space. There was a question in his mind that he didn't want to think.

What had Greta done?

But there was something else he couldn't get out of his head. Something one of the detectives said to him, tauntingly, accusingly, that still rang in his ears.

"So we hear you're some kind of fancy designer now. But you're back in the system again, huh? Right where you were supposed to be. Must feel good to be back home, huh, Mr. Ramirez?"

15

"It really is her story against yours, Joseph," said his attorney, Henry Thompson. "She admits to luring the guy into your home and keeping him there. She says she thought he was homeless—that you and she often brought homeless men into your apartment for, um, sexual purposes—" He stopped and looked down at the paper in front him. "You and she did this all the time, according to her."

"That's not true," Joey said. "Doesn't it sound ridiculous to you?"

Thompson cleared his throat. "She says you called her from Long Island, that you knew the guy was there, and you killed him because you thought he'd get away and tell people what happened. That you were concerned about the effect it would have on your fashion career." He closed the folder with a brusque finality that made Joey's heart sink.

"It's all bullshit," Joey whispered. "Why would she say that? She's completely changed her story. Doesn't that count for anything?"

"Well, when you told me she'd been acting erratic, insulting you and all that, I checked into her background, her manic-depression—"

Joey looked up. "What? She was, I don't know, excitable, moody. But she wasn't taking any medication that I knew of."

"You're right. She wasn't."

"Then doesn't that help you prove that she's making up this story?"

"You still killed the guy, Joseph. The prosecutor's going for felony murder."

"It was self-defense," he yelled. "I told you. I wasn't even there!"

"I believe you. But the cops don't believe it. A jury might, but—"

"They might not," said Joey. "Black girl and Dominican dude have some old white guy in their apartment and he ends up dead. Yeah, right."

"Are you saying you want me to make a deal?"

"I'm saying it was self-defense."

"I'll ask you one more time . . ."

Joey sighed. He felt trapped. "How much time would it be?"

The attorney cleared his throat. "Fifteen to twenty. Parole in ten."

Riker's Island. An island, sure, a piece of land distinct from the mainland, but definitely no fucking paradise.

Joey lay on his cot, waiting, straining his brain to replay the last year and a half of his life, the relationship he'd shared with Greta. Manic-depressive, Henry Thompson had said. Joey could remember dark periods around the apartment, when Greta would hide in her studio, the lights off, candles burning, down-tempo symphonic music turned low on the stereo. Then suddenly, there'd be weeks of loud highs, rock concerts and nightclubs and brash installation ideas coursing from her brain to her lips, long antic conversations about life and love and art and community. He'd taken her behavior to be just an artistic temperament, something to be managed but appreciated, if they were going to be together. But he had to admit that things had turned predominantly dark of late. After Joey began to take his designing seriously, hadn't she gotten moodier, more critical, less supportive? She had, and he didn't exactly know why, except to assume that she'd been jealous, of his new success, of Carla. And the lies, about money and work; her father's confirmation that she hadn't actually been selling her work to Europe, but taking money from him to pay bills and eat.

But would she really make up some story as dramatic as this one? And if she would, why would she do it?

"You got a phone call." Joey looked up. A tall, mean-looking officer was at his door. "You Ramirez, right? Your attorney's calling for you."

"The deal's in place," Thompson said when Joey picked up the receiver.

"What about Greta?" he asked. "She take a deal?"

"She did," said Thompson. "She'll be spending the next five to ten in a special care facility."

"And me?"

"You're going upstate, Joseph. I got them down to manslaughter. Six to twelve."

At this point the years or the place didn't mean anything. "Can I see anyone before they send me up there?"

"I'll get back to you on that."

When Joey was summoned to the visitors' area two days later, his attorney was on the other side of the glass wall, holding the telephone receiver in his hand.

He said, "Not who you expected, I guess."

"Hey," Joey said.

"Carla said she will come see you upstate."

"Tell her she doesn't have to," Joey said into the phone. "I'd rather she didn't."

The attorney just nodded.

"Did you get in touch with him?"

"Leo Bradford's out of the country. Apparently he left town a few hours after he got back from Long Island."

"Does he even know I'm in here?"

Henry Thompson shook his head. "I really do not know. I left messages at his home. But I never heard back."

"Thanks," Joey said. "Thanks for everything." He stood up to go.

Thompson banged on the glass. "Joseph! Come back, Mr. Ramirez. We're not done yet, there's some more things we need to discuss."

But Joey wasn't listening; his eyes were fixed on the big-bellied officer keying open the door that led back to the cells. There wasn't anything that anyone had to say that he wanted to listen to. He stepped through the door and started back to his cell. He felt like he was dying.

16

"Happy New Year!"

Leo hugged Pete, almost knocking the bottle of Krug champagne out of his hand and over the balcony of the suite they had at London's Dorchester Hotel.

Inside, the party was loud and boisterous, packed full of the music industry elite, artists and executives, movie stars, and hanger-on types, sipping champagne and air-kissing and loving the reflections of fabulousness they found in each other's eyes. In the middle of the room, Wild Man drummer Neil Ferguson was slow dancing to the hard beats of Janet Jackson's "Rhythm Nation" with his fiancée, a rail-thin British supermodel with hair down to her ass. As Leo and Pete headed inside, out of the chilly English air, they were assaulted by Sally, begging Pete to take a picture with one of the Bangles and a guy from Fine Young Cannibals. Pete dragged Leo with him, smiling for the photographer, chatting up the Bangle like they were old, long-lost friends. After the schmooze, he dragged Leo through the crowd toward the door.

Out in the hallway, Pete grabbed Leo in a hug and kissed him full on the lips. Leo went with it for a few long seconds, then pulled back, looking both ways.

"Hey," he said. "What is that for?"

"For you being you."

"Okay."

"And because there's something I need to tell you."

Pete pulled him down, until they were sitting on the plush, carpeted floor of the hall, their backs against the door vibrating with bass. "I'm really glad you've agreed to stay here in London with me while we record this album."

"I know you are," Leo said, his eyes narrowing with suspicion. "Wait a minute, don't tell me you're trying to go back to the States, already. We just got here."

Pete laughed. "No, just the opposite."

Leo stared at him for a full minute. "Are you serious? You want to stay here?"

Pete nodded excitedly, his long dark hair flopping in his eyes. "I wanna be based here. Full-time. We're gonna be touring less, but I'm not feeling the States right now." He held up his hand. "Think about it. I'm not trying to rush you. Just think about it. Though there is one thing I want to add."

"That is?"

"I wanna come out."

Now Leo shook his head. "Don't do that for me, Pete. Or to get me to stay in London with you."

"I'm doing it because I love you and I want the world to know it and—"

"You know what can happen, right?"

Pete pulled his legs up and wrapped his arms around them. "What? We'll lose our audience? Stop selling records? Sell out fewer venues? That's all money shit, Leo. How much more money can I make?"

Leo leaned his head back against the door. "You sure you wanna do this?"

"I'm in this with you for the long run, Leo Bradford. Don't you feel the same?"

Leo turned to face him. He had to smile. He did feel the same.

But he'd forced himself to stop thinking about the day when they wouldn't have to sneak around and hide their kisses and affection from everyone but the members of the band. The band . . . "What do the guys think of this?"

"They support me," Pete said. "They support us."

"Let's go inside," Leo said, standing up.

"You need to think about it?"

"I have thought about it," Leo said.

"So?"

"Can we get tickets to Wimbledon this June?"

Eunice Maynard took a small sip of champagne and looked around at the huge, burnished expanse of the kitchen of her new home, and the elegant dining room table just off the kitchen, where Marie and her boyfriend, Hassan, were kissing in the New Year.

Duke felt his heart expand at the sight of his mother, healthy and happy. Especially when he thought of how resistant she'd been to just about everything. Starting with his decision to take the year off. "You're an athlete," she'd said, still weak and tired in her hospital bed. "Those folks ain't gonna let you leave to take care of me."

"They'll have to," he told her, and added firmly that they weren't going to talk about it anymore, the decision had been made.

"You know this doesn't mean we aren't getting out there and walking a mile tomorrow. I'm gonna have you running by March."

"Slow it down, Daniel. Don't start with me." She stood up and wrapped her arms around him, arms that had felt thin and weak five months ago but were now stronger, firmer, eager to embrace more than just her son at the holidays.

Now, Duke took the champagne flute from her and put it on the counter. He moved to help her up from the chair but she waved him away, pulling herself to a strong standing position and heading toward the dining room. As he watched her shuffle along, he had to smile, and he could hear the voices of everyone in his head: "An *entire* year?"

Now the year was almost over and he didn't want it to end. He wished it could be longer.

The ringing phone yanked Duke right out of his sleep. At first he just stared at the ringing instrument, curious: this might have been, at best, the fourth time it had rung since they'd moved into this new house. He'd had his own line installed and given the digits to three people: his agent, Leo, and Rocky, his good friend from the team. Leo was somewhere in Europe; his agent wouldn't be calling at four in the morning; and Rocky should fucking know better. Finally he reached for the receiver and said "hello."

"Duke? I'm sorry if I woke you up, but I wanted to hear your voice."

For a second, Duke felt as if he'd lost his mind, as if his heart was hearing something his ears didn't believe.

"Duke? Can you hear me? It's me—"

"Amanda?"

17

The ringing of the wake-up call smashed into Leo's brain like a hammer. He reached out, grabbed the phone, and slammed it down into the cradle again, not even listening to the cheery wake-up message delivered in those clipped English tones he usually loved to hear. He sat up slowly, so as not to rattle the remains of what he figured must be his brains, and looked around the room. The rich damask curtains were drawn against the sunlight, but even the sliver of light that managed to creep in through the edges felt like daggers to his eyes. Leo knew this feeling: too much champagne in too few hours.

Eyes closed, he felt around the bed. No Pete. Where the heck was he? He sat still, listening for bathroom noises, a shower or razor or something, but there was only silence. He swung his legs over the edge of the bed and tried to stand up, which was much easier than he expected. He made his way to the bathroom. Empty. What the fuck?

He went out into the living room area, expecting to find the usual hungover sleeping remains of Wild Men parties, but the room was spotless.

Back in the bedroom, he suddenly felt hungry, starving, like he hadn't eaten in days, which he recognized as his usual post-jet-lagged state. He ordered room service, told them to bring it into the suite, and dragged himself to the shower. Which is where he found, hanging from the nozzle, a note from Pete.

"Sorry, luv (see I'm even using English-isms! We're bloody meant to be here, no?). Anyway, I had to shoot up north to Birmingham for an interview and radio thing. Forgot to tell ya about it last night. Just chill out, will be back by dinner time. Wait for me? Ta-ta (ha-ha). Love ya, Pete . . ."

An hour later, bathed and fed and feeling a bit more like his himself, Leo decided to head out and explore London. He hadn't been there since he was a kid, with his parents, and the excitement of cavorting around the old city filled him with an energy he hadn't felt in a long time. Perhaps Pete was right, this would be a good new start for both of them. Leaving the old shit behind in the US of A, and starting fresh, almost from scratch, as the band recorded with a new producer in a new city, and he got to write, read, and think.

First he intended to hit the streets around the hotel, the lovely well-manicured grounds around Primrose Hill. But when he stepped out of the elevator, a bellman caught sight of him and pointed him toward the tall, shiny desk of the concierge. The proper-looking gentleman gave Leo a folded sheet of paper and didn't say a word, just smiled, bowed slightly, and went back to his work.

Outside, in front of the hotel, Leo opened the note. It was from Sally. "Leo, come meet me for coffee (I HATE TEA!!!). I stayed in London, didn't go to Birm with the guys. I'll be waiting for you at Roast Harvest in Piccadilly Circus. Take the red line to the Piccadilly stop and walk north a block. You can't miss it. . . ."

He could do worse than coffee with Sally, he figured, so Leo walked over to the tube station and crowded in to go to Piccadilly. When he got there, he found the coffeehouse easily. He sat down in a window booth and waited, as one usually did for Sally, for the chic little publicist to make her appearance.

Twenty minutes later, Leo decided he *could* do worse than waste all afternoon waiting for Sally to make a fashionably late grand entrance. He went to the counter and asked if he could leave a message for someone.

"Are you Leo?" the guy asked him. "Sally said to tell you she's at Lilly's Café on Goff Lane near Westminster Abbey. You should take the green line to the Abbey stop and it's right outside the Underground. You can't miss it."

Leo thanked the guy and headed out. He looked at the gloomy London sky and felt glad that the day was just cold and not rainy *and* cold, or else he'd be heading right back to the hotel and seeing Sally another time. It didn't take long to change trains at Victoria Station and make it to Westminster Abbey. Outside the station, he stared up at the famed Abbey and asked a skinheaded girl with a ring in her nose and chain leading from the ring to a loop of her jacket belt where he could find Lilly's Café.

Inside the café, crowded with afternoon shoppers and sight-seers, Leo found a small table in the back when he couldn't find Sally anywhere inside. He opened the *Guardian* he'd bought earlier outside the hotel and read all the articles in the music section. He noticed that Johnny Marr was playing a post-Smiths concert in Brixton and made a mental note to tell Sally to get them tickets for the show.

Half an hour later, still no Sally. The day was wasting away. He gathered his stuff to go. Standing at the counter to pay for his tea, he felt a tug at his sleeve. He turned to see a short but solidly built guy standing there, waiting to pay his bill as well. He was a good-looking guy, his hair a helmet of short, spiky dreadlocks.

"Hey, mon." Thick Jamaican accent. "You're Leo, right?"

Leo said, "I know you, don't I?"

"I'm Teddy," the guy said. "I played some keys on the last Wild Men CD. We met in Mustique." He offered his hand. Leo shook it. "Nice party last night, mon."

They walked outside. Leo explained that he was supposed to meet a friend.

"Come to Bayswater," Teddy said. "I have some tapes I wanted to give Pete, and you can see a nice part of London. I mean, since your day seems pretty much shot."

By the time he and Teddy had gotten off the tube in Bayswater, Leo felt like a real Londoner, jostled as he'd been, pushing his way on and off the train like an expert. Seeing Bayswater, however, was like coming home. They had only had to travel ten minutes from downtown to get to this place with rolling lawns and quiet little lanes. He followed Teddy around a long meadow where a group of scruffy-looking kids kicked a dirty soccer ball around. Then they turned into a little lane off the high street bordered by the meadow and stopped in front of a town house with blue shutters on the windows. Teddy said, "Here we are."

Leo said, "You live here?"

"No, mon," said Teddy with a grin. "You do."

And right then, the door opened and Pete looked out, laughing like a madman.

Leo said, "What the fuck?" He climbed the steep steps and stepped into the foyer. Pete hugged him, still laughing.

"Sorry, bro," he managed to get out. "It was the only way."

Leo followed him into the main room and lying there on a smooth leather couch, her feet up, with a mug of coffee in her hands, was Sally. "Wild goose chase, huh?"

"I hate you," Leo said. "Bitch." He leaned down to kiss her.

"Stay away from my woman," Teddy said, and leaped on top of Sally, almost spilling her coffee. He smothered her with kisses as she squealed with delight.

Leo left them to their passion and followed Pete on the grand tour of their new home. "I closed on it yesterday before the party," Pete said. "I so wanted to tell you about it last night, but I couldn't. I needed you to just see it. And see where it was."

Leo said, "I love it."

"I figured it's the closest you could get to Sag Harbor and still be here," Pete said.

They had their things sent over from the hotel and had their first dinner in their new house—take-out curry, served on paper plates, with cans of Coke. But it was the best dinner Leo had eaten in a long time. He didn't even wonder what his mother had cooked for New Year's dinner.

18

"Something tells me," Barry Chambers said, "that these have just been two years that we'll look back on and think, wow, did we really deal with all that shit?"

He was sitting with Duke at a table in the back of the Shark Bar, a hip New York soul food hangout for the young, gifted, and black. Their plates were piled high with the bones of the spare ribs they'd enjoyed with creamy macaroni and cheese, tangy collard greens, and slices of corn bread.

"I hang with you one night and I'm completely off my game," Duke said, watching the plates as the waitress came over to take them away.

"What else is new," said Barry. "Remember when this was how it used to be? Just you and me, man. Chilling."

Duke nodded. "Yeah, I remember those days, bro. You stealing girls from me."

"I was young and dumb and full of—"

"Yourself."

"Well, yeah, that too, I guess." Barry gave him a goofy grin that Duke thought might have been sincere. "You forgive me, doncha, man?"

The waitress brought their coffees, decaf for Duke.

When she was gone, Duke said, "You gave Amanda my number in Long Island?"

Barry nodded.

"How did *you* get it?"

"I have my ways. Especially since you didn't deem me worthy of it."

"You certainly didn't get it from Leo."

"I haven't spoken to him since that weekend."

"That weekend," Duke said. "Have you been up there to see Joey?"

"Not yet."

"Me neither. I've been so busy with Ma. He was gonna go far, wasn't he?"

"I was hoping he was gonna take my company far with his fashions."

Duke laughed. "Since when is CoCo *your* company?"

"You know what I mean."

"What about law school?"

"September," said Barry. "I love CoCo and Gary but I'm still going to school. What about you? You going back to the NFL?"

"Next year." He sipped his coffee. "I wanna make sure my moms is straight."

Barry said, "Here comes my girl."

Duke turned to look, as did everyone else in the restaurant, as the tall, voluptuous woman made her way down the aisle, her heart-shaped, high-cheekboned face, piercing green eyes, and swiveling runway-ready hips selling sex as vividly as a neon-bright ad in the middle of Times Square. She kissed Barry and smiled her bright smile at Duke.

"Have we met before?" she said to Duke.

Duke shook his head. "I'd have remembered meeting you. I'm Duke."

"You have met," Barry said. He sipped his coffee. "That week-end, actually."

"I'm Cheyenne," the woman said. "Pleased to meet you, Duke."

"Cheyenne," said Barry with a proud grin, "is the new face of CoCo Cosmetics."

19

12 APRIL 1990

Dear Joey

I hope this letter finds you well, considering. I've been wanting to write for the longest time, but, in all honesty, I didn't really know what to say. I was very sorry to hear about things. I was even sorrier not to be in New York when everything went down. I got your message from your lawyer long after I'd heard from my mother and Carla what had happened. I'm sorry that our last interaction had to be my catty comments to your friend Cheyenne in Sag Harbor.

As you can see, Pete and I are living in London now, full-time. The springtime weather is getting better here now (it's getting slightly less rainy, but only just). We live in a nice area of London. Pete says he bought the place because it reminds him of Sag Harbor, which, he knows, is probably my favorite place in the world. When I think about it, other than my bit of time at Yale, that's the place where I was last happy. As much as I hated some of the stuff my father did and as much as I hated being fat and as much as I hated so many things, it was still a happy place.

Do you keep in touch with the guys? Duke is in NY, out in Sag taking care of his mother. Barry is a captain of industry, I guess, learning everything he can from my father. Duke says they spent some of the New Year together. He also saw his ex, Amanda, you remember her, right? It looks like they might try again, but I don't know. Duke seems like he's moved on. Then again, do you ever forget your first love?

Well, you have my address if you'd like to write me. I hope you do. It would be great to hear from you and know that you're taking care of yourself. My mother sends her love as well. Pete says to tell you "hello." Be well. Best to you. Leo.

May 1st, 1990

Dear Leo,

Thanks so much for your letter. Yes, all things considered, I am doing OK. But it's still hard. It is JAIL!!! But you take the good with the bad which has always been the way that I have handled things. Please excuse my bad writing. That's your thing, and I've never been perfect at it. So if there are commas in the wrong place or something, forgive me. Life is crazy isn't it? If anyone had told me that I would be here I would have killed them. Bad joke I guess, but you know what I mean, right? This wasn't my plan, but I guess it isn't really about what your plans are, but instead what the larger plan is for you, cosmically or something. I never used to read horoscopes, but I do now. And when it's a good horoscope I try to make it a good day here. I try. There's a bunch I want to say to you, a bunch that I wanted to say to you before I came in here but I tell myself that I will survive this and that those important things I want to share with you I will be able to do face to face. If I think any other way, it will be defeatist, as a guy here calls guys who come here and give up. I REFUSE TO BE DEFEATIST!!!. How's that for positive energy, bro????

Anyway, be well yourself. Give my love to your mom. Carla came to see me just like she said she would. I didn't go out to see her the first time, but you know what? That crazy cousin of yours came BACK! And that time I went out to see her. She brought copies of Vogue *magazine to show me. Crazy, crazy Carla. It sounds like you and Pete have a great life together and I wish you the best with that. If I know you—and I do—I know that you probably still get depressed about things that you have absolutely no control over. Don't do that. That is my word to you: Be happy. And if you don't feel happy, go out into that place there like Sag Harbor and force yourself to find something happy to think about. OK? Do that for me, Leo the Lion. I miss you and will always be your*

JOEY

12 JUNE 1990

Hey Joey—

Sorry for the delay in writing you. The Wild Men are recording their new album and I've been writing more lyrics than ever before. They've already recorded close to thirty songs and they're thinking of doing a double CD. Of course the record company says no, but what the hell, ya gotta stretch your wings sometimes, right?

Thank you so much for your words about finding happiness. You remind me of Pete in that way. So much shit comes down on him as the leader of the group, from the label, from the fans, from critics, from his folks etc, but he's always smiling, always working hard to keep real happy, positive energy in his life. I'm sure he'll live to be a hundred years old and he'll still be going to rock concerts trying to dance with the young people.

Glad to hear Carla's coming to visit you. Did she tell you she and her husband were here in Europe and came through London? They stayed with us. I still hate Reggie, though he's grown up a bit and isn't just a pretty, bourgie boy now. Well not all the time at least (smile). Carla's trying to find a life after being the CoCo girl for so long, but she'll survive, she always does, and since her father left her all that money, I'm sure she'll find something to keep her happy, even if it's just traveling around the world.

Sorry this is short but I should sign off . . . I'm actually writing this as we're about to board a plane to Brazil for a concert there. Let's stay in touch OK?

Sending love and good wishes to you, Leo (the Lion).

PS—I've included some of the lyrics I wrote for the new CD. (One of them might remind you of something from years ago. I also included a few interviews and articles I've done for a few British magazines here . . .)

PPS—You know one of the Wild Men went to prep school with Greta, right? He says she wasn't always the most easy-going girl . . . Just thought I'd tell you . . .

JUNE 20, 1990

Dear Leo—

You actually named a song "Cheyenne?" That's crazy. Like that day was crazy when we saw you and Duke at the Crab Hut. We were both pretty mean to each other. I don't know what Cheyenne is up to these days. We lost touch after everything went down. Hey, check this out: I met this guy here who knew my father. I had seen him staring at me for a long time and finally he comes up to me and goes, I think I know you. I told him I don't think so and he asks me if my name is Ramirez and says if it is I must be Jose's boy. Isn't that strange? He's an older guy, says he used to do break-ins with my father back in the day. Funny because I didn't think I looked all that much like my father. Maybe I didn't want to look much like him. But we have no control over that kind of stuff, right? Anyway, this guy, his name is Posada, he says my father was this great guy who was very loyal to his friends and all this other junk. How once the cops caught my father after they had ripped off this old lady and my father refused to give up the other guys. I tried to look all impressed but I don't think he bought it. I think he just gets off on me being here and listening to his old stories. He says he has stories to tell me about my mother as well. But I told him I don't want to hear them. Not yet at least, and it's not like I'm goin anywhere, you know?

So, you were getting on a plane to Brazil? How was it? Lotta sexy people I can imagine. Did you go anywhere else interesting? Tell me everything, every smell you smelled and food you ate and flower you plucked (smile). The details give me stuff to think about when the lights go off here.

Guess what? Greta's been trying to get in touch with me. But I don't take her calls or open her letters. I just send them back. What do you think she can possibly say to me now? Some people are very strange, right? Wasn't that the name of a rock song you liked?

Write back bro. Missing you.

JOEY

PS—thanks for the heads-up about Greta. I wish I'd have known that before!

20

That August, Duke left Sag Harbor and returned to the Redskins and the hardest training camp he'd ever experienced. He'd tried to be good and stay in shape during his year away, running and lifting, eating healthily, getting to bed early. But if he was honest with himself he had to admit that those "good" days were only when he was with his mother out in the summer house, not when he was hanging out in Manhattan, rekindling his friendship with Barry, which meant late nights at the Shark Bar and private parties in supermodels' apartments and rap concerts and anything else Barry could find for two young men on the loose in Manhattan to get into. Duke liked being a fly on the wall as he watched Barry schmooze and socialize, climbing the CoCo ladder with an ambition and deftness he didn't know even Barry was capable of. And it was weird to watch Barry as he dated Cheyenne and still cheated on her with other girls. It was like watching a master playboy at work and play.

As Duke stopped to catch his breath during the second of his two-a-day practice sessions, he had to laugh as he remembered waking up on Barry's couch to answer the door for one girl as Barry scrambled to get Cheyenne into the shower to avoid a confrontation. If anything, Duke was happy to be back in the rough-and-tumble world of the NFL. As hard as it was to get back in two-a-day mode, this was nothing compared to the high-priced, out-all-night emotional roller coaster of reckless bachelorhood that Barry was living in New York. A few months of hanging with Barry had taught him that much.

He went over to the table where tiny cups of Gatorade were lined up like soldiers.

"Nothing left in ya, Maynard?"

He turned to see Solomon Greenbridge standing near the table, his big brown body supported on a pair of crutches. It was good to see the veteran back from the injury he'd sustained the previous year. Solomon had looked out for him his rookie year, answering questions, helping him learn plays. He'd even had advice about the Amanda situation. He'd been in Duke's position, but in reverse: the black athlete with the white fiancée and all the family strife it could cause. Only he'd ended up married to Sheila, now going on twelve years. Duke asked about the wife and kids and Solomon gave him a big, relieved smile.

"I love 'em to death," he said, "but how Sheila deals with them 24/7, I'll never know. She's a saint. I'm much happier to be back around you knuckleheads." Solomon asked about Duke's mother. "That was great what you did, bro. For your mom."

"Coach doesn't think so," Duke said, swallowing a second cup of Gatorade.

"He'll get over it when you get out there scoring on suckers," Solomon laughed. "No one's worried about you." He paused. "But your brother . . . They're watching him. Which means they're gonna be watching you too, bro."

"I'm sure I'm not the only dude in the league with an ex-junkie for a brother," Duke said. After he said it, he wished he'd tempered some of the edge. He knew that Solomon was a good guy, that he was only trying to look out.

"That might be true, man, but you might be the only one who

brought one to camp with you as your assistant," Solomon said. "I'm just saying, bro, be careful. Just remember eyes are on you, that's all I'm trying to tell you." With that, he turned and hobbled away toward the clubhouse.

Coach shouted for Duke to get back to the field. He crushed the cup in his hand and jogged out to meet the rest of his team-mates.

Barry thanked them with the speech he'd rehearsed all night, con-gratulating the company on its new initiatives and for welcoming him with such open arms. *And open legs,* he thought, looking over at Gail Oliver, who refused to meet his gaze. She'd been cold to him ever since he'd cut her off, even colder when she saw Barry kissing on Cheyenne one night at Time Café. But what could she do? Especially considering that she was pregnant now. *And,* Barry thought, looking at the firm protuberance lifting the maternity smock she was wearing, *forever attached to the boring man she married.* He wanted to tell her that he hoped the baby wouldn't bore her as much as her husband did.

But now he was leaving CoCo, so what did he care?

Vernon Franklin shuffled over and shook Barry's hand, forcing himself to congratulate Barry through gritted teeth. Barry wanted to tell him to enjoy the next three years as much as he could be-cause he was coming back to take his job. He just smiled and nod-ded thanks to Vernon, who was stepping back as Gary came up to Barry.

"You did a great job for us, Barry," he said. "Even if you were about to hand over our new division to a convict."

"I still believe Joey was set up, Gary."

"You do."

"You allowed him into your house at one time," Barry said. He couldn't resist adding, "And I know you consider yourself an excellent judge of character."

"You do remember how we met Joey, don't you? Helping to kidnap Carla—"

"But ended up helping her," Barry interjected. He sipped back the last of his champagne and looked directly at Gary. He'd had his fill of Gary Bradford, even if the man had done so much for him. He knew that if he did ever come back to CoCo, there would be many changes made. And he wanted Gary to know it as well. "Listen, Gary. I've always been curious about something."

"What's that?"

"How did you find out that Leo was gay?"

Gary hesitated. "Why do you want to know?"

"Leo always thought I told you about him."

"That's none of your business, is it?"

"Come on, Gary. You've seen my ass fucking on video. I'm sure you can share a secret with me. It was Edna, right? She caught Joey and Leo and told you, right?"

Gary just looked at him. And Barry knew he was right. "Like I said, just curious."

"Is that another letter to Joey?"

Leo looked up to find Pete standing over him, munching on an apple. He had on his long suede jacket with the frayed collar. His travel-coat, he called it; he wore it whenever the band was traveling to play a one-off gig. It brought him luck, he said.

"I haven't written in a while," Leo said. "Carla said he's been asking about me."

"I think he's still in love with you," said Pete. He tossed the apple core into the wastebasket near the back door that led to the garden outside. "Two points!"

"Joey is not in love with me," Leo said, "if he ever was."

"Well, he'll never love you as much as I do." Pete wrapped his arms around Leo's shoulders and ran his stubbly cheek against Leo's. "And that's a fact."

Leo could only smile. He still couldn't believe how great life was in London now that the band had taken a few years off from touring. They recorded right in the house now, too, so there were no more late nights crammed into recording studios filled with weed smoke and groupies and the ghosts of rock stars past. He and Pete still worked on songs together but still made time to hit the theaters in the West End or just chill in the park in Hampstead Heath, wasting time doing nothing but being together. Pete had rediscovered his love of African art and spent hours digging through old antiques stores in Charing Cross Road, looking for pieces he could send to Lillian, who'd visited twice already and was preparing for another visit to coincide with the band's return from Rome in two days. Even writing to Joey was a positive thing. Leo hated that Joey was in jail but there was something oddly upbeat about most of his letters, which rubbed right off on Leo. He'd even written a song called "The Ballad of Joey," which Pete said reminded him of something Dylan might write.

Pete said, "I'm sad you're not coming to Italy with us, baby."

"Between my mother coming and finishing this article for *Spin*—" Leo started.

Pete held up his hands. "I know. It must be *so* hard being just a hanger-on to a big, important rock band these days." He kissed Leo again, then grabbed his bag from the counter. "Gotta get in the limo, it's been waiting for an hour already."

"Must be *so* hard to be a rock star and make limos wait for you," Leo said.

"If the limo driver has a man at home like I have, he'll understand."

Leo walked him to the door. Pete kissed him in full view of the street. "Bye, babe," he said. "You think Lillian's gonna be cool with the press conference?"

"She'll have to be," Leo said. "Not every day a rock star comes out of the closet."

"It should be," Pete said, "as many gay ones as there are." He ran down the steps and jumped into the limo. He stuck his skinny torso through the sunroof as the driver maneuvered the car out of their tiny lane. "Call you soon as we land," he shouted, and blew Leo a kiss. Leo turned to go inside. "Hey! You didn't catch it, man." Leo turned back and caught the kiss with his fist. He put it to his lips and waved goodbye.

Inside, he put on the advance cassette of the new R.E.M. record they'd gotten from Pete's A&R guy. By the third song, Leo was in a groove. He'd finished the letter to Joey and was now writing up the statement he and Pete wanted to make at the press conference. After that, he ordered a chicken curry from the take-out down the street and settled in to finish the article about the Stone Roses he had to fax to his editor at *Spin* in the morning. By midnight he was done. He looked at the clock and realized he still hadn't heard from Pete. Leo dialed the hotel in Italy and asked for Pete Reynolds's room.

"We have no one here by that name," the hotel operator said.

Leo laughed. "I'm sorry," he said. "Can you connect me to Bugs Bunny's room."

"No problem, sir. One second."

The attendant put him through. The phone rang seven times before Leo started to hang up. Then a woman answered.

Leo said, "Is this Pete Reynolds's room?"

"Who is this?" the woman asked.

"This is Leo. Who is this?" The sound of muffled voices answered him back. Leo said again, "Who is this?"

"Hold on," the girl said when she came back to the phone.

Leo waited a few minutes. Then he heard Sally's voice come on the line. "Leo? It's Sally. Something's happened. I was literally just about to call you—"

"Where's Pete?"

"It was an accident, Leo, a stupid fucking accident—"

Leo could feel his heart racing. "Put Pete on the phone, Sally."

There was a long pause. Leo could hear Sally breathing hard. Finally she said, "Pete's dead, Leo. He was shot at the airport."

"I said, put him on the phone, Sally. Now!"

"He was shot, Leo. A gunman mistook their plane for the Turkish ambassador's plane and as Pete disembarked, the guy shot at him, and—"

Leo had dropped the phone. Tears sprang from his eyes and he began to shake. The tea in the cup he held spilled over, flowing hotly over his fingers and dripping onto his bare feet. He didn't even feel the hot liquid between his toes. He felt numb.

1

TNT said, "You know what, Leo? I should have you talk to a friend of mine. He's a rapper and he's gay. He wants to come out of the closet. Maybe you can help him out. You seem to have a good rapport with famous people who got secrets."

"What's that supposed to mean?" Leo said.

"I think he's talking about Pete," said Duke. He looked at TNT. "Is that the point you're trying to make? You know so much about us and we know nothing about you?"

TNT just smiled. "Do you fools really think I'd ask you all here and not be prepared? I mean, considering the reason I asked all of you up here in the first place?" He twisted off the bottle cap, took a long sip. "So, Joey, what was it like doing hard time?"

"Hard," Joey said.

"Those letters from Leo must have helped, I bet." He smiled.

"Stop playing this game," Barry said. "We get it already. You know all our business. Get to the fucking point, man. Tell us what we need to know about you so one of us can answer your question. If one of us is, indeed, your father."

The room was quiet. TNT watched the four of them not look at each other. He hadn't expected this. He thought they'd all be more forthcoming about themselves, more interactive with each other. Perhaps he'd played the moment wrong. Perhaps he should have just come out and told them what he wanted them to know, to see if he could get the answer he wanted, the truth he deserved. He decided to be direct, to tell them his mother's name. Then the phone rang. They all looked at the sleek cordless phone on the low table next to the bar.

"I'm not expecting a call," Barry said sarcastically. "It must be for you."

TNT reached over and picked up the phone. "Yeah?" he barked.

2

Melissa Dellums took a deep breath and glanced over at the guy in the red sweatshirt and the black baseball cap before she answered TNT's question. "Troy, it's me," she said into the phone. "I need to see you."

"I'm in a meeting, Melissa."

"I know, Troy. But it's important. I have to see you. Can't you come down?"

"Told you I didn't wanna be disturbed. Told you how important this was!"

"He hung up," she said, handing the cell phone back to the guy in the red sweatshirt. He held it up to his ear. Silence.

"I told you it wouldn't work," she told him. She could feel the barrel of the gun pushing into her side. She took another deep breath. She looked around the street, hoping that maybe she'd see a beat cop making his rounds. But she didn't see anyone walking the street where they were parked over on the far West Side, a block from the highway. "He told me earlier not to bother him, like I told you."

"You didn't do it right," the guy in the red sweatshirt said.

"What do you want with him anyway?" Melissa asked him. Before the words were completely out of her mouth, she felt the weight of his fist against her chin. Her head banged against the window. For a few seconds she saw bright circles dancing in front of her eyes. Up to now, she hadn't really been afraid. Even with the gun, she thought this guy was just some kid with no plan. Even with the gun, she had a feeling she could at least outsmart him and get away unharmed. But now she wasn't so sure. "What do you want?" she asked him again, trying hard not to scream the words at him and agitate him any further. "Maybe if you tell me, I can convince Troy to come meet you."

He hit her again, then raised the gun from her side to her head. Melissa felt tears come to her eyes. "He stole from me," the guy said.

"Why would he steal something from you?" Melissa asked, trying to sound steady, unafraid. "Who *are* you?"

"I didn't say it happened yesterday." He pulled the gun away from Melissa's temple and rested it in his lap, his fingers still wrapped around the shiny handle.

"Tell me what Troy stole from you," Melissa said. "If I can help you get it back, I will. Just don't hurt me. Please."

He swallowed once, keeping his hand on the gun and his eyes on the street ahead of them. With his free hand he turned the ignition and started the car. They pulled off, then stopped to wait for the light to change at Tenth Avenue. He turned to Melissa and said, "My life. That's what he stole, okay? That fucking liar stole my life." He pulled off, making the right turn after a taxi hurried by. "And I want it back."

1

"Now *this* is the fucking life." Mike Maynard raised his cool glass of vodka cranberry to the powder blue Miami sky and pumped his other fist.

"I hope there's no alcohol in there," said Duke, lying back on a chaise longue.

"Course not, bro." Mike swigged back the last of the drink. He took the glass straight to the wet bar on the deck and dumped the ice into the small metal sink. "I gotta tell you, as sad as you were to leave the Redskins, I can get *very* used to this." He sat down in the other chaise longue and gave Duke a wide happy grin. "This city is beautiful, the women in this city are beautiful." He laughed. "This house is beautiful. The Miami Dolphins are beautiful! This is the fucking life," he repeated, lying back, his sunglassed face tilted up toward the sun.

Duke looked at his watch. "I gotta go get Leo from the airport."

"Can't you send a car?"

"Sure I could," Duke said. "Driven by you, my personal assistant. But Leo's coming out of a very fragile place and I wanna be there when he gets off the plane." He really wanted to say, "I don't want my best friend being driven by my drunk brother," but he didn't say it. He knew Mike had been drinking some lately, not as much as he used to, but some. He preferred alcohol to the junk Mike once indulged in, but he was still a little worried. Miami didn't seem to be a city for people who lacked self-control. He hoped he hadn't made a mistake. He had no recourse against being traded to the Miami Dolphins, but he wondered if bringing Mike with him had been such a good idea.

Leo sat on a stone bench, smoking a cigarette and wondering what the hell he was doing sitting outside Miami International Airport in August. He knew he had to get out of New York, particularly since all the litigation was done and he was finally free of estate lawyers and record company execs and press hounds barking at his every move. He'd finally gotten his share of Pete's estate, a full four years after his death, a full four years of battling Pete's family, who refused to accept Leo, after the many years he and Pete had been together, as Pete's lover. Which was weird considering how inviting they'd been when Pete was alive. But after his death, they'd decided that, if anything, Leo and Pete had been, simply, good friends, so all Leo was entitled to were the royalties he made from co-writing hits with Pete and none of Pete's estate, estimated by a battery of accountants and lawyers to be just under twenty-three million dollars, whether or not Pete's will decreed it so. Leo replayed the depositions over in his mind, the long-drawn-out meetings with his own lawyers, the interviews with Pete's bandmates who'd insisted that Leo deserved most of Pete's money and belongings, the mean-spirited quotes surreptitiously dropped to the media by Pete's family. Leo had made it clear that he didn't want Pete's money for himself, that he'd intended it to go to an educational and legal fund for troubled young gay people, but, if anything, that only made the Reynolds family even more upset, their son's hard-earned cash supporting more "scandalous" behavior.

They agreed to a settlement of ten million dollars. Leo didn't need the money. The novel he published after Pete's death was a best seller; and he had a contract to do two more. Even though he knew that his sudden literary celebrity had as much to do with the death of his rock star lover and the attendant press coverage as it did with any writing ability he possessed, it still felt good to be independent of everyone's expectations and desires and money.

2

Joey sat on the pink plastic *FashionNation* bench with the big "C" painted on the sides and stared at the wall of photographs across from him, his eyes moving from the two-shot of Carla with Whoopi Goldberg to the shot of Carla standing between Bill and Hillary Clinton to the huge black-and-white print of Carla holding a microphone up to Mizrahi.

She'd said she was going to do it, Joey thought. His mind raced back to that visit she'd made to see him up at Caledonia State Correctional Facility two years ago, her last visit. She'd recounted how she'd been dumped as the face of CoCo Cosmetics and how all she had to look forward to was a huge, lavish wedding to Reggie McFarland. And what kind of life was that? she'd asked him. Then she apologized, sorry that she'd spent so much time talking about her own problems. But Joey hadn't minded her complaining. Listening to Carla's stories had taken his mind off his own troubles. And had he known that that visit would be her last, he would have prompted her for more stories from her world, more long-winded tales of glamour and fashion and gossip. After she'd told him that she intended to ace an audition with a producer for a new fashion talk show on a local cable channel, Joey drew as much of her ebullience into himself as he could and forced himself to re-create it in his dreams at night, after lights out, when it was easy to let the stink and loneliness of his cell infiltrate his every thought.

The nights had definitely been the hardest. At least during the day, he could chill with Posada, hearing more glory-days stories about his own father's criminal past, or hang in the yard when weather permitted, lifting weights and playing basketball. Before prison, nights were when he did his stitching and creating. Nights spent lying in a jail cell, with no outlet for the bursts of ideas that careened through his brain, felt like death. But then the call had come from his lawyer with the big news: Greta had attempted suicide at her facility in Pennsylvania, but not before writing a long letter to her parents and doctors, telling how she'd kidnapped that guy on her own, that Joey had not been involved, that she'd wanted to set him up because she'd been jealous and unhappy. It took another four months before he was released but they were four months of hope rather than despair, and that had made all the difference.

The red "studio" light over the door next to the photo wall went off and a few seconds later, the door swung wide open and there was Carla, in a polka-dot tunic, her arms raised and a big smile on her face. "Joey!" she screamed, and ran right into his arms.

They both picked at Chinese chicken salads at an outdoor table at the Saloon as Carla told him all about her life. The show was going very well, especially now that it had been picked up for syndication in twelve other major cities. Married life was treating her well, even though Reggie traveled quite a bit and they still hadn't moved into their dream apartment since it was still being renovated. "Who knew it took seven weeks to get marble ordered, cut, and installed?" she said with a sigh. "But enough about me, baby boy. How are things with you?"

"As soon as I find a place and a job, I'll be fine," he said. "Edna's been nice enough to let me stay at her place but that's not gonna last forever."

"Well, we'll work on a place," Carla said. "As for a job, you know you're coming to work for *FashionNation*. Don't even worry about that, baby."

"You'd really give me a job?"

"I'd give you head if you promise to make me some more dresses, Joey."

He looked down at his salad. "I haven't stitched a thing in four years, Carla."

"Just think of that as a long hiatus," she said.

Joey laughed. "That's one way of looking at it, I guess." Rich, beautiful Carla. She had every reason to be a cynical stuck-up bitch, like so many of the snobby rich black girls he remembered meeting out in Sag Harbor. Sure, she could do the bitchy thing when she wanted to, but Joey found himself still marveling after all these years at her ability to see the bright side of everything.

"Think of it this way," she added. "You won't be influenced by any of the bullshit passing for fashion these days. You'll have a fresh perspective." She popped a piece of chicken into her mouth. "And I'll have a fresh new wardrobe."

How did the song go? Barry thought, sitting in one of the stone seating areas that surrounded the fountain outside the Lowell building on Sixth Avenue. *You can't always get what you want . . . but if you try sometime, you get what you need.* Here he was, one year out of Yale Law School, and he was miserable. Sure, he was making a ton of money for a single, twenty-eight-year-old dude, but he was also living in New York City, where a lot of money didn't go as far it might in some other, saner city, particularly when you needed to keep up with not only the Joneses, but also the Bradfords, the McFarlands, and the Olivers. And he was working more hours than any young human should be forced to work just because the old farts who called themselves partners had been hazed in the same way when they'd started their climbs up the corporate law ladder.

He bit into his turkey sandwich, which he should have been eating at his desk while he read over the brief that he'd be rewriting until six the next morning. His eyes followed the ample rear end of a sexy Latina chick in a tight skirt and high stiletto heels as she made her way toward the McGraw-Hill Building across the street. But then he pulled his eyes away. He couldn't think about sex. Otherwise he'd be walking around with a hard dick for the rest of the day, as horny as he was since he never had the time to fuck any of the girls he saw around him every day.

This cannot be my life, he thought. *This is not what I was supposed to do.* He had liked studying law. And maybe one day, he thought, he'd like practicing it. But that was far away. He'd be a glorified assistant for the next three years or so. Then he'd have to impress enough elders to be made partner. What was he doing?

He knew what he was doing. Being stubborn. Being hardheaded. Telling himself that he could make it in New York without running back to Gary Bradford. Ever since that last conversation with Gary at his going-away party, two weeks before he left for law school, he'd built Gary into an even bigger asshole than he'd already assumed the man to be. But he was a smart asshole, wasn't he? So what if he didn't talk to his gay son? So what if he cheated on his beautiful wife? He had the magic hand when it came to making money and building a business. *And he'd seen what I could do,* Barry thought. So again, he asked himself, what was he doing slaving away at some stuffy white-shoe law firm instead of loving life at CoCo Cosmetics?

He knew the answer. He wanted to be *asked* back to CoCo,

begged even. And even if he knew that Gary wanted him back he didn't want to go hat in hand, asking Gary for a position. Or did he? Was that how he was supposed to play this? Suck up to the head guy and hope to be anointed?

Fuck this, he thought.

Barry tossed the other half of his sandwich into a trash bin next to the subway entrance and dug in his pocket for a token. Before he realized it, he was on the subway, swooshing toward midtown, getting off and standing in front of the CoCo Cosmetics building. He went inside.

Nothing had changed, right down to the stick-figure-looking woman with the severe bun hairdo at the front desk.

"Hey, Marsha," he said. "I'm back."

She waved him toward the elevator and five minutes later he was standing outside of Gary Bradford's office, his suit jacket tossed over one shoulder, waiting for Gary's assistant to notice him. She spoke quietly into an intercom, then buzzed him in.

Barry found Gary Bradford sitting behind his desk, the same one he'd had four years ago, his fingers steepled in front of him, a Camel cigarette burning in the silver ashtray next to his phone.

"Hello, Barry," he said. He put out his cigarette. "What took you so long?"

3

Madonna and a bunch of music execs crowded around the table to their right. Dennis Rodman and a crew of drag queens surrounded a table to their left. Mike smiled a sly grin and waved his arms around to the remix of the Montell Jordan song that had dancers sweating all over the dance floor. "Welcome to Nocturne," he said to Leo. "Welcome to Miami, man. *This* is how we do it here, bro."

"This isn't Miami," said Francina, the tall half-Portuguese, half-Japanese model draped across Mike's lap like she was posing for a photo shoot. "This is South Beach." She tickled Mike's nose. "You better learn the difference if you're gonna be here for a while." She stood up and stretched her long arms over her head, swaying to the beat of Latin-tinged hip-hop now pumping from the huge speakers. "Let's dance, Mike."

Mike winked at Leo and shrugged, then followed Francina through the sweaty, gyrating crowd to the dance floor. Leo breathed out a heavy sigh; he was glad they'd left the table. Francina was a conceited bore, and as much as he loved Duke, and appreciated how compassionate he was being to help his brother, he really didn't like Mike. Leo looked at his watch. He hadn't planned on staying out all night, and Duke was late, if he was coming at all.

As they made their way back to the table, Leo watched Francina throw her head back, laughing loudly, wiping at her nose and sniffing. *Coke*, he thought. He couldn't bring himself to look at Mike. If he saw Mike acting the same way, he was going to explode. That was his cue to go. He said his goodbyes and got out of there.

There was a light on in the kitchen when Leo got back to Duke's.

He called out Duke's name. "You home?" He heard a woman giggle as he stepped farther into the living room. As he got closer to the kitchen, he could hear the giggle again and Duke's whispered voice shushing the woman. Leo had to smile. Duke, whom he and Mike had taken to calling the Pope because he'd seemed to be living by some vow of chastity, had a woman with him, a happy-sounding, giggling woman. Leo stepped into the kitchen, a sarcastic smile ready for Duke and his new friend.

Only the friend wasn't so new.

Leo said, "Amanda? Is that you? What are you—"

"It's me," she giggled, standing there in a Miami Dolphins T-shirt. "Hi, Leo."

Duke stepped out from behind the open refrigerator door. He was completely nude. He pulled Amanda in front of him. "We didn't know you were here," he said.

"So at least now I know," Leo said, "why you didn't make it to Nocturne." Leo just laughed and went up to his room.

4

The limo was waiting for them when the private plane landed at Miami International. As the chauffeur loaded Carla's Gucci luggage and Joey's lone garment bag into the trunk, Carla threw up her arms and screamed, "I love Miami. The heat. The men. The sun."

Joey just laughed and climbed into the limo behind her. He was excited to be in Miami, too, but for other reasons. According to Posada, this was not only where his father had gotten his start before coming back to New York City, but it was also where his parents had met all those years ago. Miami was also where, according to Posada, his maternal grandmother still lived, long after she'd disowned her daughter for marrying a drug-abusing Dominican criminal. Joey intended to find this woman and introduce himself. "Don't tell her you done time, though," Posada had warned him when Joey visited him two weeks before the trip. "Or she'll have nothing to do with you, papi."

———————

The yard outside the green clapboard house was small but well kept, with huge bursts of orange blossoms lining the boxes sitting underneath the front windows. A fence that came up to his waist surrounded the entire property. Joey could see a bicycle with a basket attached to the handlebars parked at the side of the house. A late-model Taurus was parked in the driveway. The front door stood open even though Joey could hear the hum of two air conditioners, one on the first floor and one upstairs. He stood there outside the fence staring up at the house, wondering if this was where his mother had grown up, if this was the street where his mother had played as a kid, much like the smoothly tanned kids did in the yard next door.

"Can I help you?"

Joey turned to see a tall skinny older man in walking shorts and a tank top that had sweat splotches across the chest.

"You lookin' for Eula Mae and Florence?"

Joey nodded.

"Florence went to the grocery store. Eula Mae was just out here a few seconds ago fiddlin' wit' them flowers she got there." He looked over Joey's shoulder. "There she go right there."

A short, light-skinned woman with a graying, close-cut Afro stepped out of the door, a small spade in one gloved hand, a packet of seeds in the other. She waved when she saw the old man next to Joey. But her wave died when she saw Joey.

"This here young man lookin' for you all, Miss Eula Mae."

She dropped the spade on the top step and came down the walk, her eyes firmly on Joey's face, her mouth slightly open. When she got to the fence, she just stood there for a few moments. She blinked a few times, then opened the gate. "Chile, well, I'll be," she said. "You are Joey, aren't you?" A tear crept down her cheek.

She was still tearing up two hours later, as Joey sat on a soft chenille sofa across from her on the patio deck in the rear of the house, listening more than talking, looking at pictures of his mother as a child and teenager. "See that dress right there?" Eula Mae said. "She made that with a Butterick pattern she got from the dollar store."

"My mother sewed?"

"Nola could do anything," Eula Mae said. "Why you think I didn't want her to . . ."

"Marry my father?" Joey finished for her.

Eula Mae sighed. "I'm sorry. I just always had such big dreams for her."

"I sew," Joey told her. "I make clothes. I always thought I'd got it from my father's mother. She taught me how to stitch."

"She was a nice woman," said Eula Mae, "I met her once, the one time I went to New York." Eula Mae sniffed. "The one time I ever saw you." She leaned over and hugged Joey for the fourth time since they'd been together.

"Who is this?" A voice interrupted them.

They looked up to see a tall, imposing woman in a lime green sweat suit, her graying hair pulled back in a tight bun. She had grocery bags in each hand, which she dropped to the floor. She crossed her arms over her chest. "Eula Mae?"

"Florence, this is Nola's boy."

Joey stood up.

Florence didn't smile or offer a hand or hug. "How did you find us?"

"A friend of my father's," Joey said.

"What friend? I didn't know junkies had friends." She picked up the groceries and turned around and went into the kitchen.

Eula Mae jumped up from the sofa and ran after her. "Florence? Wait a second."

Joey sat there on the patio, listening to the two women argue. He heard a door slam somewhere upstairs. He couldn't make out the words but it was obvious that Florence, whoever she was, wasn't as happy about this reunion as he and his grandmother had been. Ten minutes later the door slammed open and Joey could hear clearly the words between them. Florence's voice carried all the way to the patio.

"I don't care if he designs clothes for Patti LaBelle and Mary Magdalene, I don't want him in my house. He looks just like his father, you think he ain't got some of that nastiness inside him, Eula Mae? So when he disappoints you like Nola and his father did, am I gonna have to sit up and nurse you back to health again? I'm your sister, not your mother. This is my house and I don't care."

Joey decided it was time to go. This wasn't a good idea. He opened the patio door and stepped outside. Then he thought of something. He went back to the photo album on the table and took the picture of his mother in the blue dress she'd made for herself.

As he made his way around the house toward the front yard, he heard the front door open. Eula Mae met him near the fence. "Don't leave, Joey," she cried. "Florence is just surprised, that's all."

"I don't wanna cause any trouble," he said, hugging his grandmother.

"Come back for dinner tonight," she said. "I'll get Florence to understand."

Joey looked into her eyes, tearing up again, pleading with him to return. He smiled. "What time should I be here?"

Carla lounged across the king-size bed in Joey's hotel room in a crocheted bikini, watching him knot his tie in the mirror over the minibar. She glanced over at the television, where the O.J. trial coverage was plastered across the screen. "I think I need to give Marcia Clark a makeover," she said. "What do you think?"

Joey laughed, but more out of nervousness than Carla's remarks. He could barely process that he was going to spend the evening with his grandmother; there was absolutely no room in his head for O. J. Simpson news.

"Want me to come with you?" Carla said. "Grandparents *love* me."

"I don't think so," Joey said. "I gotta do this on my own."

Carla stood up. "Well, you should go in style. So you take the limo, then come meet us at Nocturne when you're done. Bring Granny along if she's feeling it."

"She might be. She's an athletic old lady." He turned to Carla. "How do I look?"

"Perfect," she said. "Grandsons don't get more perfect than you, Joey, baby." She kissed him on the cheek and flounced out of the room.

Joey had the limo stop at a strip mall near the house so he could buy some flowers and a bottle of wine. He'd noticed a rack of merlots and cabernets in the kitchen when Eula Mae was making tea, so he thought they'd appreciate the wine. As the limo curved through the streets of North Miami, Joey could feel his heart beating against his chest. He couldn't believe he was about to break bread with a real blood relative, his mother's mother, whom he'd dreamed about. His hands were shaking, as if they were finally realizing, like the rest of him, that an in-the-flesh meeting was actually going to happen.

The limo parked outside the house and Joey sat there for a few moments, catching his breath, soothing his nerves, not wanting to appear anxious or nervous to Florence. He wanted to impress his dissatisfied great-aunt, to show her that he was a good guy who just wanted to know his family.

No one came to the door on the first knock. Or the second. Or the third. Joey walked around the side of the house. He could see into the kitchen from one window. No one was there; it was dark, and all the lights seemed to be off in the front of the house. He saw a light in the back, so he walked farther back, toward the patio doors he'd exited from earlier in the day. Sitting there on the patio was Florence, watching TV, a tray holding a plate of food on it in front of her. Joey stood there at the patio doors, holding the flowers and wine, looking right at Florence, who kept her eyes on the TV. Finally Joey knocked once. Florence forked a bit of rice into her mouth, her eyes still on the TV. Then she slowly turned her head and looked right at Joey, her eyes flat and uninviting, as if she were observing a stray dog looking for food scraps in her yard. She turned back to the TV and continued to eat.

Joey took the receipt from the wine shop and wrote down his name and his number at the hotel. He stuck it in the door handle and stepped back from the door.

Out front the chauffeur looked surprised to see Joey coming back to the limo. He hurriedly stubbed out his cigarette, put down the paperback book he was reading, and jumped out to open the door for Joey. Joey climbed in and sat back on the plush leather seat. He felt ridiculous, sitting there in that stupid white shirt and tie, looking down at the flowers and wine. He could feel emotion well up inside him but he tamped it down. He refused to cry. He told himself there were more important things than family. What had family ever done for him really anyway, except die or go away? Anger rose within him, anger at himself for even trying. Who needed them? Who needed anyone? This was his destiny, to be alone. Wasn't that what life had been trying to teach him all this time, from his mother's car crash, to his father's drug use, to his grandmother's cancer, to foster care, to jail, to today? He would always be alone. That was just the way it would be. But there was something else, something else he realized he needed, if aloneness was, in fact, his destiny. He needed the world to know he existed. He needed the world to know that he could share the things he created even if there was no one to share his world. *Fuck people*, thought Joey Ramirez, not for the first time in his life. *I want the world.*

5

As soon as practice ended, Duke was in his Jaguar and skidding out of the parking lot. He was at the doctor's office on Meridian Avenue in twenty minutes. Amanda was standing on the front step, flipping though a brochure. As he parked the Jaguar, Duke stared at her, still amazed that they were back together, and that they'd managed to keep it a secret from almost everyone for close to a year. When she looked up and smiled at him, he knew the news was good.

She slipped into the bucket seat and tossed the brochure into her bag. She screamed, throwing her arms around his neck. "We're having a baby!"

They'd agreed to keep their reunion a secret from almost everyone until they were sure it was something they wanted to maintain. Now there were going to be no more secrets. "Can I tell Leo?"

"*Just* Leo," said Amanda. "I wanna wait another month to tell the world."

———

"Leo? Leo the Lion?"

Leo looked up from his menu and saw Joey standing at his table. "Yo!" He stood up and hugged Joey, then stepped back to look at him. "What are you doing in Miami?"

"This and that," Joey said with a smile. "What are *you* doing in Miami?"

"The same," said Leo. "I'm staying at Duke's. You should come by."

"I thought about calling him, but, you know, with the season starting and all—"

"I know he'd love to see you, Joey."

"Yeah, same here. Listen, I have to run. Maybe I could get your number?"

Leo wrote Duke's number on a napkin. They said goodbyes and Joey strolled away down Lincoln Road. He looked back at the table once, waved, and continued on.

Later that afternoon, Joey tried to concentrate on the financial information sputtering from the thin lips of Warren Cassidy, but his thoughts kept flowing back to Leo. In *Miami*? He had looked good, too. So good, Joey couldn't even make a conversation. He looked down at the napkin with the number on it and as embarrassed as he felt about his short behavior at the restaurant, Joey felt something in his chest—and his groin—stirring, memories of his good times with Leo dotting his brain.

"By the third year I think you'd be able to branch out," Warren was saying. "You listening to me, Joey?"

"Yeah," Joey said. "Go on." But he was still preoccupied. He tried to push his mind away from memories of Leo and consider this move to Miami, to remember Carla's decision to help him after

Joey told her he was leaving *FashionNation* and going to Miami to launch his own fashion line.

"It's the perfect place for me," Joey had told her. "All those vain women with their surgically slimmed-down bodies. All that South American drug money coming into town every day." He'd laughed when he said it, but he was serious. He wanted to be where the money was, but where the pressure wasn't. New York meant pressure and hype and expectations. Miami meant comfort, a place he could work at his own speed. To his surprise, Carla agreed with him and dug right in, helping him to get incorporated, introducing him to Warren Cassidy, who'd negotiate her investment, and the additional funds he'd need to get on his feet.

"What about Lillian Bradford?" he'd asked Carla. "Is she still interested in investing in me?" Carla assured him she was probably still in—if Gary agreed.

Now here he was, sitting in the Miami sun, listening to Warren's slick drone.

"What's going on with CoCo Cosmetics?" Joey asked him.

"In terms of what?" Warren shifted in his seat. "Since they fired Carla, I don't have much to do with them anymore."

"Can you get me a meeting with Gary Bradford?"

"That asshole? Why do you wanna see him?"

"He owes me a favor," Joey said.

Warren Cassidy's bushy eyebrows climbed far up his forehead. "You're more connected than Carla told me if Gary Bradford owes *you* a favor."

Joey just smiled. He'd devised a plan for making his dream come true. He hadn't even told Carla about it. But since he'd made his decision to light the world on fire with his JoeyRam designs, he'd decided it was time to call in some chits.

6

The CoCo Cosmetics offices hadn't changed much from the days when Joey visited as a teenager, stopping by to visit Edna after work or meet up with Leo after a meeting with his father. A huge photo of Cheyenne was posted outside Gary's office. Joey wondered where she was these days, who she was with. Maybe he'd have her phone number thrown into the mix of things he intended to get from Gary Bradford.

Gary's assistant gave him a big smile when he reached the alcove outside Gary's office. "We really miss Edna," she told him. "I remember when you were just a kid."

Joey smiled back but said nothing. He was still rehearsing in his mind the message he wanted to relay to Gary.

Inside the office, Gary sat at his desk and waved his hand at the empty visitor chair in front of it. Joey took a seat and sat there, saying nothing.

Gary said, "Welcome home, Joseph. We've missed you."

"Thanks," Joey said. "We being who exactly?"

"Me. My wife. Edna."

Joey nodded. "Glad you brought that up," he said. "They're just the two people I want to talk about."

Gary lit a Camel. "How can I help you?"

"You can let your wife invest in my company."

"And she should do that because?"

"Because she likes my designs and she always told me she would."

"Lillian says a lot of things, Joseph." Gary came around the desk. He went over to the couch to the right of it and waved Joey over. "I think we've done a lot for you over the years, Joseph—"

"It's Joey. Please call me Joey."

"And we'd like to help you some more. Unfortunately, with what you've been through the last few years, it doesn't really behoove us to, as you say, invest in you."

"I'm the same designer I was before I was unfairly incarcerated," Joey said. "I acted in self-defense."

"Whatever happened, Jos—, uh, Joey, it wouldn't really look good for us to—"

"Then here's what we'll do, Mr. Bradford." Joey sat forward on the couch and cupped his hands in front of him. "You allow Mrs. Bradford to invest in me and I won't tell her about those nights you spent at Edna's while I was in the other room."

Gary coughed. He sat forward himself and stubbed out his cigarette in the ashtray on the coffee table. "You came here to blackmail me?"

"Yes," Joey said. "I lost a lot going to jail, most important of which was time. There are things I want and I realize that sometimes you have to do things you don't really want to do to get the things you want."

"Why would I do what you ask?"

"Because you have too much to lose."

"This is how you repay me for all I've done for you."

"No offense, Mr. Bradford, but you haven't really done that much for me. You gave me a room to sleep in at your mistress's apartment. You paid for a couple of years of City College. Great. And thanks. A lot. But you also cheated on Edna with other women. And I had to listen to her cry at night when she found out. You also did and said hurtful things to Leo when Edna told you about him and I. You made him think that his friend Barry outed him to you because you didn't want him to know how close you were to Edna.

You can think highly of yourself if you like. But I know the truth of who you are." Joey sat back and said nothing else.

The room was quiet for a few seconds as Joey and Gary just stared at each other.

Finally Gary stood up, went to his desk, and pulled a checkbook from the top drawer. He said, "How much do you need?"

"This has to be Mrs. Bradford's investment," Joey said. "I don't want a check with your name or CoCo Cosmetics's name on it." He came over to the desk, "I want to make Mrs. Bradford a rich woman. I want her to have her own stash of cash so that when she decides to leave you she won't have to beg you for anything."

Gary fingered the silver pen next to the checkbook. He looked right at Joey. "Do you remember a girl named Towanda, Joey?"

The sound of that name threw Joey off his rhythm for a few seconds. TeeTee? How did Gary Bradford know TeeTee? Joey shivered at the thought of that night, waking up to find TeeTee on top of him. "What about her?"

"She'd probably love to see you," Gary said. "And she'd probably love for you to see her son. Or should I say your son."

"What are you talking about?" Joey asked him. "How do you even know—"

"That's not important," Gary said. "What is important, Joey, is that you understand that what you barged in here to do today is a man's game. And two can play it. Hell, I fucking invented it."

"So, what? You're not gonna give me the money?"

"You'll get it. But don't you ever forget that as much as you *think* you know about me, I probably know more about you. And I'll never hesitate to use it if I have to."

7

Joey returned to Miami still a little shell-shocked by Gary's counterpunch in their little battle of wills. Especially after he spent two days trying to locate Towanda, trying to find out anything he could about her supposed son. He couldn't believe that she'd gotten pregnant from that one night she'd pretty much raped him, but apparently she had. At least that's what she'd told Gary and Edna, which Edna confirmed for him. Towanda had followed him home after seeing him at a rap concert one night shortly after he'd moved into Edna's apartment. She showed up the next morning, followed Edna to work, and told her that she was the mother of Joey's baby. Edna had told Gary and they'd written her a check for expenses, never expecting that she'd come back for more. They'd made a pact to never tell Joey, to give him a chance at life without more burden. "You'd been through so much already," Edna told him. "Fatherhood? At your age?" And she laughed. "I told Gary there was no way I'd let you be connected to those people, not after what her mother had done to you." She'd teared up telling the story. "I already felt like you were mine, Joey. I only wanted to protect you. Do you understand?"

He understood. But that didn't stop him from taking a car to Brooklyn, to the apartment building where it had all happened, finding a family there that had never heard of Shirley Bogarde or her kids TeeTee and Carlton. A man down the street remembered them. "Shirley got murdered by some woman, musta been around, I don't know, '83 or '84, after she got outta jail for stealing," he told Joey. "Carlton's in jail somewhere, and that girl took her kid and moved away a few months after Shirley died. I heard she might be in Georgia, but what do I know?"

Ultimately Joey wasn't really surprised by all this. It was the main lesson of his life. You lose people. You lose family. You lose the people you love or who love you.

Like Cheyenne. Was it just dumb fucking luck that he was sitting in Barry's office, catching up with his old friend, when the CoCo Girl herself would strut into the office, plant a big kiss on Barry's lips, and eventually notice Joey sitting there only because of the uncomfortable look on Barry's face?

"You two?" Joey had asked.

"You went to jail," Cheyenne said, planting herself on the corner of Barry's desk. "Nothing personal."

"I'm guessing this isn't a new thing then?"

Barry tried to apologize, explaining that it was a short thing between them, that he and Cheyenne were just friends now, but Joey stopped him. "I was in jail," he said, getting up to go, in his mind already headed to Brooklyn to find Towanda. "Just like she said. When you go to jail, anything you leave behind becomes public domain, right, Barry?"

Now, he tried to force all the ugly memories of his quick trip to New York out of his head. He put on an old Stevie Wonder CD, went out to the balcony, and lit a cigarette. He could see tall tan women in halters and slick-haired guys in leather jeans milling around, the hot embers of nightlife starting to catch fire down on Ocean Drive.

I have a son, he thought. *Somewhere out there I have a son.*

8

A month later, Duke pulled up to his house and parked behind the huge white catering truck hulking in the dead center of the driveway. He sighed deeply and shook his head as he grabbed his duffel bag from the passenger seat. Hadn't he told Mike to have the caterers drive around the back and unload from there rather than tramp through the front of the house? He walked around the back. Where was the staff? He heard giggling above him. He looked up to see Mike and Francina cuddling, leaning over the rail of the deck. Mike unloosed himself from Francina. "Hey, bro. You back sooner than I expected."

"No fucking kidding," Duke muttered as be climbed the stairs to the deck. "You were supposed to be there for the new itinerar-ies, Mike."

"I had the travel secretary fax them over," Mike said.

"But you were supposed to be there for the new orientation. I left you a note on the fridge this morning." Duke pulled a soda from the wet bar fridge. "I'm not supposed to be reminding you about shit. You're *my* assistant, remember?"

Francina said, "Don't talk to him that way."

Duke took a deep breath. He was one beat away from boring right into her, but he didn't want to go there. He wanted to go up-stairs, soak in a hot tub, go get Amanda from the airport, and come back to a nice team party. He downed the last of the soda, tossed the empty can in the recycling bin, and went inside.

As he opened the door, he heard Francina say, "I fucking hate athletes."

He turned around. "Then get the fuck out of this athlete's crib and don't come back, you dumb bitch."

Mike said, "Yo, Duke! Don't talk to her like that. Whassup with that, man?"

Duke dropped his bag and stalked over to the two of them. "Up with what?" He could feel his heart beating rapidly in his chest. He took another deep breath and stopped. "I'm going to get Amanda from the airport. When I come back, I don't want to see either of you until the party jumps off tonight. You hear me? Just get the hell outta here."

Outside the airport, Amanda said, "Look who was on the plane with me," pointing to Barry, standing off to one side talking into a mobile phone. He pressed a button to end his call and grabbed Duke into a big hug.

"Yo, superstar," he said. "We got shit to talk about. I wanna make you a star."

"I'm already a star," said Duke, picking up Amanda's garment bag. "How are you, honey, you feeling all right?"

"I'm talking about daddyhood stardom," Barry said. "Hear me out, bro."

"No business," Duke said. "It's a bye week and I'm taking that very seriously." As he and Amanda started toward the car, he shouted back to Barry, "But you can come by the house tonight. We're having a party."

Barry said, "Can I bring a friend?"

"Bring two," Duke said.

In the car, Amanda said, "I think Barry's found The One."

"No such thing as The One for Barry."

"She's pretty. The woman he was with. A lawyer, I think he said. He seemed really into her."

"Then it must be a business deal," Duke said. "Barry could make a divorce settlement seem like a sex orgy."

―――――

Actually she wasn't pretty. She was beautiful. Almost every man at the party had taken a chance to speak to her when she and Barry got to the house. Barry said, "This is Monica Murphy. She does some legal work for CoCo."

Monica shook Duke's hand. "And for a couple of your teammates," she said. "Congrats on the baby."

Amanda and Duke thanked her and pushed their way through the crowd to find Leo. "See, I told you she was pretty," Amanda said. "Didn't you see how Barry was looking at her?"

"Whatever," Duke said. "I just want to eat some fish and have a good time." He pointed across the deck. "Look at your brother." Sean Holland was grinding against a curvaceous blonde Miami Dolphins cheerleader, a beer in one hand and a fish sandwich in the other. "I guess it runs in the family."

"What?"

Duke laughed. "You might be the black bourgeoisie but y'all love yourselves some white folks."

Amanda slapped him playfully as he took her into his arms.

Across the room, Joey was telling Leo about the new design space he'd rented on Meridian Avenue. "But enough about me. How are you? I still can't believe we're both here in Miami!"

Leo told him how he was still putting the finishing touches on the Pete Reynolds Foundation paperwork. "You like it here?" he said with a smile.

"It's good seeing you and Duke," Joey said.

"We're family, Joey. You know that."

"It's good to hear you say that, Leo."

"I mean it." Leo looked over Joey's shoulder. A very handsome guy with long dreadlocks walked into the party.

Joey turned to look. "Good-looking guy," Joey said. "Definitely fuckable."

"Not as fuckable as you." Leo grinned.

Joey felt heat rise in his neck. He said, "So you still think I'm fuckable, huh?"

"Forget I said that," Leo said. "It's just the beer talking."

Joey raised his beer bottle in salute and headed toward the fry pit.

"My mother needs an estate lawyer," Duke said to Monica. "I should introduce you."

"I'd love that," Monica said. She pointed to Amanda, across the room talking to her brother. "You two been together long?"

"College sweethearts," Duke said. "With a break in the middle." He sipped his beer. "How long you and Barry been together?"

Monica laughed, almost choking on her gin and tonic. "We're not together. Did he tell you that?"

"Amanda and I thought—"

"Typical of couples in love." Monica grinned. "You play matchmaker in a minute." She sipped some more of her drink. "I'm a single gal," she said. "Still haven't found Mr. Right. Barry's Mr. Right *Now*, if anything."

Duke liked how she laughed. He thought his mother would like her. He made a mental note to tell Mike to get Monica's information. Which made him remember that it was time he talked to Mike.

Barry found Joey sitting on a couch in the living room, speaking Spanish to a woman in a red tank top. He kneeled down next to him and said, "What the fuck did you say to Gary, man? He was pissed as fuck when you left CoCo the other day."

"What makes you think his mood had anything to do with me?"

Barry shrugged. "Listen, I'm sorry about Cheyenne, Joey."

"Don't be sorry," Joey said. "You just do what you do. I can't stress it." He patted Barry on the shoulder and turned back to the woman.

"What did you do now?"

Barry turned to find Leo standing next to him. "Nothing," he mumbled, getting to his feet. "Why does everybody think I'm always *doing* something?"

"Maybe 'cause you usually—" Before he could get all the words out, Leo was shoved forward, right into Barry, spilling his drink down the front of Barry's T-shirt. "What the f—"

"I want my shit, motherfucker!"

A big guy in a nice brown suit pointed his finger right into Mike Maynard's face. "I want my shit," he bellowed, his voice booming, rising above the beat of the music.

Leo said to the big guy, "Yo, man, what's going on? Take this outside."

"I ain't takin' it nowhere; this motherfucker tells me to come here for my shit and then tells me he ain't got it."

Duke rushed over and turned Mike to face him. "What is he talking about, Mike?"

Mike shrugged. "He's buggin', bro. I don't know this dude."

"You don't *know* me? That's how you wanna play this? You don't know me?"

"You gotta get outta here," Duke said, reaching for the big guy's shoulder to escort him out. "I can't have this in my house—"

The guy pushed him away. "Don't touch me, man. Just tell your brother to give me my shit or somebody's getting hurt." The room got very quiet. Partiers looked in from the deck. "This don't have to go down like this," the big guy said into the silence. "This ain't about you. This about your fuckin' brother cheatin' me."

Duke looked at Mike again. "What is he talking about, Mike?"

"I ain't in this," Mike said. He grabbed Francina's hand and pulled her through the crowd and up the stairs. Everyone could hear a door slam. The big guy started toward the stairs, but Duke and Barry grabbed him and dragged him, struggling and fighting, toward the front door. Once they got him to the door, he ceased struggling and straightened himself up.

"It's all good," he shouted as he left. "We'll fix you, Mike. You'll definitely get fixed."

Duke turned to the crowd. "It's all over, people. Go back to the party." He tried to make his voice sound light. "We got lots of food for everybody."

Some of the guests continued their halted conversations, others started to file out through the front door or onto the deck. Duke tried to ignore the rising murmur of the guests as he rushed up the stairs two at a time. He banged on Mike's bedroom door. "Open the fucking door, Mike." No answer. "Mike!" Still no answer. Duke stepped back from the door then pounded his shoulder against it, splintering the edges near the jamb and busting it open. "Mike!"

There was no one in the room. The window to the balcony was open, the curtains blowing slowly in the breeze.

The rest of the night continued with little fanfare. Teammates came and went, flirting with pretty girls, teasing each other, enjoying the generally relaxed energy of a bye week with no game to prepare for. Leo watched Duke stalk around, a plastic smile dimpling his face to make the strangers and acquaintances feel comfortable. But he knew that Duke was boiling inside. He knew that Duke was carrying around the twin emotions of guilt and anger, guilt for putting Mike in this environment and anger for not watching him more closely. But there was also disappointment there, Leo could tell, the searing disappointment that you could only feel for yourself and your family, the tight, clenched fury of feeling that you'd been let down in the worst possible emotional way.

"*I want my shit.*"

Drugs. What else could it be? What other "shit" could the guy have wanted from Mike? Money? No one calls money "shit" in a crowded room. But everyone assumed Mike wasn't doing drugs anymore. Leo wondered if perhaps Mike was dealing drugs.

"Come to my place." Joey was beside him. "I don't like the vibe after that showdown."

Leo thanked him. "But that's not a good idea, Joey."

Joey smiled. "I just don't want you here around some drug shit." He looked over at Duke, his head close to Amanda's. "I bet you Mike's involved with drugs again."

Leo nodded. "I thought the same thing." He looked over at Duke. "Duke's taking it pretty hard."

"So you coming with me or not?"

"I'm staying here," Leo said. He could feel his heart tug at Joey's invitation. Even though he knew it wasn't about sex or romance, he felt closer to Joey than he had in a long time. "Funny," he said. "*You* taking me in."

"What goes around comes around," Joey said. "If you change your mind . . ."

Leo hugged him, holding him close for an extra second, glad that they'd both ended up in Miami after the horrors they'd both been through. He was glad to be there in that house, glad that he was around family, even if that family wasn't Lillian and Gary

Bradford. He walked Joey out to the driveway. Mike's blue Corvette was parked behind Joey's Jeep. Leo went inside to get the keys to the Corvette so Joey could get out.

Duke and Amanda were in a huddle with Barry and Monica in the kitchen. "I need Mike's keys," he said. "He's blocking Joey in."

"We're gonna go, too," Barry said, jumping down from his stool. "Let me move the Corvette. I've never driven one before."

Before Barry could take the set of keys from the hook, Amanda grabbed them.

"I'll move the car," she said. "Come on, Monica. I wanna show you those plants."

"You sure, Amanda?" Leo said with a sly smile. "I mean, you are with child."

"I'll never be so pregnant I turn down the chance to drive a classic sports car."

Leo followed them out to the long gravel driveway next to the front yard. He watched Amanda fit herself into the sleek Corvette and went over to Joey's Jeep. "So what do you make of Barry's girl Monica?" he said.

"Don't talk to me about Barry," Joey said. "What did you use to say? 'Be-Wary-of-Barry'? Now I know exactly why."

Leo laughed at the memory and turned to go back to the house. Just as he reached the grass, he heard Amanda start the Corvette, then an ear-smashing BOOM, just before he was thrown across the yard, landing on his ass right next to Monica, who'd also been tossed by the fierce thrust of the explosion. Soon the Corvette was a moaning pyre of smoke and fire, sending flames high into the air over the yard and house. Leo blinked a few times to get soot and ash from his eyes and ran over to Monica, who was trying to stand, one hand clutching her forehead, where blood was gushing down into her eyes. He could hear someone calling his name over the crackling fire. It was Joey, running from around the Jeep. Leo could hear Duke's throaty cry, "Where's Amanda?" Leo tried to point to the flaming car, but he could barely lift his arm, as the pain gouged at his side.

"Where's Amanda!" Duke shouted again, as Barry tried to hold him from running straight to the burning carcass of the Corvette. The flames shot upward, like prison bars, tightly holding everything inside it, burning, damaging, encasing in its hellish fury.

The tears coursing hotly down Leo's face burned his cheeks and chin. He tried to talk, to shout something helpful to Duke, but the words wouldn't come. He collapsed into Joey's arms just as Duke folded into Barry's, howling, "Nooooooo!" It was a long, low moan of sadness.

1

The guy in the red sweatshirt still held the gun in his lap, but Melissa could see that he was so wrapped up in the confusing story he was trying to tell her that his grip on the trigger had loosened. She wondered if he'd noticed himself, but she wouldn't let him see that. She just continued to nod at his story, stopping him again to show that she was paying attention.

"Are you sure TNT is the guy you're thinking of?" she asked him, her head down, her eyes glancing at the gun. "M-m-maybe you're mixing him up with someone else?"

"What kinda question is that? Aren't you listening to me? He grew up right next door to me. We used to write rhymes together all the time."

Melissa tried to process all the information he'd been trying to impart. According to this guy, Troy had stolen his name and his rhymes, in effect, his whole rap career. And now he was trying to confront Troy, trying to reclaim what he thought of as his. He kept mentioning someone named TeeTee, and someone named Carlton. Melissa couldn't keep all the names and situations straight, concentrated as she was on trying to figure out a way out of this thing.

It was getting darker now, in that smoothly transitional way it does in summer, the light in the sky hovering between sun and moon, the air moist with the possibility of rain. She wanted to scream, hoping that someone around there would hear her, but she didn't want to risk the possible lack of results. So she sat back, laying her head against the headrest, and breathed easy, letting her mind clear as his words tumbled over her, into one ear and out the other. She let her chest rise and fall slowly, gaining more strength from his descent into memory, from his increasingly obvious disinterest in her as he recalled the supposed theft that had led him here to this point.

"I'm not a bad man," he said. "I'm not. I just want what's mine."

"Of course you do," Melissa whispered. "Of course."

Then she went for it. She didn't want the gun, she just wanted to be away from him, so she shoved at his lap, knocking the gun to the floor, reaching over him when he leaned forward in surprise to retrieve the gun. She fumbled at the lock mechanism, pushing the button and feeling her heart surge as she heard the click of the locks unlocking. But he was fast. He sat back, trying to trap her between his body and the car seat. But she was fast, too, and she pulled back, planting her back against her own door and kicking at his face and chest, again sending the gun to the floor. As he reached down, she took that as her cue and wrestled the door open, falling ass-first into the street behind her. She scurried up and slammed the door.

Then she ran. As fast as she could, she ran, toward the intersection at Tenth Avenue and Seventeenth Street, screaming like a madwoman, trying to get someone's attention.

She could hear his Timberlands hitting the concrete behind her but she was too scared to take a look back, hoping instead that she'd made a fast enough escape to put some space between the two of them. She could see a cab letting off a passenger at Fifteenth Street. She raised her hands, shaking them wildly, but the cab only sped past her, up the avenue, its VACANT light burning brightly in her eyes like an insult. Then she did turn around. He was gaining on her, breathing heavily, swinging the gun in one hand and something else in the other, something sharp-looking, though she couldn't make out what it was from her position on the corner.

She took off, across the avenue, praying that traffic would flow behind her, preventing him from getting closer. She could see the lights of the pier further down the street, out across Eleventh Avenue. *I just have to get there*, Melissa thought. *There will be people there.* She looked back one more time, but she didn't see him. She felt herself exhale a long breath, and leaned over, grabbing her knees, breathing hard, blinking sweat from her eyes.

2

The four of them sat there looking at each other, waiting for TNT to come back into the suite after dashing out to make a call on his cell phone.

Finally Leo said to Joey, "Do you think he's Towanda's son?"

Joey shook his head. "I don't know. Unless he tells us who his mother is—"

"If he's Towanda's son," Duke said, "wouldn't he know that you're his father?"

"Who is Towanda?" Barry asked. "And what are you talking about?"

Leo laughed and looked at Joey, who just looked down at the floor. "Barry," Joey said. "When you fuck over your friends, you don't stay privy to all the gossip."

Barry scowled and went over to the bar. "Oh, fuck you, Joey. I apologized for that Cheyenne crap. Get over it. You were in jail. You expect the girl to just wait for you? Hell, she didn't even know you were feeling her like that."

"Not after you scooped her up, of course she didn't," Joey said. He stood up. "But this isn't even about Cheyenne, Barry—"

"What about what Duke did to me?" Barry exclaimed. "Huh? What about the secret he kept from me all those years?"

"It all sorta worked out for you in the end," Joey said. "Didn't it?"

Leo said, "Can we please not bring *that* up?"

No one said anything for a little while. The sound of ice clicking in cocktail glasses filled the room.

Barry went over to the window and looked out over the stretch of Manhattan extending north from the Meatpacking District. "I think I know whose kid he is." He turned back to face his old friends, a coy smile on his lips. "If anyone's interested in what 'Be-Wary-of-Barry' has to say about the matter."

For a few seconds no one responded. Finally Duke said, "Okay. I'll bite."

"Funny *you* should bite," Barry said.

Duke looked at Leo, then back at Barry. "Meaning what?"

Leo said, "I think he means it's you, Duke."

Duke laughed. "If TNT's my son, I cannot possibly imagine who his mother could be. Tell me that, Barry."

"Amanda's his mother." Barry took a sip. "Or was, at least."

Leo grabbed Duke just as he leaped from the club chair. Joey scrambled across the room in time to help Leo stop Duke from pounding into Barry.

"Leave Amanda outta this," Duke said. "Are you that evil, Barry?"

"What's evil about the truth?" Barry said.

"Besides," said Joey. "When could that have happened? Amanda had an abortion, then she went back to Syracuse, right, Duke?"

Duke nodded. "Barry's just trying to start some sh—"

"She didn't have an abortion the next time," Barry said quietly.

Duke said, "What next time?"

"The next time she got pregnant," Barry said. "When she left you at Syracuse."

It became a little clearer what Barry was saying. But no one seemed to want to acknowledge it, most of all Duke, who slowly sat down in the club chair and put his head in his hands.

Leo said, "You're saying she had a baby when she left Duke?"

"How do you know all this?" Joey asked him. "Who told you?"

Barry said, "Who do you think?"

"The Keeper of Secrets," Leo said. "The Master Manipulator. Gary Bradford."

Barry refilled his drink, taking his time getting to the point. When he was done refreshing his Scotch he sat on the arm of a couch and took a sip, savoring the flavor like a connoisseur. "Amanda had a choice to make all right. Whether to marry you and have a baby or whether to get another abortion. She chose to have the baby, but she didn't choose to marry you, Duke. I'm sure her pops had something to do with that."

Duke shook his head slowly. "It's not true."

Barry continued. "When Gary saw me spending time with Amanda, after I brought her to Joey's fashion show, he pulled me aside and asked me if I knew the story."

"It's not true," Duke said again. "She would have told me."

"She had a baby and put him up for adoption," Barry said. "Last I heard the kid was taken in by some couple in Albany that couldn't have children."

"And you never saw fit to mention any of this to Duke?" Leo said. "All the time you spent together when he was caring for his mother?"

"It really wasn't my place," Barry said.

They all looked up when they heard the suite door open. TNT came into the living room, his face dark with a look of concern. "No one killed anyone yet?"

Leo said, "Is your mother named Amanda?"

TNT looked at each of them, one by one. "I have to run a short errand," he said, ignoring Leo's question and turning back to the door.

"Just answer the question," Joey said.

TNT said, "I will when I get back."

"How long do we have to wait here for you?" Barry said. "I have places to be."

TNT smiled. "You sat around this long waiting to find out. What's another hour or so until the big reveal?" And with that, he turned around and walked out.

1998

1

From *People*, July 12, 1998:

> . . .*And he's really living the good life as he preps for the opening of JoeyRam's New York store. During this interview alone, Ramirez had to make so many calls, you wonder if he spends more time on the phone than he does in the studio: Call from his lawyer about the house in Lake Como he's buying; call to his New York muse Carla McFarland to make sure everything was set up in New York; call to the publicist about MTV scoping out his apartment for an episode of* Cribs. *"Yeah," says Ramirez, smiling a shy smile, "I feel like I talk on the phone more than I design sometimes!"*

From *Sports Illustrated*, July 18, 1998:

> *The Miami Dolphins have finally severed ties with controversial wide receiver Duke Maynard, sending the aging gridiron star to the Oakland Raiders for two fullbacks and a draft pick . . .*

2

Leo fiddled with the pencil, occasionally sketching tiny doodles in the margins of the legal pad on his lap. *Blah blah blah*, he thought. *If Pete was here, he'd smack me for getting all these boring financial types involved with the Foundation.* He looked up at Lionel Whitaker, tall and slender in that patrician way that Leo had always found so annoying in boys, dating all the way back to his secondary school classmates in Switzerland. But Lionel Whitaker was an estate lawyer and the slender patrician look seemed to be the usual shape, size, and model that boring estate lawyers came in. Leo just doodled in the margins, accepting that what Lionel lacked in exciting good looks and personality he more than made up for in good financial planning sense.

Look at me, thinking about Lionel's looks. How freaking shallow am I? he thought. *Very, I guess. So sue me.*

He smiled to himself. *Sue me.* If it hadn't been for the threat of a lawsuit, he might not even be sitting here in this stuffy room listening to Lionel and his partners outline the new five-year plan for the Pete Reynolds Foundation. If it hadn't been for Monica suggesting to Joey that he bring a civil suit against Greta and the City of New York for his wrongful conviction, he wouldn't have had the extra two million dollars to invest in the building the Foundation wanted to buy in Harlem to launch its new programs. Two million dollars, thanks to Joey, of the twelve million he got in the suit, the remaining ten going into expanding the growing JoeyRam empire. Speaking of which, Leo looked at his watch. If these bores didn't stop chattering he was going to be late getting to dinner with Joey and Carla and his parents to celebrate the opening of the New York store.

"Will that work for you, Leo? Meeting two weeks from today," Whitaker said, straightening his tie. "Can you meet?"

"No problem," Leo said, standing up.

"Is everything all right?" Whitaker asked. "You seem a little preoccupied."

"I haven't spoken to my father in almost five years," Leo said. "And I'm having dinner with him tonight."

"Ah," said Whitaker.

"Sorry for my behavior," Leo said, shaking his hand. "You're doing a fine job. Pete would be proud."

"Of you, too," said Whitaker.

When he got home, his answering machine had two messages, one from his mother asking about the restaurant for the dinner and one from someone he didn't know.

"Hi, this is Emily Wallace at *Black Men's Monthly*. I'm calling because I need a writer. I loved your book and you come highly recommended. The only thing is, I want to assign you an article that needs a quick turnaround and I don't even know if you're available but if you are can you please call me and let me know . . . I'm sorry I'm rambling but if you can give me a call I'd really appreciate it." She'd left her number.

Black Men's Monthly. A new magazine, edited by Sonny Britton, a guy he'd been in Jack and Jill with back when he was still a proud member of the black bourgeoisie. Like Leo, Sonny had achieved the outcast status of being an out gay boy when he graduated from Tufts and launched a career as an outspoken performance artist. Outcast or not, though, Sonny had found some way to raise the money to start his magazine. And Leo knew that some of that money came from the deep pockets at CoCo Cosmetics. How funny would it be to write for a magazine his father partly owned?

As he showered, Leo debated calling Emily Wallace back. If she needed a writer that fast it probably meant that some other writer she wanted turned her down or pulled out of the piece at the last minute. Was he in the mood to be sloppy seconds? Well, she did say she loved his book. That at least deserved a callback, even if he did turn down her offer for an assignment. Because he was going to turn it down. He'd never write for a magazine that his father had a financial stake in, would he? He grabbed a towel from the stand near the tub and dried himself off as he made a decision on his way to his bedroom.

Emily picked up on the first ring, sounding rushed and out of breath. "Thank goodness you called me back," she said. She had a pinched, high voice with the hint of a Southern accent. "I'm tearing my hair out here. We need someone to profile Gregory Finch of the New York Knicks. Are you interested?"

"I don't really write about sports."

"That's why I'm calling you," she said. "We don't want a sportswriter. We want someone who can paint a broader picture of this guy. Someone who can go behind the hundred million contract and the whole bad babydaddy reputation. Tell us who the man is hiding back there." She paused. "Only thing is, we need the piece in about a week."

As the cab pulled up to the restaurant, he saw his mother, chic in a knee-length linen coat, standing next to his father, and Leo couldn't wait to share his news. After all the years of being on the outside of his father's life, it was an oddly satisfying pleasure to know that, even indirectly, his father now needed him. He cleared his throat, took a deep breath, and plastered onto his face the most insincere smile he could muster.

"Hey," he said as he got out of the cab. "Guess what magazine I'm writing for?"

3

A couple of days later, Leo met Carla outside the new JoeyRam store for the big opening. He was surprised to see her arrive alone.

"Where's Reggie?"

"Don't talk to me about him," she said, straightening the blouse top of the red silk JoeyRam minidress she wore. "I'm getting very sick of him."

"What now?"

She sighed, giving a forced smile to the paparazzi lined up outside the store. "He's insufferable. He won't grow up. You know he's completely jealous of all of you."

"All of who?" Leo asked.

"You guys. You're all successful. You're all smart. Joey and Barry came from nothing. Duke's a football star. Your book was a best seller. He hates all of you guys from when we were all teenagers but now that you've all done well for yourselves he's livid. I just don't get it. *And* he thinks I'm still sleeping with Barry. Behind his back."

"Jealous of us?" Leo had to laugh. "Reggie comes from more money than anybody I know," he said. "He's always had everything he's ever wanted. Given to him."

"That money may not last much longer," Carla said. "And now he wants to dig into mine!" She started into the store. She air-kissed a slender woman in a severe-looking pantsuit. "Let's talk about something else: *you*," she said as they walked through the platinum-lined doors of JoeyRam NYC. "I didn't want to tell you this at dinner the other night. I think you and Joey need to get back together."

Leo almost spit out the piece of chewing gum he'd been chomping on to get the smell of marijuana off his breath. "What?"

"Look how well he's doing," she said. "And he has no one to share it with."

"And he doesn't want to share it with me, Carla. You can believe that. Besides," Leo said. "It was a phase Joey went through. He's not gay."

"Tell that to Boo Padgett," Carla said, and pointed across the store at Joey, dressed in a black turtleneck and low-cut black jeans, trying to maneuver away from the hulking presence of Boo, the infamously amorous head buyer at Bendel's.

With a sly grin on her lips, Carla stopped to get interviewed by a TV entertainment show. Leo stood there for a few seconds, singing along with Brandy and Monica as "The Boy Is Mine" blasted from the speakers hung around the room.

He saw the lascivious look on Boo Padgett's face and the desperate look on Joey's, so he headed that way to rescue his friend. He took Joey's arm and told him the store looked fabulous, making sure to stare right into Boo Padgett's lusty gaze. Joey thanked him, then politely told Boo that he had to show an old friend around.

Joey said, "Thank you. That was a close one."

"Carla says you and I need to get back together," Leo told him.

"What do you think?"

"I think you should stop batting those long Latin eyelashes at me and show me where the bar is."

"Is Duke coming?"

Leo shrugged, following Joey to a champagne-laden bar set up near a display of babydoll dresses with brocade frontpieces. "You know how he's been."

"I was hoping maybe things had gotten better." Joey grimaced. "I gotta go greet these people from Macy's. Give me a sec, man?"

Leo sipped his champagne and watched Joey move smoothly through the crowd, shaking hands, kissing cheeks, smiling for photos.

He wondered what Duke was doing at that moment and whether he should even report for training camp with the Raiders. He tried to force the pictures of that day out of his head, but it never worked. Even today, almost three years later, he could still smell the rancid smoke floating up from Mike's Corvette. He could still see Amanda's mangled, burned body as the firemen dragged her from the wreckage. He could still hear Duke's moans and cries, and the guttural monstrousness of his shouting as Mike had the audacity to get out of a cab twenty minutes after the whole conflagration erupted and ask what had happened. Leo didn't know which was worse, Mike's insane decision to move heroin with a teammate of the brother who'd brought him back from the brink or his insensitive denial of all of it when so much evidence was carried out of his room and into unmarked Miami-Dade police vehicles two days later. Or maybe the Dolphins were the worst, distancing themselves from the situation and publicly chastising Duke, like he'd planned the whole caper, designed it to make the team and organization look bad, yet still not releasing him from his contract so he could at least make a clean break and start fresh in another city.

Leo pulled out his cell phone and dialed Duke's number out at his mother's house. He felt like hearing his boy's voice.

Duke checked the caller ID. Then he turned back to TV and grabbed the remote control.

He knew Leo was calling from Joey's opening, but he wasn't in the mood to talk. Three years later, and Duke still found himself falling into sad moods. It only partly helped to be able to come back to his mother's house in the off-season.

He remembered that first return home, the teary explanations to his mother, how he'd failed them all: Mike, her, the team. He took solace in his mother's cooing assurances that he'd done all he could, comforted only so much because he was sure that somewhere inside she felt disappointed. In him, in Mike, in herself, and Duke could hardly bear that. Yet this was still where he felt most comfortable, eating his mother's cooking, walking with her in the summer nights, never thinking about football or money or the hardships of life, instead just living it, reveling in his chance to close down and leave it all out there for others to sort through.

And for a long time afterward, it was still only Amanda that he thought about more than anything.

He made himself whisper her name every day, sometimes more than once a day. As if saying her name kept her alive inside him, around him. When he walked along the bay, he'd call her, "Amanda," and he'd think of the name they'd have given their baby, the growing life inside her, snuffed out in the flames of Mike's bullshit. Sean, after Amanda's brother, if it was a boy. Ariana, if it was a girl. Sometimes, that first off-season in Long Island, walking on the beach or through the park near his mother's house, he'd see kids running in the surf or sliding down the climbing poles and he'd feel tears well up in his eyes, the sadness gripping at his insides like someone was forcing his blood to stop flowing, freezing him in place and refusing to let him move.

The one bright spot, funnily enough, was Monica. Perhaps because she'd been there when it happened, after having spent a few hours getting to know Amanda. Perhaps because she'd been injured herself, stuck as she was in the arm cast and leg brace for almost three months from the impact of the blast. She and Leo both had broken arms, and Duke smiled thinking about the party they had the week they had their casts taken off and the pretty velvet wraps Joey stitched up for both of them to cover their arms.

And now, three years afterward, it was his own smile that warmed him deeply yet also somehow chilled him to the bone.

How could he still mourn Amanda and yet think so much about Monica?

He thought about the night he'd come to Long Island, hoping to surprise his mother, and being surprised himself, finding Monica sitting at the dining room table, across from his mother, discussing estate taxes and her will. She'd stayed for dinner that night, entertaining them with funny stories about life at her law firm, where she was the only black partner. She was easy to talk to, a good listener who sat quietly when Duke found himself crying one night, after happening upon Sean, Amanda's brother, on the television, reporting news on a cable news/financial channel. She'd let him weep, then hugged him close, understanding, caring, letting him get it all out. It was in Monica's arms that Duke figured something else out, something that confused him enough to really want to stay away from people he wouldn't know how to explain it to.

He was falling in love with Monica.

As frozen as he felt missing Amanda, like the blood pumping through his heart had congealed into some cold, lifeless sludge, he could feel a warming thaw inside himself whenever he was around Monica. How could that be? How could he feel such competing emotions, and was one overwhelming the other? Did he even want it to?

The phone rang again. Duke looked at the caller ID box. It was Monica. He picked up the phone. It was good to hear her voice. She asked him if they were still on for a late lunch tomorrow; she still wanted to give him that paperwork for his mother. He said he'd be there. As he hung up the phone, a smile lightened his face. Maybe he'd see Leo and Joey while he was in the city, call them up and see if they wanted to grab a beer. He could tell Leo how much he liked his book. Congratulate Joey on his burgeoning fashion empire. Maybe he'd even stop by Marie's place and take Starkeisha something nice. He was feeling much better already.

4

The party was launching into high-schmooze mode, and Joey felt himself rising with the energy emanating around the space. He let himself be pulled from guest to guest, graciously accepting congratulations and well wishes.

He found Leo standing in a little circle with his parents and some guy he didn't recognize. Leo introduced him as Sonny Britton. With his flamboyant mannerisms, tight Helmut Lang suit, and heavy silver rings on multiple fingers, Joey wondered who he could be; he couldn't believe Gary Bradford was having such a pleasant conversation with such an obvious queen.

Joey excused himself from the group and made his way over to his assistant Ramona, who looked a little more relaxed than she had at the beginning of the evening. Joey took two flutes of champagne from the tray of a passing waiter and thrust one into Ramona's hand.

"But your rule," she said, "about employees drinking?"

"You deserve it, girl," he said. "To our success." They toasted. "And thanks."

"It has gone well, hasn't it?" Ramona took a drink. "Do you want an update on your calls or do you want to wait till later?"

"Anybody important?" Joey said. As Ramona scrolled through the cell phone calls, he watched Leo across the room, introducing Sonny Britton to Carla and her husband, Reggie, who'd just arrived. *Leo the Lion*, Joey thought with a smile. *Wait till he finds out I named one of the sunglass lines after him.* Joey sipped his champagne, amazed at his own good fortune. He basked for a minute in the love he felt circulating around in the room, even if it was, he knew, a fashion industry kind of love with its odd blend of respect, fear, and jealousy all wrapped up in a bow most people would use to choke their closest competitor. It was good to have Leo and Carla around to support him.

"This was the only one that seemed interesting," Ramona said, handing him the cell phone and pulling him out of his thoughts. "It's from someone named Florence Thomas. She asked that you call her back as soon as possible."

Florence Thomas. His aunt who'd shut him out of his grandmother's life all those years ago in Miami. Why would she be calling?

"Did she say what she wanted?"

Ramona shook her head. "She left a message at the store in Miami. Raoul called the cell and left the message. She just said it was important. Something about your grandmother. Do you want me to return the call? Joey?"

The next morning Joey was on a plane to Miami. Mariano was waiting at the airport in the Land Rover, and took Joey right to University of Miami Hospital, where his Aunt Florence met him in the intensive care unit. She'd been up all night, since she'd brought her sister in after she'd collapsed while gardening in the front yard.

"She'd first called out for your mother, for Nola," Florence told Joey in a halting, hesitant voice that seemed edged with a kind of embarrassment. "Then," Florence said, "she started asking for the baby. She wanted to see the baby." She cleared her throat and looked down at the tiled floor. "And I took that to mean you," she muttered.

Joey could tell that she was remembering their moment at the house, when she sat and ate, ignoring him as he waited for her to respond to his knocks. But as much as he wanted to force her to acknowledge that rejection, he knew he was there now for another purpose, to provide solace to his grandmother. Florence could deal with her guilt some other time, as far as he was concerned. Now here he sat, wondering if his grandmother would completely recover, if they'd ever get to share more moments together. The doctors hadn't seemed too positive when they'd spoken to Florence earlier, murmuring their dark diagnosis with their heads bowed, clipboards in front of them like shields against the ricochets of the pain they knew they were inflicting on loved ones.

"I'm sorry, Joey." She said it again, then again, then reached for Joey's hand and clasped her fingers around it, tightening her grip until all the blood rushed out of Joey's fingers. Joey put an arm around her, cautiously, and wondered why tragic situations like this one always forced people to admit their mistakes. But then he pushed those thoughts away and felt his energy galvanize. He didn't know how much time he'd have left with his grandmother, but he vowed to make the most of it starting now. He took his arm from around his aunt's shoulder and stood.

"Where's the doctor," he asked her firmly. "I need to get some answers."

5

By the time Leo was working on his fourth article for *Black Men's Monthly*, six months after his profile of the basketball star Gregory Finch, he was seeing his father on a regular basis. He was returning from Miami, from Joey's grandmother's funeral, when he got a call from Gary, inviting him to lunch. "And it's important," Gary had said. "Don't double-book your day, Mr. Bestselling Writer."

As he sat outside his father's office waiting for a meeting to end so they could have lunch, he had to smile to himself, remembering his first visit to CoCo Cosmetics when he was five years old. He remembered holding his father's hand as they got off the elevator and walked the long maze of corridors to Gary's office. The friendly smiles from the employees trying hard to be nice to the boss's son were still imprinted on his brain with so many other fond early memories of his father. Some of those people were still here twenty-five years later and their smiles were still friendly. Leo asumed they all must have heard about the longtime estrangement between father and son, and another Leo, the old Leo, would have been embarrassed to sit outside Gary's office, knowing that the people who passed by probably had their own theories and ideas and judgments about him and his lifestyle and his relationship with Gary. But today, he didn't care at all.

As he flipped through one of the magazines left on the credenza outside the office, he wondered what today's lunch was about. After seeing each other at dinner that night, then again at Joey's opening two nights later, they'd had brunch that weekend, their initial conversation somewhat stilted by the lack of a rhythm that a more sustained relationship might have built, but Lillian's happy smiles and awkward icebreakers helped them through it. By the next week, they were meeting alone at his father's club and laughing at recollections of Bradford family shenanigans. They went to the Knicks season opener together and hung out at the after party with Barry and his latest flame, a young model from Senegal. The beginning of each meeting, Leo had to admit, was a little fraught for him, with the impending moment when Gary would bring up the sexuality thing—but he never did. For a while Leo wondered if that was good or bad. Was he *really* meeting with Gary on his own terms if the question of his sexuality, which had ripped them apart, never entered the discussion? Or had Gary just gotten over it, matured, come to terms with the fact of it, which didn't require any discussion about it? Then again, it wasn't like Leo was seeing anyone that he could tell Gary about anyway. That day would come, he knew. But until then, he also had to admit, it was good to have his father back in his life. At the very least, it meant that he and Lillian didn't have to sneak around to see each other anymore.

"Barry's going to join us," Gary said.

Leo looked up from the magazine to see his father pulling on his coat.

"No problem," Leo said. "How's he doing? Haven't talked to him in a while."

"He's been acting strangely lately, to tell you the truth." Gary shrugged. "But he doesn't tell me anything." As they waited for a light to change at Madison Avenue, Gary asked Leo about Joey's grandmother's funeral. "It's good that you two got to spend a few days together," he said.

Leo stared at the sidewalk, unsure of what to make of his father's kind words. He almost felt that if he looked at Gary, he might realize that this kindness was just a dream.

Barry was sitting at the bar when they got to Langdon's. He hugged Leo and shook Gary's hand. Leo watched Barry fidget through menu-perusing and small talk. Finally, Barry sighed and said, "Gary, can't we just tell Leo already?"

Gary put down his Scotch and said, "*Ask* him is more the case, Barry."

"Ask me what?" Leo said. "This some kind of ambush?"

Barry sighed again. "Gary wants you to take over *Black Men's Monthly*." He picked up his menu and hid his face behind it.

Leo looked from Barry to his father. "You serious?"

"That Sonny guy is nice and all," Gary said. "But the magazine needs something else. Something smarter and edgier."

Leo put down his coffee. "Edgier? Didn't even know you knew the word existed."

"I've learned a lot over the years," he said, his eyes on Leo's. "I've changed."

Leo didn't know what to say. About the offer just made to him or about the hidden meaning in his father's words. Learned. Changed. Two other words Gary Bradford didn't use often. Especially about himself, because he knew everything and because he was perfect, nothing about him needed to be changed.

"So?" he asked Leo. "Do you accept?"

"Of course he does," Barry said. "You think he won't?"

"I'm hoping he will," Gary said. "Excuse me. Duty calls."

Leo watched him walk away, then turned to Barry. "So you knew about this."

"I told you a long time ago, your father's an asshole but he's not evil."

"I remember," Leo said. He sat back in the velvet-lined chair. "My new book is due in six months. When will I find time to edit a magazine?"

"You've been dreaming about this day for years, Leo. You'll find the time."

Whatever else Leo thought about Barry, he knew Barry had never been all that wrong about reading people. But there was something else. "Are you okay, Barry?"

"I'll be all right," Barry said. "I'll be fine."

"I was sorry to hear about—"

Barry held up his hand. "Do not say her name."

"So that's what up." Leo nodded. "Heartbreak."

"I should have married Carla when I had the chance."

"*You* had a chance?"

"Fuck you, Leo." Barry looked at the menu again. "This is funny to you, right? Ol' Barry gets his heart yanked out and you think it's some kind of joke."

"I don't think it's a joke," Leo said. "But I did learn one thing."

"And that is?"

"That you actually have a heart."

When Barry got back to the office, he told his assistant Yeva to hold his calls.

He dropped himself into his desk chair and slumped down. Who cared about the Senegalese supermodel? Everyone thought he was still hung up on that chick. Yeah, she'd left to be with some Brazilian soccer player that Barry had never heard of, and it had hurt a bit at the time, but really who cared? Since her, he'd been with two soap actresses, a movie studio executive he knew from Yale, and an acrobat from the Big Apple Circus. Sure, he thought he might be able to get serious with the supermodel, but he didn't care about any of them, not really, not when he realized the real source of the odd, depressing feelings he'd been having. Something was missing, something that wasn't filled up by glasses of Scotch and long legs on showgirls and maintaining the destructive sense of control he needed to have over everything in his life.

Then one day, he figured it out. He'd come to Gary's office to show him the new TV ad campaign, and there was Leo, sitting in the visitor chair, laughing with Gary about something Lillian had said at dinner the previous night. After their long break from each other, they were laughing, making new memories that could only enhance the old ones that had built their relationship. And it hit Barry, square in his head and his heart: the father he felt like he never knew. Partly because they were both always so angry, constantly up in each other's faces yet so distant from each other in so many ways.

I want to see my father.

Looking for Earl took up a lot of time and created in Barry another level of focus to his already tightly wound demeanor. Everyone around him thought he was still mourning the loss of his love, but actually, he was just concentrating, trying to counter the loss with this new assignment he'd given himself.

After hitting dead ends himself, he gave a private detective the basic information: Earl Chambers had been born in Newport News, Virginia, arrived in New York in June '73. He gave him the names of the women he knew Earl had cheated with and the names of some of his cronies from the bar where he hung out in Sag Harbor.

"Just tell me what he's doing now," he'd told the detective.

A week later, he got some info. Earl Chambers was living in Macon, Georgia, with a woman named Jackie Parham. Barry reached for the phone on his desk. He'd read the number out loud a few times, like a mantra, as if he needed to hear the number to really believe there would be someone to answer the call when he dialed it.

The woman on the other end sounded harried and impatient. Barry asked for Earl.

Jackie Parham said, "Who is this?"

"This is Barry Chambers calling from New York. I'm looking for my father, Earl."

"He ain't here."

"Can you tell me when he'll be back?"

"You got a better chance of seein' him before I do. He up there in New York."

Barry felt his heart skip a beat. "Do you know where in New York?"

"Seein' his daughter, he tole me. Don't ask me where she stay." She yelled at someone in the background. "You need anything else?"

"Did you say his *daughter*?" Barry actually felt a buzz. *A sister? Family?*

"Yeah," said Jackie Parham. "Meanin' your sister if you really who you say you are." And she hung up.

Now, lunch with Leo and Gary behind him, his calls being held, his hands shaking like a little boy taking a free throw in the big game, Barry stared at the single folder on his desk that he'd been waiting days for, the reason he'd rushed Gary to make his announcement to Leo, then left right after finishing his meal.

There were two pages in the folder. One was a bill, neatly outlining all the fees the detective had accrued on his search for Earl Chambers. The second page was made up of two paragraphs of information. According to the notes, Earl Chambers's daughter was named Starkeisha Maynard. She lived in Queens, with her mother, Marie Maynard.

Maynard. Barry knew a Marie Maynard. Duke's sister was named Marie Maynard. Barry tried to swallow, but felt like something lumpy was caught in his throat.

Could this be right?

An hour later, Barry was standing on the lopsided steps of a shabby-looking, gray-shingled house off Merrick Boulevard in Jamaica, Queens. He hadn't called first. He wanted to surprise Marie and his father, shock them as good as he'd been shocked by the detective's news. On the drive over from Manhattan, running all kinds of scenarios through his brain, he realized that it did make sense. He did remember seeing Duke's sister Marie with his father a couple of times, once coming home from school, in the passenger seat of his father's truck. But he'd thought that Earl had just seen her walking and offered her a ride home. Another time, he could remember, he saw them talking outside the Cubby Bar, when his mother had sent him to tell Earl to come home. Had they been fucking all that time? He rang the bell, with one last thought popping into his brain: *Did Duke know?*

He could hear someone walking toward the door. When Marie opened it, he waited to see if she'd immediately recognize him. She did.

"Hey, Barry," she said, as if she'd been expecting him all day. "How you doing?"

Barry didn't know what to say.

Marie said, "You coming in?" She yelled up the stairs. "Earl? It's for you."

"**N**o," said Earl Chambers. "Your mother don't know 'bout Marie. She never did."

Barry took a sip from the can of Dr Pepper Marie had given him. "Does Duke know who Starkeisha's father is?"

"*I* never told him," Marie said.

"He caught us that one time." Earl looked over at Marie. "You remember that?"

"I remember," Marie said. "That don't mean he knows you Starkeisha's daddy."

Barry sipped some more soda, wishing he could close his ears to their squabbling. Everything had been an argument between them the whole twenty minutes he'd been in the house, from Earl's refusal to come downstairs because his favorite TV show was on to Marie's refusal to mix him a rum and Coke when he finally did come down. He looked at the two of them, his father, looking pretty much the same except for a little less hair on his head, and

Marie, who looked way older than her thirty-four years, her once shiny blond locks now hanging like dirty string, her thick legs and ass jammed into a pair of Jackal jeans. There was certainly no love between them. Had there ever been? Barry wondered for a second if he'd feel different if he had felt some love, some deep emotional connection flowing between them, instead of feeling the sheer disgust he was trying hard to harness inside him. "Is Starkeisha here?" he asked.

"She work at a day camp," Marie said. "Yeah," she continued, a haughty tone creeping into her voice, "she gotta work all summer 'cause your no-good father don't do shit for his daughter."

Earl said, "Don't say that."

"Don't say what?" Marie said, suddenly more than haughty. She was pissed. "I don't even know why I bother letting you come up here to see Star—"

"I ain't talking 'bout that," Earl said. "I'm talking about you calling me his father."

Barry looked up from his can of soda. "Excuse me?"

Earl said, "You heard me."

"Earl?" Marie sat on the couch next to him. "What you trying to say?"

"What I shoulda said a helluva long time ago. I ain't none of his father."

Barry put the soda can down on the coffee table. It suddenly felt too heavy to hold. The room suddenly felt hot and crowded with a fierce nothingness that made Barry's heart beat twice as fast. "If you're not my father," he said, "then who is?"

Earl shrugged. "Your mama never told me, if you wanna know the truth. And after a while I ain't really care anymore." He looked over at Marie. "Now, can I get back to my show?"

1

TNT stood in the lobby of the Hotel Gansevoort and dialed Melissa's cell number again. Still no answer, just her voice mail, an announcement with "Scandalize," his most recent hit, playing in the background. He was getting nervous now. He dialed another number.

"TNT Productions, this is Natalie."

"This is Troy. Is Melissa there?"

"No," said Natalie. "Aren't you supposed to be in some important meet—"

"Find Melissa," he said, and clicked the phone shut.

Something was wrong. He could feel it. And he felt like an ass for being so abrupt with Melissa on the phone earlier.

He headed out of the hotel. Outside, his Land Rover was parked across the street. He ran to it and hopped in. There was one more person who might know where Melissa was calling from. He took out his phone and dialed another number.

The woman who answered said, "Bradford residence."

"This is TNT. Can you tell Lillian it's me?"

2

Upstairs in the suite, Joey poured himself another vodka tonic and went to the window overlooking Ninth Avenue. He was tired, but he wasn't sure if it was just the exhaustion that was making his mind flash back on moments from back in the day. Could TNT be TeeTee's son, the result of that one night in Shirley's house? He shivered as the memory of waking up that night with Shirley and Carlton hovering over him. After his grandmother's death, even after building a slow but fulfilling relationship with his Aunt Florence, there was still a part of him that longed for some blood relative, for some connection that had nothing to do with JoeyRam designs or his fame or his money.

Which one of you bastards is my father?

Did TNT even know? Did anyone of them know? Was he just gonna wait them out? Wait for a confession?

There really was only one thing to do, Joey decided. When TNT came back, he'd force him to tell them his mother's name. It was only way.

Leo sat on the couch farthest from the rest of them, and he had to laugh. The idea that he was sitting here, in this suite, was funny to him. Because it was all coming back to him now. That crazy week. It felt like all hell broke loose, emotions so high in the summer home of the Bradford family that he was sure things would never be the same again.

"What's so funny?"

Leo took a sip of his Coke. "Let me ask you all a question," he said. "Why us?"

"Why us what?" Barry said.

"Why the four of us sitting here? Together?"

"He says one of us is his father," Duke said. "Weren't you paying attention?"

"That's not what I mean," Leo said. He stood up and put his Coke on the arm of the couch. "Why us? Why not four random guys? Why us? The four who basically spent every waking moment together from, what, age sixteen to college? Why four friends?"

The other three looked at each other. No one said anything.

"None of you find it interesting that it's the four of *us*?"

"Well, Sag Harbor does have something to do with it," Joey said.

"Yeah," Leo said. "But again, why us? Why isn't, say, Duke in this hotel suite with three other guys you went to high school with? Why isn't it Barry with three other dudes from Sag? Why does it happen to be the four of us?"

"The VIPs," Duke said.

"Exactly," Leo said. "Here we all are. And if you think about that, I think you'll figure out who TNT's mother is. And then, pretty much, who his father is."

Barry sat down. "Are you saying that you know?"

At that moment, the suite phone began to ring. They all looked at each other. Finally, Leo reached for the phone. He said hello and listened for a few seconds.

"Slow down," he said. "This isn't TNT; he's not here. Who is this?"

The other three crowded around him, leaning closer to hear the conversation.

"He just went out, Melissa," Leo said. "He said he had an errand to run."

Leo shrugged at the others, his forehead wrinkled in confusion.

"I don't know where he went. Did you try his cell phone? What do you mean? Who has a gun? Who are you talking about? Can you come here?" Leo took the phone away from his ear. "She hung up. She said some guy's looking for TNT, that he has a gun and he's after him." He hung up the phone.

Joey said, "What the fuck?"

"This is officially the day from hell," Barry said.

3

TNT sat in his Land Rover watching the traffic crawl down Ninth Avenue.

He looked up at the hotel. He wondered what the four of them were talking about now. Still arguing, probably. But still there. *They're all lonely*, he thought. *They all* want *to be my pops*. He wondered for a moment if this had been the right way to handle it.

He looked at his cell phone, willing Melissa to call again. He looked at the dwindling battery icon. Of course he didn't know he'd be in the Hotel Gansevoort all day. But then he also didn't expect to get a hectic-sounding call from Melissa halfway through his meeting with The VIPs.

That name. Did the four of them really know they'd end up rich New York guys, rolling around in limos and private planes, walking down red carpets and dating models and rock stars? Even Joey, the ex-con. Look at him, one of the biggest designers in the world, stores in Miami and London and Tokyo and L.A. And Duke, football player turned Internet mogul, white trash made good. He looked at himself in the rearview mirror, at his hazel eyes, so like Duke's green ones, actually.

He smiled. It had been a good day, after all the initial drama, at least. Now if only he could get Melissa on the phone—

It rang. He grabbed it and punched the answer button.

"Mel? Where are you? I'm outside the hotel. What do you mean go back inside?"

A tap on the window.

TNT turned to see a guy in a dirty red sweatshirt standing there, a smudged .45 staring at him from the guy's ashy hand.

The guy said, "Get out. Either get out or let me in."

TNT dropped the phone. He dived down and reached under the passenger seat for his own gun, but it wasn't there. *Fuck.*

He hadn't brought it with him from Westchester.

He looked up to see the guy in the red sweatshirt walking around the Land Rover.

TNT thought fast. If he jumped out of the ride, he might be able to make it across the street back to the hotel before the guy could get a real shot off from that side of the Rover. He decided to go for it. When he saw the red sweatshirt get completely around the Rover, he used his foot to open the driver's side door and scooted out.

He could hear the red sweatshirt yell, "NO!"

He was halfway across the street, dodging cabs, about to reach the door of the Hotel Gansevoort, when the shot rang out. He heard it ricochet off a wall, kept his head down, hustling toward the double doors of the hotel. Just as he reached it, another shot fired.

And it hit him. In the back. He went down.

He felt like a linebacker had pushed him to the ground.

The bright lights of the hotel started to dim.

He could feel the commotion as people began to surround him.

But it didn't stop the lights from fading.

To black.

2001

1

"Ladies, gentlemen, I'm pleased to welcome you to the launch of *Rhythm* magazine!"

The rush of applause spreading through the room felt like a wave of love. Standing there on the stage behind his father, Leo could only think about the ridiculously rough road they'd traveled in the last few months to make sure this evening would even happen. He looked over his father's shoulder at the rappers and singers and music industry executives who were hungry for a new magazine that covered them with pride and beauty. He could see the advertisers in their Armani suits, with their eager, hungry looks; the word on the street was that *Rhythm* was going to do the sort of business *Vibe* and *The Source* hadn't seen in years. And he could see Barry, sulking in a corner booth, sipping a Scotch. Which made him feel vindicated. The applause was the sound of people drowning out Barry's increasing negativity about the plan.

"I'd like to introduce someone now who you all probably know already. Ladies and gentlemen," said Gary Bradford, "the real brains behind this brilliant project, my pride and joy, my son, Leo Bradford."

Leo swallowed. He wasn't expecting this at all. "Pride and joy?" When had that become his description? As he stepped nervously to the microphone, he searched for his mother in the crowded audience. He found her, and saw a tear sliding down her cheek. His father gave him a tight hug as he stepped aside, making space for Leo.

"Uh," Leo said. "I, uh, do not know what to say. *Rhythm* has been a long time in the making, and it's something I'm incredibly proud of. And it's the perfect next step after the fabulous success we've had with *Black Men's Monthly*. It represents many of my ideas about journalism, about African American culture, about the world. But it's also, personally speaking, very meaningful because it brought me closer to my father." The audience applauded even louder. "And not just because he's the rich one with all the money," Leo added, and smiled at the roar of laughter that greeted his words. "There's not much more I want to say," he concluded, "except to say thanks to my wonderful staff, and thanks to my parents who I love with all my heart."

Gary grabbed him into another bear hug as he placed the microphone on the podium behind him. "You're a winner," he whispered into Leo's ear. "And I have so many more plans for you, son. I love you, too."

"Can I please get a picture with the three moguls?" Carla said.

She had one hand holding up the strapless bodice of her black silk JoeyRam sheath dress and the other wrapped around the wrist of a harried-looking photographer as she dragged him over to the booth in the center of the room where Leo was enjoying champagne with Joey and Duke.

In the popping glare of flashbulbs, enhanced by other photographers and onlookers joining the fray as they tried to get a glimpse of the three friends and their supermodel buddy, Leo put his arm around Joey's shoulder and pulled him in closer for the picture. Through the flash he could see Greg's tall, lanky frame hovering nearby, a glass of orange juice in his hand, which he raised in a toast when he made eye contact with Leo. Leo winked once and smiled. *Success*, he thought. *And love.* Who would have thought the first one would come and who would have ever thought that the second one would ever come again? It had taken him a long time to get over Pete, but now here was Greg, NBA star, Georgetown graduate, smart, funny, tender, and great in bed. Was it love? It must have been, Leo believed, because love came with a price as far as he was concerned. *There's always a price,* he thought as he waved Greg over. He tried to hide his frown as Greg did exactly what he thought he'd do, beg off, shake his head, step away from the possibility of anyone in public thinking they were together. It had been that way since the first date, a few weeks after the *Black Men's Monthly* interview. It had been that way during their off-and-on courtship. And it was still that way two years into what they both were finally calling a "relationship."

As the flashbulbs blasted into his eyes, Joey wished he'd worn a pair of his Leo the Lion sunglasses, the sample pair of the blue ones he was debuting in Paris next week for JoeyRam's Summer 2002 resort line. And when he thought of sunglasses he thought of other things he had to get done. Like e-mail the sketches of the costumes he was doing for Madonna's next tour to her manager. Like figure out how he was going to get out of that dinner with Puff Daddy in Saint-Tropez. Like decide what he was going to send Ricky Martin for the music program he was trying to launch in Puerto Rico. *My life,* he thought. *JoeyRam is everything I ever wanted it to be.* I'm *everything I ever wanted to be.* Well, almost. Because if he was everything he ever wanted to be, he had to ask himself: What was he doing in the relationship he was in? What was he doing in a threesome with the television newscaster and his ultra-horny wife? What was he doing spending so much time in their Long Island mansion like some boy toy? And how could he manage to be in an ongoing ménage à trois and still feel as alone as he did?

He looked around the nightclub, trying to locate John and

Melanie, the two perfect blondes he slept with whenever he was in New York. There they were: John getting interviewed by some gossip columnist, Melanie at his side like the loyal wife, that self-satisfied look on her face, secure in the knowledge that no one in town knew the freaky life they led in the Hamptons. Joey watched them and came to a decision. It was time to end it. And after that there was something else he needed to do. There was something he wanted that he wasn't sure he had any right to.

He wanted Leo. As happy as he was for Leo, he knew that Greg was the wrong guy for him. It was time for Leo and Joey to be together again.

*M*ogul, thought Duke. *I'm not a mogul, I'm a football player.*

But then he thought about the meeting he'd had with his lawyer and accountant six months earlier in Los Angeles. Murray had placed a document in front of him, a huge smile dimpling his cheeks. Duke read over the paper, not even sure he was understanding everything it said, crowded as it was with talk of investments and returns and percentages and remunerative incorporations. But when Dominic took the check from the portfolio on the glass-topped desk and passed it to Murray, who then placed it on top of the document in front of Duke, everything started to make sense.

Twenty million dollars of sense.

All from an investment of three hundred thousand dollars because he thought the twenty-year-old nephew of his old Redskins teammate Solomon Greenbridge had an interesting idea. And because Solomon had looked out for him in those early NFL days when he was the fast white boy who got all the attention from the sports world.

Duke didn't even really know anything about the Internet when he ran into Solomon and his nephew Randy two years ago, right at the end of all the Miami drama. He knew about e-mail. He knew about chat rooms and dating services, but that was about it. As he told Murray, he didn't even know where Silicon Valley was. But when he heard Randy's impromptu pitch sitting there at a barbecue at Solomon's house in Bethesda, the deceptively simple idea of a place where people who loved hip-hop and sports could congregate and trade stories, chat, share pictures, play fantasy league games—it just sounded like the kind of cool online community he would go to if he ever found the time to chill on the computer. When Solomon told him he was going to invest a couple hundred thousand because Randy was "some kind of computer genius," Duke threw his hat into the ring. His money wasn't doing anything else except taking care of his mother and sister and her kids, and hiring detectives to find Mike to make his mother happy.

And then, after a year of attracting members and getting wonderful press around the country, Randy's website, SportsandBeats .com, was bought by a large cable sports network eager to reach the young, hip audience that made up its membership. When Murray called Duke and told him the network was paying over ninety million for the site, that Duke's initial investment would net him at least fifteen million dollars, he couldn't believe it. And now, with Monica's help, that money, more than he'd ever made as a football player or soda or sneaker endorser, was invested, and growing. And apparently making him into some kind of mogul.

Now Duke scooched over on the booth seat to make room for Monica, who'd been talking to Reggie McFarland most of the night. Duke kissed her right on the lips and massaged her neck.

"Hey, baby," he said. "You miss me?"

Monica smiled. "Always, baby." She shifted closer. "But I can do without all the cameras. And Reggie staring down my blouse when I'm trying to talk business."

"Reggie will never change," said Duke, shaking his head. "Let's give this ten more minutes for Leo, then we're outta here."

"Good," Monica cooed. " 'Cause I have plans for you when we get to the hotel."

"I'm still recovering from this injury," Duke said, rubbing his shoulder with an exaggerated stroke. "So you'll have to be gentle with me."

"You know I know what to do," she whispered.

"You spoil me," said Duke.

"You need to be spoiled," said Monica. "And everyone will find out at the lunch tomorrow." She waved her ringless ring finger at him and kissed his cheek. "Everyone will know that I'm Mrs. Duke Maynard!"

Across the room, Barry watched the crowded booth where Leo and Joey and Duke were holding court. As a waitress in a short skirt and a *Rhythm* T-shirt sauntered by, Barry grabbed the edge of her skirt and yanked. "Another Scotch," he said. "Pronto, sista."

From his vantage point, Barry watched the constant flash of the camera's bulbs, trying to decide whether he should go over to the booth and congratulate Leo on a job well done, even if he really didn't believe it. Did the world really need another black culture magazine? Hardly, as far as Barry was concerned. Gary could have found some other way to spend that cash. As far as Barry was concerned, Gary was only doing it to make up for all that time he lost with Leo, to show his little boy that he could still be the most powerful and loving man in the world when he wanted to be.

But whatever. That was what fathers did for sons, right? They had the right to exert all the power they could muster to make the world safer, better, richer for their sons. *Not that I'd know,* Barry thought. He closed his eyes and remembered going back to his mother's house after his confrontation with Earl.

"It's not important," his mother had told him. "What does it matter who your father is? He's dead now. Why do you care?"

"I need to know," Barry had told her, anger pulsating through him because she couldn't understand how unmoored he felt, how empty it was to feel fatherless. It was better to think that Earl, with all his faults, as damaged and wrong as he was, had fathered him, rather than know that some other guy, some guy who never existed as far as he was concerned, had sired him.

"Why didn't you tell me?" he asked her.

"Like I said, I didn't think it was important. He ran out on you anyway, Barry. You really wanted to know who he was after that? I was just trying to protect you."

Another thing fathers did. Barry remembered all the times Gary asked him about Leo, even when they weren't speaking, even when Leo was across the ocean playing the role of what Barry liked to call Rock Star's Wife. Gary would find a way to bring Leo into almost any conversation, find a way to ask after his affairs, using Barry to get information about his son. Even when he hated to look at Leo, it seemed that Gary Bradford still couldn't stop thinking about him. Had his father done that? After he left? Had he even thought about Barry, wondered how he was growing and changing, if he even *was* growing and changing?

He'd tried to articulate these feelings to his mother, and he still felt bad for the words he left her with that night, even though he meant every one of them.

"Don't you get it?" he'd pleaded. "Do you know how many women I've screwed and asshole rich boys I've sucked up to or tried to emulate 'cause I've felt like absolutely *nothing* all these years? Huh? Do you know that? The whole Barry Chambers thing, this whole performance I've perfected since I could fucking talk? Trying all this time to be confident when all I was doing was conning people and conning myself into thinking I was this confident big shot who knew everything and *every*body. And you can't even tell me my real father's *name*? Can't you even give me that much? You can keep my Yale degrees, okay? You can keep all those awards I won in high school and debate championships and all of it! I spent my whole life like a big fucking fake, just trying to figure out who I am and why I matter and what I'm supposed to be so I wouldn't end up like Earl Chambers. And you won't even tell me who Earl Chambers was replacing? Ruining everything? Hitting you? Degrading me? I haven't even wanted to have kids with any of the women I been with. I forced one, Ma! I forced one to have an abortion 'cause I had no clue! I had no clue what it meant to be a loving father to a child. To a son. My father, Ma. My *father*. I'd just like to go see his damn grave, just to know he existed. Just to pretend maybe he thought about me every once in a while. And you can't even give me that?"

He'd left his mother's house in tears, telling himself he'd never go back there, ignoring her calls for weeks, diving deep within himself. And now here he was watching the happy reunion between Leo and Gary continue. He really couldn't take it anymore.

The waitress returned with his drink. He grabbed it from her little circular tray and swigged back the entire contents of the short glass. He felt strong. He stood up and headed over to the center booth.

"I remember," Barry said, leaning over the side of the booth, "when you didn't want anything to do with CoCo, Leo. Look at ya now, the right prince of the kingdom."

"Things change," Leo said. He looked around the booth. "You wanna join us?"

"Why would I wanna do that? So you can tell everyone how I was the main opponent to the idea of your little magazine?"

Carla said, "You need to chill out, Barry."

"And you need to mind your business, Mrs. McFarland." He looked around the club. "Maybe you should go find your husband before he bankrupts somebody else's company." He noticed the harsh look in Carla's eyes and laughed at his joke. "Oops. Was I not supposed to say that?"

"What's he talking about?" Leo said.

"Nothing," Carla said. "This is your night, lil cousin. Ignore Barry."

Duke said, "You've had too much to drink, man."

"Maybe you should go home, Barry," Joey said.

"I'll go home when I'm good and ready," Barry slurred. "You scared I'm gonna bring up some of your secrets, too?"

Monica said, "Come on, Duke. Let's get out of here."

"Why?" Barry said. "You scared I'm gonna tell Duke about us?"

"There is no us," Monica said, avoiding Duke's glance at her. "Come on, Duke."

Duke said, "What's he talking about?"

"Not now," Barry said. "Not *today*. But I'm not talking about now, am I, Monica?"

Monica stood up. "Are you coming, Duke? I'm ready to go."

"It was just once, Duke," Barry slurred. "I was down in the dumps. Monica just wanted to make me feel better. Nothing emotional. Just sex. Right, Mon?"

Everyone looked, from Barry to Duke to Monica.

"I think it's funny," Barry went on. "Let's see, Carla, Monica. All the fine black bitches that Duke has fucked? I've fucked 'em, too!" He paused. "Well, except for Amanda. Never did get those panties."

Duke leapt up from the booth and clocked Barry right across the chin. Joey jumped up and caught Barry just as he was about to fall backward. Leo pulled Duke back. A crowd of onlookers started to form around the booth.

Out of the corner of his eye Leo could see the *Post* gossip columnist Frederick Henderson creep closer to the booth. He turned to Frederick. "Nothing for you to see here, Fred. Move on." He turned back to the booth and saw that his father and mother had come over to see what was going on.

"Barry," said Gary Bradford. "I think it's time for you to go."

"I'll leave when I'm ready," Barry said. He stood there, glaring at Gary.

"Now," Gary said, his voice quiet but steely. "Get the hell out of here. Now."

"Whatever," Barry said, throwing up his hands. "Fuck all y'all."

He turned and stumbled. Joey reached out to help him, but Barry waved off his help and stood straight. "I don't need your help." He looked at each of them, his eyes falling finally on Gary. "I don't need anybody's help." He stumbled off.

2

Later that night at the Four Seasons Hotel, Duke kept his eyes on the huge flat screen television, his finger pressed against the remote control, watching the channels flip by.

Across the room, Monica sat stiffly on the footrest of the big brown club chair near the window. "Do you want to order some room service?" she asked him. "I can have them send up some soup or something."

Duke just changed the channels, stopping only when the TV flashed ESPN. "Are you going to talk to me, Duke?"

"I don't have anything to say," he said.

"Barry was drunk," said Monica. "Don't you get that? He was trying to hurt all of us at the table tonight."

"Well, I guess he was successful."

Monica walked over to the couch. "I told you already. I love you—"

"But you weren't thinking about that when you were sleeping with Barry again, right? Like you said, it was just sex. You just got caught up. No emotions. Your heart was with me." He paused. "You told me you were *done* with Barry."

"I was," she said, sitting down next to him. "Emotionally, I was."

"You don't get it, do you? And what pisses me off the most is that I've *told* you about my history with Barry. How he was. Barry has made a point of trying to be with *every* woman I've ever felt anything for. I told you how hard it was for me to even get with *you*, considering you had a history with Barry! And you still got caught up."

She moved closer to him. "Then you're really not mad at me, are you?"

Duke stood up before she could touch him. "I'm going to bed."

"Then just do one thing for me, Duke."

He stopped and turned back to her. "What's that?"

"Think about how I felt when the woman you chose to defend with your fists tonight, the one whose honor you felt so ready to stand up for, was Amanda."

Duke thought for a few seconds. Maybe she was right. He took a deep breath. "Well. You do *two* things for me. Cancel the lunch. There's no big announcement to make now. I don't want anyone to know I was stupid or desperate enough to marry you." He looked right at her. "Then call your attorney. I want a divorce."

3

"Can you please pass the butter?"

Joey pushed the small saucer of butter across the carpenter's table that John and Melanie Warrington used for meals in the breakfast nook of their Central Park West apartment. He looked around at the small kitchen, so different than the spacious luxury of the kitchen in their East Hampton spread with its hanging pots and flowering plants and expensive Sub-Zero appliances. The vibe was different here, too. Probably, Joey thought, because they hadn't had sex after returning home from the *Rhythm* launch party.

He spread some butter on his croissant and snuck a quick glance at each of them. John stared down at his plate, his tie flopped back over his shoulder to avoid stains, cutting into his bacon with a knife, raising eggs to his mouth with quick, short movements. Melanie was scooping her spoon into a bright green melon. Neither speaking, neither paying any attention to the other. So different, to Joey, than the excitable, attentive couple they usually were in the bedroom.

When their Town Car pulled up in front of the building after the party, they both had to beg Joey to come upstairs with them. Melanie massaged his inner thigh, purring into his ear, "It'll be just like in the Hamptons." Joey could feel his dick throb in his jeans but, as horny as he was, he wasn't really in the mood for their randy bedroom antics.

"How's the melon?" John now asked Melanie.

Watching them now, in this extremely domestic moment, he had to laugh to himself. Was this what they were like when he wasn't around? Not that he really cared anymore. He was trying to figure out a way to end this thing. And he couldn't help thinking about how it all got started: the dinner party last summer at the

Montauk home of the president of one of the largest ad agencies in Manhattan, the tropical drinks and flirtatious mingling with the other A-list guests on the beautiful patio deck, and eventually the tall slender woman in beige slacks and an off-white, midriff-baring wrap blouse from the JoeyRam line who cornered him and said, "I'd like to have you wrapped around me as tightly as this blouse you designed." Before he could say anything, she took a crisp white business card from her pocket and dropped it into his shirt pocket, then winked once and sashayed away. Joey watched her hips move under the linen slacks and immediately decided that he'd be calling her as soon as he left the party. An hour after that, he was coming out of the bathroom on the second floor of the massive home and he was stopped by a tall, blond guy with a perfect set of teeth and a perfect set of pecs in a tight Polo shirt. "You met my wife earlier. She's a big fan of yours," he said. Joey recognized him as the news-caster of a major TV network. Joey thanked him for the compli-ment, but couldn't shake the eye contact. It had been a long time since he'd been with a guy, but he was sure this guy was making a play for him. So Joey bit.

"The one in the wrap blouse?" he asked, thinking, *Hmm, a tag team might be fun.* "Where do you work out?" he asked John.

He named a gym on the West Side, close to the studio where he broadcast the news. "Maybe," he added, "we can work out to-gether. Break a real sweat."

The sweating certainly led to a roller coaster of good mindless sex, expensive drugs, and more sex, but now the ride was over. Joey wanted to unfasten his seat belt and go play at another park. Now, biting into his croissant, he decided honesty was the best policy. He cleared his throat, sat back in his wooden chair, and said, "I'm not gonna see you guys anymore."

They looked at each other, wonder and surprise etched across both their faces. Melanie dropped her spoon. "But we have so much fun together."

"I'm not having fun anymore," Joey said.

John said, "Is there someone else?" He said it with a serious tone, like he was interviewing some local politician on the news broadcast. "I'd really like to know."

Joey sighed. What was there to say? That he wanted to pursue his first love? See if there was a spark in the heart that he'd broken all those years ago? "Sort of," he said. "An old, uh, partner of mine."

"Male or female?" Melanie asked. She looked genuinely curious, her chin in her hand like Joey was a science experiment she was waiting to see explode.

Joey said, "Is that important?"

"I asked, didn't I?"

"Well," Joey said, pushing his plate aside and crossing his arms. "It's a guy."

Melanie slapped the table's wood surface hard, a smile on her face. She looked like she wanted to shout Eureka! "Told you," she said to John. "He's *gay*. You owe me dinner at Nobu."

Joey said, "Excuse me?"

John said, "Melanie bet me that you were really gay, not bi. That you were just pleasing her because you really wanted to be with me."

"Glad to see you guys discussed me outside the bedroom," Joey said.

"Told you, John," Melanie crowed as she flitted from the kitchen.

"You think you're our first 'boy toy'?" John said, laughing. "The guy eventually gets bored, moves on. Melanie accuses him of being gay, then gets something cosmetic done, and we find a new guy. I think she's gonna get her tits done—again—this time."

Joey looked at his watch.

John said. "You got somewhere to be?"

Joey told him he had an important meeting before his friends Duke and Monica's lunch. "They have some big announcement to make."

4

Duke rolled over in bed and winced. His shoulder was supposed to be healing but he still felt the pains in the morning. He sat up, already looking forward to the hot shower and the standing massage appointment he'd ordered when they'd checked into the hotel. As he rubbed sleep out of his eyes, the previous night's events rushed back into his mind and he shook his head to force the memories away.

He could remember hearing Monica pack her things and leave before he drifted off to sleep. Sitting on the living room couch, he now wondered if he should call everyone to cancel the lunch or just show up and make up a reason for inviting them. He turned the TV to NY1 and dialed room service.

The news anchor finished a story about a corrupt politician, then started to report a story about an explosion at an office building in the far West Village. No one was sure whether the explosion was an accident or not, but the eager-looking on-site reporter seemed intent on getting the story. When Duke heard her say "McFarland Enterprises," he put his fork down and paid attention to the TV screen. The reporter recounted the story. Explosion. McFarland Enterprises. West Fifteenth Street between Ninth Avenue and Tenth. At least two people feared dead, including the owner of the company, an Upper East Sider named Reggie McFarland, husband of model and TV host Carla McFarland.

He ran to the bedroom and dug his cell phone out of the pocket of the pants he'd worn to the *Rhythm* party. He called Carla. The phone rang, three times, five times, seven times. Finally her seductive voice announced her voice mail. "Where are you?" Duke said, after the beep. "Call me!"

Then he called Leo. Leo picked up on the second ring.

"I was just about to call you," Leo said. "I can't get Carla on the phone either. Maybe she went down there?"

"My other line is ringing, hold on, man." Leo changed lines. It was Joey.

He said, "You heard about Reggie's office?"

"I'm on the phone with Duke now," Leo said. "I've been trying to get Carla on the phone for half an hour."

"I'm on my way to you," Joey said. "Are Duke and Monica still having the lunch?"

"Good question. See you when you get here."

In a duplex four blocks north of Joey's friends on the Upper West Side, Lillian Bradford dialed Leo's number. It was busy. Still. She hung up the phone and called out to her assistant Rachel. "Can you try Gary's number again? I'm sure he has a number for Reggie's mother."

She flipped through her personal phone book but couldn't find a number. She tried to remember the number at Caroline McFarland's town house. Nothing came to her. It had been so long since she'd even thought about calling that woman.

Leo was dialing Carla's number again when his buzzer rang. He kept the phone to his ear as he hustled over to tell the doorman to let Joey up. He pressed the button on the console and said, "Send him up, José."

"She's already in the elevator," was the response.

Leo opened the door and stood in the doorway, his eyes on the elevator. A bell chimed and the doors opened. Carla rushed out onto his floor. She ran toward him and hugged him close.

"The office," she said. That's all she said. Over and over. "The office."

Leo brought her into the apartment and sat her on the couch.

Greg came out of the bedroom. "Leo. Your mom's calling you on my phone."

"On *your* phone?"

He took the cell phone from Greg's large hand and sat down next to Carla.

"Hey, Mom. Have you heard what's going on downtown?"

"Leo," she said. "Your father's down there."

Duke was still watching the television coverage when Leo called.

He said, "My father's there. He had a meeting with Reggie this morning."

"Sit tight," Duke said, "I'm on my way to your apartment now."

"What about you and Monica's lunch later?"

"Forget about it," said Duke. "I'll explain later . . . FUCK!"

"Duke?" Leo shouted. "You there? What happened?"

"I just tripped over one of Monica's shoes," he said. "I'm fine. See you in a few."

He clicked off the phone. He kneeled down and picked up the black stiletto-heeled shoe. He looked around the room, but didn't see the other one anywhere. On his way to the shower, he threw it against the wall.

———

Leo opened the door to find his mother and Joey standing there, his mother in dark sunglasses and a light trench coat. Joey carried a big Barney Greengrass bag.

Lillian pointed to the bag. "I didn't know what to do," she said. "So I went and bought breakfast. Bagels, juice, some lox . . . Have you spoken to Carla?"

"She's here," Leo said. "I'm trying to get her to wait here until she hears some news." He took the bag from Joey and went into the kitchen. Joey followed.

"Can you believe she went to get food?"

"You know your mother," Joey said. "No news about your father yet?"

Leo shook his head and began unpacking the bag, then he reached into the cabinet over the center kitchen island to get a large plate and some bowls. "No," he said tightly.

"Right," Joey said. "Here, let me help you."

Just as he reached up, Leo let go of the plate and it crashed to the floor.

"I'm sorry," he said, kneeling down to the shattered glass.

"Don't worry about it, man," Joey said, helping him to his feet. As Leo stood, Joey could see that he had tears in his eyes.

"Hey," Joey said. "Stop. Everything's gonna be all right. You'll see. We're gonna hear something any second." He took Leo into his arms and hugged him close. He could feel Leo's tears moisten the shoulder of his T-shirt. He rubbed Leo's back, massaged his neck. "Really, baby. It's gonna be fine." Leo pulled back and looked into Joey's eyes. Joey stared back. He could feel Leo's breath on his cheek as they moved closer together.

"What happened?"

Joey turned to see Lillian and Greg standing in the kitchen door.

"We're fine," Leo said, pulling away from Joey. "I just broke—"

Greg stared at Leo for a few long seconds. Then he said, "I should get a broom," and walked stiffly across the kitchen to the small pantry.

"I'll help with that," Leo said.

Greg said, "I got it."

"No, I—"

"I *got* it," Greg said again.

5

Duke arrived at Leo's to a tense, quiet scene, the only sound coming from the drone of the big TV in the center of the sunken living room and the murmur of anxious phone conversations. Monica went to Carla and held her, whispering soft words into her ear, trying to keep her calm. Lillian paced the apartment, making calls to Gary's assistant, trying to locate any information she could. Leo did the same, staying glued to his phone, calling hospitals, then calling CoCo.

Suddenly Carla said, "He's dead." She said it in her normal voice, but in the quiet of the apartment it sounded almost like a shouted declaration.

"Carla," Lillian said. "Don't."

"He's dead," she said again. "I can feel it." She shrugged the blanket that Lillian had draped around her from her shoulders and stood up. She moved close to the television and pointed at it accusingly. "He's dead. Reggie's dead."

No one moved for a few seconds, allowing her to express her emotions, letting her vent her feelings into the room. But soon

Lillian went to her and took her into the bedroom and put her to bed. She came out and said, "I'm going down there."

Leo said. "What can you do there? They're not even going to let you get close."

"If Natalie's at our house, and you're here, I should be down there," Lillian said.

"Then I'm coming with you," Leo said.

"No," Lillian said. "One of us should wait here." She went to the phone. "I'm going to call Natalie and tell her to send a car."

Greg stood up. "I think I'm gonna go get some air," he said.

"I'll come with you," Leo said. "I could use some air, too."

"No," Greg said. "I'm just gonna go—"

"Well, I'm going out, too. There's enough air out there for both of us."

Duke looked at Joey, who just shook his head and sighed deeply. Then he put his head in his hands and looked down at the floor.

Outside, Greg started toward Columbus Avenue. Leo walked a few paces behind him. Halfway down the block he caught up with Greg and said, "Nothing happened, man."

"I know," Greg said.

"Then what's up with you?"

"What's up with *you*?" Greg stopped. "No one knows where your father is. We don't know if Reggie's alive. And you and your ex-boyfriend are thinking about making out in the kitchen?"

"We weren't—" Leo stopped himself. They'd reached the corner of Columbus Avenue and Seventy-fifth Street. Leo noticed all the people casting curious glances at the 6'7" New York Knick standing on the corner. "I'm sure you don't wanna talk about this here," Leo said. "But nothing happened, Greg."

Greg turned to face him. "You know what? I always thought

that perhaps you had a soft place in your heart for Pete. I always thought that if I was gonna have you one hundred percent I'd have to wait for you to be completely over him."

"I'll never be *over* Pete," Leo said. "I loved him. You know that. But that is the past, and I'm with you now."

Greg nodded. "But you loved Joey more."

"That's not true," Leo said.

"Just be real, man," Greg said. "You were with Pete 'cause you could be. You liked being with him, but you were with him 'cause you couldn't be with Joey."

Leo felt like he'd been slapped.

"I'll never be Joey Ramirez. That's who you really love. I can read it all over your face whenever he's around."

Leo had no idea how to respond. He wasn't even sure that he should.

"You have anything to say?"

"You've said it all, Greg. I guess you just have to make your ultimate point."

"Which is?"

"Are you saying you don't want to be together?"

"Are you telling me that you don't love Joey?"

Leo thought about that moment in the kitchen. Broken glass everywhere, his father possibly hurt in an explosion, and he *was* about to kiss Joey. He felt ridiculous, that it had happened and that he'd gotten caught. But he had to admit: He felt safe with Joey, even after all this time. "I'm sorry, Greg," he said. "I really am." He watched Greg walk away.

As Leo waited for one elevator in the mirrored lobby of his building, the other elevator opened. Lillian, Joey, and Duke rushed out.

Lillian said, "Baby!" She hugged him tight. "They found your father. He's at St. Vincent's. We were coming to find you. Joey's driver is going to take us down there."

6

The drive downtown from the Upper West Side was slow and quiet, Joey's Range Rover filled only with the palpable vibrations of silent prayers and hopes.

By the time they reached Fourteenth Street to go east toward the hospital, the traffic had slowed to a virtual standstill. Cops with whistles and sad looks on their faces were directing people to reverse their courses, to head uptown, away from the site of the building explosion. Joey's driver, Emilio, leaned out of the window and told a cop that they were trying to reach a loved one at St. Vincent's who'd been in the explosion. The cop allowed them to squeeze through the standstill and turn down Fourteenth Street.

They parked on Twelfth Street and walked three blocks to the hospital on the corner. Leo held Lillian's hand. Duke walked behind them, Joey and Emilio behind Duke.

As they waited at the light, Leo pointed at the ER doors. "Isn't that Barry?"

"Looks like him," Duke said.

Lillian said, "What is *he* doing here?"

Leo wondered at his mother's cutting tone. But he said nothing, just kept walking. By the time they reached Barry, he was standing there with Amelia, one of Gary's assistants, looking to Leo oddly impeccable, considering the drunken mess he'd been the night before. Edna was there as well. Joey ran to her and gave her a big hug. He wiped tears away from her eyes.

Lillian said, "Where's my husband?" To Amelia she said, "Call Gary's doctor."

Barry raised his hand. "Lillian—"

"I don't want to talk, Barry. Take me to see Gary."

"I should tell you something first," Barry said. He looked around at everyone, his eyes lingering on Leo. "It's not looking good—"

"Just take me to see him," Lillian said, pushing past Barry.

Leo grabbed her. "Wait, Mom. Listen to what he has to say."

"I just got here," Barry said. "Amelia called me." He took a deep breath. "It's not good. Apparently he was finishing a meeting with Reggie and about to leave the building when the explosion happened. He was with a couple of people coming out of the elevator and they took shelter under a huge lamp dome in the lobby . . . and he had a heart attack. I just wanted to let you know that it doesn't look good."

Lillian yanked herself from Leo's grip and pushed past Barry and Amelia, flinging herself through the glass doors leading to the emergency care area. She pushed past a horde of people standing in the corridor and went to the woman at the intake desk.

"Gary Bradford," she said to the woman, who had a phone receiver pressed to her ear.

The woman held a finger up at Lillian, asking her to wait.

"Gary Bradford!" Lillian screamed.

The receptionist looked around for someone to help but Lillian ignored her and rushed through the swinging doors leading to the care area in the back. Barry and Leo caught up with her, following as Lillian pulled curtains back and looked into cubicles, searching for Gary's bed.

"He's over there," Barry said, taking Lillian's arm and leading her across the floor to a closed-off nook where Gary lay in a bed, an IV tube running from his arm and his face covered by an oxygen mask. The beeps and plinks of the heart monitor sounded to Leo like a morbid, mocking video game.

As soon as he saw the three of them step closer to the bed, Gary's eyes filled with tears. He reached for the mask, but Lillian shook her head and took his hand in hers.

"Don't say anything," she whispered. "We know, baby. We know."

Gary shook his head, slowly, it seemed to Leo, like his father had aged twenty years since he saw him the night before at the party.

Leo said, "I think he wants to say something, Mom."

"I know what he wants to say," Lillian whispered to him in a voice that sounded like a hiss. "He wants to tell us that he loves us, but he doesn't have to." She leaned closer to the bed. "You don't have to tell us, Gary. We know. We love you, too. We do."

Somehow, though, Gary found strength and pulled his hand away from Lillian. A single tear rolled down the side of his face and he slowly reached up again to pull the oxygen mask from his face. Leo reached over him to help him.

His voice was a whispered rasp. "Your mother is right," he said to Leo. "I love you with all my heart. And I'm sorry. For every-thing."

"Shh," Leo whispered. He could feel tears coming to his own eyes. He blinked them away. "It's all right, Dad. I know. I love you, too. Just rest, okay?"

"But there is something I need—"

"What do you need, Dad? You need me to get you a nurse?"

"I need to tell—"

"Let's let him rest," Lillian said, speaking over him. "Please, Gary. Just rest."

Gary shook his head. It seemed to cause him so much pain.

Leo looked at Barry. "Where's his doctor?"

"He said he'd meet us over here," Barry said.

Leo looked down at his father. "You don't need to tell me, Dad, I know."

"You don't," Gary rasped. "You don't know . . ."

Then he began to cough. And phlegmy fluid oozed from the side of his mouth. The coughing got louder, and wracked his body with shivers.

Lillian screamed, "Get the doctor. Somebody, get a doctor!"

Two young, harried-looking med students rushed to Gary's bedside. One grabbed his wrist to check his pulse as the other adjusted a reading on the heart monitor. Then a nurse appeared, with a syringe. She pushed Leo and Barry back and poked the needle into Gary's right arm. The coughing subsided; the bleeps of the heart monitor set back apace.

Leo stepped closer to the bed and realized he'd been holding his breath. He exhaled and looked at his mother. The stricken look on her face pained him. He went around the bed and put an arm around her shoulder.

"I love you, Gary," she said. "I've loved you all my life." She began to cry.

And as if in response to her words, the heart monitor began its shrieking beeps, bringing the young doctors back to Gary's bedside. The nurse appeared with a set of cardiac paddles and handed them to one of the doctors. They applied the paddles, Gary's body jerking from the shock. Nothing. Again. Nothing. A third time, more jolts to his chest. Nothing. Then a pause, and a flat line. The heart monitor played what sounded to Leo like a long sustained note of finality.

"I'll call it," said the other doctor. He looked at Lillian and Leo. "I'm so sorry," he said. He said the time of death, and handed the paddles to the nurse.

Lillian's quiet tears turned to a soft but persistent moan.

Leo held her in his arms.

Lillian had refused to leave Gary's bedside. The nurses agreed to let her sit there for a few moments while Leo took care of the paperwork. Two hours later, Duke and Joey sat in the Village Den diner, their food untouched. As Barry paced outside, Duke told Joey about his argument with Monica. "It's over," he said. Joey just nodded. When Barry came to the table, Duke got up stiffly and went out to the sidewalk.

"I'm sure they won't let her sit there much longer," Barry said, watching Duke walk by. "What's up with him?"

Joey just sighed and shook his head.

Leo and Lillian arrived ten minutes later. Lillian had retouched her makeup. Leo's eyes were vacant, distant, like he wasn't seeing anything, only feeling his way.

Lillian sat down in the chair Joey pulled out for her. "Thank you, Joey," she said. She ordered a hot tea from the waitress. "Thank you all for sticking around."

"Of course we would," Barry said. "Gary was very good to all of us."

"He wanted to tell me he loved me," Leo said. Tears came to his eyes again.

Joey said, "Of course he loved you, man." He put an arm around Leo's shoulder.

"No," Lillian said.

"What?" Leo said. "What do you mean 'No'?"

"I mean your father wasn't trying to tell you that he loved you, Leo. He'd said that already. You heard him say it." She took a long, slow sip of her tea. "Your father," she said, "was about to make what people call a deathbed confession."

Leo shook his head. He smiled, but only to hide the discomfort he was feeling. His mother seemed so composed, so sober, so different from the stricken fragility that seemed to envelop her body at the hospital. "What are you saying, Mom?"

"Your father was trying to tell you, Leo, that you have a brother."

"I have a what?"

Lillian just nodded. "While I was in the hospital just now I was debating with myself whether I should tell you or not, and if so, when I should tell you. I decided you might as well know today, because you're going to find out sooner or later."

Leo said again, "What do you mean I have a brother?" He looked around the table. Duke had a confused look on his face and he shrugged his shoulders at Leo. Leo looked at Barry, who looked as confused as Duke did. Joey, though, was looking at his plate, his hands crossed on the table in front of him.

Lillian noticed. "You know, don't you, Joey?" Joey nodded. But he didn't look up. "How long have you known, Joey?"

He thought for a moment. "I don't know," he shrugged. "Since I got out of jail?"

Leo said, "You've known for, what, five years and never thought to—?"

Lillian cut him off. "And how did you know, Joey?"

He finally looked up. "Edna told me."

Leo said, "Who's his mother? 'Cause I'm guessing it's not you, right?"

Lillian shook her head. "No. It's not me." She looked at Leo. "It's time you knew. Standing there, watching him struggle to get words out. I knew what he trying to say."

"So he got some other woman pregnant? And you stayed with him?"

Lillian looked up from her tea. "I actually left him when I first found out about it." She took a sip of the tea. "You were twelve. Remember when you and I went to stay with Carla and her family in Maryland for that summer?"

"The summer before I went to Switzerland," Leo said.

"Why do you think I made you go to Switzerland, Leo? I didn't want you anywhere around your father or the situation or anything." She took a deep breath. "But Gary convinced me that he'd gotten the woman pregnant just after we'd gotten together, that he'd changed since then. So I went back to him. It was the only life I knew. It was a decision I made. As long as you never met the boy, I'd be able to live with it. But the things you try to hide always eventually come out, don't they? And you loved Sag Harbor so much." She took another sip of tea. "So *very* much. Sometimes I think it was just destiny. Or the price we all had to pay—you really, that you had to pay—for your father's . . . indiscretions."

Leo said, "What does Sag Harbor have to do with it?"

She went on as if she didn't hear him. "I told your father, 'Leo's going to meet him and then what are we going to do?' But your father. He was arrogant about it. He actually laughed. And you know what he said? He said, 'Yeah, maybe they'll meet. And maybe they'll even be friends.'"

Leo said, "I've met him?"

Joey said, "Lillian, don't drag it out, just tell him."

Lillian smiled, sadly. She said, "You always did have a good head on your shoulders, Joey." She took one more sip of her tea and placed the cup on the small saucer with a final, distinctive grace. She took a deep breath. "Your brother, Leo, is sitting right next to you." She looked closely at Leo. "Your brother is Barry."

1

Which one of you bastards is my father?

The words rang through TNT's head as he felt the paramedics lift his gurney from the ambulance and wheel him into the emergency room bay of St. Vincent's Hospital.

Which one?

He groaned, not so much from the throb in his shoulder, which didn't feel as painful as it had ten minutes ago, but from the pain in his head, the swirling mass of images and thoughts colliding in his brain.

His earliest memory: sitting on the dirty steps of that brownstone in Brooklyn. How old could he have been? Three? Four? He could see the street like he was still sitting there: the chain-link fence that ran around the empty lot across from the brownstone, the rush of cars that honked horns and skidded to stops right there on Gates Avenue, the smell of the Jamaican beef patties floating up from the corner bodega where they always went to buy ice cream bars in the summertime.

And the rich lady. And him asking her who she was. And her smiling, and saying, "You can call me Grandma if you want." And he wanted to. A grandmother was nice. A grandmother did nice things for you. At least it seemed that way in the picture books he had to read in pre-school.

"Is that who I think it is? Is that T—"

The words pulled him out of his memory, coming from a short nurse with a gold ring in her nose. The look on her face was a mix of confusion and awe.

He liked the way the nurse looked. She was a cutie, a real dime. Was she Latina?

Dominican? Puerto Rican? He felt his body relax into a sleep.

At the Hotel Gansevoort, Leo's cell phone rang. He saw his mother's number flash on the phone's display and answered.

Lillian said, "Are you still with Barry, Joey, and Duke?"

Leo looked around at the others in the suite. "How did you know we were all—"

"Get down to St. Vincent's," she said.

"Mom? How did you know—"

She cut him off again. "All of you," Lillian said. "Just go. I'm on my way. I'll meet you there." She hung up.

"Wait, Mom?" Leo closed his phone.

"How is Lillian?" Duke said. "I haven't seen her in forever—"

"She says we have to go to St. Vincent's," said Leo. "All of us."

Talk of surgery.

Tall doctors in white coats and green scrubs rushing around him.

This is celebrity, he thinks. This is how they treat you when you're important.

But he wasn't important when he was an infant, when he was just born and brought from that hospital to the brownstone in Brooklyn. He wasn't important when he had to share a bedroom with that other kid, who hated him because he had a "grandma" who wore sweet-smelling perfume and wore diamond bracelets and wore soft coats that looked like an animal they saw at the Bronx

Zoo. He wasn't important when the kids on the block beat him up once a week and took the dollars his "grandma" had given him or jumped him in the playground of PS 23 because he didn't have a mother or a father and had to live with Towanda in that run-down old brownstone. And he didn't feel important when he asked his "grandma" who his real mother and father were and she told him that he shouldn't think about that, that he should just be a good boy for Towanda and help her around the house and do his homework.

When did he feel important?

He felt important when they all moved to Norfolk, Virginia, and he made friends with kids who understood how much he loved comic books and cool music and skateboarding. He felt important when his sixth-grade teacher Mrs. Loomis asked the class to write poetry and he wrote a poem about what he imagined his father and mother to be like and rhymed it in front of the class to great applause and laughter. He felt important when he ran into that guy Patsy at the deli and Patsy told him that he should come hang out at the studio near the community center and bring some of the rhymes and poems he'd been working on. He felt important when his grandmother came down to Virginia to see him and told him he could call her Lillian . . .

More talk of surgery. They had to get the bullet out of him. He'd lost so much blood already.

2

After ten minutes of debating who should ride with who, it took all of ten minutes for the four of them to get to the hospital.

As he stood outside St. Vincent's, Leo couldn't help but think about the last time he'd been standing in this same exact spot, right on Twelfth Street and Seventh Avenue, with these same people, seven years earlier. He breathed in, inhaling the exhaust-fumed aroma of New York City, so much like the way he remembered it, so different from Paris. Then he looked south, down Seventh Avenue, and saw the blank space in the horizon where the Twin Towers once stood, a sight he knew he'd never get used to.

He could see them all, still sitting in the Village Den diner down the street, seven years before, looking at each other, shocked by the information Lillian had given them.

"My *brother*?" he'd asked his mother. "Barry?"

Then he'd looked at Barry, whose face registered not just surprise but curiosity, as if he was replaying in his mind his entire relationship with Gary Bradford. But, Leo had had to ask himself, sitting there at that diner table, was he, was anyone, really surprised? Hadn't Gary taken Barry under his wing all those years ago? Hadn't he made extensive, open-armed professional and personal room for Barry in his life whenever he needed it?

"Well," Barry said, as if reading Leo's mind. "I guess that sorta explains a lot, doesn't it? I'm just sad that I had to find out on a day like this one."

"If I'd had my way," said Lillian, "you would never have found out." She took a sip of her tea. "But there are business reasons now," she said. "Things Gary thought should be yours."

"Like?" Barry asked.

"Gary left a will," she said. "You'll find out soon enough."

Duke said, "Your mom's here," and Leo was pulled from his thoughts.

Watching his mother step out of a cab across the street from the hospital, Leo thought of the cool and calm way she'd imparted the information in the diner that day, how different she'd seemed from

the mother he knew and loved. She'd spoken to them with a clini-
cal kind of coldness just after the warm final moment she'd shared
with Gary in the emergency room. Had his mother always been
that way? Looking at the regal way she stood on the corner, waiting
for traffic to slow to cross the avenue, Leo had to admit to himself
that she must have had to be, really, to live her whole married life
to Gary Bradford. At some point she must have constructed a cool,
calm self just to deal with the other women, the long hours. The
other child.

When she was standing there in front of the four of them,
Lillian leaned in to kiss Leo. She kissed Joey and Duke, and shook
hands with Barry.

"TNT's been shot," she said.

"Shot?" Leo said. "We just saw him a coupla hours ago."

Joey said, "He's in the hospital?"

Lillian nodded. "I'm going inside to see how he is." She looked
over Leo's shoulder toward the emergency room. "Then the five us
need to talk."

"About what?" Barry said.

"From what I understand," Lillian said, "he brought the four
of you together to ask you a question. Did he get his answer yet?"

The four of them looked at each other. No one said anything.

"I guess not," Lillian said. "Please meet me in the diner across
the street in twenty minutes." And she turned and went into the
hospital.

While the other three took seats at a table near the window, Barry
went to the men's room. He leaned on the sink and stared into the
mirror. He squinted his eyes. He smiled. He frowned. He closed his
eyes for a few seconds, then opened them again.

He sighed. *Which one of you bastards is my father?* He sighed again, trying to process the last few hours. Seeing Leo again after all these years was like a punch to the gut. Seeing all of them was strange, but seeing Leo was the strangest. Only because of their last real time together.

Sitting in a room in the Bradford apartment, a TV on before them, Gary's face staring back at them with that knowing, condescending grin on his face. It had been two hours after the funeral. Lillian and Gary's main attorney had pulled them aside and forced the two of them to go into the room and hear the words their father had left for them.

"Start it already," Leo had said quietly, after Lillian and the lawyer had stepped out of the room, shutting the door tightly behind them.

Barry pressed the DVD remote control button and suddenly Gary focused his gaze into the camera, at Leo and Barry, and began to speak.

"If the two of you are sitting here together, then you've both outlived me and that's the way it should be. First of all I want to apologize to both of you. Leo, to you for what I'm sure you're regarding as betrayal against your mother and you. Barry, to you for not telling you before now about our connection. But I couldn't, as you probably know by now. What I could do instead, however, was look out for you and make sure you had everything you ever needed in the world. Just because you wouldn't have my name didn't mean you wouldn't have everything else that having my name would have afforded you. From the summer mock trial camp you wanted to go to, to your Yale education and everything else. I'm not telling you this to keep score—Lord knows I like to keep score—but because I want you to know that I love you and I wanted you to have the best. Now, Leo, we've had our hard moments. I still can't believe that you and I didn't speak for nearly six years. But that didn't mean you weren't in my heart and mind at all times. Ask Barry. I asked him about you whenever I could. I forced your mother to talk to me about you even when she hated that neither you nor I were mature or smart enough to bridge the gap that lingered between us. You think I hated you because you were gay. That had nothing to do with it. I just wanted you, like Barry, to have the best. Call me old-fashioned, call me whatever you want to call me, but I just didn't want anything in your life to stand in the way of you attaining whatever it was you wanted. What did I know? I know that there are people out there who do hate gay people and I didn't want any of them to hurt you. Ever. I apologize if my actions were misinterpreted, but that's all I can say about that. I love you with all my heart and I always have, I'm proud of you, more proud than you can ever imagine. What I want both of you to know, because you'll both be fathers one day—yes, you too, Leo, I think you'll be a great father—is that being a father is terrifying. We have to be strong, and we have to be savvy and smart and protective and always be what society considers a man. But it's terrifying. Kids terrify us. Do you know that? Do you know how terrifying it is to think that this person you have to take care of may not work out the way you want him to? It's terrifying to *know* that life will throw them hardships and pain that even the most vigilant father cannot protect you from. But you both have turned out to be wonderful men. You both have your flaws, you know. Leo you are a know-it-all and you let your feelings dictate too much of what you do with your life. Barry, you are a dog—and I can tell you that with all irony, believe me. You often reach much farther than you should but that isn't always bad either. But enough with the bad stuff. I want you both to be happy. I want you both to take risks but be careful, I want you to be better men than I ever knew how to be. I want you to take care of your mothers. And most important, I want you both to run CoCo Cosmetics. You can decide how. But don't lose that company. It's ours. It's our blood and our hearts. All the details stuff is in paperwork that Finnegan and Moskowitz will go over with you. Lastly I'd like to reiterate what I said earlier. I love you both. I know I didn't always show it. I know I wasn't the best father that I could have been. But I'm proud that I leave behind me you two wonderful young men."

There had been no words between him and Leo after the DVD ended. Leo left the room, tears in his eyes. Barry sat there, tears streaming down his own face. Then he'd replayed the message, and replayed it again.

Two days later, the will was read. Leo interrupted the mono-tone reading of David Finnegan to say that he wanted nothing to do with the running of CoCo Cosmetics. Three days later, Barry found out that he'd be running CoCo Cosmetics, and moved into Gary's office four days after that. A week later, Leo was on a plane to Europe. He didn't even return for once-a-year board meetings, sending Lillian as his proxy.

Now, Barry ran some cold water and splashed his face. He looked into the mirror again, and noticed, as he had so many times in his life, that he had the same smile as Gary Bradford. And he thought: *I used to cut the man's lawn . . .*

3

Secrets, thought Lillian Bradford. *My whole life seems like it's been all about secrets.*

She sat on the hard plastic chair next to the door leading to the suite of operating rooms and clasped her hands in her lap. She watched nurses scoot by on soft shoes and doctors glare down at charts. She remembered something her own mother had said, on the day she dropped Lillian off at college so many years ago. "Here," her mother had told her, looking directly into her eyes, "is where you will meet your husband. And here is also where you will learn to always present your best self to the world. The world doesn't care about your worries or your troubles or your flaws. The world needs you to be perfect all the time. So does your husband."

"Is Daddy that way?" Lillian had asked.

Her mother nodded. "All men are that way. They will expect you to look past their flaws. No, I take that back. They will need you to look past their flaws. The good Lord got something wrong with men. He filled them with ego and lust and envy. They are essentially children. Never forget that. Whatever you do."

And Lillian never had. Sitting there in the hospital hallway, wondering how she was going to explain to the four of them what she needed to say, she could only shake her head and wonder if she'd done the right thing all those years ago. She wondered if maybe she should have taken care of this the last time they were all together at this hospital.

But she hadn't. And there was no use wondering about the past, something else her mother had taught her. The past was passed.

Now she just wondered if Troy was okay.

TNT, she thought, and she had to smile to herself, as much as she hated to. *TNT. Things always blow up when you try to hide them, don't they?*

Across the street at the diner, Leo sat with Joey and Duke and sipped a cup of hot coffee.

"Here we are," Duke said. "So which one of us is TNT's father, Leo?"

A voice behind them said, "Why do you think Leo knows the answer to that?"

They all looked up to see Carla standing a few feet from their table. Her eyes were rimmed red, like she'd been crying.

Barry came out of the rest room and stopped when he saw Carla standing there.

"Carla?" he said. "What's wrong?" He went over to her and hugged her. He guided her to the table and pulled a chair out for her. "What are you doing here?"

"Lillian called me," Carla said. "She told me to meet you all here. I live right up the block now."

"You will never believe what brought us all together today," Barry said.

"Yes," said Carla. "I will."

In the hospital, the detective took a seat next to Lillian.

"Now, let me get this straight," he said. "You said you're TNT's grandmother?"

Lillian nodded. "In so many words, yes."

"And you know who shot him?"

"His name is Lewis," she said. "Lewis Ramsey."

"And you know this how?"

Lillian sighed. "He came to me first," she said. "For money."

"Extortion?"

"More like blackmail," Lillian said. She looked at her watch. "Can we finish this later, please?"

The detective sighed. "I guess we can get more from TNT when he's out of surgery," he said. "But I'd like to talk to you some more."

"Of course," Lillian said. "Now I have to go across the street and explain it all." She stood up slowly.

"Do you need someone to escort you, ma'am?"

"I'm fine," Lillian said. "Just please make sure Troy is safe in here."

Leo and Carla sat on a bench outside the diner, passing a cigarette between them.

"It always comes out eventually," Carla said. "Doesn't it?"

"I'm confused," Leo said. "I get this call from TNT—"

"There's so much you don't know, Leo."

"So I gather," he said. He threw the cigarette into the gutter. As he stood, Carla grabbed him and wrapped her arms around him, pulling him close.

"I've missed you, Leo the Lion," she said. "I've missed you so much."

Leo pulled out of her grasp. "We just talked three days ago, Carla."

She laughed, wiping at the tears trailing down her cheeks. "I know," she said. "But I wish you lived here in New York."

"You can come see me in Paris," he said.

"After all this," she said, "I think I will. I'll have to."

"I'm still confused," Leo said.

"You won't be for long," Carla said. "As soon as Lill—" Carla stopped short.

Leo said, "What? What's wrong?"

Carla said nothing, she just looked over Leo's shoulder, her mouth open.

"What, Carla?" Leo turned to see where she was staring. All he saw was a bunch of cabs pulling up to the hospital. "What is it, Carla?"

"Not what," she said finally. "Who."

"Who, then?"

"I don't know if I'm just emotional," she said, "or just crazy."

"What is it, Carla? Who did you see?"

"Reggie," she said. "I just saw Reggie get out of a cab and go into the hospital."

"Carla," Leo said, his voice softening. "Reggie's dead."

But she wasn't sitting there any longer. She'd leapt from the bench and was making her way down Twelfth Street toward the hospital.

As Lillian stepped to the curb to cross Seventh Avenue, she saw a tall, light-skinned guy step out of a cab. She knew him. His hair was a little grayer around the temples, and he was wearing glasses, but she was sure she knew him.

Reggie McFarland.

But she wasn't completely surprised. She'd been waiting for this.

"Carla," Leo said breathlessly as he finally caught up with her at the corner.

"It was him, Leo," she said.

"But he's—" Leo didn't know what to say. Reggie was dead. They'd all gone to his memorial service after the explosion of his family's office building seven years ago.

"I don't think you should do this," he said, holding on to the sleeve of her cotton fleece jacket. "It's just someone who looks like him."

"See!" Carla pointed across the wide avenue.

Leo could see Lillian standing near the edge of the sidewalk talking to a tall guy who did, he had to admit, look a lot like Reggie. But—

"Come on," Carla said. The light had changed to red and the

traffic had stopped. Now Carla grabbed his sleeve and dragged Leo across the street.

Lillian said, "How could you come here?"

Reggie said nothing. He tried to push past Lillian, but she grabbed his arm and held firm. "Let me go, Mrs. Bradford." He tried to shrug her tight grip from his arm but she wouldn't let go.

"You should be ashamed of yourself, Reginald. Your father must be rolling in his very grave."

"Fuck my father," he hissed. "And fuck you."

"I will not let you in there, Reginald. What else can you do? You sent that boy to shoot Troy. What else will you do?"

"I didn't send anyone anywhere, Lillian. Now let me go."

As he tried to shake her grip from his arm, he heard a voice behind him.

"Reggie?"

He turned to see Carla and Leo rushing across Seventh Avenue.

Carla screamed, "Is that you, Reggie?"

Reggie yanked his arm from Lillian's hand and ran toward the hospital.

Leo ran from Carla's side and grabbed Reggie from behind, slamming him to the ground. People walking down the avenue moved away from the two of them, clearing room for the tackle happening right in front of them.

Reggie tried to shrug Leo off of him. "Get offa me," he yelled. "Get off me, Leo!"

Leo yanked him up from the sidewalk and stared into Reggie's eyes. "What the fuck are you doing here?" he said. "You were supposed to be—"

"Dead," Carla said. "You died, you bastard. You fucking died!"

She marched up to Reggie and slapped him across the face. "Where have you been all this time?"

"What the hell do you care?" Reggie said.

"Fuck you, Reggie," Carla spat at him. "What are you doing here?"

Reggie didn't say anything.

Lillian sighed. "This is turning into a nightmare," she muttered. "Reggie's the reason we're all here, Carla."

Leo said, "What does that mean?"

Lillian took a deep breath. "Who do you think put Troy up to bringing all of you together?" Lillian could see that Leo was still confused by all the information storming his way. "It was Reggie who told TNT that one of you was his father."

Carla and Leo looked at Reggie, who still had no words, just glaring looks at all of them as Leo still held him by the arms.

"Reggie is also the reason TNT's in surgery now," Lillian said. "Aren't you?"

Reggie still said nothing. His breathing was hard and angry.

"Let's go to the diner," she said calmly. "Troy should be out of surgery soon."

Joey and Duke exchanged a look of deep curiosity as they watched Leo and Carla and Lillian step into the diner, leaving Reggie outside.

Barry said, "That cannot be who I think it is."

Carla nodded as she took a seat.

Leo pulled a chair over from another table for Lillian and they both took their seats. For a while, no one said anything. Everyone just stared at each other as the waitress refilled coffee mugs around the table.

Finally Joey said, "How is he doing?"

"I don't know much yet." Lillian shrugged, but she noted the hopefulness in the tone of Joey's voice, the longing in his question. She smiled at him. She looked around the table. She cleared her throat.

And she told them a story.

4

The rapper they knew as TNT was named Troy when he was born in 1984. His mother insisted that whatever happened, he be named Troy. Because she'd always told herself that that would be the name of her first son. And when she looked into his eyes the last time that she saw him, before the nurse took him away for the very last time, she whispered the word "Troy," and wished him love.

She did this because she knew that she'd never see Troy again. Once he was born, the machinery for his future had already been forged into place. She was young, a seventeen-year-old girl with no resources to raise a child. So she'd gone to the one woman she knew would help her keep her secret, the one woman who'd been like a mother to her all her life, to help her figure it all out. Besides, unlike most other seventeen-year-old girls, Troy's mother was a public face, known for her beauty and poise, for her position as one of the best and brightest the community had to offer. In those days, you couldn't look at a black magazine or see a billboard in a black neighborhood without seeing her honey-toned heart-shaped face. A baby? No, that was all wrong, for her, for her image, for the brand of cosmetics she represented, for the community she represented across the globe.

———

As Lillian talked, all heads turned to Carla, sitting there, looking down at the table, her fingers shredding paper napkins and braiding them into strips of yellow plaits.

Leo said, "But I thought—"

Lillian said, "Leo, let me finish."

Leo held up his hand. He said to Carla, "So when I took you into Manhattan to get an abortion—"

"I didn't get it," Carla said, her voice small and tight. "I couldn't do it, Leo."

At first only two people knew about the birth of Carla's child, which took place in a small private hospital on the North Shore of Long Island. She'd spent the majority of her pregnancy stowed away in the Bradford summer house, nursed by a woman Lillian hired who worked at the local hospital. Lillian would sneak out on some days while Leo was in school and Gary at work.

Lillian spent many a night wondering what to do after the birth of the child. At first she thought she'd explain the situation to Gary and then quietly adopt the child, never letting the world know the identity of the child's mother. But Gary was against it. They were too old, he said eventually, to be parents to a baby. And why keep the child so close to Carla if she didn't want to keep it? That would never work.

Then someone came into the picture, a savior of sorts, out of nowhere.

A girl named Towanda knocked on Edna's door one day and said she was the mother of Joey's baby. She wanted to see Joey and she wanted support. Edna sent her right to Gary, who invited her to his home to meet with him and Lillian. Towanda explained her situation, that her mother had exploited Joey, but that didn't mean that his child should go without. And Gary agreed. After dinner he took out his checkbook and wrote Towanda a check for seventy-five thousand dollars. And he told her to never come back to his house, or Edna's, ever again. She was not to try to engage Joey either. He was a young man with a future and fatherhood wasn't part of his immediate plans. Towanda agreed, took the check, and went away.

But Lillian kept tabs on her. This was, after all, the mother of Joey's child. And Joey, at this point, was almost like a child to her. And Leo's best friend, the kid who had somehow made her morose, overweight son into a happy, lithe kid who laughed and made friends and engaged the world. There was good in Joey. So there would be good in his child one day. She would do all she could to nurture it.

And when Carla's baby was born, it came to Lillian one day as she walked from her car to the hospital room. *Towanda.* Towanda could raise Troy as her own. He could grow up with Joey's son, like brothers. And why shouldn't it work? From her increasingly frequent visits to Towanda's apartment in Brooklyn, she saw that the girl was clean, and careful with her own child, nothing like the stories Towanda had told her about her own mother Shirley or her brother Carlton. Towanda wanted a better life. She had a boyfriend who worked and brought home food and money. Why not Towanda?

And even better, Towanda agreed to take Troy. Especially when Lillian presented her with a check for one hundred thousand dollars. Which would help Towanda and her boyfriend find a nicer place, get a car, feed their family, start over.

Barry said, "You did all that for Carla?"

"And for the baby," Lillian said. "He needed a home."

Joey said, "But why Towanda?" A dark shadow of memory crossed his face. "You know what she did to me?"

Lillian nodded. "I do know what she did to you," she said. "And she really wanted your forgiveness. Her mother put her up to it. She was a girl. And she'd grown up so much once she had a child. Besides, to be honest, I didn't know what else to do."

"But you kept her from me," Joey said. "And when Gary told me about it finally, he used it as a chip, something to bargain with."

"We did what we thought, what we hoped even, was best for you, Joey," Lillian pleaded. "You were seventeen, you were in school—"

"But my son," Joey interrupted her. "You know where he is? Can I see him?"

"I'll get to that," Lillian said.

"No," Joey said, his voice laced with anger. "With all due respect, Lillian, it's nice what you and Gary did for Towanda and my son, and for Carla's son, but if you don't mind, I'd like to know how I can see my son."

Lillian sat forward and looked directly as Joey. "Well, that's the thing, Joey. He isn't your son."

"Excuse me?" Joey said. He sat back in his chair as if he'd been smacked across the face. "What did you say?"

"They boy Towanda came to us about wasn't your son."

"But you said—"

"Lewis Ramsey is not your son. Towanda lied. But we didn't find that out until later. Much later. And, all due respect right back at you, I think it's best that he isn't your son." She watched Joey slouch into his seat, a mingled look of dejection and confusion dancing across his dark features. "Now. May I finish?"

Everything was good, for a while, at least. Lillian visited Troy often, bringing him gifts, watching him develop into an energetic, curious little boy. Even when Towanda's boyfriend left her, taking most of the money with him, Lillian was there for them, replenishing the bank account, helping Towanda find work as a maid at a hotel run by one of her friends. Everything was good, until the day Lillian showed up at the little apartment in Bed-Stuy, Brooklyn, and found no one home.

Towanda had moved away, leaving no forwarding address. As she stood there in front of the brownstone, her heart in her stomach, angry and sad and unbelieving, a young woman next door came from her stoop and asked if she was Lillian. She gave Lillian an envelope, her name written across it in a childish scrawl. She opened it to find a short note from Troy. "Goodbye, Grandma," it read. "Towanda is taking us away from here. I don't know where but I will miss you. You are nice."

Lillian barely made it home to Manhattan, stopping several times to let the tears flow, already missing the smile and laugh of the little boy she really had begun to think of as her own grandson. When she pulled herself together, the first thing she did was get herself home and call Gary. Private detectives were hired and after a few months, Towanda was tracked to Virginia. Gary demanded that Lillian do nothing. As long as they knew where the boy was, they could keep close tabs on him. Besides, Gary told her, Towanda will need us before you know it. Just wait.

And wait was what Lillian did, for three years, until she couldn't wait anymore.

She took the CoCo Cosmetics jet to Virginia and showed up at Towanda's door, unannounced. Towanda didn't seem surprised to see Lillian standing there. But that may have been because at this point Towanda was used to women showing up at her door, with questions or concerns about her son. Not Troy. He was a model kid, going to school, getting good grades, playing sports, even making demos of rap records with a local producer who said that Troy had a lot of talent. No, the problem was Lewis, the other child. He was a challenge. He'd stopped going to school. He ran with a local gang. He'd already spent two long spells in a juvenile facility, and he was only fourteen years old.

Lillian's reunion with Troy was joyous. He played her a tape of his rap recordings, rhyming along with the music. Lillian was amazed at his charisma, watching him with tears in her eyes, computing in her brain as she watched how she could get Towanda to allow her to send Troy to the same Swiss school that Leo had attended. But Towanda wouldn't have it. Troy protected her, she'd said. From Lewis, from his rages and fits and thieving. She also confessed that Lewis was not, in fact, Joey's son.

And, as if on cue, Lewis arrived home. He sneered a hello at Lillian and went into a back room. Suddenly there was a crash and Lewis returned to the living room, breathing hard, an angry look covering his face. Apparently someone had found drugs he was keeping in the house. They were nowhere to be found. He demanded to know where they were. Towanda said nothing. Finally Troy said he found them and threw them away. Lewis was on Troy faster than anything Lillian had ever seen. Soon, the cops were barging into the house, dragging Lewis out in handcuffs, trying to restrain Lewis from attacking Troy again. Lillian begged Troy to return to New York with her. But he refused, choosing instead to stay with Towanda. He did, however, have one question for Lillian. It was time, he thought, to know who his real parents were. Lillian was torn. Was this the time to tell him? He was almost fifteen years old. He did have a right to know the truth. So Lillian took a picture from her wallet, a picture of Carla standing outside the Plaza Hotel. And his father? Lillian didn't know what to tell Troy. She didn't have a picture of Reggie. So she described Reggie to him. And Troy seemed happy with the description. He wondered why his parents had been rich yet unwilling to keep him, but ultimately he accepted the information and thanked Lillian.

"But he called us all together," Barry said. "He asked which one of us was his father."

Lillian nodded. "I know that, Barry."

"But then why did you tell him that Reggie was his father?"

"Because—"

"Because," Carla interrupted her. "At that point, that is who Lillian thought was his father. I didn't tell her till much later who it really was."

There was silence around the table. They could hear the clatter of silverware reaching from the kitchen.

Finally, Duke said, "So it's you or me, Barry. One of us is TNT's father."

"Unreal," Barry said. "Carla? I think it's up to you to tell us, don't you think?"

"Yes, Carla," a voice said.

It was Reggie, standing next to the table. "Tell them. I want to hear you tell the two guys you were fucking behind my back which one of them is the father of the son you gave up."

5

TNT slowly opened his eyes. He tried to turn his head to look around but the pain shot through him like another bullet entering his body. He let out a slight groan and lay still.

A voice said, "Don't move, baby."

He groggily opened his eyes again and focused on the face hovering over him.

"Towanda," he said. "You—"

"Don't say anything, baby. I'm here. Lillian called me."

"Where is she?"

"With her son, I think."

"I need to talk to her."

"No," Towanda said, putting a soft finger to his lips. "You'll see her soon enough. You just rest, baby."

"Lewis," he said.

Towanda nodded. "The cops should be locating him very soon." Tears came to her eyes. "It's just too much now, baby. I can't take it anymore."

"Don't cry," TNT said. "Don't." He tried to reach up toward her but the pain stopped him again. He grimaced.

Towanda wiped her tears away. "Don't you worry about me, Troy. You've spent enough of your life protecting me."

"He shot me," TNT said.

"I know, baby. But you'll get better soon. And you'll be strong enough to do what you do before you know it."

TNT lay there, looking up at her.

"My father," he said.

Towanda just nodded. "You'll have your answer soon, baby. I promise."

Barry said to Reggie, "What the hell are you even doing here?"

"I don't think that's the question we're all here to have answered," Reggie said.

"What happened to you?" Joey said. "You look like a fucking bum."

Reggie said, "Nice to see you too, Joey." But his look of defi-
ance couldn't hide the embarrassment as he looked down at the
ratty jeans and smudged polo shirt he wore. "Like I said—"

"You don't get any say here," Carla said. "Tell them what you
told me when I told you I was pregnant, Reggie. Since you're all
about the truth-telling now. Tell them!"

Reggie didn't say anything.

"I remember," Leo said. "I was there. He said, 'What punk
knocked you up, Carla, 'cause it wasn't me.'"

"Can you blame me," Reggie said. "She was sleeping with
every available boy in a three-block radius of the beach."

"And you were fucking every princess at Andover," Carla shot
back. "So what?"

"So what is you ended up getting knocked up," he said.

"What are you doing here?" Joey asked.

"He faked his death," Lillian said. "He faked his death to get
out from under his money troubles." She looked at Reggie, a mask
of pain and anger covering her face. "He killed my husband to
get out of his money problems."

Leo flew out of his chair. Soon his hands were clamped around
Reggie's neck. Duke and Joey pulled him off of Reggie as everyone
else watched.

"He's not worth it, Leo," Lillian said. "He'll get his."

"That's not the whole story," Reggie said, his own hands now
rubbing at his neck and shoulders. "Tell them everything, Lillian."

"Which part?" Lillian continued. "That you got involved with
some thugs in Atlanta and ended up in jail?"

"Lillian," Reggie said. "Please—"

Lillian stopped him. "And you know who he met in jail?"

"Lewis," said Leo. "It all makes sense now." He sat up. "You met
Lewis and found out who his brother was."

"And he came to me," Lillian said. "He told me he wanted money, that he'd go to Troy and tell him the entire story, tell him that Carla was a, how did you say it to me, Reggie? That Carla was a slut, that she had no idea who his father was."

"You're disgusting," Carla said to Reggie, cutting her hazel eyes at him. "I'd rather be the biggest slut in the world than an idiot who disappointed his father, then wasted all his money, then faked his own death. I always knew you were a big waste."

"So why did you marry me?"

"We damn near had been promised to each other from birth! I looked past your flaws as long as I could. But you just got worse and worse. Now look at you."

Duke said, "So you told TNT to bring us all together? You knew it was one of us, so you told him to gather us up and ask us which one was his father?"

"Excuse me," Lillian said, standing up. She walked out of the diner.

Reggie sat in Lillian's empty chair. "Look at all of you," he said. "All of you think you're all so special, don't you?"

"This isn't about us," Leo said. "Your problems have always been your own problems, Reggie."

"But look at you," Reggie repeated. "You're all so *successful* but what do you really have? Leo, you were handed the world on a freaking platter, thanks to Gary Bradford. And for that matter the same goes for you, Barry."

"I worked for everything in my life," Joey said.

"And you're alone," Reggie said. "And hoping that that asshole of a son that Towanda had was really yours. You too, Duke. Alone. It's sad really. All of you have always thought you were better than everyone else." He laughed. It sounded hollow and forced. "What did you call yourselves back in the day? Some corny shit. The VIPs? I don't give a fuck what you think of me. I made my choices. But I never pretended to be anything other than what I was. I may have been a spoiled brat back then. I may have been a waste, as Carla said. But I'm me. I'm not hiding behind clothes or books or cosmetics because I don't have a life. I faked my death and I have a freer life than any of you punks."

Barry clapped his hands, slowly, deliberately. "How long you been waiting to make that speech, Reg? Huh? You been carrying envy of all of us all these years and it came down to blackmailing the kid one of us had with your girl all these fucking years later? That's the great choice you made? Faking your death? Almost getting other people killed? Causing Gary's heart attack? That's your great choice?" Barry laughed now. "You're *sad*, Reggie. You always have been. I always hated you. 'Cause you treated everyone around you like they were there for your amusement. Even Carla. We may all be alone now, but you know what we are, you dumb fuck? We're alone together. Even this, you blackmailing TNT. What did it do? It brought us all together. The VIPs. Together again. And where are you? You still on the outside looking in."

Lillian came back into the diner. She waited a second while Reggie stood up slowly from her chair. Lillian took her seat.

"They've found Lewis," Lillian said. She looked at Reggie. "He gave you up, Reginald. He told the cops you told him how to find Troy, that you told him to kill him."

"I didn't—"

"But you might as well have, right?"

Reggie looked at all of them, rushed out of the diner. They all watched him as he ran right into the detective Lillian had spoken to at the hospital. He was accompanied by two beat cops who each took one of Reggie's arms and dragged him toward the police cruiser parked across the street. It would have seemed funny if any of them had been in the mood to laugh. But they were glad to have Reggie out of their lives.

"You gave Troy a picture," Duke said. "Of all of us."

Lillian smiled. "It was the only picture I had of all of you," she said. "After Carla told me, I wanted Troy to see his father, but also his father's friends."

Barry said, "So you knew Carla was pregnant, Leo?"

Leo nodded. "I did." He pushed his coffee cup away. "But I assumed the baby was Reggie's. She never told me otherwise."

"I couldn't," Carla said. "I was too scared to say anything. Then I was too scared to get an abortion. I didn't know what to do."

"And you've kept this secret all these years," Duke said to Lillian.

"I had to," Lillian said. "Carla wanted me to."

"I just didn't see the point in telling," Carla said. "I mean, it wasn't like I had a real relationship with Troy." Her voice broke as she said his name. She put her face in her hands and leaned over the table.

Lillian hugged her. "You were young, Carla. You all were. I was the adult. I handled it the best I could. And Gary, too. He was a big help." She saw the skeptical look on Joey's face. "Yes, Joey, he was protecting you. Edna agreed with him, too. All of you. We saw such potential in all of you. What if we'd told you that Lewis was your son, Joey? And then he turned out not to be. And then turned out to be a criminal who blamed TNT for his own failure? From what I understand, Lewis claims that everything TNT is he stole from Lewis. Picture that."

Leo reached over and put his arm around Joey.

"So," Joey said. "Who is TNT's father?"

Lillian said, "Let's go over to the hospital."

———

They walked down Twelfth Street in small groups, Leo and Joey taking up the rear.

Joey said, "Can you believe Reggie?"

"He was always a fuckup," Leo said. "You remember that."

Joey laughed. "Remember when he showed up at that party? Drunk off his ass?"

"You and Carlton had brought him," Leo said. "That's the night we met."

"I know," Joey said quietly. He stopped Leo, grabbing his shoulder. "Can we be friends again, Leo?"

Leo said, "We were never not friends, Joey."

"Yeah," Joey said with a hard grin. "We just haven't spoken in almost three years." He looked down, then back up at Leo. "I love you, Leo. And not just as friends."

"No you don't, Joey."

"Yes, I do, Leo. And that day in your kitchen? I wanted Greg to see us. I wanted you back." He paused. "And I still do."

"We can't talk about this, Joey."

Joey said, "Are you over me? There's absolutely no room in your heart for me?"

"Joey—"

"Answer my question, Leo."

"Why? So you can just break my heart again?"

"Things are different now, Leo." He stopped, grabbed Leo's arm. "I know how I acted back then. I was an idiot, I admit that. And I've regretted it my whole life. But I was young, man! I had no idea what I wanted. I was some foster kid in a whole new world with all these changes. I loved you, Leo. But how much did I really love myself? Or know myself?"

A woman brushed by them, carrying a bunch of Century 21

bags. Joey pointed to her. "It's a new century, Leo." He smiled. "You owe it to yourself to at least give me a chance. I've always loved you, Leo. You know that."

Leo stopped. "Maybe we can have lunch next week."

"What," Joey said. "I have to come all the way to Paris to have lunch with you?"

"I have an apartment here now," Leo said. "I'm staying in the States. I'm going back to Yale in the fall."

"You're goin' back to college?"

Leo nodded.

"Wow," said Joey. "Leo the Lion is now gonna be Leo the Coed."

"Yeah," Leo said. "Picture that." And before he could turn away, Joey grabbed the lapels of his jacket and pulled Leo into a hug, kissing him on the lips.

As they continued on to the hospital, Leo could think of nothing to say; he felt like the loud beating of his heart was all the communication he could manage.

"Yale, huh?" Joey said. "Always wanted to open a JoeyRam store in New Haven."

Behind them Carla and Duke walked together.

She said, "I can't believe all this stuff is out in the open now."

"My mother always says everything comes out in the wash," he said.

"How is your mom?"

"Good, Carla," he said. "Thanks for asking."

There was a long pause, then Carla said, "Okay, you and I have *never* had a hard time chatting."

Duke shrugged. "You're about to change somebody's life, Carla."

She nodded. "It's about time," she said. "About fucking time."

"You changed mine. A long time ago."

"Me?"

"You told me once that I could be anything I wanted to be."

"Sounds like me," Carla said. "I've always been a walking, talking cliché."

Duke laughed as they got to the corner. "You love to sell yourself short."

"I'm the most insecure egomaniac you're ever going to meet, Duke Maynard."

Just as they were about to cross the street, Carla turned to him. "Can we see each other while you're in town?" She hesitated. "I mean, if you wanna see me."

Duke smiled down at the street, then looked into Carla's eyes. He felt as connected to her as he had all those years ago. However this situation turned out, he knew he wanted to spend much more time with Carla. He reached for her hand and held it tight. "I was hoping you'd ask me that."

6

They all stood outside the third-floor recovery unit. Lillian looked at Carla and said, "So?"

Carla said, "Give me a minute." She ducked through the swinging doors.

Inside, Carla stared down at TNT. He looked so peaceful, even with the cacophony of beeps and whirrs emanating from the computerized machines around him.

Troy.

She thought the name over and over, letting the word play around her brain until it was just a rush of noise.

Forgive me, she thought. *I didn't mean to hurt you or make you wonder all these years. Please forgive me.*

TNT opened his eyes and stared back at her.

"You're beautiful," he said. "Just like in the magazines."

Carla teared up again. "Stop that," she said. "I'm an old hag now." She paused. "But I was beautiful then, wasn't I?"

TNT laughed, but caught himself. "It hurts too much," he said. "Is he here?"

Carla nodded. She stared at TNT for a few more minutes, and ran her long fingers over his shaved head. "You're beautiful," she said. "You're my son and you're beautiful. I'll be right back."

She found them still standing outside the recovery unit. She stood there for a few moments, staring at her oldest friends, her family. She said, "Duke? I am so sorry you had to go through this. I'm really sorry. Will you forgive me?"

There was a look of sadness in his eyes, but his smile was real. "Guess it's not me, huh?"

Carla shook her head. She took a deep breath.

"Barry? You want to meet your son?"

Barry could feel his heart thumping furiously in his chest. He took a couple of deep breaths and clenched his fists. He clenched his jaws, too, as he felt tears rise to his eyes and spill over on his cheeks.

He looked at the others, at their smiles, at the love he thought he felt coming from them, even Leo, who looked as if he might cry himself.

Barry cleared his throat. "You're sure, Carla?"

"I'm sure." She looked right at him. "I've known it was you since the first time I didn't get my period that summer."

Everyone laughed.

"I'm sorry I didn't tell you, Barry. I really am."

Barry took another deep breath and stepped through the swinging doors. As he did his mind raced, from the lawn outside the Bradford home in Sag Harbor, to the first time he saw Carla all those summers ago, to the nights on the beach and in the truck of the man he originally thought of as his father. He saw his freshman dorm room at Yale and the apartment where he fucked Gail and the heavy silver ashtray that sat on Gary Bradford's office at CoCo Cosmetics. He saw all the women he'd been through: Cheyenne and Fiona and Christine and Rochelle and Maya and Tiffany.

His entire life. To this moment. *My son.*

He stared at TNT, lying in the bed, the heavy bandage wrapped around his shoulder and torso. A pain seared through him that he'd never felt before. But it wasn't a bad pain, it was warm, with longing, deep pain that felt like nothing he'd ever felt.

He felt love. *He could give his heart to this person.*

He stepped closer to the bed. When he was right next to it, he looked down and held out his hand.

Neither one said anything for a moment, just stared at each other, as if they were memorizing details they wanted to know for a long time afterward.

Barry could see himself in the brown eyes staring back at him. And he could see Gary Bradford. And Leo.

"You're my son," he said to TNT.

"I am."

"My son," Barry said again.

"I have a question for you."

"A question?"

"Well," TNT said. "The first of many, anyway."

"Shoot."

"Bad word choice."

"Oh," Barry said, wincing. "Sorry about that." He leaned over the bed, closer to his son. "What's your question?"

"Who came up with The VIPs?"

SUMMER 1983: AUGUST

"Of course Joey's gonna end up in jail," Barry says. He tosses another stone into the ocean. "You know we don't really allow crooks in Sag Harbor, right, Joey?"

Duke says, "Why you gotta be like that?"

Barry laughs. "He helped kidnap Carla for chrissakes. Can't you see license-plate-making in Joey's future?"

"Fuck you," Joey says.

"See," Barry says. "Spoken like a true criminal."

The sun hovers over the edge of the ocean's horizon like a ball of melting fire. Leo pushes himself up from the sand and stares out into the ocean. "How beautiful is the ocean at this hour?"

"There's all these hot mamas walking around the beach," says Barry, "and this one is complimenting the ocean on being beautiful. How gay can you be, Leo? We seriously gotta get you some ass before the summer's up."

Leo and Joey exchange a look.

"You're sixteen, Leo. You gotta start acting like a man." Barry tosses another stone into the ocean. "That's because you got one of those fathers who babies you. I don't know what I would do if I had a father like yours."

"Yeah," says Duke. "Like *you* got the greatest pops in the world."

"At least I got one," Barry says.

Duke shoots him a look that could fry bacon. But he lets it simmer, and fade away.

"Besides," says Barry. "You're white, Duke. You don't know how black fathers are."

"I don't know how fathers are, period," says Duke.

"Whatever," says Barry.

Joey says to Leo, "I thought you guys were friends. If this is how friends treat each other, I'm glad I ain't got none."

Leo laughs. "Barry likes to be difficult." He moves closer to Joey. "I'm your friend, Joey."

"I know," Joey says. "Friends forever, right?"

He raises his hand and he and Leo do a complicated shake they'd seen on *The Jeffersons* that leaves them both nearly breathless.

"We need a name," Barry says suddenly. "All my boys out in Brooklyn got names for their crews."

Duke looks over at Leo. "You're the writer, Leo. What you gonna call us?"

"While Leo's being all gay thinking of a name, I'll go watch the honeys," says Barry. He strolls off down the beach, strutting like he owns the sand.

Duke shakes his head. "Don't pay attention to Barry, Joey. He just gets off on it. He hates being a townie more than anybody I know. He has to show off in front of summer people like Leo."

"What about The Kings?" says Joey. "I saw that in a movie."

"Nah," says Duke. "It's gotta sound important."

Joey squints in the sun and says, "More important than King?"

"You know what I mean." Duke says. "Leo knows what I mean."

Barry saunters back over to the guys. They all flop down onto the sand.

"What's a townie?" Joey asks.

Leo says, "Someone who lives here year-round."

Joey looks at Barry. "Why you hate it so much? I'd love to live here year-round."

"You *would*," says Barry. "You don't know any better. You ain't never been nowhere."

"And you have?" Duke says. He tosses a piece of seaweed at Barry's head.

"I will," Barry says. "I'm going *everywhere*. Starting with Yale."

"I'm going to Yale, too," says Leo. "I can't wait."

"Yeah," says Barry. "You're a legacy, though. It's gonna be easy as pie for your ass. Your father went there. I have to work to get in. I'm not the son of the VIP."

Leo sketches a few letters in the sand. Then he scratches them out and writes out VIP. "That's it," he says, stepping back.

"What?" says Duke.

"The name," says Leo, adding an "s" to the letters. "Our name."

"What does it mean," Joey asks.

"Very Important People," says Barry with a big grin. "I like it. It sums me up."

"It sums *us* up," says Duke. "I'm gonna be a football star. Leo's gonna be a famous writer. Barry's gonna be . . . what can you be that puts you around a lot of hot women and makes you a lot of money?"

Joey says, "A pimp?"

Even Barry has to laugh at that.

"I'll figure it out," Barry says. "What you gonna be, Joey?"

"I don't know."

"Come on," Duke says. "Think of something. What are you good at?"

Joey thinks about the pieces of fabric his grandmother used to give him that he liked to cut up and make into things. But he won't say that. They'd all laugh at him.

"Maybe I'll be a bank robber," he says, laughing. "Or a professional kidnapper."

"You got that right," says Barry. He jumps up and grabs a stick from a pile of ashes to their right. He draws a big circle around the letters. They all stand up and look at the words.

The VIPs.

They all look at each other, smiling.

"I like that," says Leo.

"Me, too," says Duke.

"All right, you punks," says Barry. "Let's go show the world just how very important we really are." He points across the beach. "Starting with those girls right over there."

About the Author

SCOTT POULSON-BRYANT was one of the founding editors of the premier urban magazine, *Vibe*. His work has appeared in *Rolling Stone,* the *Village Voice,* the *New York Times,* the *Source, Essence, New York* magazine, and London's *Guardian* and *Face.* A graduate of Brown University, Poulson-Bryant is the author of *Hung* and coauthor of *What's Your Hi-Fi Q?: From Prince to Puff Daddy, 30 Years of Black Music Trivia.* He is currently a graduate student at Harvard.